**Two brand-new stories in every volume...
twice a month!**

Duets Vol. #103

Popular Candy Halliday returns with a quirky
Double Duets volume featuring the identical Morgan
twin sisters—one who's zany and one who's serious.
Enjoy the fun as Madeline and Mary Beth encounter
double trouble with a pair of irresistible in-your-face
heroes who turn their lives upside down! Candy's
most recent Duets novel, *Winging It*, "has a number
of very funny scenes [and] a delicious hero,"
says *Romantic Times*.

Duets Vol. #104

Irish author Samantha Connolly serves up
A Real Work of Art, a wonderful story about a
heroine who impersonates her sister and goes from
uptight to fun and flirty—overnight! Samantha made
an impressive debut with her first Duets novel, say
reviewers. Joining her in the volume is talented
Jennifer McKinlay, whose writing "is fresh and funny,
with memorable characters and snappy byplay,"
notes *Romantic Times*. Jennifer's story
Thick as Thieves, a teasing road tale, was inspired
by her own cross-country trek several years ago!

Be sure to pick up both Duets volumes today!

Are Men from Mars?

"Hey, Captain, looks like our spy is a she!"

Angrier than she'd ever been in her life, Maddie pulled herself up when the force holding her down suddenly set her free. She picked up her pith helmet, which had been knocked off in the struggle, and brushed her long, tangled blond hair out of her face. It took only a split second to confirm that she really had been captured by mysterious green men, after all.

U.S. military camouflage green, to be exact. In tight T-shirts.

She hesitated a moment, staring up at the imposing figure towering above her, silently cursing herself for noticing how cute he was. "My name is Dr. Madeline Morgan," she began haughtily, "and for your information, I'm an entomologist, not a spy."

"Whatever you are, you were trespassing on restricted government property," her G.I. Joe informed her as his penetrating gaze slid over her. "I'm going to have to detain you in my quarters until I can verify your identity."

His quarters? she wondered. *Detained* with Captain Hunk? How on earth was she going to get out of this one?

For more, turn to page 9

Venus, How Could You?

"We can play this game all night, Mary Beth."

Zack played his trump card. "But then we'd miss the reunion. I thought you would like the idea of us showing up together and finally putting an end to six years of gossip."

It took a second, but the limo's tinted window slid down. Zack managed to keep the smile from his lips.

"Keep talking," she said, still looking as if she was about to scratch his eyes out.

Zack shrugged. "What more can I say? If we show up together, think how disappointed everyone will be. They won't have anything else to gossip about."

Mary Beth thought for a minute. "You mean let them think we're back together?"

He shook his head. "Once we get there, we'll make sure everyone knows we've decided to just be friends."

Her eyebrows rose. "End of story, Zack? You won't read this as something more than it is?"

He should have been ashamed of himself for looking her straight in the eye and telling a bald-faced lie. "End of story, Mary Beth. I promise."

For more, turn to page 197

HARLEQUIN DUETS

ISBN 0-373-44169-X

Copyright in the collection:
Copyright © 2003 by Harlequin Books S.A.

The publisher acknowledges the copyright holder
of the individual works as follows:

ARE MEN FROM MARS?
Copyright © 2003 by Candace Viers

VENUS, HOW COULD YOU?
Copyright © 2003 by Candace Viers

Visit us at www.eHarlequin.com

Printed in U.S.A.

Candy Halliday

Are Men from Mars?

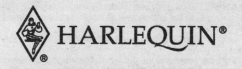

HARLEQUIN®

TORONTO • NEW YORK • LONDON
AMSTERDAM • PARIS • SYDNEY • HAMBURG
STOCKHOLM • ATHENS • TOKYO • MILAN • MADRID
PRAGUE • WARSAW • BUDAPEST • AUCKLAND

Dear Reader,

The question I'm asked most frequently is where do I get my story ideas. I wish I could tell you my mind is so boggled with fresh new story ideas, sometimes I can't even sleep at night. If only that were true.

Sometimes a story idea can be a gift, as was the case with the first book in this volume, *Are Men from Mars?* At coffee after a meeting of my local chapter of Romance Writers of America, my dear friend Elizabeth made a mild complaint that she was bored with the same old, same old heroines—the hip executives, the models and actresses, the interior designers, etc. The type of heroine she would love to see, she told me, was a serious academic research/scientist type of heroine. And presto! Dr. Madeline Morgan, devoted entomologist, began whispering in my ear before I even finished my coffee.

To offset brainy Dr. Morgan, however, I decided it would be fun to give her a zany identical twin sister. In *Venus, How Could You?* soap opera star Mary Beth Morgan is as outrageous as her professor twin is serious. Yet both sisters soon find themselves dealing with the same problem: what to do about the irresistible in-your-face heroes who turn their lives upside down and teach both sisters a valuable lesson in the subject of love.

I hope you'll enjoy getting to know Maddie and Mary Beth as much as I enjoyed letting them tell you their stories.

Best wishes,

Candy Halliday

Books by Candy Halliday

HARLEQUIN DUETS
58—LADY AND THE SCAMP
82—WINGING IT

Special thanks always to my wonderful agent,
Jenny Bent, and to my amazing editor, Susan Pezzack,
to whom I wish only the best with her move to MIRA.
And a very special thank-you to Elizabeth Fensin,
for giving me the gift of Maddie.

This book is dedicated in loving memory
of Robert H. McNeill. Uncle Bob,
I know you are kicking back in one of
Heaven's easy chairs now, reading this
with a smile on your face and still cheering me on.

1

"I'M SERIOUS, MADDIE. I'm giving you one more hour to find your mysterious bug, and then I'm heading right back to the hotel."

Dr. Madeline Morgan, devoted entomologist, didn't bother looking at her older sister. Instead she kept her eyes trained to a pair of high-powered binoculars as she scanned the barren desert terrain. She was on a mission. A mission that had brought her from Georgia to Roswell, New Mexico, and the desert wasteland they were driving through.

"It's not a bug, it's a butterfly, Mary Beth," Maddie corrected. "We're looking for a Deva Skipper. Or if you prefer, Atryonopsis deva, to be exact."

Mary Beth sent her sister a sideways glance. "Well, if you ask me, the only divas in *this* desert happen to be sitting right here in this Jeep." When Maddie laughed, Mary Beth said, "Well, at least one of us could qualify as a diva, I suppose. In that costume *you're* wearing, you look more like..."

"Someone prepared to spend a hot August day in the desert, perhaps?" Maddie lowered her binoculars and leaned back in her seat. "Only you, Mary Beth, would consider wearing a tube top and thong for this type of outing."

"These are short-shorts, sister dear," Mary Beth said, continuing their usual sisterly repartee. "Something you would know if you stopped playing professor long enough to get in touch with your feminine side.''

Maddie looked down at her own clothing. She had thoroughly researched what was considered proper attire for the time they would spend in the desert. Like her sturdy long-sleeved shirt that wouldn't allow desert sun access to tender skin, and her khaki straight-leg pants that tucked quite easily into her sturdy new high-top hiking boots.

''Of course, it's that pith helmet that really makes the outfit,'' Mary Beth said on a giggle. ''Yep, nothing turns a man on quite like a stylish pith helmet. It reels them in every time.''

''In case you've forgotten, it isn't male attention we're looking for,'' said Maddie.

Mary Beth tossed her long, pale hair back from her face and dropped her sunglasses down on her tanned nose. ''Speak for yourself. *I'm* always looking for male attention.'' She held Maddie's gaze for a moment with challenging blue eyes.

It was like looking in a mirror, Maddie always thought. They were identical twins, with Mary Beth being all of two minutes older. Yet, Maddie had always thought of them as the opposite sides of a coin.

Even as children, Mary Beth had loved the frilly dresses, the white tights and the patent leather shoes their mother had dressed them in. Maddie, on the other hand, had usually soiled her dress, torn the knees of her tights, and scuffed the toes of her shoes crawling around on her hands and knees observing insects of every size and description.

As they grew older, Mary Beth had been the social one, while Maddie kept her nose buried in the encyclopedia learning everything possible about the winged invertebrate population. Mary Beth had been the cheerleader and homecoming queen in high school, Maddie the valedictorian of their senior class. And while Maddie had plunged into college for a Ph.D. in entomology, Mary Beth had chosen an acting career.

We're identical, all right. Identical opposites, Maddie thought, but offering a truce to the sister she dearly loved, she said, "I'll make you a deal. I won't say anything else about your short-shorts, if you'll stop making fun of my pith helmet."

"It's a deal. But I wasn't kidding about heading back to the hotel within the hour," Mary Beth threw in as she gave their immediate surroundings another nervous scan. "This place totally creeps me out and you know it."

"Do-do-do-do—do-do-do-do." Maddie chanted the *Twilight Zone* theme in fun.

"Very funny," Mary Beth grumbled. "But more than one eyewitness claimed a space ship landed in Roswell in 1947. Some people even claim to have seen the bodies of those poor space creatures our government dissected for its own amusement."

"And after fifty years of extensive investigation, the government concluded all those people saw was a weather balloon," Maddie insisted.

Mary Beth sent her a shocked look. "You mean you really *don't* believe other intelligent life is out there somewhere?"

Maddie grinned mischievously. "Maybe the surest sign other intelligent life *does* exist, is the fact they've never tried to contact *us.*"

Both sisters shared a good laugh before Maddie reached out and patted her twin's shoulder. "You know, I really am glad you came with me on this trip. We never get to see each other now that you're out in L.A."

"If you want to be in pictures, you've gotta go where the action is," Mary Beth answered with her standard reply.

"I know," Maddie said with a sigh. "But we really do miss you, me and Mom and Pop. Though I have to admit they haven't seen much of me, either, these days. I've been so caught up trying to map out the migration of the Deva Skipper, I've barely had time to eat and sleep."

"And what happens if we do find this bug?"

"Butterfly," Maddie corrected again. "It's a rare species. There have been reported sightings in the southeastern part of New Mexico, but none have been confirmed. If I could find one, it could help pave the way to preserving future colonies."

"*And* also advance your career a little, maybe?" Mary Beth accused with a grin. "Like that research team you're so eager to be chosen for?"

Maddie didn't deny it. "I'd be lying if I said I wouldn't kill to make my boss's research team on…"

"On why an old bore like him can't find a date?"

For the first time, Maddie sent her sister a stern look.

"Okay. Don't get all huffy," Mary Beth said as she downshifted and picked up speed. "We'll look a little longer, but I mean it, Maddie. There's no way we're staying out here in UFO utopia after dark."

"Afraid we might get probed?" Maddie chided.

"No," Mary Beth said with a laugh. "I'm more afraid you'll *never* get probed if this is your idea of how to spend your summer vacation."

Maddie's eyes cut to the left. "That wasn't an invitation for another lecture about my love life."

"What love life? Or have you finally determined celibacy is too grim a fate even for a workaholic like you?"

Maddie took up her binoculars again and refused to answer.

"I hope you know you're fooling yourself. You think you're safely hidden behind those saintly college walls playing professor, but one day some guy is going to come along and knock your feet right out from under you."

"I'll be sure to let you know the second anything like that happens."

"But he won't be some mental wizard like those stuffy professors you hang around with now," Mary Beth predicted. "He'll be all man. Total brawn from head to toe. And you'll be so hot for this guy, even you would be willing to dance naked on CNN just to get his attention."

Maddie laughed in spite of herself.

"Besides," Mary Beth added with a sigh, "we aren't getting any younger, you know. The big Three-O is just around the corner, and…"

"Age isn't a subject I care to discuss, either."

"Nor do I," Mary Beth agreed. "I just hate seeing you waste your life away like your revered Dr. Fielding has done. And what has being devoted to his career really gotten your boss? When he's ready to retire I doubt there'll be any life left in his old *caterpillar,* if you know what I mean.''

''Mary Beth!'' Maddie scolded.

''Well, I'm sorry, but that man gives me the creeps. Any man who would devote his entire life studying the sex life of the tsetse fly has to have a major mental problem. And what scares me most,'' Mary Beth added, ''is that *your* only goal in life seems to be to follow in the old coot's footsteps. Don't you want a family some day, Maddie? Don't you want…''

''Stop!'' Maddie grabbed Mary Beth's arm and pointed up ahead. ''Ease the Jeep up that hill. Near those thistles. I saw something. Get closer.''

As instructed, Mary Beth eased the Jeep forward and up a small rise that took them even farther away from the main road and deeper into the desert.

''Don't get too close,'' Maddie warned, still using her binoculars to search a patch of brush growing by a chain-link fence that had suddenly appeared out of nowhere.

''Is that a fence?'' Mary Beth whispered, reaching for the binoculars when Maddie took the strap from around her neck.

Maddie ignored the question and substituted the strap of her faithful Nikon camera around her neck. Grabbing a small net from the knapsack sitting on the floorboard, she started to ease herself out of the Jeep when Mary Beth grabbed her hand and pointed to a sign fastened to the fence. Forcing Maddie to take back her binoculars, Mary Beth said, ''Take another look. I told you we never should have left the main road. This is government property. I think we should get the hell out of here. Fast.''

Maddie looked through the binoculars again at the weather-worn sign that was faded, yet still official looking enough to cause some concern. Government Property—Absolutely No Trespassing—Violators Will Be Prosecuted—didn't leave much room for any misunderstanding about the warning. However, Maddie made her decision when she checked the bush again and saw another flutter of movement.

"I'm not going *over* the fence," she argued, prying Mary Beth's fingers from around her wrist. "It'll only take me a minute to get a specimen."

"A specimen?" Mary Beth cried out. "I thought you said these butterflies were rare? And now you're going to capture one? Cut its tiny life short? Isn't that defeating the whole cause?"

Maddie drew her fingers to her lips in a quick sush. "The Deva Skipper only has a life span of a few weeks," she whispered. "That's why finding one is almost impossible. I have no intention of harming it, but how can I possibly save other colonies if I can't prove the Deva was here to begin with?"

Mary Beth frowned. "All of you scientists are alike, aren't you? Always hell-bent on getting a specimen. I bet that's the last words those little green men heard, too. 'Sorry we have to sacrifice your lives, you poor little green bastards, but we have to get that specimen.'"

"Save the drama for the silver screen," Maddie said as she eased herself out of the Jeep. "I'll be back in a flash."

Taking her time, Maddie crept up the hill and along the fence line, butterfly net in hand. She was literally shaking with anticipation as she eased closer, marveling at the sheer beauty of one of nature's most delicate creatures.

And it *was* a Deva Skipper, no doubt about it.

The fringe on its forewing was brown, its hind wing a whitish color, and the upper side wing a reddish-brown. And though she couldn't see the underside of the hind wing from where she was standing, Maddie already knew it would be brown with a gray overscaling and a faint dark bar across its middle. In a single word, the little Deva was breathtaking.

And it was almost within her grasp.

Inching closer, Maddie adjusted the zoom lenses on her camera and snapped a few pictures as she carefully picked her steps over the dusty desert floor. She was trained, ready and skilled to take her captive easily and without doing the tiny creature harm. Holding her breath, she could almost taste the sweetest of success on her tongue. She was only one swoop away from capturing the find of her life when the flirtatious little Deva lifted itself upward and came to a perfect landing on the *wrong* side of the forbidding chain-link fence that now stood between them.

Without a second thought, Maddie stuck the butterfly net in the back pocket of her khakis and forced the toe of her hiking boot into one of the diamond-shaped holes in the rusted fence. She could hear Mary Beth yelling from behind her, but Maddie scaled the fence like a veteran climber and dropped nimbly to the other side.

"Maddie! Get back here! I mean it, Maddie. Do you hear me?"

"I hear you. You've been trying to boss me around our entire lives," Maddie mumbled under her breath, "but this is one time I'm not leaving until I get what I came for."

Easing forward, trusty butterfly net again in hand, Maddie was even ready to sprout wings herself if that's what it took to complete her mission. "Come to me, little Deva," she cooed, but when Mary Beth's screaming grew even louder, Maddie glanced back over her shoulder in time to see the panicked look on her sister's lovely face.

In fact, Mary Beth was literally jumping up and down on the front seat of the Jeep now, waving her arms wildly above her head like a crazy person. Maddie waved back impatiently, motioning for Mary Beth to pipe down, but a large shadow suddenly fell across Maddie's path, blocking out the sun.

Startled, she looked up and immediately felt her breath catch in her throat. A huge metal object was hovering directly above her, yet the strange-looking aircraft was as silent in its flight as the tiny Deva Skipper that had lured her to the wrong side of the fence.

More curious than she was frightened, Maddie immediately grabbed for her camera. She was still snapping the shutter frantically when the aircraft swooped downward, instantly blinding her with a cloud of sand and dust. Maddie held tightly to her pith helmet, trying to shield her face from the caustic dust storm that was now choking off her airway and stinging her eyes.

She let out a strangled scream when something snaked around her waist and lifted her upward and into the air.

In less time than it took to worry about her twin

sister's safety, Maddie heard the loud clang of a door slamming shut. She soon found herself face-down on a cold metal floor, coughing up the dust as she tried to catch her breath. With her eyes still watering from the dirt and sand, Maddie couldn't yet make out who or what was holding her captive. All she could hear was the definite whir of the unidentified flying object as it whisked her away to some unknown destination.

"Let me up this minute! I demand it!" Maddie started yelling, and she began struggling with such fervor the elastic strap on her pith helmet broke free, unleashing the long, pale hair stuffed under her helmet.

"Holy hell, Captain," a shocked voice called out. "It looks like our spy is a *she*."

Angrier than she'd ever been in her life, Maddie pulled herself up when the force holding her face down on the floor suddenly set her free. And it only took a split second to confirm that she really had been captured by mysterious green men, after all.

U.S. military camouflage green to be exact.

And World War Maddie was about to do battle with everyone responsible for making her lose what could have possibly been the biggest entomological find of her career.

AIR FORCE CAPTAIN Brad Hawkins jerked his head around in time to see a finger waving ninety miles a minute while their definitely female prisoner delivered a good tongue-lashing to his copilot.

Did she look like your typical spy?

Of course, she didn't.

She looked, Brad decided, like an angry little girl

with her cheeks blazing, her tangled blond hair in a windblown mess, and her chin jutted forward in defiance as if she'd just taken a nasty spill from her bike. Classic facial features. Haunting blue eyes. A curvaceous figure that even her "Dr. Livingstone" outfit, complete with a pith helmet couldn't quite hide.

She was stunning.

And though he told himself it was only the shock of finding a woman on isolated government property that had left him so addled, it took several seconds before Brad could force himself to look away.

Turning his attention back to maneuvering the multimillion-dollar prototype helicopter he was flying, Brad aimed the large craft back toward the old air base on the outskirts of Roswell that the Air Force was using as a testing facility. She was still kicking up quite a fuss behind him in the belly of the chopper, ranting and raving about what? Butterflies? Had he heard that right? And something about a terrified sister? Was that who had blazed off in a cloud of dust so fast Brad had only caught a mere glimpse of a bright red Jeep?

Groaning inwardly, Brad picked up the microphone to his radio and mumbled, "There's a suspicious tourist in a red Jeep along the south perimeter. Apprehend the driver. Do it quickly and quietly." He signed off with, "I'll meet you back at the base."

Crap! He'd assumed they'd run across some nosey reporter. Some guy acting on a tip that the Air Force was conducting more than routine maneuvers at the old base. And that's when Brad had made the decision to apprehend their trespasser. He'd planned to take the guy back to base, destroy the film and then threaten the reporter with serious charges.

But who would have thought that within just three weeks short of completing testing on the most advanced helicopter known to modern man, a woman, wearing of all things a pith helmet, and her runaway sister would stumble upon their operation and threaten to blow the cover on their highly guarded mission straight to hell and back again?

"And another thing. If you think for one minute I'm going to overlook the senseless, barbaric way you've treated me, you're sadly mistaken. My name is Dr. Madeline Morgan. And for your information, I'm an entomologist, not a spy. I was doing nothing more than conducting necessary research on an endangered species of butterfly when you so rudely, crudely and unfairly abducted me!"

Entomologist?

He never would have pegged his lovely passenger for a lady with a bug fetish. Especially not with that sexy, Southern accent of hers. Yet, her unusual career choice made her even more intriguing.

Unfortunately her identity would only add another nail in his coffin. Apprehending a nosey reporter with a camera trained on a top secret aircraft was one thing. But hijacking a reputable entomologist? Doing nothing more than conducting important research on an endangered species of butterfly? Brad gripped the controls, just thinking about the consequences.

Not that being rudely, crudely and unfairly abducted, as she put it, wasn't her own doing. Trespassing on restricted government property might have been overlooked, but it had been that damn camera of hers that had sealed her fate. Had she treated their accidental encounter like most people would have done and run for cover like her sister, he would have had no reason to bother her in the least.

In fact, the whole point of conducting testing at the old air base in Roswell had been Roswell's tie to the UFO phenomena. Around Roswell people *expected* to see strange objects flying through the air. And it didn't matter if those sightings were real or if they were only imagined. Roswell depended on UFO sightings as the main tourist attraction that supported most of the city's livelihood.

A civilian actually having pictures of the current most top-secret aircraft in the United States military, however, couldn't be tolerated. Especially when those pictures had the potential to fall into the wrong hands.

I made the right decision, Brad told himself with confidence, then skillfully landed what had aptly been nicknamed the Black Ghost on the helipad that was protected from view by the fifteen-foot concrete barrier walls that surrounded them.

Unbuckling his seat belt, Brad pulled himself out of the cockpit. He walked to the back of the chopper and stood with his hands at his waist, looking down at his disgruntled prisoner. She was still sitting where she'd landed on the floor, but she had managed to push some of her hair out of those dark blue eyes that were now as big around as saucers. Unfortunately those full, enticing lips he'd noticed earlier were now pressed together in a line so thin they almost disappeared.

"Captain Brad Hawkins. United States Air Force," Brad said with as much authority as he could muster, and then he extended a willing hand to help his frowning passenger back to her feet.

MADDIE HESITATED FOR A moment, staring up at the imposing figure who was now towering above her. Oh, he was cute, all right. She'd noticed he was cute the second he turned around and looked at her. Yet looking at him now, Maddie realized referring to this man as *cute* was the equivalent of calling the brilliant Monarch butterfly a rather colorful moth. No, it was more like referring to Mt. Everest as a hill in the Himalayas. His dark hair was cut in that crisp, military fashion that commanded respect. The hint of a five-o'clock shadow crept up the full length of his jaw. A tight-fitting T-shirt and his camouflage fatigues only emphasized a fine-honed body that was lean, mean and nothing in between. And those arms—God, those arms. His biceps were literally bulging. Exactly the type of arms that would have the power to crush a woman to him and....

In a flash, Mary Beth's *total brawn from head to toe* comment came rushing back to haunt her.

Maddie shuddered at the thought.

She reluctantly accepted his offer and pulled herself up to a height that barely reached his shoulder, ignoring a jolt of a different nature that colored her cheeks from the mere touch of his hand.

What's wrong with me? Maddie worried. So, maybe he did have a hunkability factor of about a zillion. So what? He was also someone she should have been ready to throttle. She should have kicked both his shins and sucker-punched him soundly in the stomach. Hadn't he literally kidnapped her? Terrified her poor sister? Possibly destroyed her chances of finding the Deva Skipper again? Maybe even ruined her chances for the biggest opportunity of her career?

Yet, here she was acting like a silly schoolgirl experiencing her first legitimate crush!

Shame on you! Maddie told herself, then purposely squared her shoulders and found the courage to say, "I'm Dr. Madeline Morgan, Captain Hawkins. And I'm certain the colonel or the general, or whomever is in charge will be absolutely appalled when he learns how badly you've treated a defenseless law-abiding citizen."

His eyebrow raised slightly. "Law-abiding?" he repeated in a mocking tone. "I doubt my *wing commander* will call trespassing on private government property something a law-abiding citizen would do."

He was toying with her and Maddie knew it, she could see the hint of amusement in his dark brown eyes. Dreamy eyes, she might add. Eyes that were currently staring at her so intensely Maddie felt her cheeks flame a second time. *He's openly flirting with me,* Maddie suddenly realized. And though his flirting flattered her in one respect, it irritated Maddie in another.

"I prefer that your *wing commander,* not you, Captain Hawkins, make that type of decision for himself," Maddie was quick to tell him before she added with another lift of her chin, "and if you'll kindly escort me to his office, I'll be happy to take the matter up with him myself."

He stalled for a moment, seemingly amused that

she would question his authority. "First, I'll need to verify that you are who you say you are. Can you provide me with any type of identification?"

Maddie let him know exactly what she thought of such a stupid question. "Well, of course, I don't have any identification *on* me," she sputtered. "My purse was in the Jeep with my sister. And I'm sure you scared her to death when you had G.I. Joe reach out and grab me and then body-slam me to the floor of your stupid—" she glanced around her surroundings before she added "—your stupid whatever this flying contraption is."

He glanced at his copilot, who had suddenly found something rather interesting on the toe of his boot.

"And what is all this spy nonsense?" Maddie's hands were on her hips now. "Take a good look at me, Captain Hawkins. Do I look like a spy to you?"

When he purposely looked her up and down, Maddie wished she could snatch back the invitation to do so. She was sure he was thinking that she didn't look like a professor, either. And she didn't. She looked like hell is what she looked like, thanks to him and his partner.

Angry all over again, Maddie glanced briefly at the metal door to her left and made her move. She wasn't quick enough. Captain Hawkins had the door blocked before she could reach for the door handle. And the scowl on his face told her trying to reach around him probably wouldn't be a good idea.

Now what? Maddie wondered, worried for the first time that her impressive credentials might not be enough to get her out of her current predicament.

BRAD DIDN'T BOTHER admitting he'd already made the *spy* assessment himself. He had no doubt she was who she said she was. Even the way she carried herself let him know she was accustomed to giving orders instead of taking them. But Dr. Morgan was on *his* turf now. And the sooner she realized *he* was in charge, the better it would be for both of them.

Still, he couldn't help but notice that her beauty was genuine. No heavy makeup, no frills, no polish or jewelry. None of the usual amenities most women felt were necessary to make them attractive. And her confidence wasn't limited to her appearance, either. She'd been confident enough to make a break for the door. Which meant keeping her sequestered until he figured out what to do with her might not be an easy task.

Time to play hard ball, Brad decided. "Right now all I *know* is that you were trespassing on private government property. And," he added as he reached out and grabbed the camera strap from around her neck, "you were taking pictures on government property without permission. *Illegal* pictures," he said as he quickly flipped the back of the camera open and jerked the film out to completely expose it. "Pictures I'm personally authorized to destroy on behalf of the United States Air Force."

The color drained from her face so fast Brad was prepared to catch her if she fainted. It was then Brad realized the Black Ghost wasn't the only thing his pretty captive had been photographing on her expedition in the desert.

"Do you have any idea what you just did?" she gasped as her hand flew to her mouth.

"Yeah, I just did my job," Brad told her.

"No, you just destroyed the only evidence I had to support the research I've been working on for the last six months."

Destroying her research hadn't been his intention, but there was nothing he could do about it now. Stuffing the exposed roll of film into his pants pocket, he slipped the camera strap carefully back over her head and said, "I'm going to have to detain you until I can verify your identity. Sergeant Baker will escort you to my living quarters. You can stay there until I notify you otherwise."

"Your living quarters?" She jerked her arm away when the sergeant tried to take it. "If I'm under arrest, Captain Hawkins, then I insist you take me to the proper authorities!"

She could insist all she wanted, but Brad had his own problems to worry about. Like explaining to his wing commander how his test flight that afternoon had suddenly turned into a quasiespionage mission. A mission that had resulted in one suspect being apprehended, while a search party was now racing across the desert in hot pursuit of suspect number two.

Knowing he could no more divulge those details than he could successfully restore her ruined film, Brad folded his arms across his chest and said as calmly as possible, "Look, Dr. Morgan. If that *is* who you are. We can do this easy, or we can do it hard. It's your choice. But you *are* going to go with Sergeant Baker one way or the other until I get this whole mess straightened out. Understood?"

Another lift of her chin told Brad she wasn't even going to acknowledge his question with an answer.

Turning to his copilot, Brad said, "Wait at least

thirty minutes before you make your move. Be discreet. Take her through the back way. And don't answer any questions if anyone stops you. The fewer people who know she's here, the better.''

"You're going to regret this, Captain. I'll see to it," she threatened with a deadly look.

Brad held her gaze a second longer than necessary, then turned away. "Don't let her out of your sight," he called back over his shoulder before he opened the side door of his multimillion-dollar Black Ghost and slammed it soundly behind him.

2

"YOU DID WHAT?"

Brad squeezed his eyes shut when the powerful fist of Brigadier General Joseph Gibbons made contact with his heavy wooden desk and sent a loud crack echoing through the room. Still standing at attention, Brad took a deep breath and said, "I'm sorry, sir. We were right on top of her before I even saw her. If she hadn't picked that moment to play photographer, I could have been out of there so fast her head would still be spinning. But under the circumstances, I didn't have any choice but to bring her back to the base."

"And you destroyed that film?"

"The minute we landed," Brad said, then took the exposed roll from his pocket and gave up his straight-back pose long enough to place it on the desk in front of his commander.

Gibbons, who had seen more combat action than Brad ever planned or hoped to see, pushed back in his chair and stood up, then began pacing around his office. Standing at attention again, Brad never moved a muscle.

"And you say she's a professor?"

"A professor of entomology," Brad affirmed, still rather impressed by the fact. "I did a quick background check. She teaches at a small private college in Georgia. She's out here doing research on an endangered species of butterfly.''

Gibbons's scowl made Brad take a deep breath before he added, ''But there is another slight problem, sir. Someone else was with her. She says it was her sister. The sister split so fast there wasn't any time to stop her. I radioed ahead and have a patrol out now to bring her in. She was way off the main road. I'm sure we'll stop her before she gets back to Roswell.''

''You'd damn well better stop her!'' Gibbons bellowed. ''Do you have any idea what will happen if that woman hits Roswell screaming a strange aircraft carried off her sister? Hell, every news team in the country will be on top of us so fast we won't know what hit us!''

Brad cringed. ''That isn't going to happen, sir. They should bring her in any minute now.''

Gibbons resumed his pacing, then stopped to glare at Brad again. ''I want both of those women in my office within the hour. Do you hear me? We have a top secret operation to protect here, and I don't intend to let a couple of tourists jeopardize our testing.''

Brad nodded. ''I'm sure they can be convinced to keep silent, sir. It may take some fast talking, but...''

''Fast talking, hell!'' Gibbons shouted. ''I intend to scare the living crap out of them.''

''Well, we do have the upper hand here.'' Brad threw that in for good measure, hoping he might spare his pretty prisoner and her sister some of the old man's wrath. ''I mean, the professor *knows* she was trespassing. I'm sure if you explain...''

"You leave those details to me." Gibbons made another lap around the room, then flopped back down at his desk. "Now get the hell out of here and see if they've located that sister yet."

Brad gave his commander a salute, turned on his heel and was one step from reaching for the door-knob when a loud knock brought him to a stop. The commander's anxious-looking aide stepped into the room the second Brad swung the door open.

"Sorry to interrupt," said the young lad who barely had a trace of peach fuzz on his face. "The patrol Captain Hawkins sent out just called in to say they weren't successful in their search. They said you'd want to know."

Brad prepared himself for the rage that immediately followed.

"Get your ass to Roswell, Hawkins. And do it now," the voice of authority yelled from across the room. "And don't step foot in my office again until you have this whole mess straightened out!"

After a quick salute Brad hurried from his commander's office, already suspecting, however, that his new assignment would be his own personal version of *Mission Impossible*.

MADDIE CONTINUED TO PULL away every time Sergeant Baker tried to take her arm. "I'm perfectly capable of walking unassisted," she told him in a frosty tone that should have turned the big goon into an ice sculpture.

"Just following orders," Baker mumbled.

"Well, as far as I'm concerned your orders are every bit as ridiculous as you bailing out of the air to capture me like some common criminal,'' Maddie huffed.

"You were trespassing," Baker reminded her.

"And exactly what penalty does trespassing carry in the Air Force, Sergeant Baker? Does the rule book say jump out of the sky and pounce on your trespasser? Shove them facedown with their arms held behind them? Bruise and batter them? Does it say *shoot* those pesky trespassers if they dare try to run away?"

Baker didn't answer. Instead he continued to shepherd her along in a lumbering fashion while looking straight ahead.

"And why is your captain so concerned about someone else seeing me?" Maddie grumbled when the man towering above her stopped only long enough to look up and down a long hallway before forcibly taking her arm again and steering her down the hall.

Again, Maddie wrenched her arm free, then sent a wistful look back over her shoulder. As luck would have it, they hadn't seen a single soul since they'd emerged from the strange aircraft they'd been riding in. If they had, Maddie would have screamed bloody murder and begged for someone to rescue her. She even thought of screaming now, but the threat of being slammed to the floor again by a guy with the build of a professional wrestler kept her silent.

The big bully! Maddie thought with a frown.

Both of her knees were scraped, probably even bleeding, and it would be weeks before the skin grew back on her right elbow. And though it briefly occurred to Maddie that her injuries were mainly due to her own kicking and struggling, she much preferred to blame those injuries on her overgrown chaperone.

"Could it be possible Captain Hawkins told you to be so secretive about my existence because he knows keeping me against my will is totally illegal?" Maddie piped up again. "Tell me the truth, Sergeant Baker. Do the two of you routinely swoop down and pluck innocent women out of the desert and spirit them away to your *private* living quarters? Is Captain Hawkins the brains behind some type of illegal love slave trade the two of you have going on out here in the desert?"

Again, Sergeant Baker didn't answer, but her whimsical assessment of the situation quickly filled Maddie's mind with thoughts of what it might be like if Captain Hawkins *did* hold her captive as his love slave.

Would he be the type of man to aggressively force her into submission? *Never,* Maddie told herself, though her heart betrayed her and skipped a beat at the possibility of such unfamiliar excitement. Or would the hunky captain lure her into his arms with gentle whispers of the tantalizing things he planned to do to her while they made slow, unhurried love?

Oh, yeah. That would undoubtedly be *his* style.

In fact, her interaction with him so far left no doubt he was a man of few words, but exceedingly quick in the action department. Like the way his eyes had traveled daringly over her body when she'd made the mistake of asking him to take a good look at her. His intense gaze had left her breathless.

You idiot! Maddie scolded, when her apparently sex-starved mind began wandering again. And then she asked herself, *Why on earth am I having these bizarre thoughts now?*

She was an educated woman. A woman with the ability to stay completely focused on her career—a career that, thanks to Captain Fantasy, had possibly been sabotaged. Yet now, she was suddenly daydreaming about being this man's *love slave*.

It was completely unlike her.

Totally preposterous!

Yet, so was her current situation.

For all practical purposes, she might as well have been spirited off to another planet, Maddie reasoned. Educated and focused or not, she was totally out of her element. Could she really expect herself to act normal? Expect to remain calm and collected when she'd lost complete control of the situation?

And, of course, there was also that stupid prediction Mary Beth had made earlier about some guy knocking her feet out from under her. That had to be what was jinxing her now and turning her into some wide-eyed silly twit because some hunky soldier had paid a little attention to her.

Damn you, Mary Beth.

But thinking about her sister also made Maddie wonder what her poor twin's fate had been. She was certain Mary Beth had to have seen the soldier jump out of the aircraft and seize her. Was it possible Mary Beth was already in the commander's office now pleading for her release? Or had Mary Beth gone back to Roswell to enlist the help of local authorities?

Which might not be a good thing, Maddie reminded herself with a frown. The local sheriff probably wouldn't be any more lenient about her trespassing than the captain had been. A convicted felon certainly wouldn't be a prime candidate for a federally-funded research team. Although making the research team was the least of her worries at the moment. Thanks to her own stupidity, she could possibly end up with a new wardrobe of striped prison clothes and staring out at the world from behind bars.

Maddie was still mentally kicking herself for being such an idiot when Sergeant Baker stopped in front of a door, opened it and pushed her inside a darkened room.

She blinked when he switched on the light.

The captain's living quarters were certainly nothing like the barracks Maddie had seen portrayed on TV and in the movies. "How does Captain Hawkins rate his own suite at this inn?" Maddie wondered aloud.

As usual, Baker refused to answer.

She took another look around the room. The accommodations certainly weren't elaborate. The walls were cement blocks and painted a puke-green, and to her dismay there wasn't a window in sight. The main room was large enough for a sitting area, but the love seat and matching recliner had seen better days. A sagging bookshelf to her left held a TV, VCR and what looked like a CD player. A metal table and two metal folding chairs sat on the opposite side of the room. There was also a small apartment-size refrigerator. Instead of the standard military-issue cot, Maddie could see a double bed in an adjoining room.

She assumed the closed door off the bedroom led to the captain's private bath. And a bathroom was certainly something she could use at the moment. Not only was she covered in dust and grime from head to toe, but her scrapes and scratches shouldn't go long without attention. The way her luck had been going, gangrene could set in at any moment.

Maddie glanced at her bodyguard. "Does Captain Hawkins have his own private bath?"

"Off the bedroom."

"And may I use that facility?"

Baker nodded.

"Alone?"

Baker blushed.

"Don't you need to search the bathroom first?" Maddie jeered. "Make sure I can't shimmy out a window or something?"

She'd only been joking, but to her surprise Baker motioned her in the direction of the bathroom. Only when they were standing side by side and peering into the small bathroom did he nod his approval. "Help yourself," Baker said with a goofy smile. "I didn't think there were any windows in this old block building, but thanks for reminding me to check it out."

"You *aren't* welcome!" Maddie stomped inside the bathroom and slammed the door behind her. She could hear the sergeant chuckling to himself as the sound of his footsteps left the bedroom. It irritated her that the big buffoon thought the situation was funny, but at least he'd had the decency to allow her a little privacy. Reaching down, Maddie locked the bathroom door just to be safe, then stood staring at herself in the small mirror above the sink.

Completely covered in dirt, Maddie decided she

looked like one of those old Vaudeville comedians in black face makeup.

"God, I'm a mess." She bent forward and ran her fingers through her tangled hair. The sand that peppered the basin made her yearn for a hot shower. The thought of stripping naked in the captain's private bathroom, however, made Maddie more than a little apprehensive. Especially with the off-the-wall scenarios that seemed to spring to mind every time she thought about the handsome devil.

Like now.

Maddie could picture herself waterlogged and withered after spending hours waiting naked under a spray of water that had long since grown cold. Waiting. Hoping. Praying her mysterious kidnapper would finally burst into the bathroom to see if she had somehow managed to escape. He would throw back the curtain and grin wickedly when she only halfheartedly tried to cover herself. And then he would step into the shower with her and pull her naked, quivering body...

You, my dear, are a certifiable nut case!

Hoping to cool herself off from *that* mental image, Maddie jerked a towel from the towel bar, wet it thoroughly, then mopped it slowly over her dust-splattered face. The amount of grime and dirt she was leaving behind on his own personal towel made her smile.

After cleansing her injuries as best she could with a basin-type bath, Maddie studied the medicine cabinet above the sink. She had never been one of those nosey people who secretly went through other people's medicine cabinets.

But under the circumstances?

Well, it was the captain's own fault she needed medical supplies, she reasoned.

Boldly reaching out, Maddie opened the door and peered inside. The usual male toiletries stared back at her. His toothbrush and toothpaste told her even a big, strong soldier like him was just as concerned about the threat of gingivitis as everyone else. There was a can of shaving foam and a fancy-looking razor for that heavy stubble she had noticed earlier. And he evidently preferred aftershave to cologne, though his brand wasn't cheap; Ralph Lauren would have been proud. Picking up the bottle, Maddie's intention was to take a quick sniff.

She froze the second she saw the box of condoms.

Shoving the bottle back in place, Maddie slammed the cabinet door and stood staring into the mirror wondering how such a promising day had turned crazy on such short notice.

Instead of aliens, an overzealous Air Force Captain had snatched her out of the desert, destroyed her precious film and was holding her captive in his own private living quarters. Yet, was she fearing for her own safety? Was she worrying that her abductor might be summoning up just cause to put her behind bars?

Nope. She wasn't even thinking up ways she might *strangle* Captain Hawkins for all the trouble he had caused her. Instead Maddie's newly liberated mind kept flirting with the possibility of how much fun it might be to *wrangle* him out of those camouflage fatigues purely for her own pleasure and amusement.

"Who *are* you?" Maddie demanded of her reflection.

She hurried from the bathroom when the woman Maddie no longer recognized sent back an imaginary wink from the captain's bathroom mirror.

BRAD STEELED HIMSELF against the long stream of curse words coming from his commander's bared lips. With a grimace, Brad said, "With your permission, sir, I'll beef up security. Now that the sister has involved the local authorities, it's only a matter of time until the media starts questioning whether we're really out here on routine maneuvers as we claim."

"Well, let them question all they want," Gibbons bellowed. "Just don't let anyone step foot on this base."

Brad nodded, feeling completely chastised.

The old man, as he was respectfully called by the men who served under him, had asked for Brad specifically on this final assignment that would take Gibbons into retirement at the end of the year. Brad knew the request had been made mainly out of respect for his father who had saved Gibbons's life in Vietnam before being killed himself in a surprise attack. Brad had only been six years old at the time, but he'd been old enough to vow that, in memory of his father, he would become one of the best helicopter pilots the United States Air Force had to offer.

At thirty-four, Brad had achieved that goal by never allowing anyone or anything stand in the way of his mission.

"How soon do you think we can demobilize and move this operation?" Gibbons spoke up, jarring Brad back from memories he usually kept at bay.

"Three days. Tops," Brad told him, still saddened that thanks to him, Gibbons's exit from the military wasn't going to be an easy one. "I'm just not sure how we'll go about getting the Black Ghost out of here with a bunch of reporters watching our every move."

Gibbons dragged a hand over his weatherworn face before his black eyes flashed in Brad's direction. Though now in his sixties, he still resembled the young officer in the old photograph sitting on his desk. It was a photo Gibbons took with him everywhere he went. A group of young pilots, including Brad's father, stood with arms slung around each other's shoulders, squinting into the sun. Brad's eyes rested fondly on the picture of his dad for a moment, then back to the photo of Gibbons. Same alert eyes, Brad noted. Same crew cut, though now the old man's hair was completely gray. Same ability, Brad knew, to make split-second decisions without so much as the blink of the eye.

"We don't have much choice," Gibbons finally said, diverting Brad's attention away from the photo and back to him. "We'll take the Black Ghost out of here the same way we had to bring that spy plane back from China when we got our ass in a crack. We'll dismantle and ship the sucker one piece at a time."

"I'm really sorry, sir. About everything," Brad said with a sigh of resignation. "Unfortunately we're in an age of instant communication. Now that the sister is in Roswell yelling alien abduction, every news crew in the nation will pick up the story."

"Bastards," Gibbons swore. "Always shoving a

camera in somebody's face. Hell-bent on sensationalism."

"I hate to say it, but the public is just as much at fault," Brad mused. "Look at all those reality shows that have become so popular on television today."

"Well, *your* damn reality is going to be keeping that professor quiet until we can get the hell out of here," Gibbons said, suddenly angry all over again. "I'd intended to threaten those women with serious charges and send them on their way, but that isn't possible now."

Brad tensed. "Exactly what are you saying, sir?"

Gibbons pounded his desk in his usual *pay attention* style. "I'm saying we'll have to keep the professor here until we can move our operation. After that, she can talk to the media all she wants. Once the evidence is gone, there'll be nothing left to confirm her story."

Keep her? Brad's mind yelled in protest.

But that was crazy. They were on a temporary assignment, camped out at an old base that was virtually vacant most of the time. They didn't have any military police here, much less any type of jail cell where they could house his accidental prisoner.

"But, sir, that's impossible. If we keep her, then all hell will surely break loose. The local sheriff is bound to call in the FBI."

"I'll make a few calls to Washington," Gibbons said, obviously unconcerned about the FBI. "It's the damn media and the local-yokels who'll give us a problem."

"But, sir…"

Gibbons pointed a stern finger in Brad's direction, and Brad didn't miss the menacing twinkle in the old man's eye when he said, "The way I see it, you grabbed her. Now, *you* baby-sit her."

Under different circumstances, Brad would have shouted hallelujah at such an appealing opportunity. Baby-sit her? Hell, yes, he'd like to baby-sit her if the timing was right. He'd give those pouting Southern Belle lips of hers something to pout about. Like tempting her and teasing her until she realized there were much more exciting things in life than chasing butterflies across the desert.

But now?

When their entire top secret mission was in jeopardy? How could he possibly baby-sit the professor and make sure the Black Ghost was safely out of harm's way?

"But keep her where, sir?" Brad finally summoned the courage to ask. "We can't take the chance of letting anyone else even know she's here."

"Didn't you say you had Baker take her to your living quarters?"

"Well, yeah, but what do you expect me to do with her?"

"You're asking *me* that question?" the old man said with a laugh. "You? Mr. Love 'em and Leave 'em is actually telling me he doesn't know how to keep a lady occupied for three short days? Cut the crap, boy. I know better."

Brad flinched. Maybe he did have a reputation with the ladies. If a lady wanted a friend, he could be a loyal one. If she wanted a fun date, he was her man. A little sex? Sure, he could be persuaded to rise to the occasion.

However, it wasn't likely Dr. Morgan would be

interested in him, period. She was already fit to be tied over him destroying her film. But if Brad had to inform her that the two of them were going to be *confined* to his living quarters for the next three days? Hell, he'd come closer getting to first base with an angry barracuda than he would with the comely professor.

"We're not talking about some lady I'm taking on a date here, sir. We're talking about me keeping a highly educated woman in my own bedroom against her will. Aren't you concerned about the lawsuit she's bound to bring against us when we do let her go?"

Gibbons grinned. "What's the matter? Afraid the professor is too smart for your usual lady-killer charm?"

Brad frowned. "I'm saying this isn't your typical situation."

"Damn right this isn't your typical situation!" Gibbons boomed. "So the typical rules don't apply. Got it?"

"But, sir…"

"Handle it, Hawkins."

"How? Keep the professor handcuffed to me for the next three days?"

His outburst sparked another threatening gleam in the old man's eye. "Hand me my briefcase."

Brad obeyed his order. Gibbons searched through his briefcase for several seconds, then eventually produced a set of steel-gray handcuffs. Brad caught them easily when Gibbons threw the cuffs in his direction. A second later, Gibbons tossed Brad a key.

"I knew those would come in handy one day,"

Gibbons said with a lopsided grin. "I took them from a snotty M.P. in Saigon one night when he tried to arrest me and your father for disturbing the peace. We'd just flown fourteen helicopter missions straight through the bowels of hell. We both decided no M.P. with a cushy security job was going to do anything but give us the respect we deserved. I took his cuffs away from him, and your father stuffed him in a trash can outside the bar. It still makes me laugh when I think about it."

Brad wasn't laughing. "And you really expect me to use these?"

"What part do you not understand, Hawkins? Handle it."

"Sir…"

"That's an order, Captain Hawkins. I don't care how you do it. Just do it. Dismissed."

Defeated, Brad saluted the man he had always called *Uncle Joe* in private. The man who had become a surrogate father to him after his father was killed. The man who had been his mentor, his confidant, his pal.

The same man who was grinning back at Brad now with an openly sadistic smile.

"Isn't it standard procedure that all prisoners get at least one phone call?" Maddie asked Sergeant Baker who was now standing in front of the only door in the room with his legs wide apart and his hands clasped behind his back in a typical guard-type pose.

Still guarding *her,* of course, the accused *spy* whose only mistake had been to climb a fence in pursuit of an elusive butterfly that could have possibly furthered her career.

"You'll have to take that up with Hawk when he returns," Mr. G.I. Joe-cool finally answered.

"Hawk?"

"Captain Hawkins. It's his nickname. But not just because of his last name," Sergeant Baker added with a sly grin. "We call him Hawk because there isn't a chick in anybody's coop safe when Hawk's around. The hens simply can't resist him, if you know what I mean."

Maddie felt her own feathers ruffle at that comment. She even clucked her tongue a few times before the lie slipped out in protest, "Then I guess I'm not your typical *hen,* Sergeant Baker. Because Captain Hawkins doesn't appeal to me at all."

Baker's smirk challenged her statement. "Then I'll be sure and pass it along that Hawk has finally met his match."

Maddie was ready to cackle out a plea that Sergeant Baker do no such thing, but the door suddenly opened and the handsome hen thief himself stepped inside the room.

She was on her feet in a flash.

And how long had it been now? One hour? Two? Looking down at her watch, Maddie was shocked to see it had now been four long hours since she had unwillingly lost her freedom.

"I'm worried about my sister," Maddie was quick to tell him before he had time to say a word. "And I'm sure she's frantic wondering what happened to me. Now, please, Captain Hawkins. Take me to your commander so we can get this whole mess straightened out."

His answer was to stroll across the room and force what appeared to be a neatly folded pair of camouflage pants and a T-shirt with the same irregular markings into her hands. On top of the T-shirt sat a new toothbrush, a tube of toothpaste, a small bottle of shampoo and a brush and comb.

"Standard government issue," he said matter-of-factly. "These clothes were the smallest I could find. I'm sure you'd like to clean up and get rid of some of that dust and sand."

Refusing to let an act of kindness deter her in the least, Maddie looked down at the bundle, then back up at him. "You seem to be under some misguided notion I'm going to need these. But I assure you, as soon as I get to see your commander that won't be the case."

He accepted the bundle when she pushed it back in his direction, but they continued to face each other like two gunslingers prepared for a shoot-out. Maddie stared at him. He stared back. She tried to step around him and head for the door. He purposely blocked her path. With only inches left between them, Maddie had nowhere to look but up. And the second she did, she became lost in the dark brown depths of his eyes.

"I'm sorry, Dr. Morgan, Commander Gibbons isn't available at the moment."

"He isn't?" Maddie managed to squeak.

She didn't object when he took her gently by the elbow and began leading her away from the door and in the direction of the love seat. Just the touch of his hand was enough to make her knees weak. The faint smell of his aftershave didn't do much for her addled thoughts, either. In fact, Maddie was mentally fabricating a letter of complaint to Mr. Ralph Lauren in protest of the intoxicating effects his products had on women, when she glanced back over her shoulder at Sergeant Baker's grinning face.

In an instant, the words *hawk* and *henhouse* sobered her faster than a bucket of ice water.

"Now listen, Captain," she said, pulling away from him in the nick of time. "Like you told me earlier, we can do this easy, or we can do it hard. It's your choice. But I *am* going to see this Commander Gibbons one way or the other. Is that understood?"

He had the nerve to laugh.

"You think that's funny?" Maddie demanded, shaking her finger in his direction. "You think you can hold me against my will, and I won't march right out of here the first chance I get?"

He didn't bother answering her question. Instead he turned to his buddy and said, "Why don't you head over to the mess hall, Baker. I'm sure Dr. Morgan is hungry. Pick up a few sandwiches, some fruit and anything else you can find. And give us at least an hour alone. We need to have a little talk."

Maddie sent an anxious glance after her bodyguard when he disappeared through the door. "What now, Captain Hawkins?" she asked with false bravado. "Is this where you send away any witnesses so you can rough me up? Are you going to force me to admit I'm some international spy when I'm not? Use some type of Chinese water torture, maybe? Try some shock therapy on me?"

Better yet, why don't you just kiss me to death?

Maddie panicked. She couldn't have these thoughts now. Not with him standing less than ten feet away! Still, her mind kept yelling *I'll admit to anything, for just one kiss. I'll admit to being a spy. I'll even admit to being a pistol-toting gun moll. You name the role. I'll play it!*

He kept looking at her so strangely Maddie feared she had actually spoken the words aloud. She breathed a thankful sigh of relief when he slowly shook his head and said, "You've seen too many old war movies if you really expect me to use any type of torture on you, Dr. Morgan."

You're torturing me now, just looking in my direction!

He walked calmly to the opposite side of the room and placed the clothing on the table. Then he reached inside the small refrigerator and pulled out two cans of soda before turning back to face her. "I think you'd better sit down for this conversation."

Maddie accepted the soda, but not his suggestion. "I'll stand, thank you," she told him, deciding it might be safer if she stayed on her feet. Besides, she wasn't taking any chances. Now that her usually suppressed libido had assumed a life of its own, something as innocent as sitting on the love seat might quickly turn into something else. Something like her stretching out seductively in a come-on pose and beckoning him to follow.

When he seated himself in the recliner a safe distance away, Maddie felt like cheering.

"First, I want to apologize," he said, never taking his eyes from her face. "I'm sorry I had to destroy your film."

He caught Maddie off guard with that statement. Especially since she could tell he was sincere. There was no trace of mockery hiding in those dark brown eyes of his. No hidden agenda. No game playing. No deceit.

"Apology accepted," Maddie told him. She assumed his apology meant she was no longer a spy suspect. "I owe you an apology, too. For climbing that fence and for causing you all this trouble. And if there's a fine for trespassing, Captain Hawkins, I'll gladly pay it. But I can't stress enough how important it is that I'm released as soon as possible. If I'm detained much longer I could lose any chance of finding—"

He cut her off before she could finish. "I'm sorry, Dr. Morgan, but there are a few complications you don't understand."

"What kind of complications?" Maddie asked suspiciously.

By the time he got to the *top secret* part, Maddie deeply regretted her question.

3

BRAD HAD KNOWN HE WOULD BE taking a big gamble if he told his prisoner the truth. In fact, under different circumstances he could have even been facing a court martial for divulging classified information. But like the old man had said himself, this wasn't your typical situation. Typical rules, therefore, simply did not apply.

And that had been the deciding factor for Brad to place all the cards right out on the table. They were caught up in a bizarre situation. If he wanted her full cooperation, Brad knew he needed to tell the professor the truth. Instinct told him her own integrity wouldn't let him down.

By the time he finally finished his lengthy explanation, Brad noticed she had wandered over to the love seat after all, and was now sitting stiffly on the edge of her seat with a panicked expression on her face. And then, from out of the blue, came the overwhelming urge to comfort her; to take her gently into his arms and kiss away the lines of worry that were now marring her beautiful face.

Whoa! Talk about a red alert.

He wasn't the comforting type. Sure, she'd been handed a raw deal, but she'd have to suck it up and deal with it. Besides, only seconds earlier comforting her had been the last thing on his mind. He'd have to be dead not to find her attractive. Earlier, as he'd watched her pace around the room, all he could think about was wanting her naked. Plain and simple. Naked he could handle.

But being tempted to comfort her?

That was scary.

Purging any thoughts of comforting her from his mind, Brad said, "I hope you'll agree protecting national security takes precedence over the research you were doing on your butterfly."

She nodded, but continued sitting on the edge of the love seat with a vacant stare.

"And not to make light of things, but this is one of those situations where you happened to be in the wrong place at the wrong time."

She glanced in his direction this time. "I don't agree with *that* statement," she said defiantly. "In fact, I think I was in the *right* place at the *right* time, or I never would have found the butterfly I was searching for."

"We could argue the point for hours, but it wouldn't change the situation," Brad tossed back. "The fact still remains protecting this mission has to take top priority."

She frowned. "Tell me, Captain. If this mission is so top secret, how did you get permission to tell me all of the details?"

Brad smiled, having anticipated she would ask that very question. "What was the point in insulting your intelligence? You've already seen the Black Ghost. You've even ridden in it. You had to realize it wasn't your everyday run-of-the-mill helicopter."

She seemed pleased with his answer. "You're right. And then when you destroyed my film..."

"You realized it was the helicopter I was trying to protect?" Brad finished for her.

She nodded. "I suspected as much."

"I was counting on the fact that if I explained the seriousness of the situation, you'd be willing to give me your full cooperation," he added for good measure.

"Well, of course, I'll give you my full cooperation now that I know the circumstances," she said, sounding insulted that he might think otherwise. "I *am* a responsible citizen, Captain Hawkins, despite my one bad decision to climb that fence."

"Good. Because I'm going to need your full co-operation. And that's an understatement."

She sent him a blank stare. "Do I dare ask why?"

Brad tossed his empty soda can in a small waste-basket sitting by the recliner and left his chair. Walking toward the bookcase, he hoped what little ground he'd been gaining over the last few minutes wouldn't be lost when the full magnitude of the situation was finally revealed to the woman with whom he was destined to be spending the next three days.

However, just to be on the safe side, Brad purposely sent her an apologetic look when he picked up the television remote and reluctantly punched the button.

MADDIE GASPED WHEN A close-up of Mary Beth instantly filled the screen.

"Thank you for being so patient with me," Mary Beth told the handsome TV reporter in what Maddie immediately recognized as her sister's *theatrical* voice. "I'm still shaking so badly, I can hardly sit in this chair.'' As proof, Mary Beth held out her trembling hands for the reporter to see.

Maddie frowned.

''Well, of course, you've been shaken up,'' the reporter sympathized as he reached out to pat those poor shaking fingers. ''Who wouldn't be after what you've been through?''

Mary Beth dabbed daintily at her eyes with a tissue one of the adoring police officers standing beside her suddenly produced, then sent another pitiful look directly at the camera.

''For those of you just tuning in, we're here at the police station in downtown Roswell this evening with actress and model, Mary Beth Morgan, who most of you will recognize as the *Evershine Girl*,'' the reporter said.

''The Evershine Girl?'' Hawkins repeated, looking back in Maddie's direction. ''Hey, I remember that commercial.''

Maddie rolled her eyes. ''Yeah, you and every other man in the country who happened to be tuned in to the Super Bowl last year.''

Though his eyes turned back to the screen, Maddie knew that damn commercial was already running like a film strip through the captain's head. Mary Beth riding out of the fog on a coal-black stallion. Steam pluming from the horse's nostrils with every breath it took. Mary Beth holding on to its long black mane like Lady Godiva, with nothing to cover her nakedness but long blond ringlets of her damn *Evershine* hair.

In fact, it wouldn't have surprised Maddie if the company had gone bankrupt from a legion of lawsuits filed by all those guys who probably choked on their tortilla chips when Mary Beth rode nude across their television screen.

"Was your sister really nude in that commercial?" he had the nerve to ask.

Maddie held her hand up to silence him when the reporter patted Mary Beth supportively on the shoulder and said, "I know this is very difficult for you, Miss Morgan." His sympathy prompted another sniffle from Mary Beth. "But could you please tell our viewers exactly what happened a few hours ago on the outskirts of Roswell?"

When the reporter pushed the microphone in her direction, Mary Beth took a deep breath and squeezed her eyes shut, trying, Maddie suspected, to produce a genuine tear. It worked. The camera zoomed in to watch the droplet roll down her sister's flawless cheek.

"I was with my sister, Dr. Madeline Morgan, whom I might add is one of the most respected entomologists in her field," Mary Beth told her viewers, making no effort to wipe the fake tear away.

"And…" the reporter urged.

"We were out in the desert searching for…" A few false sobs erupted before she added, "An endangered species of butterfly. A species my sister is absolutely passionate about. One she even hoped to save by proving that they did exist right here in southeastern New Mexico."

There were more pats on the hand, more eye dabbing before she added, "And Maddie thought she saw one. The butterfly, I mean. That's when she left the Jeep."

Hawkins glanced back in her direction again.

"Maddie, huh? Yeah, Maddie suits you much better than Madeline."

Maddie left the love seat long enough to drop her own empty soda can into the trash, then came to a stop beside him. "I'm sure *Hawk* suits you better, too."

He laughed. "Sergeant Baker has a big mouth."

"Well, I'm one *chick* Sergeant Baker won't have to worry about," Maddie said right back. "*My* hen-house is hawk proof."

He sent her a we'll-just-see-about-that grin, but the reporter spoke up again and turned their attention back to the television screen.

"Please go on," the reporter encouraged.

Mary Beth's lip did a little quiver before she looked straight into the camera again. "And that's when I saw it."

"The spacecraft, you mean?" the reporter clarified.

Mary Beth nodded, her eyes growing wide in an expressive fear mode. "It was huge," she whispered. "Silent. Deadly. It swooped down so fast Maddie never knew what hit her. I couldn't do a thing to help my poor sister. All I could do was scream."

When Mary Beth dramatically covered her face with her hands and burst into tears, Maddie said, "I'm going to kill her."

He sent her a puzzled look. "Kill her? But you said your sister would be hysterical about this."

"Yes, but I *know* my twin sister. And what you see now is nothing more than a fine piece of Mary Beth Morgan acting. Probably her finest piece of work to date, if you really want to know the truth."

"Twin?" he echoed in disbelief.

"Identical twin," Maddie clarified with a frown that only got deeper when Brad looked directly at her chest then back at the screen as if he certainly didn't believe her story.

Of course, she didn't know why she would expect *him* to be any different. Like all of the other men hovering around Mary Beth on the screen, the dear captain had obviously been dumbstruck by the ample cleavage Mary Beth didn't mind flaunting. And why did *she* care if the man standing beside her was ogling her sister's partially exposed size 36D bosom? He was no one *she'd* ever be interested in, at least not seriously. A man nicknamed *Hawk* because of the way he swooped down on innocent women? Forget about it!

His look was questioning. "So? You don't think your sister really believes you were carried off by aliens?"

"Of course, she doesn't!" Maddie said a little too sharply. "Mary Beth's an actress. She's not an imbecile."

"Then why is she making all the fuss?"

Maddie threw her hands up in the air. "Who knows? Maybe she was afraid to admit I was trespassing on government property. Maybe she thought if she told the police I'd been carried off by aliens they'd be more willing to take up the search. Maybe…"

"Maybe she couldn't resist getting her own fifteen minutes of fame?" he threw in.

Maddie looked back at the screen. The thought *had* crossed her mind. "Well, she's certainly getting that, isn't she?"

"She certainly is," Captain Hawk agreed. "And that's why you can't be released."

Maddie paled. "What do you mean I can't be released?"

He jerked his thumb toward the screen again. "That sister of yours has the entire country convinced you were carried off by aliens. We have no choice but to keep you here until we can demobilize our entire operation."

"But how can keeping me here possibly solve anything?" Maddie cried out. "The only way to clear this up is to let me go back to Roswell and prove I'm safe."

"I'm sorry, but we just can't risk it."

"Risk what?" Maddie demanded.

He took a deep breath. "To put it bluntly, we can't risk you cracking under the pressure of the media." His eyes softened a bit when he added, "But you have my word. As soon as we get the helicopter out of here, I'll personally see you're returned safely back to Roswell."

"But how long will that take?"

"At least three days."

"Three days?" Maddie repeated.

That would give Mary Beth three full days in front of the cameras. Three days to play her grief-stricken sister act to the hilt. Three days with the entire world convinced that Dr. Madeline Morgan, respected entomologist, had fallen prey to renegade aliens....

And only when her entire life started crumbling right before her eyes, did Maddie quickly turn to face him. Grabbing the front of his T-shirt, Maddie literally dragged him two steps in her direction.

"Are you nuts? You have to let me out of here! This is my *life* we're talking about."

BRAD TURNED OFF THE TV and pried her fingers from his shirt, then led his shaken prisoner back in the direction of the love seat. In spite of the lecture he had given himself earlier, he couldn't resist placing a comforting arm around her shoulder. He winced inwardly, however, when she leaned against him for support, pressing her warm, curvaceous body against him.

You can't get personally involved with this woman, Brad kept telling himself as he guided her back to the love seat and took a seat beside her. He managed to ease his arm from around her shoulder, but she only grabbed it again and sent him a pleading look.

"Don't you realize my career could be ruined if you don't let me out of here?"

Brad almost missed the question. She kept squeezing his arm, making him imagine for a moment those same slender fingers caressing his back. Then clutching his shoulders. Her nails finally digging in, signaling he was close to pushing her up and over the next wave of passion.

"And what about my poor parents?" she worried, sending another anguished look in his direction. "While one daughter is trying for an obvious Emmy nomination, my poor parents will be worrying that daughter number two is being dissected by little green men from outer space!"

When she finally let go of his arm, some of the blood that had been directed elsewhere slowly returned to his brain, allowing him to respond.

"You're right," Brad agreed. "This is a very unfortunate situation to be in, but..."

"Unfortunate?" she wailed, jumping up from the loveseat again. "It's much worse than *unfortunate!* If you don't let me out of here, I'm going to be a worldwide laughing stock! Everything I've worked for my entire life could go right down the drain."

"I know, and I'm sorry, but..."

"Then if you won't let me leave, at least let me call Mary Beth at the hotel and get this whole thing straightened out!"

Again, Brad shook his head. "I'm sorry. I really am. But it's totally out of my hands now."

Her voice grew even more pleading. "Then let me see Commander Gibbons. Please. Give me the chance to tell him *my* side of the story."

Brad squirmed at that particular request. He could tell she was finally beginning to see the big picture for what it actually was.

"Wait a minute," she said slowly, her eyes narrowing. "I'm never going to *see* Commander Gibbons, am I?"

Brad didn't answer.

"No. Of course, I'm not going to see him," she said, slapping her forehead with the heel of her hand. "This is going to be 'I never had sex with that woman' all over again, isn't it? If your commander never *sees* me, then he can technically deny knowing I was ever brought to this base."

Brad knew his guilty look said it all.

"But what if I don't cooperate?" she threatened. "What if I *don't* keep this helicopter of yours a secret when you do let me go?"

"It won't matter then," Brad said simply. "It will

be your word against the United States Air Force. And the more you force the issue, the less credible you'll become. Especially since your sister has already gone overboard with her alien abduction story.''

If looks could kill, Brad knew the Air Force would have been making arrangements for his full military funeral.

"So, you've got it all figured out, haven't you?'' she huffed. "You'll discredit me and ruin my reputation even further if I expose your top secret helicopter. And you'll claim my sister is just some weirdo with a screw loose.''

"I wouldn't exactly put it like that.''

Brad was on his feet now. She was getting all riled up again and he needed to keep her as calm as possible. He tried to take her hand so he could coax her back to the love seat, but she quickly smacked his hand away.

"And stop trying to pull your ridiculous henhouse magic on me. It won't work.''

Wanna bet? Brad thought, and to test her, he took another step in her direction. He smiled inwardly when her eyes suddenly grew wide with concern.

Yes, his military training had taught him well. He had always been good at finding his adversary's weak point, though he found it rather funny that a woman with a degree in entomology turned into Little Miss Muffet when he got too close, acting as if he were some spider trying to frighten her away. Her obvious concern about his intentions, however, would be his trump card in keeping her under control. He would keep her flustered. Off balance. Keep her mind off everything else by making her deal with him one-on-one. Making her do the one thing Dr. Madeline Morgan obviously didn't have an impressive degree in: interacting with the opposite sex.

"I'm always open to suggestions," Brad teased, reaching out to run his finger along the curve of her chin. "Why don't you tell me what *will* work to put you in a friendlier mood?"

"Your head on a silver platter, maybe?" she said and slapped his hand away again.

Brad only grinned. "Sorry, but you're stuck with me. And if you'd lighten up a little, you'd realize we could have a pretty amazing time playing house together over the next three days."

PLAYING HOUSE TOGETHER? While my entire life is going down the toilet? Maddie was so shocked by such an absurd suggestion words completely failed her. Unfortunately her wanna-be playmate took her silence as an invitation to step forward again.

And that's when Maddie knew she really was in trouble.

He was standing so close she was sure he could hear her heart thumping wildly in her chest. She tried to move away, and she would have, had he not surprised her by reaching out to gently push a wayward strand of hair away from her face.

"So? How about it?" he asked, his voice husky and dangerous. "Wanna call a truce and play house?"

Maddie stiffened when one of his powerful arms slipped around her waist. He pulled her to him, forcing her to acknowledge every inch of his rock-hard body that was pressed against her own. A little afraid, but deliciously excited, for some reason pushing him away never entered Maddie's mind.

And from that moment on, she was helpless.

She was powerless.

She was nothing but another willing chicken, after all, surrendering shamelessly to the ruthless hawk who now had her in his more than capable clutches.

Closing her eyes in breathless anticipation, Maddie waited for the kiss of a lifetime. His warm breath inched closer, teasing her, tempting her, and then finally cheating her when a loud knock on the door produced not a kiss, but a curse from his lips.

"Let go of me," Maddie demanded when her eyes snapped back open. She did try to push him away this time, but Hawk held her against him long enough to whisper, "Make yourself at home, Sweet Maddie. This is just a sample of the fun we can have together over the next three days."

BRAD WALKED OUT INTO THE hallway and closed the door behind him. He turned to face his copilot and found Baker holding a tray loaded down with enough food to feed half the men who were staying on the base.

"Anyone question you about the food?"

Baker, who was six-four and tipped the scales somewhere around two-fifty, looked down at the tray and laughed. "Are you kidding? Everybody knows I can eat this much food for a snack."

"Good." Brad ran a hand over his short-cropped hair. "Because we're going to have an extra mouth to feed until we can demob and get the Black Ghost out of here."

Baker sent a worried look at the closed door.

"You mean the old man plans to keep her here on base?"

Brad nodded.

"Where?"

"Right where she is."

"She's going to bunk with you?" Baker barked in disbelief.

Brad frowned. "Yeah. You got a problem with that?"

"You're the one who's going to have a problem with it, Hawk," Baker said, frowning back. "Hell, man, you might as well be sleeping with the enemy."

Brad stared at the man who had been his closest friend since they were in boot camp together. They'd seen their share of good times over the years. Chased the ladies together. Held fast in their belief that the Air Force did and always would come first in their lives. But this was the first time Baker had ever voiced a concern that Brad couldn't hold his own where a woman was concerned.

"What are you saying? That you don't think I can be confined with a woman and keep my pants zipped?"

"It's not your zipper I'm worried about, Hawk. There are ladies you play around with and ladies you don't. This lady is your worst nightmare. If you're not careful, you'll end up chasing her right up until the time *she* catches *you*."

Brad laughed. "That isn't going to happen and you know it."

Baker didn't seem convinced. "Trust me about this, Hawk. Get this woman under your skin and the next thing you know, you'll be back in civilian clothes and hurrying home every night so you can help out with the kids.''

Brad really had a good laugh that time. Him? Running home to a wife and kids? Not a chance. He'd made himself a promise when he joined the Air Force that he'd never make the same mistake his father did. Brad knew first hand how devastated he and his mother had been when his father was killed. His mother never really recovered. The doctors claimed her heart was weak, but Brad knew better. Her heart had been broken. And rather than hand down that same legacy himself, a wife and a family would never have any place in his future.

Jabbing a finger in the big man's chest, Brad said, ''Stop worrying about me and keep our prisoner confined while I go check on the Black Ghost. No one knows she's here but you, me and Gibbons, and we need to keep it that way. But she's determined to get out of here, Baker. Don't let that happen. Got it?''

Baker sent another worried look toward the door. ''Why don't *I* go check on the Black Ghost, and *you* stay here?''

Brad laughed. ''What's the matter? Afraid *you'll* fall under the professor's spell?''

''Hell, no,'' Baker grumbled. ''But you weren't the one trying to hold her down earlier. She's stronger than she looks.''

''You have at least one hundred and thirty pounds on her,'' Brad scoffed. ''I think you can handle it.''

''That's easy for you to say,'' Baker argued. ''I'm telling you, Hawk, she's a real handful.''

Believe me, she's more than a handful, Brad thought with a frown, remembering the feel of her ample bosom pressed against his chest. He hated to admit it, but Baker was right about the danger he'd be facing over the next few days. Especially if he stuck to his plan to keep her off balance by coming on to her. There was always the possibility a plan like that one could backfire. But he assured himself he could handle the situation. "Stop stalling and get back inside. Someone might get suspicious if you're guarding my door."

Baker groaned, but finally nodded in agreement.

Brad gave him a playful salute and headed down the hallway. "Have fun," he tossed back over his shoulder with a wink.

4

SLUMPED ON THE LOVE SEAT, munching from a bag of popcorn Baker had brought back from the mess hall, Maddie ignored the big gorilla who was again standing guard in front of the door. She was still stewing over the disastrous little tête-à-tête that had occurred earlier with the Hawk, though Maddie mainly blamed herself for letting her guard down. Which she positively wouldn't do again, thank you very much!

Liar! the little voice inside her head yelled out with a snicker.

Okay. So maybe she wasn't as strong as she thought she was. Maybe it would take everything she had to keep from *clucking* her silly head off when Mr. Let's-Play-House walked back into the room. She was, after all, just a normal, healthy, still on the back side of thirty female.

Normal?

Okay. So maybe she wasn't exactly your *typical* twenty-something female. She could admit that. She was dedicated to a fault. Focused more on her career than she was on life in general. But she still dated occasionally. She had to earn some points for dating.

Occasionally?

Okay. So maybe *rarely* was a better word. But

she did date. And she did like men. She did! She just never had any time to fit them into her life.

What about the next three days?

Maddie pushed *that* question to the back of her mind, and continued to channel surf through a multitude of cable stations. She jumped to her feet when Headline News flashed her faculty picture, taken straight from the McCray-Hadley annual on the screen.

All Maddie could do was stare in horror.

She wasn't sure if her terror was because they had chosen to display her absolutely most dreadful and unflattering picture of all time, or because Mary Beth's idiocy had now been picked up by *national* television news.

"An all-points bulletin has now been issued for Dr. Madeline Morgan, a professor of entomology at McCray-Hadley College, one of the most acclaimed private colleges in the South," the pretty newswoman said with a serious look when the camera switched from Maddie's horrid picture back to her. "As reported earlier, Dr. Morgan was allegedly abducted earlier today by an unidentified aircraft near Roswell, New Mexico. Anyone with any valid information on the whereabouts of Dr. Morgan is urged to contact their local police authorities...."

"Can you believe this insanity?" Maddie cried out, prompting only a sheepish look from her bodyguard.

"And joining us now direct from a fraternity house near the McCray-Hadley campus is our own reporter...."

"Dear God," Maddie moaned as a live shot of the Alpha Beta Pi fraternity house came into view.

"We're here in Morgan City, Georgia, tonight," the handsome reporter told the world, "but so far we've been unsuccessful in getting any statement from the dean of McCray-Hadley, or from Dr. Melvin Fielding, noted entomologist and current Department Chair, who is also Dr. Morgan's immediate supervisor."

"Of course, they don't have time to make a statement, you idiot!" Maddie yelled at the screen. "They're too busy trying to figure out how they're gracefully going to fire me."

"But we have been fortunate to locate several of Dr. Morgan's students," he added and the camera panned to a group of grinning students waving madly at the camera. One boy mouthed "Hi Mom" before the reporter extended the microphone in his direction.

"Are you a student of Dr. Morgan's?"

"Yeah, man. She's a really happening teacher."

"Too bad your *grades* aren't just as happening," Maddie grumbled, digging into her popcorn bag again.

"Do any of you think it's really possible Dr. Morgan *has* been kidnapped by aliens?" the pushy reporter inquired.

As luck would have it, a student known as "Reefer" for a very good reason jumped forward to answer that question. "Wow, man. I'm totally psyched over the possibility Dr. Morgan really has been abducted by aliens," Reefer said in his usual far-out way of speaking. "Of all the people in the world, the aliens chose one of our very own faculty members right here at McCray-Hadley to represent our entire planet. It's totally awesome, man. Totally awesome.''

''And do you have any speculation about why Dr. Morgan would have been chosen, if, in fact, she *has* been abducted by aliens?'' the reporter said with a sinister smile that could have easily been caused by the overwhelming aroma that was usually reeking from Reefer's wrinkled clothing.

''You bet I do,'' Reefer said with a completely serious expression. ''Butterflies, man. Dr. Morgan knows all there is to know about butterflies. Ask anyone on campus. That's how she earned her nickname. Madam Butterfly.''

Maddie felt like she'd been slapped. Nickname? Reefer was the one with the nickname! Not her. Surely not her!

''Well, you've heard it here folks,'' the reporter said with a lopsided grin as he practically shoved Reefer back into the crowd. ''Students at McCray-Hadley are certainly wishing the best for Dr. Madeline Morgan, who is known around campus as Madam Butterfly.''

Maddie switched off the TV, smashed the popcorn bag with her fist and threw the remote control across the room. It landed on the love seat with such force it bounced several times, then toppled to the floor.

''I can't believe this is happening,'' Maddie kept saying as she paced around the room. ''This morning I was a respected entomologist, on the verge of the biggest discovery of my career, and in the blink of an eye a snide reporter on national news has the audacity to refer to me as Madam Butterfly!''

Maddie did a little more pacing, tossed the bag

into the trash, then tentatively looked around the room for something to destroy. Her intentions must have been reflected in her frown, because her body-guard suddenly cleared his throat to get her attention.

"I wouldn't let that reporter bother me if I were you, Dr. Morgan. This will all blow over soon enough," Baker said calmly from his post at the door.

Maddie whirled around to face him, hoping he couldn't detect thc wheels that had also started whirling around inside her head. She hesitated for a second, and then she said, "You know, Sergeant Baker, you're absolutely right. Thanks for helping me put things into perspective." Maddie sent him her most brilliant smile.

He seemed surprised, but he smiled back. Then he shrugged. Then he did a little shuffle from one foot to the other, more than a little embarrassed under her praise. "Hey, don't mention it."

Gotcha! Maddie thought. And though she certainly wasn't proud of herself for turning on a big dose of feminine charm, Maddie knew she had to get back to Roswell before her career was so badly ruined she'd never recover.

"You poor, poor, man," Maddie said, forcing herself to even bat her eyelashes a few times. "I've been so focused on my own problems, I never stopped to think how tired you must be standing at the door hour after hour."

Baker stood up a little straighter and puffed his massive chest out a bit further, if that were possible. "Don't worry about me. I'm fine."

"Don't be so modest." Maddie walked across the

room toward the table. "The least I can do is bring you a sandwich. I'm sure Captain Hawkins doesn't care if you eat something, as long as you guard the door."

Baker licked his lips, watching as Maddie rifled through the contents on the tray. "That's okay." But there was a lot of uncertainty in his voice when he added, "I'll get something later."

Maddie waved a tasty-looking ham and cheese sub in his direction. "This is what I had earlier. And believe me, it was scrumptious."

"Well, I am kinda hungry," Baker admitted, just as Maddie hoped he would.

"And what about a soda to go with your sandwich?" Maddie asked in the sweetest voice she could muster.

"Yeah, that would be great," Baker said, grinning back in appreciation.

Maddie withdrew a can of soda from the small fridge, popped open the top, then walked toward Baker with what she hoped was a pleasant smile on her face. "Here you go," she said when she handed over the sandwich, but she purposely let go of the can before he could take it.

The contents splashed all over him.

Baker automatically bent down, grabbing for the can, and when he did, Maddie gave him a push with everything she had. Caught completely off guard, Goliath hit the floor with a thud.

Maddie never looked back.

She yanked the door open and headed down the hallway at a breakneck speed that would have put any Olympic sprinter to shame. *Which way?* Maddie kept asking herself frantically. The long hallway stopped at an intersection up ahead. Baker had brought her in from the left, through an exit door that would only lead her back outside to the helicopter pad. But if she went right, where would she be? Deciding her only choice was to take that chance, she turned right at the last second.

Colliding head-on with Hawk gave Maddie a glimpse of how her insect friends felt when they didn't see the windshield until it was too late.

The impact bounced her backward like a rubber ball and landed her flat on her back. By the time she pushed herself up on her elbows and stole back her breath, both Hawk and Baker were standing above her.

Neither seemed amused.

"Dammit, Hawk, she tricked me," Baker explained.

Hawk didn't answer. Instead both men reached down simultaneously, hooked Maddie under each arm, and literally carried her back down the hallway. Once back inside her prison, Maddie was plopped down in the recliner before Hawk uttered a word.

"Give me your shoes," Captain Hawk ordered.

"I most certainly will not!"

He bent down and had Maddie's hiking boots off faster than if she'd been wearing a pair of slippers.

"Take these with you. I'm in for the night," he told Baker who wasted no time grabbing her boots and making a hasty exit out the door.

Bracing herself for the lecture she knew was coming, Captain Hawkins didn't disappoint her. Coming to a stop directly in front of her chair, he glared down at her with his hands at his waist. "You think this is some kind of a game, don't you?"

"Game?" Maddie jumped up to face him in her stocking feet. "My entire life is being ruined, you're holding me against my will, and *you* have the nerve to ask me if I think this is a *game?*"

They glared at each other for several seconds as if the brief intimacy they'd shared earlier never happened. Maddie was too worried about her career to even think about the kiss that almost transpired between them, and judging from his serious expression, Captain Hawk wasn't in a playful little mood, either.

He surprised her when he said, "You're right. You *are* the one who has the most to lose in this situation. That's why I decided a call to your sister might not be such a bad idea."

Maddie couldn't believe her eyes when he pulled a cell phone from the pocket of the jacket he was now wearing.

"Get your sister to call off the search," he instructed. "Tell her you're okay, but nothing else. Understood?"

When Maddie nodded, he asked, "Where is she staying?"

"The Hampton Inn. Room 402," Maddie told him, then held her breath when he called information for the number.

He checked his watch before he dialed the hotel. "It's almost midnight, so it should be safe to make the call. Make sure she's alone. If she isn't, hang up."

Maddie nodded in agreement again.

"Room 402," he said when the hotel operator answered, and Maddie eagerly took the phone when he handed it over. He was standing so close, Maddie decided she'd be wise to follow his instructions to the letter. The second Mary Beth answered, Maddie said, "Are you alone?"

"Maddie? Is that you?" came the startled cry on the other end of the line.

"Answer me, Mary Beth. Are you alone?"

"Well, of course, I'm alone. My God, Maddie, are you okay? How much trouble are you in?"

"Not nearly as much trouble as *you're* going to be in when I get my hands on you," Maddie seethed.

"Now wait just a minute," Mary Beth protested. "I've been worried to death about you. Where are you, anyway? Tell me! I'll come and get you this minute."

"Come and get me?" Maddie shouted. "I've been carried off by aliens, remember?"

"Okay, okay. I admit things have gotten out of hand. But you weren't the one being chased across the desert by jeep full of soldiers with bazookas on their shoulders."

"God, Mary Beth, how could you do this to me?" Maddie broke in, no more impressed than she usually was with her sister's outrageous dramatics.

"I swear, it wasn't my fault, Maddie. I was petrified when I saw that soldier grab you. And then when I realized I was being chased myself, I headed for Roswell so fast I had to be doing a hundred miles an hour."

"And?"

"Well, that was the problem. After I hit the main road, I was pulled over by the local police for speeding. The second the officer walked up to the Jeep, I blurted out that my sister had been abducted."

"Dear God," Maddie groaned.

"I know. Saying the word *abduction* in Roswell is like saying you saw something strange swimming around in Loch Ness."

"But why didn't you explain what you meant, Mary Beth?"

"I tried to explain," Mary Beth insisted. "But think about the answers I had to give them. A weird-looking aircraft? Out near the old Air Force base? Everyone got so excited, I decided if I just went along with the hysteria, those goons who grabbed you would forget all about your trespassing and send you straight back to Roswell to clear things up."

Wishful thinking, Maddie thought. "And what about Mom and Pop, Mary Beth? Have you at least had the decency to call and tell them the truth?"

"They're up at the cabin for the next two weeks. Didn't they tell you? And you know Pop's rules when they go up there. No radio. No TV. No phone. No outside communication, period."

Maddie breathed a sigh of relief. "Well, at least that's one thing in our favor. Hopefully this will all be over once you make a statement to the press in the morning."

"Statement?"

"Yes, Mary Beth, you have to tell them you were mistaken," Maddie stuttered. "Tell them you've heard from me and that I'm okay."

"And *are* you okay? You still haven't told me exactly where you are. Why haven't they let you go, Maddie? Tell me what's really going on."

Maddie hesitated. "It doesn't matter, Mary Beth. Just call off the media."

"What do you mean, it doesn't matter?" Mary

Beth yelled so loudly Maddie held the phone out from her ear.

"Of course, it matters. Tell me where you are and I'll come and get you. Then we can *both* talk to the press. Don't you realize we're celebrities now, Maddie? There's no telling where we could go with this. Think about it. Identical twin sisters? The media will love us. You could get a book deal. Maybe I could even get a picture out of this."

"Have you gone crazy?" Maddie said through clenched teeth. "You have to call off the media, Mary Beth! Do it first thing tomorrow."

"And if I don't?"

"Just do it, Mary Beth."

"Why? What's really going on, Maddie? Tell me."

"I can't," Maddie admitted, sending an anxious look in Hawk's direction.

"What do you mean, you *can't* tell me? You mean you're being held against your will? By our own damn government?"

Maddie took a deep breath. "Something like that," she said, but a warning look from Hawk told her she was already skating on thin ice.

"Then you can tell those camouflage-wearing morons for me that I'll call off the media when I get my sister back!"

Maddie saw red. "Dammit, Mary Beth. My entire career is on the line here!"

"It's always about *your* precious career, isn't it?" Mary Beth accused.

"What's that supposed to mean?"

"What about *my* career? Have you stopped to consider the exposure I'm getting right now?"

"Exposure?"

"Yes, exposure. This is finally the big time for me. I've had calls from Larry King. From Letterman. Even Oprah's people have been ringing my agent's phone off the hook."

Maddie didn't answer.

"Don't you see what this can mean to me? When all of this is over, you'll still be Dr. Madeline Morgan and you'll still have that impressive Ph.D. flowing behind your name. But what about me? If I don't make the most of this opportunity right now, I'll slip back into obscurity and spend the rest of my life scrambling around for occasional two-bit commercials."

When Maddie still didn't answer, Mary Beth said softly, "Don't hate me for putting *my* career first, just this once. I've never hated you for always doing the same thing."

"You know I could never hate you, Mary Beth." Maddie let out a long sigh. "No matter what you did."

"Then tell me the truth, Maddie. Are you really safe? Are you really going to be okay?"

Maddie took another look at the man who made her pulse race every time he looked in her direction. "I'll be fine," she lied. "I should be back at the hotel by the end of the week. Wait for me there. I'll explain everything then."

"Don't worry, I'll be here. My agent wants me here in Roswell where I'll draw the most attention. He's even working out details for satellite interviews he plans to sell to the highest bidder. Can you believe this, Maddie? Me? Being interviewed by…"

Mary Beth was still rambling when Brad reached

out and took the phone, then disconnected the call. He then promptly removed the battery and slipped it into his pants pocket before he placed the now useless cell phone on top of the bookcase. Maddie watched every move he made, but she never said a word.

He leveled a look in her direction. "What about your parents?"

Maddie shrugged a shoulder. "They're up at our family cabin in the mountains. My father insists on total solitude when they're up there. But since Mary Beth won't call off the search, it's only a matter of time until someone from Morgan City heads up to the cabin to find them."

"Any connection between the name of your hometown and your family?"

"Afraid so," Maddie said with a sigh. "My ancestors founded Morgan City. My father's the mayor. Of course, in a town the size of Morgan City, being mayor is more of an honorary title than anything else."

His look was sympathetic. "And this sister of yours? She would really jeopardize your career and never give it a second thought?"

Maddie walked back to the love seat and flopped down with her head in her hands, the events of the day finally catching up with her. "I'm too exhausted to even think about that right now," she told him truthfully. "But thanks for letting me at least *try* to talk some sense into her."

She could tell he had hoped she could convince Mary Beth to call off the media. Without the media figuring into the situation, his helicopter would have been safe and his commander would have had less reason to keep her there. And he had to be just as eager to get rid of her as she was to leave. They couldn't get along for more than five minutes at a time, mainly Maddie suspected, because they both liked being in control.

Well, I'm not giving in, Maddie vowed as she massaged her throbbing temples. But now that she had attempted to escape *and* he knew Mary Beth wasn't calling off the bogus search, what would he do?

"How do you usually sleep? On your back? Or on your side?"

Maddie's head came up to look at him. "I beg your pardon?"

"Do you sleep on your back? Or do you sleep on your side?" he repeated.

"Why on earth would you want to know that?" Maddie's mouth dropped open when he reached into his jacket pocket and pulled out the handcuffs. "Don't even think about it," she warned, but he quickly cut her off.

"I've already thought about it," he said with a frown. "After that stunt you pulled with Baker, I'm not taking any chances. And now that you know your sister isn't going to cooperate, you have even a bigger reason to run. But I'm worn-out, and so are you. We're both two mature adults, so let's simply walk calmly into the bedroom and try to get a little sleep."

"You can't be serious."

"I'm dead serious." And the expression on his face confirmed it. "Now, answer my question. Do you sleep on your back or do you sleep on your side?"

"I sleep on my side," Maddie admitted, sending him an icy look.

"Right side or left?"

"Left," she finally answered after a second to ponder.

"Good. I sleep on my left side, too," he said. "This should be easy."

He took a step in her direction, but Maddie moved farther away. It was the wrong thing to do. When she saw the muscles flex in his jaw, Maddie worried she may have pushed him a little too far.

"Are you purposely trying to be a pain in the ass? Or is this normal for you?" he asked with a grim expression. "I've gone out of my way to make you as comfortable as possible. I've seen that you have food. I've made sure you have clean clothes. And, against my better judgment, I even let you call your crazy sister. Now, I don't know about you, but I think it's *your* turn to do a little compromising. After all, I'm not the one who climbed that fence and set this whole fiasco in motion. *You* are."

The flush of shame crept up her neck. "I don't suppose you would take my word if I said I wouldn't try to escape again?"

He threw his head back to laugh.

"And I guess it doesn't matter that you've already taken away my boots?"

"It doesn't matter in the least."

"And you wouldn't consider sleeping on the love seat, maybe? We could push it in front of the door. You'd be sure to wake up if I tried to climb over you."

He looked over at the love seat and back at her.

"I'm six foot two. How much rest do *you* think I could get on a four-foot love seat?"

"Well, you're crazy if you think I'm taking off my clothes," Maddie sputtered.

His grin was as wicked as his laugh had been nasty. "Suit yourself, but I'm taking off mine."

"Fine. I'll sleep on top of the covers."

"It gets chilly out here in the desert at night," he warned.

"Not that chilly."

He shrugged, then motioned toward the bedroom. Reluctantly Maddie marched ahead of him like a prisoner on her way to the gallows. Dear God, what was she going to do now? He had rendered her senseless with the mere possibility that might kiss her. And now she was going to be *handcuffed* to him. In bed. With him naked.

Good Lord, Maddie thought, *how am I ever going to survive the next three days?* Stopping when she reached the side of the bed, Maddie turned around and faced him with both arms held out in front of her.

"Just the right arm, please," he said, grinning from ear to ear.

Maddie rolled her eyes, but did as he instructed. However, when the cold steel clamped around her wrist, Maddie wondered if Hawk realized once he handcuffed them together *he* couldn't escape, either. The thought of him being *her* prisoner brought a faint smile to her lips.

"Now, let's see." He rubbed a hand over the shadow on his chin that only emphasized his maleness. "If we both sleep on our left sides, that means I need to cuff our right hands together. Correct?"

"Don't ask me, I'm just the prisoner," Maddie was quick to point out. "You're the mastermind behind this catastrophe."

He ignored her comment, then bent down long enough to take off his boots. Then he turned her around and stepped up behind her so close, Maddie could feel his warm breath on the back of her neck. A tingle spread through her body so fast it almost made her swoon.

"Should it concern me that you just happen to have a pair of handcuffs in your possession?" Maddie quipped, trying to disguise her rapid breathing.

The chuckle was low in his throat. "I'm not into bondage, if that's what you're asking. Pleasure's always been my game."

Forcing her eyes shut at *that* comment, Maddie bit down on her lower lip, hard. She was trying with everything she had *not* to let her traitorous mind wander into the pleasure department. Not now. Not when she was only seconds away from crawling into bed with a naked man.

To her surprise, instead of shedding his fatigues, he clamped the cuff around his own right hand, leaned over and pulled back the covers and switched off the bedside light.

The room instantly became pitch-black.

"I thought you were getting undressed," Maddie mocked when he didn't go through with his threat.

He leaned closer, resting his chin on her shoulder. "I wouldn't want to tempt you. You might take advantage of me."

"By putting a pillow over your face until you pass out, you mean?"

He laughed, then found the small of her back with

his free hand. "Be a good girl and climb in first. I'll climb in right behind you." Maddie didn't move until he gave her a gentle push. "And then we'll be just as snug as two bugs in a rug," he added with another one of those husky chuckles that unnerved her. "Which is an appropriate way to be if you're sleeping with a famous entomologist, I would think."

"I wouldn't give up my day job," Maddie scoffed. "A comedian you *aren't*." She slid under the covers and scooted as far to the opposite side of the bed as humanly possible. It didn't work. He scooted right in behind her. A piece of paper couldn't have been wedged between them. *Okay, you can do this,* Maddie told herself. *Like the man said, we're both two mature adults. We're both exhausted. And there's no reason why we shouldn't get a little sleep.*

Not that Maddie intended to fall asleep. After all, she was handcuffed to a total stranger who had her sexual motor running faster than a turbo-charged Indy race car! But she would get some rest. Rest was important if she wanted to survive the next three days. Yes, she would just lie there in the darkness awake, still as a mouse, and *pretend* she was asleep. Maybe then he would stop all the snuggly-buggly crapola that was driving her out of her usually focused mind.

But God, he did feel good pressed up against her, she admitted with a mental moan. In fact, they were a perfect fit. She would never have pictured Hawk as a *cuddler* kind of guy. But lying there in the darkness in that intimate spooning position, suddenly made the whole point of cuddling crystal clear to Maddie. Until she felt an unmistakable bulge pressing against her backside.

"Okay, soldier. That better be a hand grenade in your pocket," Maddie warned, hoping the nervousness she felt wasn't evident in her voice.

The second he moved away, Maddie let out a deep sigh of relief. Or was it regret? Whatever! Maddie was simply too exhausted to sort it all out. Unable to suppress a yawn, she mumbled, "It's going to be a long three days."

"Hopefully, long enough," he said with a yawn of his own.

Maddie didn't dare ask, "Long enough for what?"

She had a feeling she already knew the answer.

5

THE SOUND OF THE BEDROOM door closing launched Maddie into a sitting position. Thankfully her iron bracelet and her bed-buddy were now both gone.

"God, what a night," she groaned, glaring at Brad's beside clock. It was only 6:00 a.m., but he had been up and on the move for at least an hour while she kept her eyes closed, pretending to be asleep. Amazingly she had managed to stay awake most of the night, long after the sound of Brad's even breathing told her he was out for the count; a fact that upset her whether Maddie wanted to admit it or not.

Yes, her, she mused. Dr. Madeline Morgan, the woman who only had time for her career, had actually been a bit disappointed that the handsome hunk who had taken her prisoner hadn't been a little more persistent about his boastful house-playing threat.

And what would you have done if he had tried to get a little frisky? her pesky libido wanted to know.

Refusing to even ponder that question in her sleep-deprived state, Maddie scrambled from the bed and made a mad dash for the bathroom. The reflection she saw in the mirror a few seconds later, however, sent her fist to her mouth to stifle a scream.

Her hair, which had never fully recovered from

the helicopter wind storm, looked as if she had contemplated dreadlocks but left the task only halfway completed. An ugly purple bruise the size of a quarter had popped out above her right eyebrow. And worse yet, the skin now seemed to be missing on the very tip of her nose. Praying her bloodshot eyes were only distorting her image, Maddie leaned closer to the mirror, then reached up and tweaked the bright red spot. An instant stab of pain told her bloodshot or not, her eyes still had perfect 20/20 vision.

"If this isn't a day for heavy makeup, I don't know what would be," Maddie grumbled aloud, then remembered all she had with her were the clothes on her back.

Wonderful, she thought, frowning at her horrid reflection. No wonder she had awakened to an empty bed. The way she looked, she suspected Mr. Air Force was probably in the other room now, still hyperventilating over the shock of waking up next to Medusa, snake hair and all! Of course, the minute she thought of Brad, Maddie hurried back to the door to click the lock safely into place. And it wasn't until she turned back around that she noticed the items he had offered her the night before were now sitting in a neat little bundle on the closed toilet seat.

Atop the bundle was a note.

Maddie walked over and picked it up. *Shower and get cleaned up. By the time you're dressed, I should be back with breakfast. Baker is back at his guard post in case you get any bright ideas about trying to escape again.*

"Cute, real cute," Maddie said aloud.

Yeah, he was a real riot, that Hawk.

She tossed the note into the wastebasket beside the sink, shed her rumpled clothing and pulled back the shower curtain that was still damp from the shower Brad had taken earlier. Stepping under the hot spray, she winced slightly when the water found the tender places from the manhandling she had suffered the day before. Too bad her arms and legs weren't the only things bruised. She hated to admit it, but her ego was a little bruised, too, from the manhandling that *hadn't* taken place the night before. And that's what had her so puzzled.

Maddie couldn't explain it, but in less than twenty-four hours she felt as if her entire life had done a gigantic flip-flop. Even finding a Deva Skipper seemed unimportant at the moment, although that could easily be explained thanks to Mary Beth and the media. Now, just holding on to her job had to be her main priority.

But what about all of the fantasizing? The funny feeling she got in the pit of her stomach every time she looked at Hawk? Not to mention the sudden concern over her appearance, which had never mattered one way or another to Maddie before.

Those weren't her normal concerns.

Which was why, Maddie decided, she had to pull herself together and she had to do it fast. Captain Brad Hawkins was a luxury she simply couldn't afford. Not if she intended to remain in control of her emotions *and* in control of her life. So, she simply wouldn't give in to any further fantasies. Nor would she allow herself to obsess over her ratty hair and whether or not she had a big red wound on the tip of her nose. What she would do was start acting like the woman she really was. A competent woman. A focused woman. A confident woman. A woman with a kick-ass attitude, who knew what she wanted out of life and what she had to do to get it.

''Will the *real* Maddie Morgan please step forward?'' Maddie said aloud, and stepped from the shower a woman renewed.

Thirty minutes later, however, she certainly didn't look like the real Maddie Morgan. Her standard military issue fatigue pants were so large around the waist they fit like hip-huggers, and the T-shirt was so small it strained across her ample bosom like something you would wear to a wet T-shirt contest. Not that it mattered whether the T-shirt was wet or not. Since she'd rinsed out her bra and her undies along with the rest of her clothes that were now hanging discreetly behind the shower curtain, there was nothing to encumber the two distinct protrusions winking back at Maddie as she stared at herself in the mirror.

So much for getting back to my old self, Maddie thought. If anything, she looked exactly like Mary Beth.

Maddie rubbed her hand over her exposed midriff, thinking that all she needed now was Mary Beth's belly-button ring. Yet, knowing there wasn't a damn thing she could do about the situation *or* her new clothes, Maddie stomped from the bathroom like the true survivor she was, in search of one thing and one thing only.

Breakfast.

AFTER MAKING A MORNING check on Operation Demob, Brad had made a stop by the mess hall himself, then quickly returned to relieve Baker of his morning guard duties. He had chosen things he thought Maddie might like: cream cheese, bagels and a variety of fruit. He'd also picked up two containers of orange juice and a couple of disposable cups of hot coffee. He'd even remembered to grab a few packets of artificial sweeter and some creamer, since he found women rarely liked their coffee black the way he did himself.

Baker's confirmation that he'd heard the shower running earlier told Brad his prisoner was already awake. Had she been one of the usual women he found in his company, Brad would have probably wandered into the bathroom and maybe even into the shower with her. But Brad had to remind himself that Maddie wasn't one of his dates. She was his prisoner. And the fact they'd already shared a bed didn't change a thing.

Especially since the bed sharing had been totally platonic; a fact Brad was still struggling with, even though common sense told him he needed to maintain the same resolve over the next few days. And that was going to be the hard part. Just like last night. He'd been teasing her, trying to keep her off balance, until the proximity to her got out of control and he accidentally let her know what was really on his mind. But who could blame him? What red-blooded American male could snuggle up with Maddie Morgan and *not* get aroused?

Smiling to himself over the comment she'd made about the hand grenade, Brad knew she had spent most of the night awake, most likely worried that his male urges would eventually get the better of him. Even when his own internal alarm clock had awakened him at 5:00 a.m., he could tell she was only pretending to be asleep. When he'd switched on the bedside light, he'd seen those long eyelashes of hers flutter ever so slightly like the butterflies she was so passionate about.

He'd been tempted to rattle her chain a little, let her know he was on to her by cuddling up next to her again, until thoughts like those evoked a response that sent him straight to the bathroom for a long, cold shower. In fact, just thinking about her now was enough to make Brad wonder if he shouldn't come up with a Plan B and back off on the sexual advances. Those damn advances left him teetering on the fence every time he got close to her.

And falling for Maddie Morgan wasn't an option. He was a lifer. A military career man. He had made a solemn vow there would never be any room in his life for a serious relationship. Maddie was no exception.

At least, those were Brad's convictions until the bedroom door opened and she stepped into the room. Then all thought of the Air Force *and* his convictions evaporated faster than a jet engine vapor trail.

Sweet Maddie, hell! Brad thought. The way her T-shirt was clinging to every curve, all he could do was stare at the two delectable mounds that seemed to be begging for his immediate attention.

"Yes, I have boobs. Now, close your mouth and stop staring at them."

Brad swallowed, hard. "Hey, you surprised me, that's all," he lied.

She didn't answer. Instead she padded barefoot across the room in his direction and headed straight for the local paper lying on the table. Her eyes narrowed when she picked the paper up and read the bold headlines **THE SEARCH FOR MADAM BUTTERFLY CONTINUES.**

"Were you expecting your sister to change her mind and call off the search?"

"Not really."

"Well, I was sure hoping she'd change her mind," Brad admitted. "If she'd been willing to cooperate, we might have been able to put an end to this predicament."

When she didn't comment, Brad changed the subject by motioning to the table he already had set and waiting. "Hungry?"

"Starving," she said and tossed the paper into the trash can before she seated herself at the table.

Okay, Brad thought as he seated himself opposite her. He couldn't quite put his finger on it, but she was acting differently this morning. Sure, she had never seemed nervous or too timid to take up for herself, but still, there was something different about her. She was acting more…well, more aloof. Yeah, that was it. Today she seemed detached. Distant.

Which might be a blessing in disguise, Brad decided when his eyes wandered back to the two perfect peaks responsible for the activity that was going on under the napkin he had just placed on his lap.

"I hate to keep harping on your sister," he said, testing the water a little further, "but you're certainly being more charitable about her behavior than I would be if I were in your shoes."

The look she sent him was as unyielding as the material stretched across her chest. "You don't know the first thing about my sister. Mary Beth has

been through some hard times. She craves valida-
tion…attention.''

"Don't we all? In one way or another?''

"Not like Mary Beth,'' she argued. "How would
you feel if your childhood sweetheart left you standing at the altar in front of your entire hometown?''

Brad tried to answer truthfully. "That's a difficult
question for me. Because standing at the altar is
something I never intend to do.''

She blinked. "Nor do I. But you have to admit
being left at the altar could certainly shake a person's confidence.''

Brad was still hung up on her first sentence.
What? She never wanted to get married? He didn't
know why that would bother him, but it did, so he
asked, "You mean you honestly don't see a husband
and a family in your future?''

She surprised him when she bypassed the cream
and sugar and took a long sip of black coffee straight
from the cup. When she put the cup back down, she
sent him another frosty look. "Is that so hard to
believe?''

Brad grinned mainly because he knew his answer
was going to irritate her. "I have a hard time pic-
turing *you* as an old maid.''

"Why?'' she challenged. "Because you find it
hard to believe a woman would *choose* to dedicate
herself to a career rather than to a man?''

He purposely sent her a leering grin. "I was under
the impression women today could have both a career and a family without having to make a choice.''

"Most women do want both.'' Her chin lifted. "I
just don't happen to be one of them.''

Again, her answer struck a raw nerve. He decided

to probe a bit deeper. "Any particular reason why you don't see marriage and a family in your future?"

The look she sent him was challenging. "I could ask you the same question."

Brad hesitated, and when he did a smirk crossed her lips. "Why, Captain. I do believe your double standard is showing," she accused. "How dare a woman suggest giving up a family for her career. But *don't* dare suggest a man should give up his career for a family."

Brad didn't care for her new attitude, or for the fact that she had obviously stereotyped him as some military grunt with a chauvinistic outlook on life. Before he could stop himself, he said, "Like you told me earlier about your sister, you don't know the first thing about me, Dr. Morgan. But I'll be happy to tell you why I never intend to get married. My father was killed in Vietnam when I was six. I grew up without a father, and my mother died with a broken heart. Every time I get behind the controls in a cockpit I risk the chance of not coming back. Leaving behind a devastated wife and family is not a scenario I care to repeat."

He could tell he'd embarrassed her, and that hadn't been his intention. Nor had he intended to blurt out his deepest feelings. She'd pushed the wrong buttons at the wrong time and ....

Dammit to hell! Now I've made her cry.

And if there was one thing in the world that tore Brad's heart out, it was the sight of a woman's tears.

"Hey, don't cry," he pleaded. "I overreacted...."

She shook her head. "No, I'm the one who overreacted,'' she sniffed, dabbing at her eyes with her napkin. "I'm so used to defending myself because my goal in life isn't to snag a husband and help populate the world, I assumed you were as judgmental as everyone else. But I am really sorry about your parents. Losing both of them had to be horrible for you."

Now he was the one who felt uncomfortable. And he certainly didn't need or want her sympathy. Pushing another napkin in her direction, he tried to change the subject. "Hey, forget it. We're both on edge, and who could blame us? You're anxious to get back to your life, and I need to get back to mine. Anyway you look at it, this whole situation sucks."

She managed a slight smile. "I guess we're really a lot alike, you and me. We're both dedicated to our careers and we're perfectly satisfied with our lives just the way they are." Unfortunately her face clouded over when she added, "I guess I should say, I'm satisfied with my life the way it *used to be,* shouldn't I? Before yesterday."

Brad swore under his breath when she left the table and headed straight for the television. "Don't you think it might be better if you *didn't* know what was going on out there?" he suggested. After all, they were just beginning to find common ground.

She ignored his plea and switched on the set. As luck would have it, the first thing that popped up on the screen was a picture of Madam Butterfly herself. "God, I hate that picture," she groaned.

Brad glanced at the TV. He had to admit the picture wasn't flattering in the least. Wearing horn-rimmed reading glasses, and with her hair pulled back from her face, she looked exactly like the old maid schoolteacher type she claimed she wanted to be. Which suited Brad just fine, when he thought about it. In fact, the idea of men ogling Maddie the way he knew they ogled her *Evershine* sister, didn't sit well with him at all.

"The search for Dr. Madeline Morgan is ongoing," the news commentator announced, "and has been expanded to a hundred-mile radius around the location where Dr. Morgan was last seen. Air Force troops conducting routine maneuvers outside Roswell have now joined in the search...."

She immediately whirled around and sent him a shocked look. "And whose idea was that? Yours? Join in the search so no one would think to look for me here on the base?"

Brad shrugged. And the only thing he could think to say was, "Sometimes a guy's gotta do what a guy's gotta do."

She frowned. "I hate clichés. Can't you come up with a more original excuse than that one?"

Here we go again, Brad thought, cursing himself for not realizing she would never calm down enough to ride out the next two days as long as she had access to the outside world. And because he still hadn't come up with a Plan B, he did what any soldier would do when he found himself with his back against the wall.

Pulling himself up from his chair, Brad's grin was slow and deliberate when he said, "I've always been rather fond of clichés, myself. In fact, another one of my favorites is a bird in hand is worth two in the bush. Or would you feel more comfortable if I changed it to *a butterfly* in hand is worth two in the bush?"

"No, changing it only makes me angry all over again," she said, staring him down. "If you remember, I almost *had* a butterfly in hand until *you* zoomed in out of nowhere."

"And if *you* remember, I was exactly where *I* was supposed to be. *You're* the one who zoomed in out of nowhere." He surprised her when he grabbed the remote from her hand and switched off the set. He purposely looked her up and down before he said, "You know, I meant to tell you earlier it really should be illegal for anyone to look that good in military fatigues."

She tossed her hair back over her shoulder. "You're out of clichés, so now you're going to try pickup lines?"

Brad grinned. "No, I'd rather point out something else I just realized."

"That your usual techniques aren't working with me?" she said with her hands on her hips now.

"You said yourself you have no intention of getting involved with anyone."

"What a relief. From the way you're acting, I didn't think you heard that statement."

"But don't you see?" Brad insisted. "You have no intention of getting involved with anyone, and neither do I. So why not make the most of a bad situation?"

"Now you're right back to the clichés," she said, stepping around him. "And here's another one you might want to add to your collection—"'If sex is the question—no is the answer!'"

Brad flinched when the bedroom door slammed behind her. He'd been messing with her again. He wasn't proud of it, but at least he'd taken her mind off the field day the media was still having with the ridiculous abduction story. Still, he felt guilty. Especially since their conversation earlier dispelled Baker's theory about her being the type of woman who would have him back in civilian clothes and changing diapers. Hell, they weren't even likely to cross paths again. Could he picture himself hanging out on a college campus in hometown Georgia? No way. That was as unlikely as her giving up her research to follow him around the country while he bounced from base to base.

Wandering back to the table, Brad dumped the leftovers from breakfast into the trash, fully ashamed of himself for forcing her to flee back into the bedroom. The hours that stretched out before them were going to be long enough without her sulking alone in one room and him in the other. And with that thought in mind, Brad grabbed a box off the bookcase shelf, walked across the room and rapped softly against his bedroom door.

MADDIE JUMPED AT THE SOUND of the knock. She was still leaning with her back against the door, wondering when to expect the next close encounter of the *dangerous* kind when Brad called out, ''Come on out, Maddie. I'm sorry, okay? I'll behave myself. I promise.''

You're not the one I'm worried about, Maddie wanted to yell back. She was worried about herself. One minute she'd been determined to stay cool, calm and collected around him, and the next minute all she could think about was hugging him to her breast over the hurt he'd suffered at the loss of his parents. Was she having some kind of an identity crisis? Is that what was wrong with her?

More like a no-life crisis. This guy might help you get one. "Shut up!" Maddie said aloud without thinking.

"Hey, I don't blame you for not believing me," he called back through the door. "But the day is going to be long enough without you barricading yourself in the bedroom. Open up. I have an idea I think you're going to like."

After a few seconds, Maddie reluctantly opened the door. The second she saw that irresistible grin she was tempted to slam the door right back in his face.

"How about a game of chest? I mean, chess?"

Maddie *did* try to slam the door after that faux pas, but he thrust his foot forward, keeping the door open with his heavy boot. "I was just kidding. Lighten up."

Maddie sent him a warning look, then sent an idle glance at the box he was holding out for her inspection.

"Am I right in suspecting an educated woman like yourself would know her way around a chessboard?"

"I've played my share of chess," Maddie admitted. "And I never lose."

He stepped aside and made a sweeping motion in the direction of the table. "Then we should have a good game. Because I never lose, either."

As Maddie walked past him, she heard him mutter under his breath, "and I'm not just talking about chess."

"Did you say something?" she asked innocently as she sat down at the table.

"No. I didn't say anything." He sent her another grin that would have made her knees buckle if she hadn't already been sitting down.

You big fibber, Maddie thought as he walked over to where she was sitting and placed the box on the table. Funny that chess would be his game, she decided. She would have picked poker instead, in a smoke-filled room with a bunch of his buddies like Baker huddled around the table. Chess was a game that required more brains than brawn and complete concentration. Yet, when she thought about it, being responsible for the current most top-secret helicopter in the military took a good deal of brainpower and concentration as well.

"How about a game of skittles first?" he asked as he took the board out of the box and began sorting out the carved pieces into two groups.

Maddie shook her head. "Absolutely not. I never play chess just for fun."

And then she had a brilliant idea.

"In fact," Maddie added, amazed at her own resourcefulness, "I think we should make this a high-stakes game."

His eyebrow raised slightly, telling her she'd gotten his attention with that request. "High stakes?"

Maddie smiled. "Exactly. When I win, you'll take me to Commander Gibbons and let me see if I can't put an end to this madness."

He shook his head. "I've already told you, that isn't going to happen."

Maddie frowned. "Then, when I win, you'll let me make one more phone call to my sister."

He looked at her for a moment. "You keep saying *when* you win, and I assure you, that isn't going to happen. But say I do grant you that phone call *if* you lucked out and won this game. My idea of a high-stakes game, means *I* have something to gain from the bet, too. What do I get when you *lose?*"

"*If* you win, I'll never ask you for another favor."

"Not good enough."

"I'll give you my word I won't try to escape again."

He shook his head. "How about when *I* win, you'll accept your fate and start behaving yourself?"

Maddie hesitated. "And that translates to mean?"

"Only that you'll stop being so uptight and relax a little. Give yourself the chance to see if we can't be compatible roommates while we ride out the next two days."

I'm sure you mean compatible bedmates, Maddie thought, and with more confidence than she felt, Maddie said, "It's a deal. Because this is one game I don't intend to lose."

"I don't intend to lose, either," he said. "In fact, I'm so confident you can't beat me, I'm even going to let you make the first move."

"And I'm going to accept that offer," Maddie said with a grin of her own, "because the first rule in being a good chess player is to always take every advantage that comes your way."

"Touché," he conceded, and Maddie forced her concentration back on the board. She could still feel him staring at her, unnerving her to the point she was afraid everything she knew about the game of chess would disappear from her memory. She was even hoping that he *was* staring at her disheveled hair and her red nose. Better her bruises than the fact that she was braless. It really would have the potential of turning into a *chest* game if his careful scrutiny caused her dang nipples to spring to life.

"That move might have given you a slight edge," he said when Maddie finally reached out and moved one of her pawns. "But I should have warned you," he added. "They don't call me the king of counterattack for nothing."

Maddie frowned at the board when Brad proved his point. Okay. So, he was sharp. So, what? She was pretty sharp herself. She just needed to focus on what she was doing. She needed to study the board carefully. Make every move count....

"Hey, stop it," Maddie said when he reached under the table and pulled her bare foot into his lap. When he began gently massaging her foot, his touch was so sensuous Maddie had trouble catching her breath.

"I heard somewhere the best thing for concentration is a good foot massage," he said, never batting an eye.

"And where did you hear that? Letterman's Top Ten list?"

"I never would have figured you for a Letterman fan."

Maddie wrangled her foot free. "Admit it, Hawk. You're trying to break my concentration because I've got you running scared after only one move. If you're really afraid I'm going to beat you, why don't you let me make that phone call now?"

"No way will you ever beat me," he said, leaning back in his chair. He stretched his arms over his head, making his T-shirt ride up to expose incredible six-pack abs tanned a deep bronze. "In fact, I'm even willing to extend our bet to two games out of three."

Maddie quickly averted her eyes away from his stomach and back to the board. "That won't be necessary. I intend to beat your pants off first time out."

Yikes! Wrong choice of words. Maddie knew it the second they rolled off her tongue.

"With an offer like that, I might be tempted to throw this game," he said, wiggling his eyebrows up and down.

"Damn you. That was just a manner of speech and you know it."

"I thought you didn't like clichés."

"Just play the game," Maddie warned.

And he did. Maddie knew he played his heart out, but this was one time the captain's best just wasn't good enough.

"Checkmate!" Maddie finally cheered. She stuck her arm out and wiggled her fingers in his direction. "Show me the cell phone." When all he did was sit there and stare back at her, Maddie frowned.

He pushed back from the table and folded his arms across his chest. "I don't have it with me," he finally admitted.

"What do you mean you don't have the phone with you?" Maddie snapped. "You should have told me that when we first made the bet."

He scowled in her direction and Maddie actually laughed for the first time since she'd been taken prisoner. And once she started laughing, she couldn't seem to stop. Chess pieces began bouncing all over the board every time she pounded the metal table.

"What's so damn funny?"

Maddie pointed her finger in his direction. "You really didn't think I could beat you, did you? Admit it."

His dark eyes flashed a menacing look back at her. "Okay. I admit it. But you did beat my pants off, didn't you? So, why don't you walk over here and get them?"

And in that instant, the strategy he'd been using on her all along became as clear to Maddie as one of her specimens under a high-power microscope. She'd been acting like a naive schoolgirl since the minute she'd met him, allowing Hawk to intimidate her with his come-ons. It was just another area where she'd lost complete control since the infamous Black Ghost had flown in and turned her world upside down. She had no control over her sister, she had no control over the media, nor did she have any control over the fact that she might not even have a faculty position when she finally made it back home to Morgan City.

But Hawk was a different story.

For the first time in her life, Maddie threw caution to the wind and forgot all about being reserved, devoted, stick-in-the-mud Dr. Madeline Morgan. "You know, I think I will," Maddie said before she lost her nerve.

He sat up a little straighter in his chair. "Yeah, right."

"You don't think I'm serious?" Maddie said, sending him a coy little smile as she pushed back from the table and stood up. "Well, I *am* serious.

You've finally won me over, Hawk. You said it yourself, there's no reason why we *shouldn't* have a little fun while we're forced to spend this time together.''

''You're bluffing and you know it,'' he gulped, giving Maddie the courage she needed to be even bolder.

When she reached his chair, Maddie snapped her fingers and pointed to his pants. ''I'm not kidding. Hand them over.''

He laughed and looked up at her with a cocky grin. ''You're playing a dangerous game here, Professor. I should warn you, I don't believe in underwear.''

''That's your misfortune,'' Maddie said, trying to control the tremor in her voice. ''I couldn't care less about the status of your underwear.''

His grin evaporated. ''You think I'm not on to you, Maddie? You really think I'm going to hand over my pants so you can make another split for the door?''

Maddie stepped even closer, actually forcing herself between his legs while he remained seated in the chair. Mercy me, wasn't *that* a stimulating experience? So stimulating, Maddie pushed the envelope a bit further when she let her fingers do a slow walk up the front of Brad's T-shirt. ''Don't worry, Hawk. I'm not going *anywhere*.''

He stuttered for a response, but Maddie ran a fingertip slowly around his mouth before bending down and silencing him with a kiss so thorough she felt him stiffen like a week-old corpse. The fact that she was also digging her own grave was a moot point. She was drunk on power, and she discovered she liked being the aggressor. This time, the game was going to be about what *she* wanted, not what Hawk wanted her to give him.

"Stop it," he said, and managed to push her away. He stood up then and frowned down at her. "You've proved your point, okay? You've beaten me at my other game, too. I admit it."

"Your other game?" Maddie said, feigning surprise. "But, Brad. I said I agree with you. Why waste time playing chess, when we could…"

"Didn't you hear me? I said you've proved your point."

"Oh, no, I haven't," Maddie purred, stepping closer to circle her arms around his neck. "Now take those pants off, Captain, and let's play house."

He grabbed her roughly by the shoulders and pinned her arms to her sides, forcing her to look at him. "Don't tempt me, Maddie. Don't think I won't march your brainy little butt right in that bedroom and show you…"

"And show me what?"

He glared at her for a second longer. Then he pulled her to him and kissed her so passionately she melted like butter on a hot iron griddle. They stared at each other again when their lips broke apart, but their lips didn't stay apart long. Maddie quickly pulled Brad's head down for more, lost again in another mind-blowing kiss that had every muscle in her body tuned in, turned up and turned on for anything Brad wanted to offer.

She didn't resist when his hands found their way beneath her T-shirt. Nor did she resist when he started backing up, taking her with him as they both stumbled blindly in the direction of his bedroom. He closed the bedroom door and pushed her roughly up against it, smothering her again with kisses so urgent Maddie had trouble breathing. She wasn't sure how they made it to the bed, but Brad had her T-shirt off faster than he'd removed her hiking boots. She bit down on her lower lip when his hands slid down to cup what he was seeking, and when he lowered his head and his hot mouth covered her bare flesh, the pleasure Maddie felt was more than she ever dreamed it could be.

She was still lost in the sheer magic of the moment when a knock on the door snatched her from outer space and sent her crashing back to earth like the alleged spacecraft that was responsible for making Roswell so famous.

"Dammit, Baker. Go away," Brad yelled, prompting Maddie to wiggle out of from under him and take refuge in the darkened bathroom.

"The old man wants you, Hawk," Baker called from the other room.

When Maddie peeped out from behind the bathroom door, Brad sent her a pitiful look and said, "Tell him I'll be there shortly."

"He said pronto, Hawk. I wouldn't keep him waiting."

"Go," Maddie urged, motioning frantically for Brad to toss over her missing T-shirt.

All it had taken was one knock on the door to pop that big bubble of desire she'd been lost in and bring her right back to her senses. Now, standing behind the bathroom door half-naked, all she could think about was how fast flirting with danger had almost coerced her out of more than her T-shirt.

Maddie shivered.

And not from the chill in the room.

6

BRAD FINALLY RELENTED and tossed the T-shirt in her direction. The second she caught it, Maddie slammed the bathroom door shut. *Talk about lousy timing,* Brad thought, rubbing a hand over his face. But was the timing really lousy? Maybe Baker's interruption was a blessing in disguise.

He was upset just thinking about how quickly he'd lost control of the situation. As did the way his ability to reason disappeared the second Maddie kissed him. It had taken only one kiss to throw him into a tailspin. And if he wasn't careful, Brad knew keeping her out of his heart would be as hopeless as jumping from a plane with a parachute missing its damn rip cord.

He walked across the room, then paused for a second before he rapped softly on the bathroom door. "I shouldn't be gone long," he called through the door, and the minute he said it, Brad felt like a complete idiot.

But what could you say at a time like this?

Sorry, honey, but duty calls? Hold that thought, sugar, we'll pick up where we left off when I get back?

Yeah. Like that was going to happen.

"Just go, Brad," she called back, her voice sounding desperate. "Maybe Commander Gibbons has finally decided to release me."

Excuse me?

Sure, he knew she was embarrassed. What woman wouldn't have been embarrassed to have someone burst in on such an intimate moment? But was Maddie really that eager to get away from him now that they'd finally stopped playing mind games and acted on their attraction for each other?

Resting his forehead against the closed door, Brad took a deep breath. "Don't analyze what just happened between us to death while I'm gone, Maddie. We'll talk when I get back."

He suddenly wondered if *he* was ready to let *her* go.

MADDIE KNEW BRAD WAS GONE when she heard the bedroom door close behind him, leaving behind Baker, she was sure, to keep her captive. Baker, who Maddie would now have to face alone, knowing the big goon had to be laughing his head off over Hawk's latest coup d'état of the henhouse variety.

Dammit! How could she have been so wrong? She had always scoffed at Mary Beth's romance novels, and even at the movies when some otherwise rational female was suddenly swept away by a wave of raw passion that Maddie had never believed was real. But dear God, there really was such a thing a raw passion! How else could Maddie explain what had just happened to her, a totally rational woman?

Her basic instincts had simply taken over.

Basic instincts! God, she felt so stupid. She had even devoted her thesis to the similarities of insects and humans in the mate selection. Comparing a process known to evolutionary biologists as runaway selection with what Charles Darwin called sexual selection for humans, Maddie had argued that regardless of the species, the male always has a certain trait, whatever it might be, that attracts the female. And that's what had been happening to her from the moment she laid eyes on Captain Brad Hawkins. She had finally met a man who completely stimulated all of her basic instincts. She hadn't gone crazy, after all. Nor had she lost sight of her goals. She was just normal. Wonderfully, delightedly and deliciously normal.

Maddie felt like shouting for joy. She also felt like dancing into the other room and sticking her tongue out at her bodyguard with a nanna-nanna-nanna-na pose. Because the last thing she was going to do was remain hidden out in the bedroom like a kid caught doing something naughty until Hawk returned.

She had finally experienced the thrill of being a woman. Not a woman completely devoted to her career. Not a professor of entomology with no time for anyone or anything in her life but her work. A woman who had no intention of being embarrassed about having a healthy sexual appetite, whether Sergeant I-told-you-so Baker liked it or not.

Opening the bedroom door, Maddie headed straight into the adjoining room like Joan of Arc returning from another victory. She purposely sent Baker a triumphant smile.

He sent her a triumphant smile right back. "I brought you some lunch," he said, motioning to the table.

Maddie glanced at the tray sitting on the table. "Thanks. Maybe I'll eat later."

He grinned knowingly. "Maybe after Hawk gets back you'll work up more of an appetite."

Despite her big pep talk, Maddie felt her cheeks flame.

"You know," Baker said with another teasing grin. "I had a feeling you might change your mind about my old buddy, Hawk. Once you *really* got to know him, I mean."

"Now listen here, Baker..."

Baker held his hands up. "Whoa, Dr. Morgan. Don't get all riled up. I'm just making my own observation, that's all. *And* trying to save you a little embarrassment later on."

"Embarrassment?"

"Yeah," Baker said, grinning from ear to ear. "I hate to point this out, but your T-shirt's on wrong-side out."

Maddie stomped back into the bedroom and slammed the door to show Baker exactly what she thought about his keen observation. She put her T-shirt on the right way, made herself as presentable as possible with the limited resources she had at her disposal, then busied herself tidying up the bedroom, straightening up the bed and pausing long enough to inhale the heady aroma of Brad's scent from his pillow.

Sitting cross-legged in the middle of his bed, she hugged Brad's pillow to her breast, trying *not* to do exactly what he'd warned her about before he left. But why *had* he warned her not to analyze their situation to death? Because he knew he'd do the same thing once they were apart?

Yes, that had to be it, Maddie decided. They were, after all, two of a kind. Brad knew as well as she did there would never be any possibility for a real relationship between them. They'd been caught up in the moment, that's all. Overwhelmed by the overpowering physical attraction they felt for each other. Unaware of how quickly taunting and teasing each other could push them farther than either of them had ever intended to go.

Unfortunately her handsome captain had certainly punched a giant hole in her theory that sex was a rudimentary fact of life she could do quite nicely without.

But now she felt like a kid who'd been given one lick of a lollipop, only to have it snatched away.

Maddie didn't know what would happen when Brad did come back but she did know there wouldn't be any more lighthearted teasing between them. At least, not at first. When he came back they would have to face each other seriously and decide if they wanted to pick things up where they left off, or...

"Dr. Morgan? I think you'd better come watch this," Baker yelled from the other room.

Tossing the pillow aside, Maddie left the bed and hurried into the other room. She came to a screeching halt when she found not only Mary Beth, but Brad staring back at her from the television screen.

"What's this all about?" Maddie asked, turning to Baker.

"The best I can tell, your sister's making allegations that the Air Force is holding you captive."

"Allegations?" Maddie shouted.

"You know what I mean." Baker shifted uncomfortably from one foot to the other, then jammed his thumbs into the front pockets of his fatigues. "Your sister's stirring things up. She's demanding that someone come out here and search the base."

Maddie frowned. *Search the base?* Not now. Not yet. Not until she and Brad could have that talk. She looked back at the screen when Brad said, "I want to assure Miss Morgan *and* the citizens of Roswell the Air Force is assisting in every way possible to assure Dr. Morgan's safety...."

"Then why won't you let anyone search the base?" Mary Beth cut in. Her arms were folded stubbornly across her chest. A chest that was now completey covered, Maddie noticed, since today instead of a tube top, Mary Beth was wearing a modest.... "That's my best linen suit!" Maddie yelled before Brad turned a cold stare in her sister's direction and said, "As I told you earlier, Miss Morgan, searching the base would be a total waste of time. And time is of the essence in this matter."

The reporter spoke up. "You're referring, of course, to the harsh desert elements threatening Dr. Morgan. Right, Captain Hawkins?"

Mary Beth didn't give Brad time to answer. "I didn't suggest we should *stop* searching the desert, Captain Hawkins. I merely suggested we should search the Air Force base, as well."

When Brad frowned, Maddie watched her twin turn on her usual winning Mary Beth charm. Batting her eyelashes innocently, she added, "I mean, it's possible my sister is scared and confused after such a trying ordeal. Maybe she's hiding somewhere on the base, afraid to show herself because she's not sure what that strange aircraft really was. And what about you, Captain Hawkins? Do you have any idea what that strange aircraft could have been?"

"A figment of your imagination, maybe?" Brad said, making several members of the curious crowd that surrounded them chuckle at his reply.

Mary Beth's eyes narrowed. Shaking her finger in Brad's direction, she said, "Your willingness to make light of my sister's disappearance, Captain Hawkins, only confirms my suspicions. Tell us the truth. The reason the Air Force doesn't want us on that base is because you're holding my sister against her will. Admit it!''

When the tense-looking reporter shoved the microphone back in Brad's direction, his words came out as a hiss through his clenched teeth. ''I was not making light of Dr. Morgan's disappearance. I was only pointing out that maybe you should stick to one story at a time, Miss Morgan. Yesterday, the aliens abducted your sister. Today you say the Air Force is responsible. Who will it be tomorrow? The World Wrestling Federation?''

''Why you...''

Maddie gasped when Mary Beth pulled off one of her shoes and lunged in Brad's direction. The nervous reporter quickly stepped between them, trying to hold Mary Beth at bay, but a big, burly biker-looking guy in a leather jacket suddenly rushed from the crowd to Mary Beth's rescue. The biker pushed the reporter down, then shoved his big hand over the camera lens, forcing the cameraman back and out of the way.

In a split second there was total pandamonium.

The cameraman finally recovered long enough to keep panning the crowd. Maddie watched in horror as the situation quickly turned from bad to worse. Mary Beth was still waving her shoe in the air, and the leather-clad barbarian was now poking his finger forcefully against Brad's chest.

''You, sir, need to calm down,'' Maddie heard Brad say, but the big guy drew his fist back and landed a punch that sent Brad sprawling backward into the startled crowd.

"Hawk never should have made that comment about the WWF," Baker mumbled absently as the crowd pushed Brad back into the big bruiser's path.

"Why isn't someone stopping this?" Maddie screeched.

"Don't worry. Hawk can take care of himself," Baker said with a chuckle.

Maddie bit her lower lip when Brad and his grinning opponent began circling each other, ready for battle. "But won't Brad get in trouble? Surely your commander won't condone this type of behavior."

"Hawk didn't start this," Baker said with a snort. "If anything, that bum in the leather jacket would be in trouble for striking an officer."

When the big man lunged in Brad's direction again, Maddie covered her eyes with her hands. She didn't look until she heard a loud groan. When she peeped back through her fingers, Brad was rubbing his right hand, but the biker was lying facedown in the dirt, leaving the words on the back of his leather jacket face-up for all the world to see: Go Ahead. Make My Day.

And then the screen went blank before the broadcast returned to the regular programming.

Maddie frowned at Baker who was doubled over with laughter.

"That was priceless. Absolutely priceless. Make my day? Hawk sure made his day, all right."

"You should be ashamed of yourself," Maddie scolded. "Brad could have been hurt."

Baker stopped laughing long enough to say, "You still have a lot to learn about my old buddy, Hawk. Trust me. If there's ever a fight, you want to be on *Hawk's* side."

Maddie didn't comment, but Baker's advice suddenly made her stomach queasy. Mary Beth had been begging her for years to stop playing book-worm and take notice of the opposite sex. Well, she'd finally taken notice. And what had happened? Her twin and the only man who'd ever made her heart flutter had practically gotten into a fistfight on national TV.

Now, they hated each other.

And if she ever had to choose sides between them?

Well, if that ever happened, Maddie feared she'd end up much like the biker, facedown in the dirt while Mary Beth and Brad stood snarling at each other over her poor lifeless body.

HOURS LATER, MADDIE WAS awakened by a gentle shake of her arm. "Brad?" she mumbled, raising herself up on one elbow to push her hair out of her eyes.

It was only Baker, who switched on the bedside light and plopped her hiking boots down on the bed. "You need to change into your own clothes, Dr. Morgan, and you need to hurry."

"Where's Brad? Have you heard from him?" She glanced at the bedside clock, shocked to see the digital readout: 4:00 a.m.

Baker didn't answer. His only response when he left the bedroom was, "Hurry, Dr. Morgan. I need to get you out of here and we don't have much time."

Get me out of here? Maddie wondered. In the middle of the night? Without seeing Brad again? She was furious that this was how he'd chosen to deal with the short spurt of intimacy they'd allowed themselves. To have his boy, Baker, do his dirty work for him, and get rid of her so he wouldn't have to face her again.

With an imagination jumping to conclusions faster than a desert jackrabbit, Maddie wiggled out of her standard government issue duds and made the transformation back to Dr. Madeline Morgan. All that was missing was her pith helmet. What had happened to it? The last time Maddie even remembered having the damn thing was when she finally pulled herself out from under Baker's massive form when they were in the helicopter.

When a rap on the bathroom door told her she wasn't moving fast enough, Maddie opened the door with fire in her eyes. "Tell me right now if you're letting me go, Baker," Maddie said with her chin jutted forward. "Because if you're only moving me to another location, you're going to have one hell of a fight on your hands."

"You're free to go now, Dr. Morgan. I swear," Baker gulped. "I just need to get you safely outside the base without you being seen."

Seconds later, Maddie found herself creeping silently along behind Baker, who stopped at every corridor to check for any signs of life. He then motioned her forward as he slipped into the shadows. If she hadn't been so irritated that Brad hadn't seen fit to at least escort her off the base himself, Maddie would have laughed at the two of them tiptoeing across the base like two thieves in the night. It was on the tip of her tongue to go ahead and ask Baker exactly where his old buddy, Hawk, happened to be when Baker motioned her to stop and drew his finger to his lips. He pushed her backward and flattened her against the block building. They both remained hidden in the shadows until two soldiers on guard duty strolled past them, never detecting their presence.

When they were well outside the fence surrounding the base, Baker led her up a small hill. It wasn't until they reached the bottom of the hill on the other side that Maddie could see the outline of a vehicle in the bright moonlight. Propped against it was a silhouette she had no trouble identifying. Maddie almost shouted for joy, but Baker extended his hand and said, "Good luck, Dr. Morgan, this is as far as I go."

"Thank you, Sergeant Baker," Maddie told him, then reached out and shook the big man's hand. When he turned and slipped back into the shadows, Maddie had to force herself to keep from running straight toward the man waiting for her in the moonlight.

Of course, the scene playing out inside her head was a different story. Like in the movies, Maddie imagined them running to each other in slow motion, Brad lifting her off the ground when he pulled her into his arms, then swinging her around in a circle, overcome with joy that they had finally been reunited.

But a movie this wasn't. This was real life. And when she finally reached the expensive Humvee that was waiting to take her back to reality, Maddie was so uncertain about how she should react at seeing him again, she didn't walk toward the handsome captain who had stolen her heart. Instead she seated herself primly on the passenger side seat without even saying hello. It wasn't until Brad pulled himself into the seat beside her that the moonlight gave her a perfect view of the ugly bruise around his right eye.

"Oh, Brad, I'm so sorry," Maddie cried. "For everything. For climbing that fence. For taking those pictures. For trying to escape. For this…" she added and reached out to gently touch his swollen eye. "Does it hurt?"

"It hurt my pride," Brad said, laughing slightly. "Getting punched in the face on national TV isn't something I'm going to live down anytime soon."

"That was my fault, too," Maddie apologized. "You were nice enough to let me call Mary Beth, and then she…"

"Hush," Brad said, reaching out to put his finger to her lips. "The only thing I'm sorry about is that we don't have any more time together."

Maddie didn't pull away as he leaned forward and kissed her lightly on the lips. "About what happened, Maddie…I just wish…I wish things were different…that we were different…that…"

"Don't," Maddie spoke up, unwilling to listen to everything she already knew herself. "We got caught up in the moment, that's all. Nothing more, nothing less. Let's leave it at that."

"You're probably right," he said with a sigh.

You could at least argue with me, Maddie thought grumpily. Instead he turned on the ignition. In a matter of seconds they were racing across the desert in the moonlight, with Maddie biting her lower lip to keep from crying every time Brad squeezed her hand.

Stop acting like a big baby, Maddie kept telling herself. Like Brad said, their time was up. There was no point in crying over what might have been. No reason for her to feel as if her whole world was ending. If anything, she should be rejoicing that she could finally put an end to the silly nightmare Mary

Beth had started. Maddie knew all of this, just as well as she knew she wouldn't have had a future with Brad if they had acted on their emotions. They were two of a kind, destined to spend the rest of their lives devoted completely to their careers.

Yet, thirty minutes later when the Humvee finally came to a stop and Brad turned to face her, all Maddie wanted was a little more time.

"Is your Black Ghost finally safe now? Is that why you're letting me go early?" *Too early, as far as I'm concerned,* Maddie wanted to add.

Brad shook his head. "Not yet. And after what happened yesterday, it will be a miracle if the whole town of Roswell isn't climbing over the fence when I get back to the base."

"But..."

"Gibbons is letting you go because I gave him my word you could be trusted. And I *can* trust you. Can't I, Maddie?"

"Completely," Maddie said and she meant it.

He reached out and took her hands in both of his.

"I've been honest with you from the beginning, and I'm not going to lie to you now. The Black Ghost isn't fully dismantled and we can't risk anyone searching the base."

"But if I'm found..."

"There won't be any reason to search the base," Brad finished for her.

Maddie sent Brad a somber look. "Well, I hate to point this out, Brad, but that's exactly what I've been saying from the beginning."

"I know you have. I tried to point out that same thing, but Gibbons was convinced you'd talk to the press the second we let you go. I've promised him you won't do that, Maddie. We need your cooperation."

"Well, pardon me if I'm not elated because your commander suddenly wants to promote me to some Air Force emissary! I could have solved this problem two days ago, and maybe even salvaged my reputation. But *nooooo*. Gibbons wouldn't have any part of that."

His nod was sympathetic. "You have every right to be angry, and I don't blame you. But I'm asking you to keep the Black Ghost a secret for one reason and one reason only. Because it's the right thing to do, Maddie. I think you already know that."

His expression was so wounded, Maddie couldn't bring herself to torture him any further. "Fine, you have my word. No one will ever hear about the Black Ghost from me."

The relief on his face turned to concern when he said, "You realize, of course, this isn't going to be easy for you. You're going to be bombarded from all sides. The media, the police, the public. It's going to be a regular three-ring circus for a few days. And I swear, Maddie, I would spare you all of that if I could."

"That's what has me worried," Maddie admitted. "How am I going to explain where I've been for the past two days? Everyone will expect me to be near death's door. Sunburned. Dehydrated…"

"I could give you a plausible story. There are a few cottonwood trees you could have used for shelter. I could even provide you with an explanation about how you took nourishment from the plant life in lieu of water…"

"But?"

"But no matter what story we could contrive,

there's the possibility someone would challenge it and ask you for more details that you wouldn't have. That's why it's best if you don't say a thing. Let them speculate all they want, but don't admit to anything. If you refuse to say a word, they can't poke holes in your story.''

Maddie blinked. "But, Brad, if I refuse to give them any kind of an explanation, the media will exploit this alien abduction story for all it's worth.''

"I don't think that will happen,'' Brad insisted. "The media is too ratings-oriented. The second they realize you aren't going to talk to them, they're going to drop you and move on to the next story of the hour.''

Maddie let out a long sigh. "I sure hope you're right.''

Brad dragged a hand over his face and let out a long sigh himself. "You're a remarkable woman, Maddie Malone. I hope you know that.''

"I'll try to keep that in mind when I'm being chased down the street by *The National Enquirer*,'' Maddie said, trying to lighten his mood.

It didn't work.

His expression looked as miserable as she felt.

"That was a joke,'' Maddie said, trying to lighten the weight on her heart. "Are you purposely trying to be a pain in the ass? Or is this normal for you?''

BRAD LAUGHED, BUT HE WASN'T laughing on the inside. On the inside he felt like a first-class jerk. He felt guilty for leaving it to Maddie to clean up this mess. He felt helpless, because unless he was willing to hand over the Black Ghost, he couldn't do a damn thing to protect her from the media. And he felt cheated. He felt cheated because he'd realized Maddie was the only woman he could ever love.

And how fair would it be to tell her that?

I'm never falling in love, Maddie, but if I did, it would be with you?

No, just as she'd said herself, it was better for both of them to leave things the way they were. Besides, what type of future could he ever offer Maddie? He'd already spelled it out for her loud and clear. Every time he took to the air he was risking his life. Maddie deserved more out of life than being made a young widow. And any children they might have together deserved to grow up with a father. Like it or not, he'd never expect anyone else to suffer for the career choice he'd made.

Bittersweet as it might be, it would be best for him simply to go back to his life. She'd go back to hers....

"In spite of everything, I'll always be thankful I met you," she said, bringing Brad's eyes back to her lovely face. "You've made me look inside myself and realize being devoted to my career doesn't mean I can't be a desirable woman, too."

What? That's not what he wanted to hear! How was he going to wallow in his own self-pity, slobbering into his beer and longing for Maddie, if Maddie was out kicking up her heels and seeing how desirable she could be?

Her face took on a radiant glow when she added, "In fact, this entire bizarre situation is probably the best thing that could have ever happened to me."

"Well, I don't know if I'd go that far," Brad grumbled.

"But don't you see?" she argued. "My life was in a safe rut with only one focus. Now I've had the opportunity to take a long look at myself. And do you know what I've discovered?''

I have a feeling you're going to tell me, whether I want to hear it or not, Brad thought with a frown.

''I've realized my entire life I've been struggling to acquire my own identity. Aside from my twin, I mean. Since Mary Beth was so feminine, I played down my femininity. Since Mary Beth didn't give a flip about an education, I made it my mission in life to earn a Ph.D. Since…''

Brad cut her off. ''What are you saying, Maddie? That you no longer care about your career?''

''Of course not,'' she said, looking back at him as if he were crazy. ''I'm just saying I realize I'm only cheating myself if I continue to be so…well, you know, *rigid.* You've been telling me yourself I need to lighten up.''

A stab of hope forced him to ask, ''Meaning what? You've decided you really do want the husband, the kids, *and* the career?''

Maddie laughed. ''No. I still don't see a husband and kids in my future, but I do plan to…''

''Good for you,'' Brad snapped, cutting her off.

He sat there still stewing over everything she had just told him. Not interested in being so rigid, she'd said. But also not interested in a husband or kids. Just interested in…what? Wild sex with the first stranger she met? Hanging out with that crazy sister of hers so she could take her pick from a pack of bozos like that biker who had punched him in the face?

His blood pressure shot up just thinking about it.

And what was so wrong with being rigid? Hadn't the rigid lifestyles they'd chosen for themselves been mainly responsible for getting them both where they were in their careers today? Being rigid could be a good thing.

Unfortunately Brad was reminded that *rigid* could apply to more than one meaning when he glanced in Maddie's direction again and took in her flawless profile. The desert wind lifted her silky hair away from her face for a moment, turning the long strands into spun gold in the early-morning light. Brad wanted her so badly it was all he could do to keep from showing Miss I-don't-plan-to-be-so-rigid just how rigid *he* could still be.

He was still struggling to get his emotions above *and* below his waist under control when Maddie turned toward him and asked, "Now what?"

Brad gripped the steering wheel and forced himself to look straight ahead. "Now, I'll make an anonymous call to the police. I'll tell them I saw a woman matching your description on the main road into town. After that, it should only be a matter of minutes until they charge out here to the rescue."

"Sounds like an excellent strategy to me," she said, and when Brad dared to look in her direction again, she flashed him a smile that under different circumstances would have warmed his very soul.

WHEN BRAD DIDN'T RETURN her smile, Maddie turned back around in her seat. The highway leading into Roswell was only a few yards away from where Brad had pulled the Humvee over on the side of the road. It stretched out before her like a silver ribbon, leading her back to her freedom and back to her specimens and her microscope. And leading her *away* from the one bug Maddie had never expected to encounter in the desert when she came to New

Mexico: the infamous love bug that had infected her with a serious case of hopeless desire.

Not that her love-bug virus was going to do her any good. That was obvious. He'd seemed irritated with her from the moment she'd made her soulful confession, though she wasn't sure why. She wasn't even sure why she'd blurted out everything she'd been sorting in her mind over the past two days. She certainly hadn't blurted them out to make him angry. Actually it had been more of a desperate attempt on her part to let him know maybe there *was* room for something more in her life than just her career.

Not a full-time relationship, of course. Neither of them had time for that. She just wanted him to know that someday, if he did choose to look her up again and finish what they started, she certainly wouldn't turn him away.

Of course, he'd made it clear he wasn't really interested in what she had to say. He'd even cut her off before she'd had time to finish her sentence. Before she'd had time to say "but I do plan to keep my options open if you ever find yourself in Georgia."

That's how she'd planned to leave things. On a light, yet slightly flirtatious note. Not begging him to come find her, but also not giving him any reason to think she wouldn't be receptive if he did show up.

Fat chance of that happening, Maddie decided. She stole another quick glance in his direction. He was sitting ramrod straight in the seat beside her, hands clutching the steering wheel in a death-grip, and the shadow on his jaw even more pronounced as the muscles in his face flexed back and forth. Anxious, she suspected, to get rid of her as quickly as possible so he could race back to his precious Black Ghost and make sure no one was lurking around the base ready to climb over the fence.

Well, far be it from me to detain him any longer! Vaulting herself out of the jeep, Maddie sent him a brave smile and said, "I guess this is where we say goodbye."

He searched her face with such intensity Maddie stopped breathing for a second. "You take care of yourself, okay? This should all be over in a few days, and…"

"Sir, yes, sir!" Maddie teased, cutting him off when she snapped to attention and gave him a phony salute.

Laugh, dammit, Maddie kept praying. *Don't make me turn and walk away from you with that stony look on your face!*

He did smile slightly, and then he reached for something behind his seat. Seconds later, he was standing beside her, holding the bottom half of a clear plastic bottle that had been cut in two. A rubber band secured a piece of paper over the top. Several holes had been poked in the makeshift lid.

"I stopped on the way back from Roswell and tried to find your butterfly," he said, handing over his gift.

Maddie was so overcome, it took her a minute to say, "You did that? For me?"

"Of course, I had no idea what I was looking for," he admitted with a silly grin. "This was the only butterfly I could find near the fence where I found you."

Maddie leaned forward and kissed him, and when she did, Brad kissed her back, pulling her to him with so much force the plastic bottle was almost crushed between them. When they finally broke apart, he looked down at the bottle. "Not the right one, huh?"

Maddie shook her head. He had captured a Mournful Duskywing, common to the area and ironically appropriate for the way she was feeling at the moment. "It doesn't matter. The fact you would do this for me is enough."

Removing the rubber band, Maddie returned the delicate Duskywing back into the desert. They watched as the beautiful creature flitted away, and when she found herself in Brad's arms for the last time, Maddie was certain no two people had ever poured more emotion into one kiss. It was, after all, a kiss they both knew meant goodbye.

Forever.

When the kiss was over, Maddie simply walked away from her handsome captain and back to reality, making it a point not to turn around so she wouldn't betray both of them by begging him to make her his captive forever.

7

BY THE TIME MADDIE REACHED the next mile marker, the desert came alive with so much activity it looked as if a bomb had exploded, scattering people in every direction. And the first person out of the patrol car that came to a skidding stop in front of her was Mary Beth, who almost knocked Maddie down when she threw her arms around her neck and yelled loud enough to bring the camera crews running. "Thank God, you're alive!"

"Cut it out, Mary Beth," Maddie warned against her twin's moist cheek. "Your acting debut is *over.*"

Unfortunately, by the time Maddie freed herself from her twin, she was immediately seized by two concerned EMT's who practically body-slammed her onto a stretcher. Maddie was still trying to fight them off when they made a mad dash past a group of excited cameramen and headed straight for a waiting ambulance. In the background, Maddie could still hear Mary Beth gushing out excited thank-yous to everyone involved in the search.

"This isn't necessary," Maddie kept yelling as she clung to the sides of the gurney for dear life.

Her protests fell on deaf ears.

She soon found herself shoved, gurney and all, into the back of the ambulance. EMT number one disappeared to the front of the mobile medical vehicle, while EMT number two vaulted himself into the back with Maddie. And just when she thought things couldn't get any worse, Mary Beth managed to hop aboard before the double doors slammed shut.

In an instant, the vehicle lurched forward with its siren blaring full volume and with her conscientious rescuer hovering above her, his little black doctor's bag clutched in his hand. When he pulled out a hypodermic the size of a knitting needle, Maddie sat straight up on the gurney.

"There's no way you're sticking me with that thing," she said, shrinking back from his outstretched hand.

"Now, calm down, Dr. Morgan. I'm going to start an IV, that's all."

"I said no," Maddie told him when he reached for her arm. "I'm not unconscious. I'm totally coherent. And I have the right to refuse medical treatment. Now, get that thing away from me."

When the EMT frowned, Mary Beth inched closer to him and held on to his arm for support. They stood there, swaying back and forth as the ambulance sped toward Roswell. For a moment, Maddie was afraid Mary Beth was going to help him hold her down. But she leaned closer to the guy and whispered loud enough for Maddie to hear, "Poor thing. My sister's always been terrified of needles. Can't we wait until we get her to the hospital? Maybe the doctor can give her a sedative before you start poking her with all kinds of sharp objects."

It didn't surprise Maddie when Mary Beth's close proximity made the poor man forget all about his unruly patient. Why wouldn't he forget about his patient? He was elbow-to-elbow with the *Evershine*

Girl. And from the way the sweat was popping out on his forehead now, Maddie suspected all he was thinking about was Mary Beth's nude body on the back of that damn black stallion.

Mary Beth sent a pitiful look back in Maddie's direction. "Besides, we really don't know what my poor sister has been through, now do we?"

Maddie could almost see the lightbulb clicking on above the guy's head. "Oh, uh…you mean you think the aliens might have already…"

"Shush," Mary Beth said drawing her finger to her shiny, red lips. "Let's not upset her. Okay?"

When he nodded, Mary Beth began to escort him away from Maddie and toward the front of the ambulance. "I'll have a much better chance of calming her down if we're alone. And the hospital *is* only a few miles away. Will you do that for me? Will you let me try to calm her down before we get her to the hospital?"

"I don't know. I'm supposed to…"

"Please?" Mary Beth begged.

Maddie almost gagged at the stupid grin that immediately replaced his frown. "Okay," he finally said with an "aw-shucks" expression. "But I'll be right up front in the cab. I'm Dave. Just yell for Dave if you need me."

As soon as dumbstruck Dave left the back of the ambulance, Mary Beth turned to Maddie and said, "See? What would you ever do without me?"

"Your new friend Dave is going to be starting an IV on *you* after I get through with you," Maddie threatened.

Her comment didn't affect Mary Beth in the least. She flopped down beside Maddie on the gurney. "What you should be doing is *thanking* me. I thought it was rather brilliant of me to put pressure on the Air Force so they would have to release you."

"Yeah, you're a real genius, Mary Beth."

Mary Beth frowned. "Oh, stop playing the victim, Maddie. We need to get our heads together before we make a statement to the press. I don't know about you, but I'm ready to kick some serious military butt. And I'm especially going to enjoy going for Captain Brad Hawkins's jugular. You're not going to believe the nerve of that jerk, Maddie, why…"

Maddie flinched at the sound of Brad's name. "We're doing no such thing, Mary Beth. All we're going to do is keep our mouths shut. Is that clear?"

"Keep our mouths shut?" Mary Beth cried. "Yeah, like that's a possibility. The police will want to question you. The media will want some answers. The…"

"And the only thing I intend to say is 'no comment.' And that's final."

Mary Beth laughed. "No comment? The entire state of New Mexico has been searching for you for two days, and you expect to get away with *no comment?*"

"And whose fault is that?" Maddie said right back. "Did I make up the stupid alien abduction story? Was I the one sobbing into my hands on national TV one minute, and waving my shoe in the air the next?"

"You saw that?"

"Yes, I saw it," Maddie seethed. "I've had to sit by helplessly for the past two days while you made us look like dumb and dumber on national TV. And now I'm going to put a stop to it, Mary Beth. Once and for all!''

"But you have to tell them something, Maddie," Mary Beth insisted. "Look at you," she added, letting her gaze travel over Maddie in one sweeping glance. "You certainly don't look like someone who's been lost in the desert for two days. Your clothes aren't even dirty."

"Don't even get me started on my clothes," Maddie said, glaring at her own blouse and slacks her twin was wearing. "From the way you've been dipping into my wardrobe, I probably don't even have anything left to change into."

Mary Beth sent her a sheepish grin. "Sorry. But my agent thought with all the national exposure I was getting, I should tone down my clothing a bit."

"Oh, we're going to tone down more than your clothing, Mary Beth, and that's a promise," Maddie vowed.

"But, Maddie," Mary Beth whined. "If you don't blow the whistle on the Air Force, everyone really will think you were carried off by aliens."

Maddie refused to answer.

"Please, Maddie, don't do this," Mary Beth pleaded. "Don't let the Air Force blackmail you. You were held against your will by our own government while they knew full well there was a search party combing the desert for you. What's the real story here? Tell me."

Maddie shook her head. "I can't. Someday I'll tell you everything. But right now you're going to have to trust my judgment."

"But what about all the interviews my agent already has lined up for both of us? What about...''

Maddie grabbed Mary Beth's arm and gave it a

hard shake. "Stop it! Your mediafest is over, Mary Beth. And that's final. Understand?"

When Mary Beth refused to agree, Maddie shook her arm again, forcing her twin to look at her. "I've never been more serious than I am right now. If you value having me as your sister. If you love me. If you want me in your life from this day forward, you'll do exactly as I say."

Mary Beth's face turned ashen. "You mean if I don't do as you say, you're threatening to disown me?"

"No, Mary Beth, I'm *promising* to disown you if you insist on continuing this travesty at my expense."

It was several seconds before Mary Beth said, "Then I guess I'll keep my mouth shut. You already know I'd never choose any career over my own sister."

Maddie breathed out a long sigh of relief, but her mind was already speeding forward to the incredible ordeal she'd have to endure before she could comfortably sink back into her safe, boring, respectable Dr. Madeline Morgan kind of life. A life without renegade sisters or drummed-up aliens. Without police departments and rescue teams. Without pushy reporters and nosey cameramen trying to scoop each other for the astounding details of her mysterious disappearance. And sadly, without a certain adorable Air Force Captain who had attempted to capture a Deva Skipper because he knew how much finding one meant to her.

You gave him your word, Maddie reminded herself when the ambulance came to a stop. And if she was going to keep her word, she would have to face the waiting public, offering nothing more than "no comment'' to the myriad of questions everyone was going to ask her from the local sheriff, to eventually her own parents.

Pulling herself up from the gurney, Maddie didn't wait for Mary Beth or for EMT Dave. She opened the back door of the ambulance, hopped off the back of her unwanted chariot and started walking toward the sea of people who were all staring in disbelief at her noticeably unsunburned face.

SHE HAD KNOWN HER RETURN to society wouldn't be easy, but nothing could have prepared Maddie for the media onslaught the minute she stepped out of the ambulance. Not that there hadn't been other hungry sharks in the water, as well. Maddie had been poked and prodded at the emergency room until one doctor finally took pity on her and pronounced her fit as a fiddle. Then she had been spirited away by a surly sheriff, who had interrogated her for hours, only to become so outraged by her refusal to give him any information that he'd assured Maddie she would be receiving a hefty bill for the expenses his county had suffered conducting a false search and rescue mission in her behalf.

She shook her head. As if she could ever pay back that kind of money on a measly professor's salary! That is, if she even still had a faculty position when she got back to McCray-Hadley.

And then, of course, there'd been the urgent call from her parents, with her mother crying hysterically and her father demanding to know what in the hell was going on. Now, she was traveling incognito, wearing dark glasses and with a stupid scarf tied around her head, sitting in the first-class section of a plane only minutes away from landing in Atlanta.

Her parents would be waiting at the airport to drive her home. It briefly crossed Maddie's mind that she almost preferred the media hounds to the thought of facing them alone.

Mary Beth, her escape artist twin, was now headed happily back to Los Angeles to make the most of her brief stint in the spotlight. Although Maddie did have to give her sister credit for finally throwing the press off her track. By leaking information that a limousine would be taking both of them to L.A. to meet with Mary Beth's agent, Maddie had been able to leave Roswell without being detected. Maddie could picture the long convoy of news crews that were most likely in hot pursuit of Mary Beth's limo now, while her dear sister lounged comfortably in the privacy of the dark tinted windows, quietly sipping champagne and congratulating herself for her brilliance.

Hurrying from her seat the second the plane landed, Maddie found her parents waiting in stony silence as she entered the terminal. She hadn't expected them to be overjoyed to see her under the circumstances, but she honestly hadn't seen them this angry with her since her spider collection got loose when she was ten and her parents had to have the entire house fumigated.

Her father, big hulk of a man that he was, dwarfed both her and her mother, who was still as slim and trim as her twin daughters. "Let's get out of here as fast as possible," he ordered, and they miraculously made it through the crowded terminal without being noticed.

Once safe inside her father's sedan, Maddie leaned her head against the back seat and closed her eyes, thankful that in a little over an hour she would finally be home. Home to her own three rooms on the third floor of a rambling old house that had been turned into apartments within walking distance of the college. One of the reasons Maddie had never seen the necessity to spring for the expense of her own car. The other reason being that in addition to his honorary position as town mayor, her father had the only reputable automobile dealership in town. A fleet of cars had always been at Maddie's disposal any time she felt the urge to drive one.

"I still can't fathom you being involved in anything that would jeopardize your career, Madeline," her mother spoke up from the front seat of the car.

Maddie didn't even bother opening her eyes.

"You might as well stop harassing her, Helen," said her father. "She's already told you she has nothing to say."

Thank you, Pop, Maddie thought until George Morgan added, "But I agree with you, dear. I've learned to expect just about anything from Mary Beth. But never in a million years would I have expected our *sensible* daughter to go along with that harebrained publicity stunt Mary Beth just pulled."

Whatever, Maddie thought, tempted to remind them she was a grown woman, not some little kid they could shame into fessing up to all of her sins. She was also tempted to remind them, especially her mother, that for most of her life she'd been encouraged to be *more* like her twin sister. "Get out and have a little fun," they always said. "Stop taking life so seriously," her mother always told her.

Maddie briefly wondered how her mother would react if she knew her *sensible* daughter had actually slept handcuffed to a total stranger.

Don't even go there.

In fact, she didn't want to think about Brad at all. And she definitely couldn't afford any more fantasizing. Her father had already told her that her boss, Dr. Fielding, had been ringing the phone off the hook, demanding to meet with her the minute she arrived back home.

Like that wasn't a given.

But if the old toad, as Mary Beth called him, thought he was going to push her around, he was in for a big surprise. Because naive, reserved little Maddie Morgan wasn't so naive and reserved anymore. She'd been accosted by more people in the past two days than Dr. Fielding would probably meet in his lifetime. If he tried to give her a hard time, he'd find out real quick she had learned to stand her ground with better men than he. Imagining Dr. Fielding lying facedown in the dirt wearing the biker's jacket, with her standing above him massaging her swollen right hand made Maddie laugh out loud.

"Care to let *us* in on what's so funny?" her mother said in her I'm-extremely-upset-with-you voice.

Maddie only laughed harder, prompting her mother to reach over the seat and swat her no-longer sensible daughter rather forcefully on the knee.

MUCH TO HER DISMAY, MADDIE soon found she was more naive than she thought. Instead of finding refuge in her own home town, Maddie was the victim of a surprise attack the minute she set foot on the McCray-Hadley campus. News crews and cameramen were everywhere, and leading the chase was none other than Arnold Purdy, editor of Morgan

City's own newspaper and former classmate of Maddie and Mary Beth.

"Madeline. Wait up," Arnold called out when Maddie hurried on her way to the administration building.

Unfortunately, ignoring the little worm was pointless. When he kept snapping closely at her heels, Maddie stopped and faced the menace long enough to say, "I have nothing to say to you, Arnold. Now please leave the campus before I call security."

Her threat didn't work. "Give me a break, Madeline." He glanced back over his shoulder to make sure the cameras were running. "It's me. Arnold Purdy. We've been friends for years. You can tell me the truth."

"Go away, Arnold," Maddie warned, wondering how being Nerdy Purdy's lab partner in tenth grade science class suddenly qualified them as lifelong friends.

"I'll go away if you tell me what really happened out in Roswell," he said, flashing a grin that verified he still had a space the size of her thumb between his two front teeth.

Maddie was on the verge of punching him in the mouth and seeing if she couldn't bring those two front teeth closer together, until she glanced up at the second floor window in the administration building. When she saw her boss glaring down at her with his hands at his waist, all Maddie could think to do was *run.*

"She's getting away," Arnold yelled to his entourage who quickly took up the chase.

"Tell us about the aliens," someone behind her called out.

"Are you really going to stop teaching and become an actress like your sister?'' someone else yelled.

Maddie never looked back. She could hear the heavy breathing coming from the mob that was running right behind her. And she was only seconds away from being completely overtaken when two campus security officers rushed from the administration building and motioned the crowd back and away from the steps.

''You can't hide in there forever, Madam Butterfly,'' Arnold yelled after her, but Maddie sprinted up the steps and headed down the hallway, finally ducking into the safety of Dr. Fielding's own private office.

Unfortunately, leaning with her back against the door and panting like a scared rabbit being chased by a pack of wild dogs was not the entrance the new and enlightened Dr. Madeline Morgan intended to make. Before she could even catch her breath, Dr. Fielding slammed down the phone he had obviously used to call the campus security police, then glared back at her over the top of his wire-rimmed reading classes.

''Well?'' toad face croaked with disdain. ''What do you have to say for yourself, Dr. Morgan? Have you come to turn in your resignation so you can pursue an acting career? Or did you stop by to propose that you head up a new department on the study of extraterrestrial beings?''

''Neither,'' Maddie tried to assure him, but he quickly cut her off.

''And to think I was under the impression you were serious about your career here.''

''I *am* serious about my career, Dr. Fielding,'' Maddie spoke up in her own defense.

He scowled in her direction. "Well, you obviously weren't thinking about your career when you decided to go along with your sister's outrageous publicity stunt."

Thank God, Maddie thought. At least Dr. Fielding was accepting her father's only explanation for her disastrous desert adventure. With the way the media had been playing up her alien abduction, Maddie feared her boss might demand a report on the information she'd been able to pump from the little green men about the various insect life on the planet Mars.

"I'm truly sorry, Dr. Fielding," Maddie began. "All I can say is that there's been a huge misunderstanding, and…"

His bushy eyebrows came together forming a fuzzy gray line across his forehead. "Then I suggest you find a way to put an end to your huge misunderstanding, Dr. Morgan. And I also suggest you take a leave of absence for the next two weeks. The entire college can't be left in turmoil while the media plays hide-and-seek with you around campus."

"But…but, s-sir," Maddie stammered. "The fall term starts next week."

"Exactly," he said, still looking at her over the top of his glasses. "The fall term does start next week. And any disruption whatsoever simply cannot and will not be tolerated. Do I make myself clear?"

Defeated, Maddie nodded. Even she had to agree with his position. Orientation for the new freshman class would be in full swing and parents galore would be milling through the campus during visitation week. She had almost been trampled to death herself by the media herd that had just stampeded across the McCray-Hadley commons. Having parents worried about the students' safety couldn't be tolerated.

"And my classes?" Maddie was brave enough to ask.

He hesitated for a moment, rocking back and forth on the worn heels of his scuffed penny loafers, the way Maddie had seen him do numerous times when he was struggling to make a difficult decision. "The best I can do is make arrangements to have your classes delayed for the next two weeks, Dr. Morgan. But if this ridiculous drama continues any longer, I'll have no choice but to find a substitute to take over your classes for the remainder of the semester."

"I understand your position, Dr. Fielding."

"Good," he said. "Then I suggest you begin your leave of absence immediately. Do so before those hooligans with the cameras burn down the administration building in order to get their story."

"Thank you, Dr. Fielding. For giving me a chance to straighten this mess out. And for holding my faculty position for at least the next two weeks."

"Let's put it this way. *If* your love affair with the media is over at the end of two weeks. And *if* you haven't been spirited off by aliens to Jupiter or Mars again, you'll still have your faculty position here at McCray-Hadley."

And with that said, he promptly dismissed Maddie with a wave of his hand, leaving her no choice but to again face Nerdy Purdy and his media vigilantes who were still waiting when she stepped back out into the bright morning sunlight.

WHEN THE CABIN CAME INTO view, childhood memories of a happier time flooded Maddie's mind. She smiled. Taking her father's advice and hiding out in the mountains for the next two weeks had been the right thing to do.

Though her parents still spent a good deal of time at their home-away-from-home, Maddie hadn't been to the cabin in years. Surprisingly, she found nothing much had changed. Other than a new flower bed her mother had added along the flagstone walkway, the old two-story cabin with its rustic cedar siding still looked as enchanting as Maddie remembered. She suddenly wondered why she didn't spend more time there.

Turning off the ignition, Maddie hopped out of the new Explorer she had borrowed from her father's car lot and took a leisurely stretch. She then opened the back passenger-side door and retrieved her suitcase. Everything else she needed for her two-week stay was already there. There would be plenty of staples in the pantry and plenty of meat in the big freezer in the basement. And rather than argue with her father, she had even brought along her mother's cell phone, since a cell phone was another luxury Maddie had never found necessary.

Sadly, because she really didn't have anyone to call.

As she grabbed the cell phone and her briefcase from the front seat, a wistful tug pulled at Maddie's heart. If only Brad had given her a number where she could have reached him, she would have someone to call now.

Of course, he hadn't given her his number. Nor had she jotted down any information for him. And why would they exchange numbers? It wasn't as if they were dating, for God's sake. And keeping in touch had certainly never popped up in any of their conversations.

"If only things were different."

Isn't that how Brad had phrased his statement?

So, forget about him, Maddie told herself as she opened the cabin door and let herself inside. She had much more to worry about than Brad Hawkins, she reminded herself as she placed her things on the overstuffed sofa facing the fireplace. Her career was on the line. And thanks to Dr. Fielding's order to take two weeks off, she would now be behind when she did start her fall classes.

Of course, the old toad had also given her an excellent opportunity, whether he realized it or not. Rather than have him yawn over the planned outline of her classes as he'd done last semester, she now had two distraction-free weeks to revamp her class curriculum so thoroughly, even her esteemed boss would have no doubt that she was serious about her career.

And that's exactly what she was going to do. She was going to lose herself in her work. She was going to focus on a revised outline for her fall classes. And she wasn't going to spend another second even thinking about Hawk. Especially not the way his hot mouth had traveled over her body, driving her crazy. Or the power he had to render her senseless the second he took her in his arms.

No, she wasn't going to think about that.

She wasn't going to think about that mischievous twinkle in his eye when he was teasing her, either. Or how natural it had felt to have his body pressed against her own the night they slept handcuffed together. And she certainly wasn't going to spend any more time thinking about how difficult it must have been for him growing up without a father, or how devastated he must have been when his mother died, too. She also wasn't going to think about how completely she could identify with his inner determination to set a goal for himself and stick to it. Because in that respect, they were exactly alike. Just like Hawk, she was determined to stay completely focused on her career.

Which was why she wasn't going to spend another second thinking about him.

She wasn't going to think about how good he tasted, and how wonderful he smelled, or how terrific he looked. Nor was she going to think about the way the sound of his voice could get dangerously husky, or the way the touch of his hand made her skin prickle with excitement. She wasn't going to think about his thoughtfulness, either, in trying to find a butterfly to replace the one his own flying machine had caused her to lose. And she especially wasn't going to think about how perfect it would be to make love to him in front of the fire she would build later in the evening when it came time to stave off the cool, night mountain air.

No, she definitely wasn't going think about that.

Or the cute way Brad cocked his head at a certain angle every time he looked in her direction.

Or...

Oh, who am I kidding? I'm in love with the guy. Admit it.

And when she couldn't bring herself to admit any such nonsense, Maddie stomped upstairs to put away her things, hoping the distraction would allow her to lie to herself at least a little while longer.

8

___

AFTER MADDIE *HAD* BUILT the fire she wasn't going to think about making love to Brad in front of that evening, she put in a call to her parents to assure them everything was fine. She had just closed the bottom half of the palm-size device when Mary Beth rang through, bubbling with excitement because she had an audition for a leading role in a hot new day-time soap opera.

As soon as Mary Beth asked, Maddie admitted her own good news: that she hadn't been fired on the spot.

"See? What did I tell you?" Mary Beth said. "Even an old grump like Fielding realizes what an asset you are to his department."

Mary Beth rambled on for a few more minutes, but before she hung up, she added with a giggle, "Just promise me you won't get attached to Nerdy Purdy now that you're spending so much time to-gether, Maddie. There's no way I could ever tolerate having Nerdy Purdy for a brother-in-law."

Maddie laughed for the first time in days, but after she and her twin said their goodbyes, Maddie was tempted to call Mary Beth back and ask what choice she would make between Nerdy Purdy and the man she had threatened to hit over the head with her shoe. She was still smiling to herself over the choice words Mary Beth would have for candidate number two, when a distinct squeak turned her head in the direction of the cabin's front door. The second step leading up to the cabin's front porch had always squeaked "loud enough to wake the dead" according to her mother, yet for some reason her father had never found the time to fix it.

"Damn you, Arnold," Maddie mumbled under her breath, certain the little worm had followed her to the cabin still hoping for an exclusive interview.

She launched herself off the sofa, unconcerned that she was wearing nothing but a flimsy pair of shortie pajamas Mary Beth had given her for Christmas last year. Grabbing the poker from its stand by the fire place, she stomped across the room, flipped on the porch light, opened the door and stepped out on the porch.

Wielding the poker like a power-hitter for the New York Yankees, Maddie yelled into the darkness, "I'm tired of this, Arnold. Do you hear me? You're on private property and I *will* have you arrested."

When her intruder stepped out of the shadows at the end of the porch, however, Maddie lowered the poker.

"Who's Arnold?"

For a second, Maddie thought she was only fantasizing again. But when the step squeaked a second time as Brad made his way up the steps and onto the porch, Maddie almost screamed like an excited five-year-old on Christmas morning.

And dear God, but he did look fabulous in street clothes. Faded jeans tight enough to make her mouth water and a pale yellow polo shirt that made his tan look two shades darker than it was. *Oh, yeah.* The only way he could look any better was if he was stretched out naked on her bed upstairs.

All Maddie could do was stand there and stare.

When he took a step closer, Maddie asked, "How on earth did you find me?"

He sent her the same cocky grin she remembered. "With today's technology I could locate a postage stamp on the sidewalk in Moscow if I wanted to, Maddie dear. Finding you was a piece of cake."

Her eyes dropped to the duffel bag he held in his hand. "And is that what you have stashed away in your bag, Captain? A piece of cake?"

"Why don't you invite me inside and I'll show you?"

Maddie hesitated only for a second, then lowered the poker and leaned it against the porch banister. He followed her inside, and when she closed the door behind him he took a long look around the room.

"Great cabin," he said, and Maddie watched his gaze drift toward the fire in the fireplace before he placed his bag on the bar that separated the small kitchen from the great room.

When he unzipped the bag and pulled out her pith helmet, Maddie laughed.

And Mary Beth claimed you couldn't reel a man in with a pith helmet!

SHE STILL HADN'T EXPLAINED who Arnold was, but Brad had already forgotten the question. The only thing on his mind at the moment was the perfect body hidden beneath two pieces of fabric that might as well have been made of cellophane.

"You forgot this," he said handing her the helmet, wondering at the same time what his chances were of getting her out of that cellophane.

"You could have mailed it," she answered.

"I could have. But I also wanted to tell you in person that you didn't have to worry about owing anything to the state of New Mexico. Those expenses will be taken care of quickly and quietly behind the scenes."

"Hush money, I think they call it," she suggested.

"A small token of appreciation for keeping the Black Ghost a secret," Brad countered.

"Anything else?"

Brad stalled for a second. "I'm being sent out of the country on a training assignment, Maddie. And…"

"And?"

"Damn, you're making this hard," Brad muttered, running a hand through his short dark hair. "What I'm trying to say is that I couldn't leave the country without…"

She closed the distance between them so fast, Brad didn't even have time to finish his sentence. And when his mouth found hers, Brad's mind went blank and he lost all sense of reason.

He wasn't even aware she had led him across the room until she pushed him backward over the back of the sofa. And when she landed on top of him, she kissed him again before she said, "Okay, Captain. I'm taking *you* prisoner this time. We can do this easy, or—" Brad moaned when her hand slid down the front of his pants "—or we can do this the hard way. It's your choice."

Reversing their positions, Brad pinned Maddie

beneath him instead. "I think you just made that choice for me, didn't you."

Brad knew the time for playful teasing was over, he could tell from the hungry look she gave him before she pulled his head down and kissed him so thoroughly the thrill turned him inside out and upside down all at once. And when their feverish kisses reached even a higher level, nothing short of an atomic explosion could have forced them apart.

How they ended up naked and on the floor, Brad wasn't certain, but the sight of Maddie's nude body and her hair shining like glitter in the firelight, was almost more than he could stand. This was one time, however, he had no intention of giving in to his own selfish needs first.

"I told you once that pleasure was my game," Brad whispered, delivering a series of tiny kisses along her neck that made her gasp. "I think it's time I showed you what I meant."

MADDIE WAS AFRAID TO OPEN her eyes. Afraid if she did, she would find she had only been dreaming. But when a strong arm slid around her waist and pulled her closer, she smiled. They were still lying on the braided rug in front of the fireplace, covered with a throw from the sofa, but the fire had burned down only to a flicker. She wasn't sure what time it was, but judging from the number of hours they'd spent making love, Maddie knew dawn couldn't be far away.

Talk about a pleasure marathon!

She still wasn't sure how she was going to get the maple syrup Brad had found in the kitchen cabinet out of her mother's braided rug, but she'd never be able to look Aunt Jemima in the face again without blushing from head to toe. She also knew she'd never have to hear the word satiated again and not fully understand exactly what it meant.

Of course, *staying* satiated was a different matter altogether. And with that thought in mind, Maddie rolled over with the intention of waking the handsome hunk sleeping beside her to request a refresher course on the subject of pleasure. She never got the chance. The alarm on his wristwatch beat her to the punch.

He sat up and silenced the alarm, then shook his head as if to clear it. "I didn't mean to doze off," he said, sending her a sleepy grin.

Maddie sat up, too, trying to cover herself with her portion of the throw. When his gaze fell to her partially exposed breasts, she said, "There's a fabulous feather bed upstairs that is much more comfortable than this hard wooden floor."

He might as well have slapped her when he reached for his jeans and said, "That sounds great, but I'm really pressed for time."

Pressed for time? Maddie felt like screaming.

Is that why he had turned her every which way but loose from the moment he arrived? Because he was pressed for time?

He stood up and turned his back to her while he pulled on his jeans, giving her a perfect view of the naked rear she personally felt like kicking. Instead of giving him the satisfaction of knowing she was even angry, she stood up herself and wrapped the throw around her body like a tight-fitting cocoon. No way was she going to flounce around naked *or* in her sexy pjs while he gathered up his possessions to leave.

She decided to go upstairs, get fully dressed, and pray to God he'd already be gone when she came back down. And what she *wasn't* going to do is let him know she'd been stupid enough to believe his surprise appearance was anything more than just a one-night stand. Well, a half-night stand, if you really wanted to be technical about it.

The sun hadn't even reached the horizon yet, for God's sake!

How she could have been so stupid was beyond her. Yet, when she thought about it, what did she really expect? She had attacked him almost the second he stepped inside the door, which only increased Maddie's angst further remembering how she had practically body-slammed him onto the sofa and rammed her hand down his pants. *God, how humiliating!*

Not that he'd tried to fight her off, she reasoned. No, he had been more than willing to take her off on that pleasure cruise he was so anxious to show her. Well, she could be just as nonchalant as he was being. They'd had hot, uninhibited, mind-blowing sex. Nothing more, nothing less. And as soon as she accepted that fact, the better off she'd be.

When she reached the stairs, she prayed she looked cooler than she felt. She turned back to him and smiled. "There's a bathroom down the hall to the right, Brad, and you'll find clean towels under the sink. I'm sure you could use some coffee before you go. I'll get dressed and make a pot."

I'VE JUST BEEN DISMISSED! Brad thought angrily when Maddie bounded up the stairs as happy as a lark.

He'd expected her to at least ask where he was going and how long he might be gone. He'd even been foolish enough to think they would keep in touch. Call each other, write, e-mail, whatever. This day and age global communication was as common as a bad cold.

But instead, she'd let him make love to her for hours on end, and now she was through with him and ready for him to be on his way.

Checking his watch again, Brad decided Madam Butterfly wasn't the correct nickname for Maddie, at all. Madam Praying Mantis fit her much better. Wasn't that the female insect that always bit the male's head off after they mated?

Grabbing his duffel bag from the kitchen bar, Brad stomped off down the hallway in search of the downstairs bath, wondering what had happened to her previous declaration that she wanted more out of life than just her damn career. He'd done his own amount of soul searching after he'd watched her walk away that morning, and he'd come to the conclusion that he didn't have much of a life without Maddie in it. Not that the feeling was mutual, obviously. She was physically attracted to him, sure, he'd received that message loud and clear. But to not even care where he was going or when he'd be back?

Damn, that hurt.

"Suck it up and get over it," Brad mumbled to himself as he stepped into the shower. Isn't that what he'd always done? He was tough and he could take it. They'd been attracted to each other and they'd acted on it. Nothing more, nothing less. At least maybe now he could purge her from his system.

Ten minutes later, Maddie only confirmed everything Brad had been thinking when he emerged from the bathroom and found her waiting for him with his coffee in a plastic cup to go.

"I assumed you would want to take your coffee with you, since you're *so* pressed for time," she said in a voice sweeter than the maple syrup he'd dribbled over her body only a few hours earlier.

Ah, so that's the problem, Brad finally realized. He was slow. He'd admit it. At least when it came to understanding how in the hell a woman's mind worked. Evidently *pressed for time* was listed somewhere in the *Woman's Guide for What Men Aren't Supposed to Say.* How he was supposed to know that, Brad didn't have a clue, but it proved one vital point he'd known all along.

Personal relationships took too damn much out of a man!

Reaching out, Brad accepted the cup and drained it completely in two easy gulps. The fact that the coffee was hot enough to make his eyes water couldn't compare with the heat steadily rising under his collar. "Thanks," he said, as he plopped the empty cup down on the bar.

"You, too," she said with a taunting little smile.

Brad clenched the strap on his duffel bag so tightly, he was surprised it didn't break in two. He'd practically moved heaven and earth to get a forty-eight-hour furlough because he didn't want to leave the country without seeing Maddie first. He'd had to change planes twice, rent a car in Atlanta for the drive to Morgan City, only to learn from the buzz at the Morgan City Café that Maddie was still another hour away hiding out in the northeast Georgia mountains. Now, he would have to retrace every one of those steps, and yes, he was pressed for time.

But rather than admit any of this to the woman who had stolen his heart, Brad leaned forward and gave her a quick peck on the cheek. "Take care of yourself," he told her, and walked out the door while he still had the courage to leave.

BY THE END OF HER TWO-WEEK hiatus at the cabin, the media *and* Nerdy Purdy had lost interest in Madam Butterfly, and had promptly crossed Maddie off as yesterday's news. When she returned to McCray-Hadley, she'd been surprised to learn that all her fall classes had been filled to capacity, though Maddie suspected some of the students had signed up mainly out of curiosity about her. Only two days earlier, she had even received the astonishing news that she had been chosen for Dr. Fielding's esteemed research team, which had been her main goal in life when she had gone in search of the Deva Skipper to prove herself worthy of such an appointment.

So why am I so damn miserable? Maddie kept asking herself.

Two words sprang to mind.

Brad Hawkins.

She hadn't heard a word from him since he left the cabin that morning, though it didn't really surprise Maddie that he hadn't tried to get in touch with her again. Why would he? After she'd had time to think about her actions, even she had to agree she'd been a real pain in the ass, which evidently *was* normal for her, at least when it came to dealing with him.

As the weeks slipped by, she'd thought of trying to contact him instead, but Maddie knew she couldn't take that risk. The Black Ghost-alien abduction saga had finally been put to rest. If she called around trying to find him, there was always the possibility someone would link her name with his and bring the whole ugly story to the surface again.

But a day didn't go by that Maddie didn't wonder where Brad was and pray for his safety. And a day didn't go by that she also didn't curse herself for being too stubborn to ask for any details about where he was going. Of course, he was pretty stubborn himself. Not to mention he'd been too irritated with her to offer any information before he left. And that's why it was probably better that they had parted like they did, Maddie kept telling herself. They were two control freaks. Neither would ever be willing to hand over control to the other. In a nutshell, theirs was a relationship doomed before it really began.

C'est la vie, Maddie thought sadly when the announcement came over the loudspeaker that her twin's plane had landed.

"Well, don't you look fat and sassy!" were Mary Beth's first words when she bounced into the Atlanta terminal.

"Happy Thanksgiving to you, too," Maddie grumbled, but she didn't pull away from the big hug her twin sister gave her.

Mary Beth stepped back and looked Maddie up and down. "I'm not kidding, Maddie. I don't think

I've ever seen you looking so lovely. You're almost glowing.''

Maddie rolled her eyes. When they linked arms for a stroll to the baggage claim area, however, Maddie did briefly finger the strained button at the waistband of her favorite wool slacks. Leave it to her twin to notice she had put on a measly five pounds.

"Did you do that little piece of detective work I asked you to do for me?" Mary Beth wanted to know.

"Don't worry, Mary Beth. I got the information straight from his aunt. Zack is *not* coming home for Thanksgiving."

"Good," Mary Beth said. "Because the next time my ex-fiancé sees me, I'll be on CBS in the lead female role on *The Wild and the Free.*"

"You mean you got the part!" Maddie exclaimed.

"Damn straight," Mary Beth beamed. "From here on out, you can call me Fancy Kildare. And I'm going to be the hottest femme fatale on daytime TV.''

"Congratulations, Mary Beth," Maddie said, trying to muster up as much enthusiasm as possible.

Mary Beth wasn't fooled. "I know you think I'm only pursuing this acting career to spite Zack," Mary Beth said, reading Maddie's mind. "But I really want this, Maddie. And I need it. Just for me."

Maddie squeezed her hand. "Then I'm happy for you, Mary Beth. I know you'll knock their socks off."

"And how about you? Any hunky new professors on the faculty at McCray-Hell-hole this year?"

Maddie laughed. "Not this year."

"Then plan on spending Christmas out in L.A. with me. I'm going to be the new toast of the town. Our men-meeting possibilities will be limitless."

Maddie tensed. The last thing she wanted was to meet anyone. She'd be lucky if she ever recovered from her brief encounter with the man she had met. "I'm sorry, Mary Beth, don't count on me for Christmas." Maddie wanted to put an end to that invitation before Mary Beth started making any plans. "Dr. Fielding finally asked me to join his research team."

"I knew you'd never get a life if you made that damn research team," Mary Beth complained as she tugged her luggage from the revolving conveyor belt.

Maddie took one of the bags when Mary Beth handed it over. "You need to stop worrying about me, Mary Beth. I've told you a million times, I'm perfectly satisfied with my life just the way it is."

THE INSIDE OF A TOILET BOWL, Maddie decided, had to be one of life's most disgusting places. But it didn't stop her from bending forward again to revisit the revolting location early the next morning.

"Are you okay?"

Maddie glanced briefly at Mary Beth, who had stumbled to the bathroom door, wiping the sleep from her eyes. "Too much turkey and dressing," Maddie managed to say, waving Mary Beth away from the door.

"Well, if I didn't know it was *impossible*, I'd think you were pregnant," Mary Beth said with a yawn. She walked over and took a washcloth from beneath the vanity, wet it and handed it to Maddie before she disappeared back into the bedroom.

Pregnant? Oh, God.

Just the sound of the word made Maddie pay homage to the porcelain god again. But like Mary Beth had said, it simply wasn't possible. She and Brad had been so careful. Maybe they *had* gone through an entire box of condoms, but they'd never had unprotected sex. Never. Just because they couldn't get along, didn't mean they were stupid!

She hadn't even had any symptoms. Not really. Sure, maybe she *had* gained a few measly pounds, but she always indulged herself when she was depressed. Those buckets of Rocky Road ice cream she'd been wolfing down while she pined away for Brad could easily explain the weight gain.

Running the damp cloth over her face, Maddie tried to remember when she'd had her last period. She couldn't. But that was even normal for her. Her periods had never been regular. She'd always skipped a month here and there and never worried about it. *That was because you never had anything to worry about before, you idiot!* Maddie thought in a panic and promptly dunked her head in the toilet bowl again.

It took another thirty minutes before the nausea finally subsided. When it did, Maddie pulled herself up from the floor, brushed her teeth and took a shower. She then tiptoed into the bedroom she'd shared with Mary Beth most of their lives. Staying with their parents over the holidays had always been a family tradition, and one Maddie had actually been grateful for this year. The thought of sitting alone in her apartment all weekend staring at a phone that wasn't going to ring had not been that appealing.

She managed to get dressed without waking Mary Beth again, then slipped downstairs and helped herself to her father's car keys. Minutes later she was driving like a madwoman through the heavy traffic that plagued even small-town Morgan City on the busiest shopping day of the holiday season. The second she reached Morgan City's minimall on the outskirts of town, Maddie zoomed into a parking spot ahead of a Volkswagen, ignoring the loud blast from the irritated shopper's horn. She then marched into the pharmacy, returning only minutes later with the little kit that would finally put her mind at ease.

Tearing out of the parking lot with the same urgency that had brought her to the mall in the first place, Maddie didn't have the slightest clue she'd stolen the parking spot right out from under an old friend of hers. Nor did she realize Nerdy Purdy was heading straight for the pharmacy as Maddie roared away, determined to find out exactly what had Madam Butterfly in such a full-blown tizzy on the day after Thanksgiving.

A FEW HOURS LATER, Mary Beth found Maddie sitting on the living room floor of her apartment, staring at the little circle with the plus sign in the middle.

"My God, Maddie. You scared us to death running off like that," Mary Beth started ranting until she noticed the plastic stick Maddie was holding in her hand.

In one quick swoop, Mary Beth grabbed it from

Maddie's hand and stared at it in disbelief. "Please tell me this is some new type of IQ test."

"It's an IQ test, all right," Maddie assured her twin. "And *my* IQ just came back negative. The plus sign in the circle proves it!"

When Maddie burst into tears, Mary Beth dropped to the floor and let Maddie cry on her shoulder. "Oh, Maddie, you poor little thing. Who did this awful thing to you?"

"I just can't understand it," Maddie sobbed, pushing away from her sister long enough to wipe away the tears with her fingertips. "We were so careful."

"We?" Mary Beth bellowed.

"Well, you don't think I got pregnant all by myself, do you?" Maddie cried back.

"Then who was it?" Mary Beth demanded. "Tell me, Maddie. Tell me and I'll personally..."

"Hit him over the head with your shoe?"

Mary Beth's mouth dropped open. "You've got to be kidding me! So, that's what was going on out at that Air Force base when you couldn't tear yourself away."

"It didn't even happen at the base," Maddie sobbed. "Brad followed me to the cabin when I was hiding from the media."

"Why, that no-good jerk!"

Maddie bristled. "Brad isn't a no-good jerk, Mary Beth. I love him."

"Love him? Are you nuts? You only just met him!"

"You don't have to know someone your entire life like you and Zack did to fall in love," Maddie insisted, then immediately burst into tears again. "I just can't understand it,'' she kept saying between sobs. ''We used protection every time.''

''*Every* time?''

''Well, yes. I admit we got a little carried away that one time with the maple syrup, but...''

''Maple syrup?''

''But that was one of *my* pleasure moments.''

''Pleasure moments?''

''Brad didn't even...you know...''

''Climax?''

Maddie nodded. ''Brad's wonderful like that, Mary Beth. He was adamant about putting my pleasure first, and...''

''Whoa, this is way too much information!''

Maddie blushed. ''I know condoms aren't always one hundred percent effective. Maybe the syrup....''

''You idiot,'' Mary Beth yelled, shaking her head.

''There's no need to shout,'' Maddie said, looking up at her twin who was now pacing around the room.

''I just can't believe this. And you're the one with the freaking Ph.D!''

Maddie ignored her and let out a long sigh. ''What in the world am I going to do, Mary Beth?''

Mary Beth frowned. ''You're not thinking about...''

Maddie shook her head. ''No. Of course not.''

''Would you really marry this guy?''

''Marry him?'' Maddie wailed. ''I don't even know how to find him.''

Mary Beth's eyes narrowed. ''So, he pulled a hit-and-run on you, didn't he?''

''Not really. Maybe. Oh, I don't know,'' Maddie

cried. "He had to leave and I got angry. Then he got angry because I was angry, and..."

"Well, if you think he was angry then," Mary Beth said with a snort, "wait until he finds out—"

Maddie cut her off. "But he isn't going to find out. I'd never try to trap Brad into..."

"Are you nuts?" Mary Beth screeched. "When news gets out that Madam Butterfly's pregnant only three months after she was carried off by aliens, the whole world is going to be talking about this baby you're carrying."

Maddie paled. "Don't even talk like that, Mary Beth."

And before Mary Beth could answer, Maddie made a mad dash to the bathroom with her hand over her mouth.

9

BRAD PURPOSELY ignored the pretty blonde Fräulein when she returned to his table and placed another frosty stein in front of him. "Dark beer for a dark mood, *ja?*"

"I won't argue with that statement," said Brad.

In the past, he'd always looked forward to any training assignment that would take him back to Frankfort. Germany had always held a special place in his heart. He loved the old city, the ancient buildings, the fastidious nature of the German people who were so clean they even swept the sidewalks on a daily basis. Der Braau Haus, the quaint brewhouse he was sitting in now, had been one of his favorite places the last time he spent a few months in Frankfort, whipping a group of new helicopter pilots into shape.

He'd spent many pleasurable evenings sitting exactly where he was sitting now, at a table in front of the massive stone firplace, enjoying the warmth of a roaring fire. Back then, he'd soaked up every ounce of the rich Alpine atmoshere and flirted with the pretty waitresses dressed in their traditional barmaid's costumes, with their long hair braided neatly and pinned on top of their heads. He'd also managed to sample most of the superb German beers the establishment had to offer. But most of all, he'd enjoyed sitting around the table with his men, eating bratwurst and telling tall tales, most of which were more fiction than fact.

But that had been P.M.

Pre-Maddie.

Now, Brad decided, he might as well be sitting in a fast-food joint in Nowhere, Minnesota, with a Cyclops tramping drinks to his table.

Missing Maddie had certainly taken the enjoyment out of many things he'd once held sacred. Like the camaraderie that usually existed between him and his men. Since he left Maddie, he'd been so damn ornery none of his men would even get near him. Not even Baker, after they'd practically come to blows when his friend made the mistake of saying "I told you so" in reference to what a woman like Maddie would do to him.

And she'd certainly gotten under his skin; deeper than shrapnel would have done had he stepped on an enemy land mine.

He should have left things the way they were when he and Maddie parted in the desert, he kept reminding himself. Maybe then he could have returned to his old life and been satisfied playing the role of the adventurous pilot who didn't have a care in the world.

Without Maddie, nothing made sense anymore.

Being in love sucks, Brad thought and put the stein to his lips for another long swallow. He continued to ignore his attentive barmaid, hoping she would take the hint and move on to her next customer. She didn't. Instead she stalled a bit longer, taking a red-and-white checked towel from across her arm to wipe away thie riglet of moisture left behind on the table.

"Your wife? You are missing her?"

She bent over the table far enough that in his past life he might have been tempted by the ample cleavage her off-the-shoulder white peasant blouse revealed. Her forest green weskit had the drawstrings cinched so tight a man's hands could fit around her small waist. But that didn't tempt Brad either. Especially since her question about a wife only made him remember how much it had bothered him the day Maddie told him she never intended to marry.

"No wife," Brad admitted with a frown, but he realized he should have lied about a wife when she immediately sent him a hopeful smile.

"I am Freda," she said brightly. She hesitated for a moment, then ran her finger suggestively over the back of his hand. "If you are lonely..."

Brad looked up from his beer stein prepared to dissuade her, but the first thing that caught his attention was the TV above the bar.

What the hell?

Maddie!

The volume was turned up loud enough that he could hear the excitement in the newscaster's voice, but Brad's German wasn't good enough to make out what the man was saying. "I know her," Brad said, quickly pointing to the television. "Can you translate for me? Can you find out what's going on?"

Eager to please, Freda rushed back to the bar and closer to the TV. She returned a moment later with a surprised look on her face and her hands at her tiny waist. "You know this Madam Butterfly?"

"Yes, I know her," Brad said, motioning impatiently for her to continue. "What's going on?"

"She is pregnant. By the aliens."

"Pregnant!" Brad thundered, causing Freda to jump.

He was so shaken himself, Brad grabbed for the stein and drained the mug to the bottom. *Pregnant? Could Maddie really be pregnant?* He knew he had to get back to the base, and fast. But he also knew it could take forever if he tried to pay his tab with a credit card. Digging into his pocket, he threw down enough U.S. currency to make Freda's blue eyes grow even wider than they had at his outburst.

"Do me a favor and pay my tab," Brad told her as he grabbed his flight jacket form the back of his chaor. "Keep the rest for your trouble."

Freda looked down at the five twenty-dollar bills he had thrown on the table, then back at him when she picked up the bills. "One hundred American dollars for two beers? You are joking, *ja?*"

"No joke," Brad assured her and headed toward the thick wooden doors at the front of the brewhouse before Freda could argue.

The second he stepped outside, he was hit by the brisk November wind zipping around the corner. Brad turned up his collar and hurried down the old cobblestone street, heading straight fo his borrowed jeep. Seconds later he was on his way back to the base, assuring himself the media was only up to its old tricks again. But the possibility that Maddie *could* be carrying his child was enough to make sweat pop out on his brow even in the sub-zero climate.

"Damn," Brad swore, pounding his fist against the steering wheel. He'd been too stubborn to call her. And he'd been too proud to take a chance that she might brush him off if he did try to contact her again. But pregnant? The fact she might be pregnant had never entered his mind. They'd used protection, dammit! He wasn't stupid.

Yet, why all the hullabaloo with the media again?

Something was going on. Brad knew it. Just as he knew it would take nothing short of a miracle to get back to the States so he could find out the truth for himself.

He didn't bother stopping for idle chitchat the way he usually did with the main guard, who was practically the only one on base talking to him at the moment. Instead Brad produced his ID, then zoomed past the guardhouse the second the arm of the barricade lifted to let him through.

"Dammit, Maddie, why haven't you tried to find me?" Brad mumbled under his breath, too worried to dwell on the fact that Madam Butterfly hadn't seemed the least bit interested in where she might find him the last time he'd been in her presence.

MADDIE WAITED until the last of her students filed out of the lecture hall, then let out a long sigh of relief, thankful that her early-morning class was her only class for the day. Tomorrow, the long Christmas break would begin. It was a break she hoped would give her time to pull herself together and make some concrete plans. She had just put her lecture notes in her briefcase when her mother stormed into the lecture hall and slammed one of the tabloids down on the desk in front of her.

Maddie looked down at the computer generated picture of an infant with huge, vacant eyes staring back at her from an otherwise normal-looking human face. The caption below the picture read: What Madam Butterfly's Offspring Will Look Like: A Baby Only A Woman Who Likes Bugs Could Love.

"What are you going to do about this, Madeline?" her mother demanded.

Maddie ripped the tabloid to pieces and threw it into the waste can beside her desk. "Don't start with me, Mom."

"I'm not interested in *starting* anything. I'm interested in you putting a *stop* to this nonsense."

Maddie pushed back from her desk and stood up. "We'll talk about this later. I have a meeting in five minutes."

"The only meeting you *should* be having is with the press," Helen Morgan snapped. "I don't know who you're protecting or why, but I do know if you don't give people some answers, and soon, my grandchild will never be able to walk down the street in this town without someone whispering something ugly behind its back."

"You think I'm not aware of that?" Maddie wailed in protest. "You think it doesn't tear my heart out knowing everyone is making fun of this child I'm carrying?"

"Then act like it," Helen ordered and tossed one end of her scarf over her shoulder for effect. "A mother's first responsibility is always to protect her own child. Now grow up and take charge of this situation!"

When her mother stormed out of the lecture hall the same way she'd blown in, Maddie felt like screaming. How dare her mother act like she wasn't upset about the ugly pictures and the ridiculous story that her child was an alien! She might not have had time to embrace motherhood fully yet, but Maddie knew no one could ever love her child any more than she did.

She briefly ran her hand protectively over her stomach, then grabbed her briefcase and headed for the door. She hadn't bothered to tell her mother the meeting she had to attend was a special meeting called by Dr. Fielding and the dean of the college. She'd been expecting such a meeting since Arnold Purdy announced on the front page of the *Morgan City Times* that she had purchased a pregnancy test at the local pharmacy. And then the story had escalated, just as Mary Beth predicted it would.

She should have suspected they would wait until the Christmas break to ask for her resignation. They would say, of course, that McCray-Hadley couldn't afford the bad publicity, yadda yadda yadda. What they *wouldn't* mention was her pregnancy, or the fact that being unwed and pregnant in small-town America today was every bit as scandalous as it had been fifty years earlier. Maddie was well aware of that fact, as were the two members of the moral majority who were patiently waiting for her behind closed doors now.

Maddie knocked on the door and held her head high when she walked into the dean's office. If either man was impressed by her resolve, he didn't show it.

"Please sit down, Dr. Morgan," said the dean, pointing to the proverbial hot seat.

Maddie did as the dean instructed, but she had her own agenda for this meeting. "I have something to say before this meeting begins," Maddie told her persecutors, looking at the dean, and then at Dr. Fielding.

The dean glanced at his cohort for approval. When Dr. Fielding nodded, the dean said, "Yes, Dr. Morgan? What is it you have to say?"

"I have fulfilled my obligations to this college to the letter and my performance record is spotless. However, if you choose to remove me from my faculty position for any other reason than my performance, gentlemen, then I'm sure my child and I will be able to live quite comfortably on the huge settlement I'll win from you in court.''

With that said, Maddie stood up and walked politely out of the room. She didn't even bother slamming the dean's door for effect. But she did feel totally exhilarated for the first time in days. In fact, she was on such an incredible high, Maddie practically skipped along the sidewalk on her three-block walk back home.

Her incredible high disappeared, however, when she saw what was waiting for her on her living-room sofa.

"How DID YOU GET IN HERE?" Maddie demanded.

Brad didn't even bother answering her question. He pulled himself up from the sofa and stood looking at her with his hands at his waist. "I want to know the truth, Maddie. Are you pregnant or not?"

He watched her wilt like a marionette without any strings. And he was there to catch her in his arms before the first tear spilled over her eyelashes. "It's okay, Maddie. Please don't cry," Brad pleaded as she sobbed against his shoulder.

"Oh, Brad, it's been so terrible," she said between sobs. "I was so shocked when I took the test…and I never would have bothered you about the baby…but then the press picked up the story…and my parents were livid…and my sister called me an idiot because I'm not some authority on the effect maple syrup could have on condoms…and…''

"Whoa," Brad said, pushing her away so he

could look at her. "What's this about syrup and condoms?"

She wiped at her eyes. "Don't make fun of me Brad...I'm still so confused. We were so careful...and..."

Brad pulled her to him again. "We obviously weren't careful enough," he said. "But I can't believe you weren't going to tell me about the baby."

She wrestled away from his embrace. "But Brad, you told me from the beginning you never wanted..."

"It doesn't matter what either of us *wanted*, Maddie. The fact is..."

"That we have to clear up this crazy alien baby story immediately," she finished for him. "And now that you're here, I want to hold a press conference as soon as possible. I won't have people thinking our son is some offspring from outer space one second longer."

"Son?" Brad echoed. "You mean you've already had one of those ultrasounds?"

She shook her head. "No, but I know this baby is a boy, Brad. Call it mother's intuition. Call it anything you like. But I know this baby is a boy."

Feeling more than a little shaky, Brad walked over and lowered himself slowly onto Maddie's sofa again. *A boy.* Maddie had just confirmed she was having his child, and she was positive the baby was a boy. During the time he'd been making arrangements for an extended leave of absence, he'd had plenty of time to consider the possibility that Maddie was pregnant. And his emotions had run the full gamut and back again.

He'd gone from being totally overwhelmed because he'd vowed never to have children, to feeling fiercely protective of his unborn child and the woman he loved completely. He'd also thought a lot about something Joe Gibbons had told him at his mother's funeral when, in a fit of rage, Brad had cursed his father for being so selfish. "Your father loved you and your mother with every ounce of his being, and he had that same passion for his country," Gibbons had told him. "I'd hate to think he gave his life defending his family and his country for a son who can't appreciate the ultimate sacrifice he made."

Brad had only been twenty at the time, too young to understand the magnitude of what Gibbons had been trying to tell him. Now he realized his father hadn't been selfish at all. His father had been a man passionate about his family and his country. *He* had been the selfish one, walling himself off from the rest of the world and never allowing himself to love or be loved.

Brad had no intention of being selfish any longer. He loved Maddie and he would love his son with every ounce of his being, just as he loved his country. *His son.* Even the sound of those words sounded foreign, yet Brad's heart filled with so much pride he thought he might burst. He was still trying to process such astounding information when Maddie said, "I don't expect any kind of commitment from you, Brad."

No commitment? Had Maddie gone crazy?

"You can be as involved, or as uninvolved in our son's life as you choose to be."

Uninvolved? Did she really think he wouldn't want to be involved in his own child's life?

"All I'm asking is that you stand at my side when we both explain to the press that it was the Black

Ghost, not a space ship, that picked me up in the desert. And I want you to state categorically and unequivocally that you are the father of my child, and not some alien.''

That snapped him out of his trance. ''The Black Ghost is scheduled to be unveiled next May, Maddie, and I promise you, we'll hold a press conference the very same day.''

Her mouth dropped open. ''Next May? The baby's due next May, Brad. Surely you don't expect me to go through this entire pregnancy with the media announcing on a daily basis that our baby is an alien.''

Brad's look turned pleading. ''All I'm asking, Maddie, is that...''

''Well, I'm sorry, Brad, but I'm not spending another six months in media hell. In fact, I'm not interested in waiting even another minute. We're holding a press conference today, Brad. Today! And not one minute longer.''

Brad was on his feet again. ''Maddie. Honey. You have to be reasonable about this...''

''Reasonable?'' she yelled. ''Being reasonable is what got me into this mess! If I hadn't let you talk me into keeping your stupid helicopter a secret, no one would be implying I was having some alien's baby right now.''

Her sharp tone made Brad react before he could stop himself. ''Now, dammit, Maddie. I didn't exactly have to twist your arm to swear you to secrecy, and you know it.''

''I don't remember it being my *arm* you were interested in,'' she accused. ''In fact, I'm beginning to wonder if I haven't been just another one of your top secret assignments from the beginning. Was that your real assignment, Brad? Did the Air Force ask you to make love to the pitiful old maid professor as a double guarantee she'd never say a word about your damn helicopter?''

Brad was stunned. "How can you even make such an accusation? Look me in the eye this minute and tell me you really believe that.''

"All I know is that you can unveil your precious Black Ghost *after* the press conference, Brad. It's as simple as that.''

"Simple? There's nothing simple about it, Maddie. I don't have any control over when the Black Ghost is going to be unveiled. It's not my decision.''

She crossed her arms stubbornly across her chest. "Then make it your decision. Call your commander and tell him this is another one of those circumstances that doesn't qualify as your typical situation.''

"Or what?''

Maddie didn't waiver. "Or I'll tell the world about the Black Ghost myself.''

"You gave me your word you wouldn't do that, Maddie.''

There was no warmth in her eyes when she said, "We weren't having a child when I gave you my word, Brad. But we are having a child now. And if you haven't worked things out by the end of the week, then I'll have no choice but to hold my own press conference on Friday.''

Brad threw his hands up in the air. "I can't believe you're overreacting like this.''

"And I can't believe you'd continue to let the world think your own flesh and blood was an alien! I know we've always said our careers come first, but we have someone else to think about now.''

"I'm not choosing my career over our baby, Maddie, and we will put an end to the alien story. All I'm saying is that we have to wait a few more months so..."

"And I'm telling you the longer this myth is allowed to circulate, the more real it becomes, Brad. Do you really want your son to grow up..."

"I want my son to grow up with two rational parents, and you aren't being rational at the moment. I said we'll hold a press conference. We'll even get married..."

"*Even* get married?" she yelled. "Well, thank you, Captain Hawkins. How gallant of you to make such a noble sacrifice!"

Damn! He had to get a copy of that phrase book.

He had made her so angry now, Brad could see she was literally shaking. He quickly softened his tone. "I didn't mean it like that, Maddie. You didn't let me finish what I was trying..."

"No, you're definitely finished as far as I'm concerned." Her voice was calm. Too calm.

"Maddie, please. You have to realize there are standard Air Force policies and procedures...."

"Please leave," she said, pointing to the door.

Brad took a step in her direction.

"I mean it, Brad. I want you to leave. There's no room in our baby's life for you, if you can't be more concerned about him than you are about your stupid helicopter."

"Maddie, please..."

She walked across the room and threw her apartment door open wide. "Goodbye, Brad." Her voice wavered. "If I don't hear from you by Friday, I never want to see your face again."

Brad hesitated for a moment, but then he stomped

across the room and slammed Maddie's apartment door behind him.

He'd always heard pregnant women could be irrational, but Maddie was being downright impossible. As if he could do a damn thing about when the government planned to unveil the Black Ghost.

Call the old man, she'd said. Ha! And say what? *Sorry, but I'm in a bit of a jam with the mother of my unborn son. How about letting me borrow the Black Ghost on Friday so the woman I love won't cut me out of my own child's life?* Yeah. As if that would change anything.

"Women," Brad mumbled as he headed for the rental car parked in front of Maddie's apartment house. He'd known from the second he laid eyes on her she was trouble. Yet, what had he done? Hell, he'd practically handed her the rope so she could place the noose around his neck.

And she certainly had him twisting in the wind now.

He was screwed any way he turned. The woman he loved would break all contact with him when he didn't show up for her press conference, and he'd be in deep trouble with the Air Force when she told the press about the Black Ghost.

Cursing under his breath, Brad turned on the ignition and roared away from the curb. All of his life he had sworn he would never have children. And why? Because Brad couldn't bear the thought of any child of his growing up without a father the way he'd been forced to do himself. Yet, that's exactly what was going to happen. She would never back down when he didn't show up at her damn press conference on Friday. He also knew demanding that the Air Force unveil the Black Ghost early because he was having personal issues wouldn't change a thing.

Unless...

Instead of heading south toward Atlanta to make arrangements for an international flight back to Germany, Brad turned north when he reached the outskirts of Morgan City. North to I-85, the stretch of interstate that would take him to Arlington, Virginia. Home of the one man Brad had always turned to in the past when he found himself with a problem and no possible solution.

DURING THE TEN-HOUR TRIP from Morgan City to Arlington, Brad had plenty of time to decide exactly what he was going to say to the man he had always called Uncle Joe in private. However, when he pulled the rental car into the circular driveway of an impressive Tudor home at eight o'clock that evening, Brad couldn't remember a single word of the speech he'd rehearsed all the way from Morgan City.

As he sat in the car, Brad's gut instinct told him to drive away and go back to Germany and his current assignment, and he probably would have done so had the front door not opened before he had a chance to change his mind. The tall, slender woman known to him as Aunt Bess hesitated on the porch for a second. She squealed with delight when the outdoor spotlights illuminating the driveway allowed her to see who was sitting in her driveway.

"Joe! Look who's here," Bess Gibbons called over her shoulder before she headed down the front porch steps. She had Brad in a bear hug the minute he stepped out of the car.

Following along behind his wife with a scowl on

his face, Joe Gibbons shook Brad's hand before he said, "What the hell are you doing in the States? I thought you were in Frankfurt."

Brad opened his mouth to answer, but Bess swatted her husband on the arm. "Can't you at least say hello before you start interrogating the boy, Joe? Besides, who cares where Brad was? He's here now, and that's all that matters. Now I won't have to mail his Christmas present. We can celebrate early."

Brad accepted another hug from the woman who was still pretty enough to be a fashion model, but the silent look he exchanged with his uncle Joe left the old man no question that Brad had a problem. Before either of them could say a word, Aunt Bess turned her salt-and-pepper head in Brad's direction and said, "I've just persuaded this old goat to take me to dinner, Brad. I'm so glad you're here so you can join us."

"Well, I..."

"No excuses," Bess said with authority as she linked her arm through Brad's and began leading him in the direction of the Cadillac that was parked in front of Brad's rental car. "I haven't seen you in ages, and I can't wait to hear what's going on in your life."

Brad cringed at that remark. "I really came to talk to Uncle Joe."

"Then while you boys talk shop, you can ignore me completely. But you're not leaving me behind and that's final."

Minutes later Brad found himself sitting in the back seat of his godparent's Cadillac, still trying to remember the speech he'd rehearsed all the way from Morgan City.

"WELL, YOU'VE GOT yourself in one hell of a mess this time," Joe Gibbons said with a concerned look on his face.

Brad sent a nervous look around the restaurant, afraid his uncle Joe would start pounding the table at any second.

"Nonsense," Bess spoke up. "Our boy's in love and I think it's wonderful." She reached across the table and patted Brad's hand. "I can't wait to meet your Maddie in person, Brad."

Brad let out a long sigh. "I doubt you're ever going to meet Maddie, Aunt Bess. She's hysterical about this alien baby story. She's demanding I hold a press conference immediately—" Brad stopped short and glanced at Gibbons. Gibbons shook his head slightly, but not so slightly that Bess didn't pick up on the gesture.

She pushed back in her chair and shook her head disgustedly. "Obviously, you two have forgotten that I've been a military wife for forty years. Surely you don't think I'm so stupid I didn't put two and two together when that alien abduction story first hit the news. I knew both of you were in Roswell. But on routine maneuvers? Please. The second Brad appeared on television, I knew the Air Force was involved somehow."

Brad looked at Gibbons. Gibbons frowned.

"But, I'm not going to ask for any specific details," Bess continued. "After forty years I know better than to ask. But I do agree with Brad's Maddie. Brad needs to do whatever it takes to clear up this alien baby story. And he needs to do it now."

Brad shook his head sadly. "I'm sorry, Aunt Bess. That's impossible. At least right now."

"Damn right it's impossible," Gibbons confirmed.

"Nonsense," Bess said with the authority of a four-star general. "Nothing is impossible when you put your mind to it."

Gibbons sent her a patient smile. "I'm afraid you don't quite understand what's involved here, dear."

"Oh, I understand perfectly, Joe," Bess corrected. "How dare I suggest the Air Force bypass standard procedure for something as unimportant as a woman's reputation and honor."

Brad didn't like where the conversation was heading. He'd expected a little sympathy from the woman he loved like a mother. He'd expected his aunt Bess to comfort him, to agree that Maddie was being totally impossible about the situation. But now Aunt Bess was sending him the same beady-eyed glare Maddie had given him when she threw him out of her apartment.

Women, Brad thought. He'd never understand them in a million years.

"Now, Bess," Joe Gibbons spoke up.

"Don't now, Bess, me! I don't blame Maddie for being livid. And don't you dare sit there, Joe, and pretend you wouldn't have caught pure hell from me if you'd expected me to sit idly by while any of our three children were being called aliens by the press. I never thought I'd say this, but at the moment I'm ashamed of *both* of you."

Gibbon's face turned beet-red. "And what do you expect me to do about it? Permission to straighten this mess out would have to come straight from the horse's mouth."

"And you play golf almost every weekend with

the President now that you're back home waiting out your retirement.''

Brad looked at Gibbons. Gibbons glared back at Brad.

"You know what the problem really is here, Bess?"

"You bet I know what the problem is. You big, tough Air Force men are so busy trying to prove to each other how macho you are, you forget there are times when the women in your lives need a little old-fashioned understanding.''

"Bull. The problem is you women watch too many damn soap operas,'' Gibbons accused. "Maybe in one of your daytime delusions a guy would jog over to the White House to tell the leader of the free world all about the personal problems he was having with his girlfriend, but this is the *real* world, Bess. And if you think either one of us is going to worry the President with…''

Bess threw her napkin down on the table. "Then I guess I'll just have to take the matter into my own hands.''

This time Gibbons did pound the table. "Now, dammit, Bess. I will not have you barging into the oval office and…''

"Oh, you don't have to worry about me going to the President, Joe. I'm sure he'd only give me the same glazed-over stare Brad probably gave Maddie and you just gave me. I'm going to have a nice little chat with someone who has the power to do something about this dilemma. And I'm sure the First Lady will give me her full attention!''

When Bess left the table in a huff, Brad shook his head in amazement. "I'm shocked. I've never heard Aunt Bess raise her voice in my life.''

"Bess? Are you kidding?" Gibbons snorted. "That woman's been a spitfire from the moment I met her."

"But...but how have you stayed married all these years?" Brad asked in wonder.

Gibbons leaned closer and said, "Don't ever tell her, but I wouldn't have her any other way. A little conflict gets the old juices flowing, if you know what I mean."

Brad could certainly identify with that statement. Maddie had had his juices flowing one way or another since he helped her up from the floor of the Black Ghost. *Maybe there is hope for me and Maddie,* Brad was thinking when Gibbons ran his hand over his face and said, "I should warn you Bess never backs down from a threat. We'll be lucky if we're not both thrown in prison after the First Lady gets through with the President."

Brad hung his head. "Well, at least if Maddie knows I'm behind bars on her behalf, she might bring little William Joseph to see me now and then."

Gibbons sent him a puzzled look. "William Joseph?"

Brad nodded. "I want my son named after the two finest men I've ever known."

Brad pretended not to see his uncle Joe reach up to swipe at the corner of his eye. But after several seconds of silence, Gibbons finally said, "Your father would be proud to have the boy named after him, Brad. And so will I."

10

MADDIE PUT ON HER MAKEUP with particular care on
Friday morning. At ten o'clock every major news
affiliate in the nation would be waiting at Morgan
City's courthouse square for the notorious Madam
Butterfly to finally make a public statement. The
press could believe her, or not. And the Air Force
could deny the story, or not. But at least she was
finally offering an explanation that would counteract
the alien abduction theory. Not that being picked up
by a top secret helicopter and then having an affair
with the man who held her captive didn't sound just
as ridiculous.

Having to break the promise she made to Brad
bothered Maddie deeply. But when another queasy
feeling overtook her, she was quickly reminded that
she had something more important than just a few
butterflies in her stomach.

As for Brad himself, Maddie hadn't heard another
word from him. Not that she really expected to hear
from him again. In the back of her mind she knew
Brad's hands were more or less tied, but her heart
kept telling her the least he could have done was try
to reason with his superiors. Had he called her, saying
he'd made his plea to the Air Force and had been
turned down, Maddie might have even considered
riding out the storm for another six months. But

it had been Brad's cut-and-dried no-way-in-hell-am-I-going-to-inconvenience-the-Air-Force response that had made her so angry. Not to mention his infuriating accusation that she was overreacting to the situation.

How did he expect her to react?

No mother in the world would be able to sit by and allow anyone to call her baby ugly, much less an alien.

Pulling on the skirt of her best navy wool suit, Maddie found she would have to rely on a safety pin to span the gap her once twenty-four-inch waist hadn't needed. She then tugged at her white silk top just enough to blouse it over the waistband and hide the telltale pin. It really shouldn't have surprised her that the jacket to her suit also felt snug when she buttoned the center button. She opted to leave her jacket open, then ran a brush through her hair one final time.

In less than an hour, she would face the world in an effort to protect her baby, and ultimately betray the man she loved at the same time. With each stroke of the clock, Maddie prayed for a miracle, and a shrill ring gave Maddie one last hope as she ran for the phone.

Caller ID erased that hope when she saw her twin's number come up on the screen.

"I just wanted to wish you luck," Mary Beth said when Maddie picked up the phone. "And I want you to know I feel like a real witch because I can't be there with you, Maddie. Especially since I'm the one responsible for resurrecting the alien awareness that's turned my sister into the queen of the tabloids."

"And I'm the one who wouldn't listen when you told me not to climb that fence," Maddie reminded her twin with a sigh. "You just concentrate on shooting the pilot for your new soap opera."

"Well, at least Mom and Pop are going with you to the press conference this morning."

Maddie groaned. "Please, don't remind me. I can just see Mom now, dragging a tissue out of her purse to wipe away some imaginary smudge on my nose while the cameras are rolling. And Pop taking this opportunity to hand out campaign buttons for his reelection next year."

Mary Beth laughed. "But you have to give them credit for being excited about the baby, Maddie. Mom's ecstatic you've decided to stop renting out the house Granny Morgan left you and move into it yourself. You were smart to hold on to that property. I sold the condo Granny left me and can't even remember how I spent the money."

"I never needed a big house before," Maddie said as she ran her hand over her stomach. "But the house is far enough away from Mom and Pop to keep them from breathing down my neck, and its close enough so I can drop the baby off on my way to work."

"They're both really looking forward to looking after the baby, you know. Did Mom tell you Pop's already bought two boxes of cigars to hand out when the baby arrives?"

"There'll be no smoking around the baby," Maddie said with authority.

Mary Beth laughed. "Just listen to yourself, Maddie. You've turned into supermom overnight. Have you asked Pop to order your minivan yet?"

"Very funny," said Maddie, but she was often amazed herself at how quickly she'd embraced the new role she was about to undertake. She was even looking forward to a shopping trip with her mother next week for baby furniture. Especially since after the press conference, she'd be free to roam the streets of Morgan City without fear of being accosted by the paparazzi.

"Gotta run. Someone's calling my name on the set," Mary Beth said. "But you be brave, little sister. Be brief. And most of all, be proud of yourself for doing what's best for my nephew."

Maddie checked her watch when she hung up the receiver. It was nine forty-five. Brad's time was up. Without another thought, she opened her apartment door and closed it soundly behind her, fully confident that she and her baby would do just fine without him. Of course, being a single mom and raising a child alone certainly wasn't the way she had her life planned out. But Maddie's big wake-up call had been the realization that there were no guarantees you got to live life exactly as you planned it.

She was definitely a walking testimony to that fact.

Relieved to see her father's sedan already waiting at the curb, Maddie headed to the car, but an overeager reporter suddenly jumped out at her from behind the hedges blocking her path. Maddie threw her arm up to shield her face from the camera and pushed past him. Flashbulbs were still going off like strobe lights when Maddie jumped into the back seat of her father's sedan.

"Thank Heaven, this will all be over after today,"

her mother said as her father sped away from the curb.

Maddie didn't comment, but she was thinking to herself that more than the media madness would be over at the end of this day. Any chance of having a relationship with the man she loved and the father of her child would also be over. And as if in apology to their unborn child, Maddie patted her slightly protruding stomach and said a silent prayer that her son would eventually forgive her for making the decision to bring him up without a father.

"Good Lord. I haven't seen this many people in town since Georgia's native son, Jimmy Carter, stopped in Morgan City when he was campaigning for president," Mayor Morgan said when the courthouse square came into view.

Maddie gazed out the back seat window at the beautiful old square that was as big as a football field. It still served as the meeting place after church on Sunday, when families brought their blankets and their baskets for an old-fashioned picnic on the green. The thought that she would want to bring her own son to the square for a picnic one day gave Maddie the courage she needed when her father stopped the car and every eye turned in her direction.

Not bothering to wait for her parents, Maddie pulled herself out of the back seat and started walking in the direction of the slew of reporters eagerly awaiting her arrival. And standing at the front of the pack was Nerdy Purdy with his gap tooth grin, looking like a hungry jackal ready to move in for the kill.

Refusing to be intimidated, Maddie stared the little creep down and kept walking straight in his direction. They were practically nose to nose when someone let out a blood-curdling scream.

People started running in every direction.

But not Nerdy Purdy. Poor Arnold remained frozen to the spot, with his eyes bugged out and a look of sheer terror on his face. It wasn't until Maddie followed his gaze upward that she saw what was responsible for the chaos. The imposing Black Ghost was making a silent landing not far from where they were standing. Nerdy Purdy's eyes rolled back in his head and he passed out right in front of her. Without a second thought, Maddie stepped over Arnold's splayed body and started running. *He came!*

The only thing on her mind at the moment was getting to Brad. He was actually there, with his Black Ghost, and that told Maddie everything she needed to know: the man she loved had come to her rescue.

The second Brad dropped from the cockpit to the ground Maddie threw her arms around his neck and kissed him. And once everyone realized Morgan City hadn't been invaded by little green men from outer space, they surrounded Brad and Maddie like a swarm of hungry locusts.

Pulling her close to his side, Brad waited until the din of the crowd faded away. "I'm Captain Brad Hawkins of the United States Air Force," he announced with authority. "And I want to introduce you to the top secret aircraft that has kept Dr. Morgan silent since she stumbled upon a testing facility in Roswell, New Mexico, last summer."

Everyone started shouting at once.

Brad held his hand up and waited until the crowd

fell silent again. "Dr. Morgan agreed to do her part as a responsible American citizen and not reveal any details about our top secret operation. Unfortunately, the media has harassed her to the point where the President himself asked me to attend this press conference today and put an end to the alien abduction story once and for all."

The crowd went wild.

Questions were being thrown at Brad and Maddie from every direction.

"But what about the baby?" someone from the crowd yelled.

And when that question surfaced, Brad surprised Maddie by taking her by the shoulders and turning her around to face him. "I love you, Maddie. Completely. Do you think you could love me?"

Maddie blinked. "Yes. I mean I do. I love you already, Brad."

"Then marry me. I'll be a good husband and I'll be the best father I can be to our child."

The crowd grew so quiet Maddie could hear her own heart beating. She reached up and wiped a tear from her cheek. "I didn't think you wanted to get married and have a family."

Brad held her gaze. "I remember you saying exactly the same thing."

Maddie's chin came up. "I don't intend to give up my career."

Brad shrugged. "Neither do I."

Maddie smiled. "Then our marriage would be rather unconventional, don't you think?"

Brad smiled back. "We're rather unconventional people. With a little compromise, I'm sure we can work it out."

"Madeline Ann Morgan!" a voice Maddie had no trouble recognizing as her mother's yelled from the back of the crowd. "Say *yes* before this nice young man loses his patience and changes his mind."

"Yes," Maddie said, and the crowd cheered with approval when Brad pulled her into his arms for a long, searing kiss.

"What's going on? What have I missed?" Nerdy Purdy kept shouting as he ran from place to place, trying to push his way through the crowd.

"Captain, can you tell us more about the helicopter?" a reporter from CNN called out.

"The new F-211 Black Ghost will be officially unveiled at the Pentagon next week," said Brad. "The details will be given to the public then."

"When are you going to set a date for the wedding?" came another shout.

"Are you going to be married here in Morgan City?" someone else yelled.

"Of course, they are," Mayor Morgan spoke up. And when the cameras turned in his direction, he said with a broad politician's smile, "Her mother and I wouldn't have it any other way."

"It looks like your father has things under control here," Brad whispered in Maddie's ear. "Why don't we see if we can make our escape?"

"I'll call you later, Mom," Maddie said with a wave when Brad boosted her up into the cockpit of the helicopter.

"When is the baby due?"

"Is it a boy or a girl?"

"Do you have any names picked out for the baby?"

Brad pulled himself into the seat beside Maddie and sealed off the flurry of questions when he slid the door of the Black Ghost into place. "And *do* you have any names picked out for our son?" he asked when he turned to face her.

Maddie leaned over and kissed him before she said, "No. Do you?"

Brad flipped several switches, bringing the powerful machine to life. "If it's okay with you, I'd like to call him William Joseph. William for my father, and Joseph for Joe Gibbons."

"Commander Gibbons? You mean the man who made you hold me captive against my will?"

Brad sent her a worried look as he lifted the big machine into the air. "Would that be a problem?"

Maddie laughed. "Are you kidding? How much more Southern can you get than Billy Joe?"

"Now, wait a minute, Maddie," Brad began to argue. "Billy's fine. So is Joe. But I don't know about calling any son of mine Billy Joe."

Maddie raised an eyebrow when he looked back in her direction. "Oh, really? What happened to all that compromising you were ready to do a few minutes ago, Brad darling?"

Brad hesitated. "How about calling him B.J.? I could live with B.J."

"B.J.," Maddie repeated. "B.J. Hawkins."

"Sure has a nice ring to it," Brad threw in for good measure, then leaned forward and kissed Maddie again.

"And exactly where are you taking me and little B.J. at the moment?" Maddie said, running her hand possessively down the full length of his arm.

"First, we're going to take the Black Ghost home

so it won't miss the big ceremony next week," Brad told her, "and then we're going to have lunch with two wonderful ladies who can't wait to meet you."

"But, Brad. Look at me. I'm a mess."

"You look beautiful," Brad insisted, unaware that Maddie would threaten to kill him later when she found out he was taking her to the White House for lunch.

"And after lunch?"

"After lunch we'll rent a car and I'll drive you back home. From what your father just said, it sounds like we have a wedding to plan."

"A Christmas wedding," Maddie mused happily. "My favorite time of year." She added with a smile, "And you really don't mind if we get married in my hometown?"

"Not at all," Brad said, but he sent Maddie a sultry look when he added, "just as long as I get to plan the honeymoon."

"I've seen that look before, Hawk," Maddie warned. "Do I dare ask what you have in mind for this honeymoon of ours?"

Brad grinned. "I prefer to surprise you. But I will make you one promise. The honeymoon I'll plan for us will be so spectacular, your alien buddies from outer space will turn even *greener* with envy."

Maddie rolled her eyes. "If it's okay with you, I never want to hear the word *alien* again as long as I live."

"Really?" Brad said, sending her a sideways glance. "Then I guess the trip I was planning for us next summer will be totally out of the question."

Maddie turned in her seat to face him. "What trip?"

"Oh, a trip out west to a little town called Roswell."

"Roswell?" Maddie echoed.

"Yeah. I ran into this famous entomologist once who was out in the desert looking for a butterfly."

"Oh, you did, did you?" Maddie said with a laugh.

Brad nodded. "But because of me, she lost that butterfly."

Maddie reached out and took Brad's hand. "I bet your famous entomologist would tell you what she did find out in that desert was far more important than the butterfly she lost."

"And what would that be?"

"She found herself *and* she found the man who is going to make her life complete."

"You think?"

"Absolutely," Maddie said, placing Brad's hand gently on her stomach. "Don't ever doubt it."

Candy Halliday

Venus, How Could You?

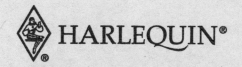

HARLEQUIN®

TORONTO • NEW YORK • LONDON
AMSTERDAM • PARIS • SYDNEY • HAMBURG
STOCKHOLM • ATHENS • TOKYO • MILAN • MADRID
PRAGUE • WARSAW • BUDAPEST • AUCKLAND

Special thanks to Bobby, Jennie and Juanita
for always believing in me.

"I HAVE WONDERFUL NEWS! I'm going to be in a coma for the next two weeks." Mary Beth Morgan grinned when her sister let out a squeal of delight on the other end of the phone.

"And just how did you manage to get yourself written out of the script of *The Wild and the Free?*" There was a slight hesitation before her sister added, "Or do I really want to know?"

"Don't worry, Maddie. I didn't end up on the director's couch, if that's what you're implying. All it took was a little crying, a little pleading and a whole lot of groveling at the feet of the head writer for the show, who happens to be a very understanding woman, thank you very much. And besides, if I'm going to take any time off, I need to do it now at the end of the summer, before fall sweeps week."

"I'm so glad you're coming home, Mary Beth. I couldn't bear the thought of you not attending our ten year high school reunion. You're all everybody's talking about here at home."

"Like that's something new," Mary Beth grumbled, thinking back to the most embarrassing day of her life

"I meant your new soap opera, silly. Not..."

"Not the day Zack Callahan left me standing at the altar?" Mary Beth heard her sister breathe out a long sigh on the other end of the line. "I'm only kidding, Maddie. You're right. I *should* come home for our reunion. It's time I stopped worrying about the jilted bride stigma that's been attached to my name since Zack walked out on me."

"Not to mention rubbing a few noses in your success as an actress, big sister," Maddie threw in. "And if you don't, *I* will."

Mary Beth laughed at her twin who was younger only by two minutes. "Okay, Maddie, let's not get militant. You're a mommy now, remember? And how is my adorable little B.J., by the way?"

Mary Beth automatically glanced at the most recent picture of her darling nephew that was framed and sitting on the bar in her kitchen. Listening while Maddie launched into a typical mother's account of the amazing things her one-year-old son could do, she walked through the sliding glass doors onto the deck of her Malibu beach house and stood staring out over the Pacific.

How ironic, Mary Beth kept thinking, that her life and Maddie's had ultimately traded places. Her identical twin, an esteemed professor of entomology who had once been totally obsessed with her career, was now a loving wife and mother. While Mary Beth, who had never thought past being a wife and a mother until Zack walked out on her, was now focused on nothing but her career.

"And that handsome brother-in-law of mine?" Mary Beth broke in when Maddie pause for breath.

"Is Captain Hawkins still making it home on a regular basis?"

"Are you kidding? Since Brad's been assigned to the Pentagon, he's home practically every weekend. In fact, he's underfoot so much I'm sometimes tempted to volunteer him for some top secret assignment just to get him out of my hair."

"Liar," Mary Beth accused and they both laughed.

"So?" Maddie wanted to know. "When can we expect you?"

"Well, I've already taken my dog to the kennel. I've arranged for my neighbors next door to pick up my mail and water my plants. Will tomorrow be too soon?"

Maddie squealed again. "Just tell me when to pick you up at the airport, you gorgeous soap opera star, you."

Mary Beth recited her flight number and waited until Maddie found a pencil and wrote it down. "I really am looking forward to coming home for a few weeks, Maddie."

"I'm glad you're coming home, too."

Mary Beth didn't miss the concern in Maddie's voice. "But?"

"It's just that...well, this *is* our ten year class reunion, Mary Beth. You don't think..."

"That Zack will have the nerve to show up?" Mary Beth finished for her sister. "Not on your life. I asked Mom to make sure his aunt knew I was coming home for the reunion. You know he won't come home if he knows I'm in town. Just like I never come home when he's there.''

"But Zack *was* our class president, Mary Beth. What if he does show up?"

"Then my character on *The Wild and the Free* won't be the only one in a coma!" Mary Beth vowed.

Maddie was still laughing when Mary Beth hung up the phone. Still smiling herself, Mary Beth placed the phone on a table by her lounge chair and stretched out in the chair in her skimpy bikini. Closing her eyes, she turned her face up to the bright California sun, wondering why she felt more guilty than usual about not finally coming clean with Maddie after six long years. About not finally admitting she really blamed herself for any humiliation she suffered over the day Zack Callahan broke and ran.

The truth was, Zack had begged her right up until the night before the wedding to postpone it. He'd even told her loud and clear he wasn't going to show up at the church. She had just been too sure of herself to take Zack seriously. Mainly because since the first day she'd marched across the playground when they were ten years old and told him he was going to be her boyfriend, Zack had never said no to her.

Never!

And from that moment on, they had started planning their life together.

Well, maybe most of those plans had been her own. Mary Beth could admit that now. But Zack had never let on he had a problem with the way she'd carefully planned out every aspect of their lives. They would be married, after college, of course. Then they would live in the adorable little condo on the outskirts of Morgan City that her Grandma Morgan had left her free and clear. She, with a degree in theater arts, would take a job teaching drama at the local college until they were ready to start their family. Zack, with his degree in business administration, would be groomed to take over her father's automobile dealership. They would have three children. Zack, Jr. would come first, followed by his two sisters, Annie and Betsy. And then she and Zack would raise their children in the small home town where they both had grown up themselves.

Yes, those had been the plans of the starry-eyed twenty-two-year-old Zack Callahan had left standing at the altar.

What she hadn't planned for was being "discovered," so to speak, by a talent agent only two weeks before the wedding when she was in Atlanta doing some last minute shopping. She'd been extremely flattered, of course. What woman in her right mind wouldn't have been flattered if a big-shot Hollywood talent agent stopped her on the street and offered her a contract to star in a Super Bowl commercial—one of the highest priced and most viewed advertising on television?

She'd been so shocked *and* flattered she'd agreed to exchange names and numbers. The decision was one Mary Beth had regretted a million times since. Being flattered was one thing, but cutting her honeymoon short and leaving her new husband behind while she ran off to Hollywood to shoot a commercial hadn't even been an option as far as she'd been concerned. She'd been planning out her life with Zack since they were ten years old. Those plans were written in stone. Or so she thought.

Unfortunately, when she returned home to Morgan City later that evening, she found her mother hysterical because some strange man had been calling for her every hour on the hour.

If only she hadn't tried to act so glib when she'd returned the call. And if only Zack hadn't wandered into the room and overheard her say she would head to Hollywood in a heartbeat if she wasn't getting married.

She still remembered how shocked Zack had looked when she turned around and found him standing behind her. She had tried to laugh it off, tried to explain she was only being polite, tried to convince Zack she didn't want the guy to think she was so stupid she didn't realize what an incredible opportunity he was offering her. But the harder she'd tried to explain, the deeper she kept digging herself into a hole.

"If you really think this is such an incredible opportunity, Mary Beth," he'd said, "and if you really would go to Hollywood if we weren't getting married, then maybe we should postpone the wedding."

And he wasn't being smart or trying to make her feel guilty over anything she'd said. He was just being himself. Practical Zack, as he was fondly called by everyone who knew him, the guy who always had the ability to analyze the situation thoroughly and eventually come up with a plausible solution.

Except she hadn't seen a dang thing practical about postponing their wedding. In addition to the fact that she loved Zack completely, their wedding was only two weeks away, for God's sake! The invitations had gone out. She had the dress. He had the tux. All the preparations had been made *and* paid for. But when she'd brought up each of those reasons why they *shouldn't* postpone their wedding, especially the fact that she loved him and wanted to be his wife more than anything else in the world, he'd looked at her and said, "I want you to be my wife more than anything else in the world, too. I just think our timing's off."

He'd gone on to remind her that he really did believe computers were the wave of the future and that he knew he could be successful in the computer field if given half a chance. But his fascination with computers had been old news to Mary Beth, and a subject she always refused to discuss. She and Zack both knew there wasn't any such career opportunity in small-town Morgan City. And that's where they always reached a stalemate. Back then, moving to a big city hadn't been an option for Mary Beth, either. And so the arguing continued right up until the night before the wedding when Zack's last words were: "Postpone the wedding, Mary Beth. I'm not going to be there."

That was six years ago.

And Zack had become successful. Extremely successful. On the front page of *Forbes Magazine* successful, for having the vision to see what the Internet could mean to the world, and for going in with two other bright computer wizards to buy up huge chunks of the web.

And the more successful he'd become, the more determined Mary Beth had been to prove herself. To prove to Zack that she *would* succeed in the career he was so determined for her to have. To prove to her family and her home town that the *zany* Morgan twin, as she'd often been called, was just as capable of having a successful career as her *brainy* professor sister.

And to prove to herself...what?

Well, she really wasn't sure what she was still trying to prove to herself, but she had come to believe that going off to Atlanta on a final shopping spree two weeks before her wedding hadn't been just a whim. She also believed it hadn't been an accident that her agent's taxi just happened to stop at a traffic light at the exact same time she came strolling across the street. No, fate had stepped in, she was sure of it. And thanks to Mother Venus, ruler of Libra, her astrological sign, she now had a life filled with glitz, a life filled with glamour, and a life filled with a certain amount of fame.

A storybook life by most women's standards.

In fact, she should probably *thank* Zack if she ever saw him again. After she punched him in the nose, broke both of his arms and legs and left him for dead, of course. He might have been responsible for saving her from a sink full of dirty dishes, a house full of screaming kids and a mundane existence, but that didn't mean she was ready to forgive and forget the hurt and embarrassment he had caused her.

Not that she was going to see Zack again.

At least, not anytime in the near future.

Zack showing up for the reunion, now that he knew she was coming home, was as unlikely as George W. asking Laura if he could hire Monica Lewinsky as his personal White House intern.

But just to be on the safe side, Mary Beth sat up and reached for her morning paper and flipped to the daily horoscope section. *Libra: Don't let uncertainty about an unresolved situation shake your confidence. Surround yourself with friends and loved ones and bask in the glow of being admired for your talent. Someone dear to you is looking forward to your visit.*

Reassured by such comforting words, Mary Beth tossed the paper aside and stretched out on the lounge chair with a smile on her face. She was finally going home to Morgan City a success *and* to make sure everyone knew how wonderful her life had turned out without Zack Callahan in it.

Zachary Thaddeus Callahan was known around Morgan City, Georgia, only as the dirty rat who left his pretty high school sweetheart sobbing at the altar. The fact that he'd recently been named one of Chicago's most successful businessmen didn't mean a thing.

Sitting in a bar on the outskirts of town, in a booth in the back where he couldn't easily be seen, Zack was grateful no one in the bar seemed to recognize him. He nodded a polite thank-you to the bleached-blond waitress wearing false eyelashes and blue eye shadow as she plopped a beer down in front of him. She was dressed in a short denim shirt with a red bandanna tied around her throat. Zack couldn't help but notice her white cowgirl boots had seen better days.

"You must be new in town, handsome," she said, trying to smile and pop her gum at the same time. "We don't get many guys in here wearing suits and ties."

"Yeah, I'm new," Zack lied, still watching the front door and praying his new admirer would go away before she managed to draw any attention to him.

"I've only been in Morgan City a few weeks myself," she told Zack with another pop of her gum. "What's your name, honey?"

Zack stalled for an answer, but forgot about keeping a low profile when he saw his younger cousin, Greg, step through the door. Standing up, Zack waved wildly in Greg's direction, prompting the waitress to send him a sour look before she stomped off mumbling something foul about his sexual orientation.

"Okay, Mr. Espionage," Greg said with a frown as he slid into the seat on the opposite side of the booth. "I took the back roads, changed cars three times and sat outside for thirty minutes to make sure no one followed me. Happy?"

Zack cast his eyes toward the ceiling. "Very funny."

"No, I'll tell you what's funny," Greg said as he grabbed a peanut from the bowl on the table. He smashed the shell with his fist for effect. "What's absolutely hysterical is this game of hide-and-seek you and Mary Beth have been playing for the last six years. You won't come home if she's in town. She won't come home if you're in town. You'd think you were back in grammar school. You both need to grow up and bury the hatchet."

Zack waited until Greg picked through the shell and popped the peanut in his mouth before he said, "I agree. And I can't think of a more perfect time to clear the air between us than our high school reunion."

Greg choked on the peanut. He grabbed Zack's beer bottle and took a long swig. When the peanut finally went down, his words came out in a croak. "What are you? A masochist? You really want Mary Beth to scratch your eyes out in front of your entire high school senior class?"

Zack leaned back against his seat in the booth. "I'm willing to suffer that kind of embarrassment. I know it doesn't compare to being left at the altar, but—"

Greg cut him off. "Why now, Zack? Why have you decided to make peace with Mary Beth after all these years?"

Zack reached up and loosened his tie. He was only a year older than Greg, and he and Greg had been raised as brothers after Zack's folks died in a house fire and his aunt and uncle took him in. People even said they looked like brothers. They both had the same sandy hair, same athletic bodies that neither of them had let turn to flab after their high school football days. They were also as close as brothers. Knowing Greg would see right through a lie, Zack said, "Why now? Because I'm successful now. I own my own business. I've made more money than I ever dreamed possible. And..."

"And you didn't want to face Mary Beth again until you could prove you didn't need her father to give you a handout?"

Zack had been right. Greg knew him well. "Yeah. That pretty much sums it up, I guess."

"Then you must not think much of a moocher like me."

Zack frowned at his cousin's description of himself. In a few more years, his uncle's hardware store would be handed over to Greg lock, stock and barrel. Which was exactly how it should be. But a family business being passed down from father to son was one thing. A son-in-law accepting charity from his wife's family was another.

Mary Beth's determination that he was going to take over her father's business had always bothered Zack. Just as it had bothered him that she intended for them to move into the condo her grandmother had left her. She'd had everything planned out right down to what furniture, linens and kitchen utensils they'd be accepting from her parents. And what could he have contributed to their marriage? Not much. And certainly not enough that he wouldn't have felt less of a man because he couldn't provide for his wife and his family on his own.

The sad fact was, he'd loved Mary Beth enough that he *would* have sacrificed his own self-respect in order to make her happy.

That is, until the talent agent saw Mary Beth walking across the street in downtown Atlanta and offered her a contract on the spot. Once Mary Beth had the opportunity to expand her own horizons, Zack knew he wanted the chance to do the same thing. He'd used some of the insurance money he'd received from his parents' death to reimburse the Morgans for the wedding expenses, and he'd used the remainder of the money as capital for the business he'd started.

"I don't think you're a moocher, Greg, and you know it," Zack said a little too sharply. "You've worked your butt off in that hardware store since we were kids. The store is your heritage. You deserve it. But George Morgan handing me a business because I married his daughter is a different story."

Greg sent him an apologetic look, then motioned for the waitress. Cowgirl Annie walked over and took Greg's order. She looked them both up and down and rolled her eyes before she wandered back to the bar.

"What's up with her?"

Zack ignored the question. "Tell me. Mary Beth *is* coming home for the reunion, right?"

Greg laughed. "You know she is. I'm sure you've already gotten that information from the church choir pipeline, or I wouldn't be meeting you in this dump right now.''

Zack didn't deny it. His aunt Lou and Mary Beth's mother had been close friends for years and had sat next to each other in the church choir every Sunday for as long as he could remember. He hated to admit it, but he had relied on his aunt Lou all these years to keep him up-to-date on what was going on with Mary Beth. In her personal life, that is. Hell, all he had to do was turn on the television or pick up a newspaper or one of the tabloids to know what was going on in her professional life.

He'd almost had a damn coronary when her *Evershine* commercial hit the air. Then, her sister's alien abduction saga had dominated the front page for months. And he'd never admit it to anyone, but he always taped every episode of her new daytime soap opera, then spent most of his evenings with takeout from whatever fast food place he had chosen, sulking as he painfully watched her wrapped up in the arms of a different handsome costar every week. *And* wondering if those steamy love scenes were ever continued in private after the cameras stopped rolling.

At least he knew she'd never been seriously involved with anyone else, thanks to Aunt Lou, who never missed the opportunity to tell him, ''True love waits, Zack. You and Mary Beth will find your way back to each other when the time is right.''

Did true love wait?

Was *now* the right time?

Zack believed it was. They'd both experienced

life outside Morgan City and they'd both been successful. And that's why he'd come home for the reunion. He'd come home to find out if they *could* possibly find their way back to each other.

"You're right," he admitted to his cousin. "I already knew Mary Beth was coming home. And I asked you to meet me here because I didn't want anyone else to know I was in town. Especially not Aunt Lou. Not yet. I need the element of surprise in my favor. And I'm going to need your help."

"Like hell I'm going to help you," Greg vowed and jumped back in his seat when the waitress slammed a bottle of beer down in front of him, sloshing foam all over the table. When she stomped back in the direction of the bar, Greg looked at Zack and said, "Seriously. What's up with that crazy chick?"

Zack only smiled. "Forget about the waitress. But you *are* going to help me, Greg. Just like I helped you when you called me in the middle of the night demanding I tell Lucy I'd come home unexpectedly and that you'd been with me all weekend. I never asked where you really were. When you put your girlfriend on the phone, all I did was cover your butt and lie through my teeth."

Greg grabbed his beer bottle and swallowed most of the brew in one long gulp. "Yeah, and if you run into Lucy while you're home, you stick to that story. She still gives me hell at least once a month because she couldn't find me that weekend."

Satisfied he had Greg right where he wanted him, Zack leaned back in the booth and motioned for their surly waitress again. "It might take a few more beers," Zack told his cousin with a grin, "but before we leave this bar, you're going to help me figure out a strategy that *will* keep Mary Beth from scratching my eyes out before I can get within ten feet of her."

Greg leaned back in the booth himself and sent Zack a suspicious look. "Why does my gut instinct tell me there's more to this story than just clearing the air with Mary Beth, Zack?"

Zack refused to answer.

"Because you're nuts if you think she'll ever take you back."

Zack shrugged and took another slow sip from his bottle. "Let's just take one step at a time, okay?"

"That's what I thought," Greg complained as he grabbed up another handful of peanuts. "I know you too damn well."

2

LIBRA: TAKE COMFORT IN familiar surroundings and enjoy the simple pleasures in life. Busy Librans often forget to take time out for themselves. Take a long walk and enjoy the beauty of the day. Relaxation invites harmony. Harmony invites peace within.

Satisfied that everything was clear on her horizon, Mary Beth put aside the morning paper, polished off her bagel and drained the last drop of her mother's freshly squeezed orange juice from her glass. After clearing the table, she took her dishes to the sink and smiled at the woman who she saw as an older version of her and Maddie. Though a little color was now needed to hide the gray in her hair, her mother's figure was still trim, and only a few noticeable wrinkles marred her pretty face. She looked smart and fresh as usual, in her pink blouse and matching slacks that had creases sharp enough to cut a finger. Mary Beth knew unless she was careful, her own clothes would fall prey to her mother's iron before her two-week stay was over. She cringed, thinking what that iron could do to the delicate beadwork on the red silk top she was wearing. Having creases down the front of her new white DKNY jeans gave her another shiver.

I'll have to keep my room locked, Mary Beth thought at the same time her mother turned to her and said, "And what do you have on your agenda for the day?"

Mary Beth slid her dishes into the soapy water, knowing it was useless to point out that the electric dishwasher to her mother's left was there for a reason. She watched her mother make a few efficient swipes over the plate, rinse it and then place it in the drain rack. Mary Beth picked up the dish towel from the counter, dried off the plate and put it in the cabinet beside the sink. She checked the clock on the kitchen wall before she said, "Maddie's invited me to lunch, but since it's only ten o'clock, I think I'll walk downtown. I haven't had a morning to myself since we started filming the show."

Helen Morgan lowered her dishcloth into the sink again and expertly washed Mary Beth's glass. "And that's what worries me. You work too hard. All those hours on the set. Never having time for yourself *or* your family."

Mary Beth had to bite her tongue, but she reached over and gave her mother a long hug. "I'm home now, Mom. Doesn't that count?"

A mild harrumph escaped Helen's lips before she said, "Well, there isn't a mother alive who doesn't want her children close by."

"And Maddie and your grandson are right down the street," Mary Beth teased.

Helen removed the stopper from the sink and turned to face her. "Maddie and B.J. aren't a replacement for you, any more than you could be a replacement for them. I miss you, that's all. And I never dreamed you'd be living anywhere but right here in Morgan City.''

Mary Beth leaned forward and kissed her mother's smooth cheek. "Neither did I, Mom. But that's how my life has turned out, so stop trying to make me feel guilty about it.''

Helen shooed Mary Beth out of her path. "Oh, go on to town. I can see I'm not getting anywhere with this conversation.''

Mary Beth laughed and headed toward the back door at the rear of the kitchen. She opened the door and paused standing halfway in and halfway out of the doorway. "You haven't heard any news I should know about from Lou Callahan, have you?''

Helen turned back around with her hands on her hips. "No, I haven't heard from Lou, but we both agree you and Zack are being plain silly. You both grew up in this town. It was big enough for both of you then, and it's big enough for both of you now.''

Mary Beth rolled her eyes. "But you did remember to tell Lou I was coming home for the reunion, right?''

"Yes, I told her,'' Helen said with an exasperated sigh, and Mary Beth scooted out the door before her mother could launch into another lecture.

Maybe it *was* silly, Mary Beth decided as she strolled down Mulberry, this unwritten law she and Zack had about never coming home at the same time. After all, it had been six years. Of course, it could have been six hundred years and she still wouldn't be ready to see him again.

Not yet.

She was over Zack. It had taken a long time, but she was definitely over him. She just had one more goal she wanted to reach before she saw Zack Callahan face-to-face again. Call it a pipedream, but she wanted an Emmy nomination. She didn't have to *win* the Emmy, she wasn't stupid enough to set a goal for herself that was totally out of her reach. But she was going to do everything in her power to get that nomination. Then, she could face Zack with the satisfaction of knowing she was at the top of her field. That she was a successful Emmy-nominated actress. That she had achieved something she was sure he, nor anyone else for that matter, ever dreamed she could achieve.

Thinking back to the day of their wedding, she remembered how devastated and how angry she had been at Zack for pushing her to do something she really had no interest in doing. Oh, she'd heard the version he had told his aunt, the one his aunt had quickly passed on to her mother. About how Zack wanted both of them to experience life so they'd never have any regrets when they did settle down and get married.

Not that Zack hadn't tried to talk to her himself after he didn't show up at the church. He'd rung the blasted phone off the hook and he'd practically beaten her parents' door down until her father finally had no choice but to threaten to have him arrested if he didn't back off. And then, after she'd gone to Hollywood to shoot the *Evershine* commercial, he had sent flowers to her hotel room every day for a solid month, begging her to at least talk to him.

He'd finally given up after she mailed him a note. *You made your choice, now live with it. I'm certainly going to!* That's when Zack had moved to Chicago, and that's when their unwritten rule about not showing up in Morgan City at the same time silently fell into place.

Mary Beth smiled, remembering the satisfaction she'd felt when his aunt told her mother Zack really had flipped out over the commercial. She hated to admit it, but she still got the same type of satisfaction every time she stepped in front of the camera on her soap opera set, thinking that Zack might be tuned in and hopefully eating his heart out. Yes, that is what usually helped her get through the day, since her mother had been right about those long days on the set.

She'd never admit it to anyone, but Hollywood wasn't nearly as wonderful as she wanted everyone to believe. At least, not for her. In fact, she was quickly becoming disillusioned with the whole Hollywood scene. Most of the other actors were wrapped up in their own egos, and the actors who didn't have egos were willing to do whatever it took in order to develop one. She often felt like an outcast instead of a cast member, never fitting in with either group. But she would prevail. She had to. And Mary Beth suddenly realized exactly what she was trying to prove to herself. She was trying to prove she wasn't the scatterbrain, the crazy Morgan twin, after all.

She knew it was childish to let an idle comment Maddie had made at her own wedding stick in her side like a troublesome thorn, but it had. Someone had brought up the alien abduction story and Maddie had said, "While Mary Beth was dreaming of an Emmy nomination, I was just trying to figure out how I was going to save my career."

Everyone had laughed.

Mary Beth had been angry enough to ask, "Is everyone laughing because you can't imagine zany me getting an Emmy nomination? Or because you can't picture brainy Maddie without her career?" No one had been brave enough to answer her question, but from that moment on, Mary Beth had a goal to reach.

And after she did get the nomination?

Well, then…

"Mary Beth Morgan! Come here and give me a neck hug."

Mary Beth waved to her third-grade teacher, Mrs. Pope, who pulled herself up from her flowerbed and began tottering in Mary Beth's direction. Well into her eighties, the old widow was still spry enough to keep her yard immaculate and win the garden club's prize every year for her pansies. "You look wonderful, Mrs. Pope," Mary Beth said truthfully.

The old woman wiped her hands on her apron, then drew Mary Beth in for a long, hard squeeze. "I heard you were coming home," she said, stepping back to take a long look. "And we're all so proud of you. I watch your soap opera myself every day."

Mary Beth couldn't help it, she blushed. Her new soap opera had been called *The Wild and the Free* for a reason.

"And I just love Fancy Kildare," Mrs. Pope gushed, fanning her face a bit with the gardening glove she'd just removed from her wrinkled hand. "What I wouldn't give if I could turn back the clock. I'd wear the same outrageous clothes Fancy wears and—" she paused and motioned for Mary Beth to lean in closer before she whispered "—and I'd seduce all those handsome men, too. Just like *you* do."

The heat grew even hotter on Mary Beth's cheeks. She wasn't ashamed of the show, and she wasn't ashamed of her character Fancy Kildare, but she was talking to her third-grade teacher, for God's sake!

"You realize Fancy is just a character I play," Mary Beth said for clarification. "And those bedroom scenes. You know those aren't real, right?"

"Oh, yes, I know. And what a pity for you, my dear," Mrs. Pope said with a cackle. "What a pity for you."

Mary Beth couldn't help but laugh when the old woman shuffled back in the direction of her flowerbed still chuckling to herself.

She'd taken only a few more steps when Mrs. Davis, a tiny little lady who barely reached Mary Beth's shoulder hurried across her lawn, waving the latest copy of *Soap Opera Digest* over her head that had Mary Beth's picture on the front. "I heard you were coming home and I saved my digest so you could autograph it personally."

"You're flattering me, Mrs. Davis," Mary Beth told the woman and looked up to find that Mrs. Truitt from across the street didn't intend to be out-done. Known for being the biggest gossip in town, Mrs. Truitt tipped the scales somewhere around three hundred and completely dwarfed Mrs. Davis. She practically pushed the smaller woman out of the way and thrust a copy of the digest in Mary Beth's direction. "I want your autograph, too, Mary Beth. And write something that's Hollywood chic on mine," she said, making her huge stomach jiggle like Jell-O when she laughed. "I want to show it off at bingo next week."

Mary Beth chatted with both women until Mrs. Davis's questions got a little too personal. She made it all the way to Main Street before the postman flagged her down. "Hey, Mr. Gordon," Mary Beth said when he came rushing across the street in her direction.

"I heard you were coming home," he said, taking off his cap long enough to mop his face with a hand-kerchief he pulled from his back pocket. "And I've got a big favor to ask."

"Ask away," Mary Beth beamed.

"My wife watches your soap opera all the time. Do you think you could send her some autographed pictures from the cast members on your show?"

"Sure," Mary Beth told him. "No problem."

"You're a lifesaver," he said, shifting the weight of his mailbag to the opposite shoulder before he ducked into the barber shop, the next stop on his route.

If everybody else in town knew I was coming home, then I know Zack got the message, Mary Beth thought with confidence, then headed directly across the street to a place where she could definitely find the comfort in familiar surroundings that her horoscope suggested.

Like every other business in town, the Dairy Hut opened promptly at nine and closed promptly at five. Mr. Gruber's smile greeted his first customer of the day the second Mary Beth walked through the door. She walked up to the counter and climbed onto the same stool she had sat on hundreds of times as a kid. The red leather seat was worn and faded now, but the chrome base of the stool was polished to a gleam like the chrome tables and chairs scattered around the rest of the small room.

Even Mr. Gruber hadn't changed a bit. He was still as round as he was tall, still wore a white uniform and a red bow tie, and still kept a crisp white paper hat perched on his bald head. And though she knew he greeted all of his customers the same way, his warm smile had always made Mary Beth feel special, as if he saved that kind of smile just for her.

"How's it going, Miss Movie Star?" he asked, but his tone wasn't mocking, there was pride in the way he said it.

"Who me?" Mary Beth asked, pretending to look back over her shoulder. "I'm just Mary Beth Morgan. Hometown girl. You must have me confused with someone else."

His laugh was as jolly as Santa's. "Yes, I believe

you are still a hometown girl at heart." He reached out and patted her hand. "Always be proud of it."

Without even asking, he went to the dairy case and came back a few minutes later with a sugar cone heaped with ice cream and sprinkles. "One scoop of pistachio, one scoop of French vanilla, and double sprinkles."

"My absolute favorite," Mary Beth said, gladly taking the cone when he handed it over. "I'm flattered you remember."

"How could I forget?" he said, waving off her remark. "You and Zack Callahan were the only kids in town who ever came bursting through the door this early in the morning begging for ice cream."

Mary Beth flinched at the sound of Zack's name.

Her heart stopped when Mr. Gruber looked past her and said, "Well, speak of the devil. Look who just walked in."

Mary Beth whirled around on her stool so fast, both scoops of her absolute favorite tumbled from the sugar cone that was now crumbling to pieces in her clenched right hand. When she jumped down from the stool, the pistachio slid down the front of her new white DKNY jeans and the French vanilla did a back flip right down the scoop neck of her red silk top and momentarily landed in her bra before falling out the other end. It didn't make any difference that Zack looked as shocked to see her as she felt. Nor was a chunk of ice cream still melting between her breasts cold enough to keep her temper from rising. Just the sight of Zack's face made Mary Beth madder than hell.

How *dare* he show up when he knew perfectly well *she* was coming home for the reunion! She was also furious that Zack had managed to catch her completely off guard. She'd had no warning, and she'd had no time to think about what she should say or what she should do when they saw each other again for the first time.

If Zack Callahan knew what was good for him, he'd walk right back out the door without so much as saying a single word to her.

Purposely turning her back on him, Mary Beth willed him to leave and gave him the opportunity to do so. She dumped what was left of the sugar cone on the counter and grabbed a handful of napkins to dab at the front of her jeans. She was relieved Mr. Gruber suddenly found something to do at the back of the store, and she was amazed that she'd been able to take in every inch of Zack in that nanosecond they'd spent staring at each other.

And dammit, but he did look good.

He was still gorgeous, of course. Still had the same sun-streaked hair that fell across his forehead in that little-boy style that instantly made her want to reach out to push it out of his eyes. But the youthful face and soft cheeks she remembered had matured into the face of a man with chiseled features and a strong angular jaw. He was even dressed like a man—in an expensive camel-colored suit Mary Beth recognized as Armani the second she twirled around on her stool.

And here *she* stood with a bright green crotch and a bra full of French vanilla!

Venus, how could you? Mary Beth's mind screamed. Her daily horoscope certainly hadn't warned her about this type of catastrophe.

When a familiar voice from behind her said, "It looks like I owe you an ice-cream cone," Mary Beth decided the ruler of her astrological sign must have taken a short vacation too.

ZACK'S FIRST IMPULSE was to walk out the door and march back across the street to the hardware store and punch his cousin in the nose. He should have known Mr. Gruber hadn't called and asked someone to come over and see what part he needed to fix the drain in his sink. And he shouldn't have let Greg goad him into coming out of his hiding place by saying he was a fool if he thought anyone in town cared enough to run tell Mary Beth he was home. Greg had obviously seen Mary Beth enter the Dairy Hut from the hardware store's front window. And that's when the dirty coward had seen his chance to get out of participating in the scheme Zack had been plotting from the moment he arrived in town.

He's a dead man, Zack thought at the same time Mary Beth yelled, "You owe me more than an ice-cream cone, Zack Callahan!"

Poor Mr. Gruber darted to the back door, making Zack wonder if he was too polite to eavesdrop on their conversation, or if he had headed out the back door for the sheriff because he didn't want one of his customers murdered in cold blood in the middle of his ice-cream shop.

Because a murderous intent is exactly what he

saw reflected in Mary Beth's ice-blue eyes. She slammed a handful of napkins down on the counter and Zack could see she was literally trembling with anger.

"What you owe me is the common courtesy of walking back out that door and going back to Chicago," she fumed. "You knew I was coming home for the reunion."

All Zack could do was stand there and stare.

He already knew the girl he remembered, the innocent girl-next-door type with the ponytail, had matured into a woman with curves so voluptuous grown men would be willing to throw themselves at her feet to worship her. Hell, he'd watched those soap opera tapes so many times, every inch of her was permanently etched into his memory. But actually seeing her face-to-face literally knocked the breath from his lungs. He was also sorry all the careful planning he'd given to the first time they saw each other again would never come into fruition now.

"You're right," Zack finally admitted. "I did know you were coming home for the reunion."

"Then what in the hell are *you* doing here?"

Zack could have sworn he'd seen steam coming from her nostrils as she spit out those words, but he took a chance and said, "I'm here, Mary Beth, because it's time to make peace between us."

"Time to make peace between us!" She marched right up to him and stood so close Zack could see a white puddle of ice cream trapped between the miraculous mounds of her more than ample cleavage. She stuck her face close to his, making him jerk his head back. "The only way you'll ever have peace with me, Zack, is when you're six feet under. Got it?"

She pushed him out of her way then, but when she got to the door, Zack said, "Please, Mary Beth. At least hear me out."

She spun back around to face him. The expression in her eyes was cold and deadly, but it couldn't mask the hurt he saw hiding behind the anger. Her lips twisted into a cynical smirk that was so unlike the warm, caring, wonderful girl he remembered. *My God,* Zack thought. *What have I done to her?*

"There's no reason to hear you out, Zack," she said with a toss of her head. "Because I'm not interested in anything you have to say."

She said those words with conviction, but she was doing a lousy job keeping her lower lip from quivering. What Zack wanted to do was take her in his arms and hold her and beg her to forgive him, because the thought that he had hurt her was like a dagger straight to his heart. As strange as it might seem, it had never occurred to him how much he had hurt her. Mainly because she had split for Hollywood only three days after he wouldn't go through with their wedding. And then he'd received the note after she did get a taste of the limelight. The note had only confirmed his belief that what she'd told the talent agent had been true: that she'd head to Hollywood in a heartbeat if it weren't for him.

But now Zack realized that he had hurt her, deeply. And the knowledge that he'd hurt the woman he still loved more than life itself, broke Zack's heart and filled his soul with sorrow.

He didn't try to hold back the tears welling up in his eyes when he said, "I would do anything, Mary Beth. Anything. If I thought it could make up for hurting you."

He saw a flicker of compassion in the look she gave him, but it disappeared when she tossed her silky blond hair over her shoulder and placed her hands on her hips. "Don't flatter yourself, Zack. You didn't hurt me, you *embarrassed* me. And that's something you can never make up for as far as I'm concerned."

"Then I'll rephrase what I said. I would do anything if I could make up for the *embarrassment* I caused you."

Her laugh was bitter. "Oh, really? You would do anything?" The cynical smirk that looked out of place on her beautiful face returned. "Then why don't you stand on Main Street handing out one-hundred-dollar bills all day, Zack? Maybe even hang a sign around your neck that says 'I'm the idiot who walked out on Mary Beth Morgan and now I'm paying for it.'"

Zack didn't falter. "I'm serious, Mary Beth." But he was having a hard time staying serious every time he glanced at the bright green circle standing out like a bull's-eye right in the middle of her tight-fitting jeans.

"Oh? You don't like that idea?" She tossed her head again. "Then why don't you trying hanging upside down from the Deep River Bridge, whistling here comes the bride until your face turns blue?''

She was toying with him and enjoying every minute of it. And if for no other reason than to keep her there as long as possible, Zack decided to play along. ''I'm afraid of heights, Mary Beth, and you know it.''

Her smirk vanished. ''Then what would *your* brilliant plan be, Zack? Pitch a tent in my front yard until I called a truce?''

Zack couldn't hide his own smirk. ''Would pitching a tent in your front yard *make* you call a truce?''

Her eyes narrowed to tiny slits and her finger came up under his nose as she shook it. ''Forget the truce, Zack. It isn't going to happen. Not now. Not ever.''

And before Zack could stop her, Mary Beth stormed out of the Dairy Hut.

''IF THAT'S A NEW FASHION statement, Mary Beth, I don't like it.''

Mary Beth kicked her sandals off onto Maddie's clean kitchen floor, unzipped her jeans and stepped out of them, then tossed them into Maddie's kitchen sink. ''It's not a fashion statement. It's ice cream. And I'm *not* in a humorous mood.''

''Then I guess asking if you've been in a wrestling match with Ben & Jerry's isn't a good idea.''

Mary Beth sent her sister a warning look, then pulled her top over her head and tossed it in the sink with her jeans. When she unfastened her favorite Victoria's Secret bra and tossed it in the sink with the rest of her clothes, her nephew let out a squeal of delight from his high chair and held both chubby arms straight out in front of him, begging Mary Beth to take him.

"Sorry," Maddie said glancing over at her son. "He's a boob man, just like his father."

Having forgotten about the baby, Mary Beth instantly crossed her arms to cover her bare breasts and sent an anxious look at her nephew. "Will you stop with your stand-up routine, Maddie, and at least find me something to put on before I scar your son for life!"

Maddie put her finger to her chin. "Umm, maybe you're right. B.J. having memories of his aunt standing in the kitchen wearing nothing but a thong might not be such a good idea."

When Mary Beth sent her another mean look, Maddie hurried from the room and was back in a flash with a terry-cloth robe that Mary Beth quickly slipped into. "Now," Maddie said when Mary Beth flopped down in a chair at her kitchen table, "Why are you in such a black mood? Other than spilling pistachio on your new Donna Karan jeans, I mean."

Mary Beth opened her mouth to speak, but burst into tears instead. How could she have been so stupid, she kept asking herself. How could she have ever believed anything, even a damn Emmy nomination, would make it okay to see Zack again? The second she saw him, all the old feelings she thought she had put to rest came zooming out of their hiding places and hit her like a two-ton truck. And the only thing that kept her from falling into his arms when he apologized so sincerely for hurting her, was the fact that she was kick-ass mad.

She was still kick-ass mad, which only made her sob louder.

Startled, little B.J. let out a wail that sent Maddie scurrying to the high chair. When she walked back to the table, she had her crying child propped on one hip. She jiggled B.J. up and down in one arm to quiet him, and patted her sister's back with the other hand as Mary Beth sobbed into her hands.

"I ran into Zack," Mary Beth said quietly when she managed to stop crying long enough to wipe her eyes on the sleeve of Maddie's robe. She reached over and tickled B.J.'s bare foot as an apology for scaring him. His crying turned into a choked-off giggle.

"You saw Zack?" Maddie gasped. "Where?"

"At the Dairy Hut of all places," Mary Beth said with a sigh.

"And you got into an ice-cream fight?"

"In a way, I guess we did." Mary Beth stood up from the chair and walked over to the sink. She tore off a paper towel, wet it and slowly wiped her face, then down her neck and across her chest to remove what was left of the sticky French vanilla. She turned around to face Maddie and leaned back against the sink. "I was so shocked when he walked through the door I dropped my ice cream, and then he had the nerve to say, 'It looks like I owe you an ice-cream cone.' Can you believe that? We haven't seen each other in six years and he has the nerve to say 'It looks like I owe you an ice-cream cone!'"

Maddie shook her head sympathetically. "I need to mail Zack a copy of Brad's phrase book." When Mary Beth sent her a puzzled look, Maddie smiled and said, "Brad's always teased me that there should be a phrase book for things men shouldn't say. So, I made one for him. Believe it or not, he looks at it quite often."

"Then be sure and add 'It looks like I owe you an ice-cream cone' to that phrase book, and underline in red 'not to be said to the woman you left standing at the altar when you haven't seen her for six damn years!' "

They both burst out laughing, prompting a gleeful squeal from little B.J.

Maddie put her son back in his high chair, then took a box from the cabinet and sprinkled some Cheerios on the tray. She waited until B.J. popped one into his mouth. Once her child was occupied, she turned back to Mary Beth. "So? What happened then?"

"We pretty much got into a shouting match after that, or I guess I was the one doing all the shouting. Especially after he told me the reason he came home was because he felt it was time to make peace between us."

Maddie sent her a guilty look.

"And don't you dare agree with him, Maddie," Mary Beth warned.

"Even though we both know Zack told you up-front that he wasn't going to be at the church?"

Mary Beth gasped. "You knew that? And you let

me feel guilty about it all this time because I didn't tell you?''

Maddie walked over and put her arm around her twin's shoulder. ''We all knew. Me, Mom and Pop. You were just so upset, we didn't want to push you closer to the edge than you already were by making a big deal out of it.''

''Would you believe me if I told you I really did think Zack would show up at the church?''

Maddie squeezed Mary Beth's shoulder. ''I know you did. So did I.'' When Mary Beth let out a long sigh, Maddie said, ''So? Where did you leave things with Zack?''

Mary Beth pushed away from the sink and started pacing around the kitchen. She didn't dare admit to Maddie that seeing Zack again had her so confused she didn't know what she was feeling at the moment. She still had her pride.

''I just hope you won't let your pride get in the way of finally settling things with Zack,'' Maddie said, reading Mary Beth's mind and making her groan. ''You know you and Zack still love each other, even if neither of you are ready to admit it. You don't try to avoid someone for six years if you don't still care about them.''

Mary Beth sent Maddie a what-do-you-know look. Sure, she might be willing to agree to a truce, eventually, after she made Zack suffer a little. But agreeing to nod politely if they passed each other on the street was one thing. Taking him back was totally out of the question. That nagging doubt would always be there in the back of her mind. She would always be afraid Zack would decide at some point he needed more than what they had together. Just like he did when he left her at the altar. She hadn't been enough, he'd wanted more. She couldn't go through that again.

She *wouldn't* go through that again.

"I left things with Zack exactly where they were," Mary Beth finally told her sister. "Over."

Maddie hesitated for a second and sent her a worried look. "Please tell me you aren't thinking about skipping the reunion and going back to L.A."

She *had* thought about it, but only briefly. "No way," Mary Beth said with conviction. "I'm sure everyone already knows we're both in town. The last thing I'm going to do is give Zack, or the rest of Morgan City, the satisfaction of running away like a frightened puppy with my tail between my legs."

3

MARY BETH PICKED UP the Friday morning paper and read the first line of her daily horoscope: *Avoid confrontations that could lead to embarrassing situations.*

"You're a little late, sweetie," Mary Beth grumbled.

"What did you say, dear?" her mother said from across the table as she passed the plate of homemade biscuits to her husband.

"I was just thinking out loud, Mom," Mary Beth said, and continued reading: *The scales bearer, Libra, strives for balance. Someone demanding justice could tip the scales and not in your favor. Keep a low profile and the danger will pass.*

Mary Beth read over the words again, then flipped back to the front page and frowned when she saw the editor's daily column: Class Of '91: Will King Of Internet And Soap Opera Queen Show Up For Reunion?

"That little slimeball," Mary Beth grumbled. The article went on to say what everyone in town already knew about her and Zack's ill-fated relationship.

"If you're talking about Arnold Purdy's article this morning, I'm angry with Arnold myself," her mother spoke up and dabbed at the corner of her mouth with her napkin. "But Arnold really isn't a slimeball. He's actually a good Christian boy."

"And what am I, Mom? A born again pagan?"

"Don't be ridiculous." Helen Morgan threw her napkin down on the table. "I just meant Arnold has recently been appointed as a deacon in our church. And the men chosen as the leaders of the church have to have exemplary moral character."

"Well, I don't call dragging up other people's dirty laundry exemplary moral character, Mom. And we both know the reason most of the men in our church are chosen as deacons is directly related to how much money they dump in the collection plate every Sunday."

"Now, that's the truth if anyone ever told it," George Morgan spoke up.

Helen sent her husband and her daughter an annoyed look. "Well, maybe if you kids hadn't always teased Arnold so much when you were in school, he wouldn't be tempted to use his newspaper to even the score now."

Mary Beth didn't deny her mother's accusation. Arnold had always been everyone's target. Mainly because he was so incredibly intolerable he just begged to be teased. "Oh, come on, Mom. Maybe we did tease Arnold in school. But Arnold Purdy's so damn annoying even a boomerang wouldn't come back to him."

"Save the cursing for L.A., please."

Mary Beth rolled her eyes and looked across the table for her father's support again. George Morgan was hunched over his bacon and eggs, looking like the big bear Mary Beth had always likened her father to. He was a little heavier around the middle than she'd like for his health, and his dark hair was slowly getting thin on top, but he was the sweetest, most loveable man she'd ever known. And he almost always took her side. "Don't you agree that Arnold Purdy is a pain, Pop?"

Mayor Morgan looked up from his plate long enough to say, "That man is a human boil on the butt of society if there ever was one."

"And I'm stupid enough to wonder where Mary Beth gets her foul language," said Helen with a sigh.

Mary Beth laughed. "Maybe you're right, Mom. Maybe Arnold is using his paper to finally get back at the classmates who teased him. But I swear, he asked for most of it. Like that stupid question box he always insisted on keeping in the cafeteria. 'Ask Arnold' is what he called it."

"Ask Arnold what?" Mayor Morgan wanted to know.

"He wanted us to ask him anything. And he was arrogant enough to brag he couldn't be stumped for an answer."

"Sounds like he was very studious to me," Helen argued.

"And did you ever put a question in that box?" her father asked.

Mary Beth couldn't keep from laughing. "Dozens of questions, actually."

"Like what?" her father asked.

Mary Beth grinned. "Like, if we can measure the speed of light, what is the speed of dark? Where do we keep the whales that we save? But the one I remember that really flipped Arnold out was, what's so great about taxation *with* representation? He practically wrote a thesis on that subject, shaming all of us for not being civic minded enough to support our own government."

Her mother looked puzzled, as if she were actually pondering the answers to those questions, but her father was laughing so hard he was pounding the kitchen table.

"Well, I'm certainly glad everyone's in a good mood this morning," Maddie said when she came breezing into the kitchen with little B.J. on her hip. "Because..."

"If you're talking about the paper, Maddie, don't worry. We've already seen it." Mary Beth reached out for her grinning nephew.

Maddie handed her son over to his aunt, but her look turned serious. "It's not the paper I'm talking about, Mary Beth. It's Zack. I just heard on WKZM that he's causing quite a commotion over on Main Street. The radio said he was handing out one-hundred-dollar bills to every one who drove by. And you're not going to believe this, but apparently he has a sign around his neck that says..."

"Oh, God. I already know what the sign says," Mary Beth gasped. She was suddenly so weak she handed B.J. to his grandmother before she dropped him.

She forgot all about avoiding conflicts that could

lead to embarrassing situations, and about keeping a low profile until the danger passed. Instead she was already running for the door when she heard Maddie say from behind her, "I swear, Mom, I think Zack's gone crazy."

MARY BETH HADN'T EVEN thought to ask for the keys to her father's car. You could cover the entire town of Morgan City in a thirty-minute walk. And even if she had taken her father's car she wouldn't have gotten very far. By the time she reached the end of Mulberry Street, there was already a long line of traffic inching its way slowly toward Main.

She ignored the open stares people were sending her through their car windows, and she pretended not to hear the questions being thrown at her as she hurried down the sidewalk.

"Hey, Mary Beth? Is Zack handing out money on Main Street just another one of your publicity stunts?" someone had the nerve to call out from the other side of the street.

"The paper says people are taking bets on whether you and Zack will both show up at the reunion. What's Zack doing, paying people to bet on him?" someone else yelled.

"Get a life and stop worrying about two people who already have one," Mary Beth yelled back to no one in particular.

And then she kept on walking.

When a motorcycle roared up beside her, Mary Beth sent a dirty look at the rider until she saw who it was.

"I guess you've already heard what my demented cousin is doing at the moment," Greg Callahan said as he coasted along beside her.

"Making a fool of himself, you mean?"

"That, and handing out one-hundred-dollar bills like it was Monopoly money."

"Can't you stop him, Greg? Can't you do something?" Mary Beth pleaded.

"I was going to ask you the same thing." Greg motioned to the space on the seat behind him. "Hop on, Mary Beth. Maybe between the two of us we can talk some sense into the crazy lunatic before he goes bankrupt."

Mary Beth swung a long jean-clad leg over the back of Greg's motorcycle and held on for dear life as he roared away from the curb. Greg weaved in and out of traffic so fast it made her head spin. She almost lost her balance when he jumped the curb several minutes later and landed on the sidewalk where Zack was standing at the corner of Main and Palmetto.

Zack, however, never even acknowledged their arrival.

Instead, he kept talking rather amicably with Toby Martin who ran the local gas station. He handed Toby a crisp new hundred-dollar bill before he said goodbye and Tony drove away.

"Next," Zack called out and motioned the next car forward.

When a Volkswagen rattled to a stop, Mary Beth hopped off the back of Greg's motorcycle and marched up to stand beside Zack. "You're making a real ass of yourself, Zack,'' she said, glaring at the driver of the car who immediately sent her a satisfied smile. "Keep moving, Arnold," Mary Beth warned.

"Gladly," Arnold said, flashing her a gap-tooth smile as he held his palm out for Zack to grease.

Zack placed a bill in Arnold's hand but Mary Beth reached out and snatched it right back. "Don't you dare give that little weasel a dime."

Zack turned and looked at her for the first time. "I'm sorry, Mary Beth. But I don't remember there being any restrictions about who I gave the money to when you came up with this idea."

"Mary Beth told you to do this?" Arnold quizzed, quickly reaching for a notepad on the seat beside him. He took a pen from the pocket protector he'd probably been using since high school and poised it over the pad. "So you think handing out money on Main Street is payment enough for leaving you at the altar, Mary Beth?"

Mary Beth ignored the question, grabbed the bill back from Zack's hand and tossed it through Nerdy Purdy's open car window. "Get out of here, Arnold. Get out of here before I personally pull you out of that car myself and..."

"I would take some anger management courses if I were you, Mary Beth," Arnold said in his usual superior tone before his old Volkswagen coughed and sputtered and finally rattled away.

Before the next car could advance, Mary Beth grabbed Zack's arm and swung him back around to face her. "And just how long do you plan to keep this up?"

"Have you changed your mind about calling a truce?"

"Does Arnold Purdy have straight teeth?"

"Nope."

"That's my answer."

Zack shrugged. "Then I guess I'll keep standing here until the cars stop coming, or the money runs out. Whichever comes first."

"That sign around your neck really is true, Zack. You really are an idiot," Greg said as he walked up beside them.

Zack took a brief look down at the sign around his neck and said, "Yep, that's what the sign says. I'm the idiot who ran out on Mary Beth Morgan. And now I'm paying for it."

Zack turned his attention back to the next car in line. A bright red head appeared when the tinted window came down. "Hey, Zack," said Sally Hughes, one of their old classmates who had always had a crush on Zack. She looked briefly at Mary Beth and managed a curt nod.

Zack automatically peeled a bill from the huge stack of money he held in his hand, but Sally said, "I don't want your money, Zack. I heard you were home and I stopped to see if you'd like to come to dinner at my place tomorrow night."

Mary Beth fought back a pang of jealousy, but answered the question before Zack could say a word. "Zack would love to have dinner with you, Sally. What time?"

Zack quickly shook his head. "Sorry, Sally. I'm going to be tied up for the next few days." He sent a challenging look back at Mary Beth as if to imply *she* would be involved in whatever was going to have him tied up.

Not in this lifetime! Mary Beth vowed silently.

The thick makeup couldn't hide the disappointment on Sally's pinched face. "How about dinner next week, then?"

Zack leaned forward and took Sally's hand, then closed her fingers around the bill she had refused the first time. "I'll see what I can do," he said, and sent her one of those heart-stopping smiles Mary Beth thought she'd forgotten.

The smile worked like a charm. "Great!" Sally said in a bubbly voice. "See you next week, sweetie."

"Liar," Mary Beth said when Sally drove away. "You're never going to have dinner with Sally Hughes and you know it."

"But at least I'm a sweetie," Zack said with a grin.

Mary Beth felt like slapping him. She frowned when she saw the local town wino stumbling across the street in their direction.

"Here you go," Zack said, handing over a bill to the toothless old guy who held the money up to the sunlight, kissed it like a long-lost lover, and then headed off down the street.

"Shame on you," Mary Beth said. "You know he's heading straight to the liquor store."

"Nah, old Charlie's sobered up," Zack told her.

"I had a long talk with him yesterday. I think he's finally seen the light."

Mary Beth was skeptical until she saw the old man bypass the liquor store completely and head into the local diner. *St. Zack*, she thought. Too sweet to hurt a woman's feelings that he doesn't want to date. Taking time out to counsel old winos and show them the light. What would it be next? Risking his own safety to rescue a helpless kitten stranded in a tree?

Give me a freaking break.

She glared at him. "Tell me the truth, Zack. What are you really trying to prove?"

His expression was as wounded as it had been the day before at the Dairy Hut. "I'm trying to prove there's nothing I wouldn't do for your forgiveness, Mary Beth. And that's the honest to God truth."

Great.

Of all the questions in the world, she had to ask that one. And of all the answers in the world, his couldn't have been more perfect.

Except for the fact that he was wasting his time.

And so Mary Beth said exactly what she'd been thinking to herself. "Sorry, Zack. You're wasting your time."

And then she turned around and left him standing on the corner of Main and Palmetto, still handing out crisp one-hundred-dollar bills to the long line of cars waiting patiently for the best deal to hit Morgan City in a long, long time.

"FIFTEEN THOUSAND DOLLARS," Greg kept saying. "I still can't believe you gave away fifteen thousand dollars in one short morning."

Zack ignored his cousin and reached for the bowl of mashed potatoes his aunt Lou had just placed on the table before him.

"And some of those cars came by twice. Not to mention that church activity bus," Greg continued with a snort. "It wasn't enough to give fifteen screaming little league ball players one hundred dollars apiece, Zack felt the need to give their coach another five hundred to help with new uniforms."

"Money well spent," Aunt Lou said, looking fondly at her nephew. "Zack always was a good boy."

Greg frowned at his mother. "Well, in case you haven't noticed, Mom, Zack isn't a boy anymore. He's a man. A man with a screw loose, if you ask me."

"Well, look on the bright side," Uncle Jim spoke up. "Zack spread a lot of money around Morgan City this morning. And we'll most likely get some of it back down at the hardware store over the next few days."

Greg wasn't appeased. "I wish the two of you wouldn't encourage him," he grumbled. "Don't either of you realize what your nutty nephew is really up to?"

When both of his parents sent him a questioning look, Greg jerked his thumb in Zack's direction. "Your crazy nephew has come back home because he thinks he can talk Mary Beth into taking him back."

"Is that true, Zack?" Lou Callahan asked, her face lighting up with hope.

Greg groaned.

Zack gave his aunt a warm smile. "Someone once told me true love waits." He and his aunt exchanged knowing looks.

"True love waits until you leave her standing at the altar," Greg scoffed. "Then *she* waits until she can have you castrated and serve your…"

"Greg Callahan!" Aunt Lou scolded. "We're trying to have lunch here."

Greg frowned and grabbed the bowl that Zack was handing over. After scooping up a spoonful of fluffy mashed potatoes, he bent his head over his plate with a scowl on his face.

Zack ignored him and speared one of his aunt's famous melt-in-your-mouth fried chicken breasts with his fork and tried to concentrate on his lunch. But he couldn't help but worry that Greg's prediction might be right. He could tell Mary Beth was a little flattered that he was actually willing to carry out the hypothetical scenario she'd thrown at him, but she had still walked away without changing her mind about them calling a truce.

Looking across the table at his cousin, Zack asked, "Did Mary Beth say anything when you went after her and took her back to her parents' house?"

Greg put his fork down. "As a matter of fact, she did. She told me not to worry about you when I said I was afraid you really were cracking up."

"Not to worry about me?"

"Mary Beth reminded me how practical you've

always been. She said you were practical enough to realize the two of you were too young to get married six years ago. And she assured me you were practical enough to realize you didn't have a chance in hell of getting her back now.''

Zack grinned and reached for another helping of mashed potatoes. *Practical? So, Mary Beth was counting on him being old practical Zack, was she?*

Sending Greg a twisted smile that immediately made his cousin frown, Zack said, ''Tell me, Greg. What are you doing first thing tomorrow morning?''

''YOU HAVE TO ADMIT WHAT Zack did was terribly romantic, Mary Beth.''

''I don't call giving Arnold Purdy more fodder for his bull crap column, romantic.'' Mary Beth glared at the Saturday morning headlines.

Wild, Free and Merciless?

That's what Morgan City is saying about soap-opera star, Mary Beth Morgan. At Miss Morgan's suggestion, her ex-fiancé, Zack Callahan, was more than willing to humiliate himself Friday morning by handing out hundred-dollar bills in an effort to end the six-year feud that's been going on between them....

''You said yourself you were the one who gave Zack the idea,'' Maddie threw in.

''What I said was only a joke, Maddie, and Zack knows it.''

"But the fact that Zack actually did what you told him was terribly romantic, just the same."

Mary Beth let out a sigh. "You call it terribly romantic. I call it terribly too late."

"Are you sure, Mary Beth?"

Mary Beth eased herself up from Maddie's front porch swing, careful not to wake a sleeping B.J. who was being cradled in his mother's arms.

After pacing the porch for a few minutes, Mary Beth finally said, "I'm sure."

When Maddie only smiled and kept swinging, Mary Beth put her hands on her hips. "What? Are you saying you think I *should* forgive Zack? Pretend we can go back to being just friends?"

"It doesn't matter what I think, Mary Beth. Whether you forgive Zack or not is a decision only you can make."

"I can't believe this," said Mary Beth. "My own sister thinks I should forgive the man who left me standing at the altar."

"I didn't say that."

"Then what *are* you saying, Maddie?"

Maddie hesitated. "I'm just trying to point out that I think it's rather odd that not once in six years have you brought any of those fabulous men you're always dating home to meet your family."

Mary Beth laughed. "And why do you think that is, Maddie? Maybe because the men I date happen to be over three thousand miles away in California? Which just doesn't make it possible to drop by for coffee with my parents and my sister after we take in dinner and a movie?"

Ignoring her twin's sarcasm, Maddie said, "No. I think the reason we've never met any of those to-die-for dates of yours is because after dinner and a movie you never bother seeing them again."

"Meaning?"

"Meaning maybe you haven't found anyone else you care about the way you care about Zack."

"*Cared* about Zack," Mary Beth corrected. "And okay. I admit it. That special someone just hasn't come along yet."

"Hasn't come along? Or hasn't come *back?* Until now?" Maddie challenged.

"Stop trying to confuse me, Maddie," Mary Beth grumbled. "It's bad enough Venus has suddenly decided to play games with my life. Don't you start making me doubt myself, too."

"Puh-lease," Maddie said. "Don't start with that Venus, ruler of your destiny nonsense again. It's just too ridiculous for me to even contemplate."

"Ridiculous?" Mary Beth echoed. "You? The woman who thinks nothing of spending two years trying to determine if gnats really have facial expressions, has the nerve to call me ridiculous because I read my horoscope on a daily basis?"

Maddie laughed. "The study I was doing on the fungus gnat had nothing to do with facial features, silly."

"Seriously, Maddie. How could she do this to me?"

Maddie rolled her eyes. "I can't believe I'm even asking this, but how could Venus do what to you, Mary Beth?"

"Hand me my stardom in one hand, and then turn around and push Zack back into my life with the other. It's just not fair."

Sending her sister a sympathetic look, Maddie said, "Sorry, hon. But sometimes life isn't fair."

"Life," Mary Beth said disgustedly. "The ultimate sexually transmitted disease."

"And one we all have to face sooner or later," Maddie added.

"What's this about sexually transmitted diseases?"

Mary Beth turned around to see her brother-in-law approaching wearing nothing but a pair of cut-offs. He toweled off his impressive torso to remove the perspiration he'd worked up mowing the lawn, then bent down and kissed his wife before he placed a loving kiss on the forehead of his sleeping son.

I might throw up, Mary Beth thought.

What she *didn't* need at the moment was to witness the perfect setting for a Norman Rockwell painting. Especially a painting with two of the most unlikely candidates she could imagine in the picture. A top gun flyboy? With his microscope-obsessive wife looking down at their angelic child like Lady Madonna?

It was enough to make Mary Beth say, "Well, I'd better get going."

"Can't you stay a little longer?" Maddie called out as Mary Beth started down the porch steps, but her sister's protest sounded rather feeble to Mary Beth.

"No, I'd better get back to Mom and Pop's. Besides, you guys need some family time alone together.''

And it was true. Weekends were all the time Brad and Maddie had together. As usual, Brad would be leaving on Sunday for his flight back to the Pentagon.

"And church tomorrow?" Maddie reminded her twin.

Mary Beth grinned. "Don't worry. I wouldn't miss church tomorrow for anything. Especially since I intend to make it a point to sit next to our old friend, Arnold Purdy, and make goo-goo eyes at our newest deacon through the entire service. Then we'll see how *he* likes being gossiped about for the rest of the week.''

"Mary Beth! You wouldn't.''

Mary Beth's only answer was to toss a final wave over her head. Then she jammed her thumbs into the front pockets of her jeans and started walking back to her parents' house.

But as she walked, she kept thinking back over the conversation she just had with her twin. It was just like Maddie to be right on target about her never dating the same man twice. Yet, her one-date-only policy was actually a defense mechanism Mary Beth had implemented without even realizing it. Probably because there were never any complications on a first date. First dates were…well, they were usually fun. She could have a great time, give the guy a polite good-night kiss at her door and then bid him a fond farewell. And if he did call again she simply kept putting him off until he got tired of calling, always using her hectic schedule as a plausible excuse.

It works for me, Mary Beth told herself with confidence as she neared Mulberry Street. Besides, what had being in love with the same guy since she was ten years old done for her? As far as Mary Beth was concerned, being in love was highly overrated. She'd already been there, done that, even got the T-shirt, so to speak. A T-shirt that would have read: Girl Meets Boy. Girl Plans For A Life Together. Boy runs like hell.

Well, now it was her turn to run.

4

"I THINK YOU SHOULD READ the interview Arnold did with Zack, Mary Beth. It's really touching."

When Mary Beth shook her head in protest, her mother forced the paper into her hands. Mary Beth let out a disgusted sigh but read the headlines: "Fifteen Thousand Dollars: A Small Price To Pay For Forgiveness As Far As Morgan City's Prodigal Son, Zack Callahan, Is Concerned...."

"I don't care if Zack handed out fifteen *million* dollars, Mom." She threw the paper down on her bed. "He's wasting his time."

"But I know he still loves you, Mary Beth. And I know you still love him."

"You know nothing of the kind," Mary Beth was quick to answer.

"Well, the least you could do is talk to him. His aunt Lou called me this morning, really excited. She said she was certain Zack had come home to win you back."

"Win me back?" Mary Beth shouted. "He doesn't want me back, Mom, he's just trying to soothe his own guilty conscience."

Helen shook her head. "Oh, no, dear. You need

to read that interview. Zack doesn't come right out and say he wants you back, but Lou says…''

"Hush, Mom!" Mary Beth warned. "I don't want to hear another word." She was standing in the middle of her bedroom wearing nothing but her underwear, but she held her mother's gaze. "But I do promise you one thing. Arnold Purdy just sealed his fate with that interview."

And Mary Beth meant every word. Her threat about seeking Arnold out at church had been an idle one. Until now.

"Now, Mary Beth, what does that mean?"

Mary Beth turned her back on her mother and walked to her closet. "It means the very nerve of that little creep calling me merciless and making Zack look like the injured party just pushed me over the edge."

"It's always better to turn the other cheek, dear" was Helen Morgan's Sunday morning advice as she started out of her daughter's bedroom.

Still flipping through her closet, Mary Beth mumbled under her breath, "The only cheek I'm interested in is the one I plan to leave bruised when I kick Arnold Purdy's bony little ass."

"No cursing while you're getting ready for church, please" came the warning from the hallway, reminding Mary Beth that age evidently hadn't affected her mother's hearing in the least.

When her eyes finally landed on the perfect outfit, the smile that spread across Mary Beth's face was almost as wicked as the plan she had in store for Arnold. She pulled the dry cleaning bag from her closet, then walked back to the bed and laid it down to pick up the newspaper. It only took a few seconds to read Zack's candid confession about how sorry he was for causing her any embarrassment. At the end of the article, he even alluded to the hope that Mary Beth would eventually forgive him, but there was certainly nothing mentioned about Zack wanting her back.

No, that was obviously his aunt's wishful thinking.

Which was just as well, Mary Beth reminded herself. Not only could she never trust Zack again, but people were finally beginning to see her in a different light. She was a star now, not Maddie's flighty twin, and not the girl Zack left at the altar. And she certainly never wanted to be known as the idiot who took Zack Callahan back the second he crooked his finger in her direction.

Not that he wanted her back, she kept reassuring herself. No, she couldn't deal with that thought. Not now. Not when she still had a personal goal to reach.

Quickly flipping to her horoscope, Mary Beth read: *Taking control of the situation is sometimes your best defense. Go straight to the heart of the problem and squelch further attempts to discredit you. Taking up for yourself is imperative. Make your move and make it now.*

Humming a happy tune, Mary Beth picked up the dry cleaning bag and hurried into her adjoining bathroom, fully convinced that Venus had just given her the green light on Project Nerdy Purdy.

WEARING A HOT-PINK SUIT with a skirt short enough to stretch the boundaries of being suitable enough for church, Mary Beth walked into the sanctuary behind her parents. She had done her hair up in a sleek French twist and applied a tad more makeup than usual.

Canvassing the happy congregation, Mary Beth kept looking for the one person she had come there to see. When she finally located Deacon Purdy standing at the front of the church, the jerk had the nerve to send her a victorious little smile.

Mary Beth immediately blew him a kiss.

She almost laughed out loud when Arnold's cheeks turned as pink as the suit she was wearing. In fact, he became so flustered he dropped the church bulletins he'd been handing out and started scrambling around on his hands and knees in a hurried effort to pick them back up.

Charge, was the mental battle cry that echoed through her head when Mary Beth walked politely past her own family's pew and headed straight for the front row where only Nerdy Purdy and the other I-can-buy-my-way-into-Heaven deacons of the church were allowed to sit.

"Excuse me, gentlemen," Mary Beth said, flashing the other four men a brilliant smile. "Could you please slide down? Arnold asked me to sit with him in church this morning."

"I did not!" came an indignant cry, but Mary Beth bent down, took Arnold's beet-red face in both hands and delivered a loud smacking kiss straight to the center of his forehead. "Of course you invited me to sit with you, Arnie. Remember? When I was leaving your house late last night?''

Several women on the row behind them gasped.

The other deacons looked at Arnold disapprovingly, but they did slide down, giving Mary Beth more than enough room to take a seat on the sacred front-row pew that was reserved strictly for the men in the congregation with exemplary moral character.

Mary Beth wasted no time cuddling up so close to Arnold he began hyperventilating. And when he finally caught his breath, she forced her fingers through his for a little friendly handholding during Sunday morning service.

''Have you gone mad?'' Arnold growled, looking nervously around the church.

''Not at all,'' said Mary Beth, knowing every eye was cast in their direction. She snuggled even closer. ''You've just been so fascinated with me and my sister over the past two years, I thought you might like to get better acquainted with the Morgan twin who is still single.''

''Well, you thought wrong,'' Arnold said through clenched teeth, and he was still trying to pull his hand out of her grip when Reverend Spindal walked to the pulpit and opened his Bible.

The frown the reverend sent the unlikely couple sitting on the front row delayed the Sunday morning sermon for a moment, but it really didn't matter. Because the back doors of the church suddenly swung open and old Charlie, the town ex-wino, stumbled into the sanctuary with a terrified look on his unshaven face.

"Hurry, Reverend Spindal," the old guy yelled to the startled congregation. "Zack Callahan's trying to kill himself. He's hanging upside down from the Deep River Bridge!"

Mary Beth jumped up so fast she pulled Arnold with her. She pulled her hand free so violently that Arnold landed on the floor with a thud. By the time she reached the back of the church, she stopped only long enough to remove her six-inch heels. Then Mary Beth started running, staying well ahead of the other church members who were all filing out of the church faster than a swarm of bewildered hornets fleeing from a knocked-down hive.

"HOW ARE WE DOING FOR TIME?" Zack asked his cousin.

Greg shook his head and reluctantly looked down at his watch. "If you're really going through with your version of stupid human tricks part two, I'd say you have two more minutes before you have to fling your crazy ass over the side of this bridge."

"Damn straight I'm going through with this," Zack said with more confidence than he felt; he still hadn't found the courage to look over the side of the railing.

The Deep River Bridge had once been the main thoroughfare through town, but now only served as a foot path to the paved bike and walking trail that eventually ended up at the courthouse green. Built back when Deep River had been given that name for a reason, the structure reached seventy-five feet across the middle, which was plenty high enough to send chills up and down his acrophobia-impaired spine. Now Deep River was nothing more than a trickle in the sandy river bottom below, another concern since there wasn't much water to buffer a fall.

The things you do for love, Zack thought. He adjusted the straps of the sturdy harness he and Greg had crafted at the hardware store Saturday morning. Then he gave the bungee cord a couple of hard tugs to make sure it was secure. "You're sure this thing will hold my weight?"

Greg laughed. "I'm sure. But maybe if I dropped you on your head, it would finally knock some sense into that thick skull of yours."

"Ha, ha," said Zack and finally took a step forward to look over the railing. He felt like Jimmy Stewart's character in *Vertigo*.

If Greg noticed he'd broken out in a cold sweat, he didn't mention it. Instead, Greg checked his watch and said, "It's show time Evel Knievel. Now get your butt over that rail."

Slinging one leg over the railing with a grimace, then the other, Zack held on to the railing with one hand and gave his cousin a feeble thumbs-up sign with the other. And though Greg had to practically pry his fingers from the railing, no one in the history of modern man had ever done a better imitation of the Tarzan yell than Zack did when he finally let himself free-fall backward off the Deep River Bridge.

Still trying to recover from being upside down with the world spinning around him, Zack's only salvation was the thought that he would soon hear the sound of thundering footsteps overhead, telling him that good old Charlie hadn't let him down.

And if he didn't fall and kill himself first, he knew Mary Beth would be among the group of spectators old Charlie had rounded up to witness yet another example of the self-induced lunacy he was willing to put himself through for the woman he loved.

BY THE TIME MARY BETH covered the short distance from the church to the Deep River Bridge, her sleek French twist was falling apart in every direction and her feet felt like she'd run through a field full of blooming Brillo pads. She stopped long enough to push the hair out of her eyes and brush away the gravel stuck to the bottom of her feet. When she put her shoes back on, she marched straight toward Greg, who immediately started backing up when he saw her coming.

"I can't believe you'd let Zack pull such a stupid stunt," she yelled, sending him a threatening glare. "You know he's always been terrified of heights."

"Hey, it was your idea," Greg replied calmly.

They both glared at each other for a second longer, then leaned over the railing at the place where a bright blue bungee cord disappeared over the rail.

"This isn't funny, Zack," Mary Beth called down to him. "Now get yourself back up here."

Zack's only reply was to whistle a few bars of "Here Comes The Bride."

Glaring back at Greg, Mary Beth said, "Get him back up here, Greg. I mean it. Do it now."

They both looked over the railing again. Zack was swinging slightly back and forth every time the wind blew. "I don't know how to pull him back up," Greg admitted.

Mary Beth sent him a look threatening enough to make Greg realize *he* might be the next one to go over the railing. "What do you mean you don't know how to pull him back up?"

Greg sent her a sheepish look. "If I pull on that bungee cord, all it's going to do is turn Zack into a human yo-yo."

"You mean to tell me you let him go off the side of the bridge without figuring out how to get him back up?" Mary Beth's tone was deadly.

"Serves him right," said Greg. "Let him hang upside down for a few hours. Maybe it will get the blood circulating back to his brain again."

Mary Beth was only one second away from placing her hands around Greg's throat when Zack's Aunt Lou came rushing up beside her. "Do something, Mary Beth. Do something before my nephew falls from this bridge and kills himself."

What do you want me to do? Climb over the railing and pull the human yo-yo back up with my teeth? Mary Beth felt like shouting, but instead she put her arm around Zack's sobbing aunt and patted her shoulder. "Don't worry. We'll get him back up somehow, Aunt Lou. But I can't promise you I won't kill him myself when we do get him back on solid ground."

"Zack, honey? Can you hear me," Aunt Lou called out with a sniff as she looked over the railing with Mary Beth. ''We're going to get you up from there. Just hang on.''

''Do you realize your crazy cousin doesn't have a clue how we're going to pull you back up, Zack?'' Mary Beth called down to her ex-lover.

The second those words left Mary Beth's mouth, Aunt Lou abandoned her post and stomped toward her son shaking her finger in Greg's direction.

Mary Beth wasn't left standing on the bridge by herself very long. A white-faced Maddie, followed by her parents and Brad who was holding little B.J., walked up beside her. Maddie's eyes were wide with concern. ''Please tell me this isn't another one of those theoretical examples you gave poor Zack, Mary Beth.''

Poor Zack? In spite of the large crowd that was now leaning over every inch of the bridge railing, Mary Beth was prepared to give her sister a good tongue-lashing for taking Zack's side again, but the sound of screaming sirens jerked her head around. A patrol car, Morgan City's one-truck fire department and the only ambulance in town roared into the parking lot just below the bridge.

''Are you happy now, Zack?'' Mary Beth called down to him. ''Everyone's here but the freaking national guard.''

Zack stopped whistling. He craned his neck up to look at her. ''Have you changed your mind about calling a truce?''

Mary Beth glared down at him. ''What do you think?''

Zack started his incessant whistling again, tempting Mary Beth to give his bungee cord a good shake that would hopefully make his teeth rattle. The only thing that stopped her was the fact that Morgan City's sheriff was now making his way steadily in her direction.

"Back up, folks. Back up," Sheriff Wilson kept saying as he made his way through the crowd and finally came to a stop beside Mary Beth. They both looked over the railing at Zack. Sheriff Wilson called down, "I hate to do this, Callahan, but I'm placing you under arrest."

"Under arrest?" Mary Beth snapped, narrowing her eyes. "For what?"

Sheriff Wilson sent her a disapproving look and said, "Bungee jumping off this bridge just happens to be against the law in Morgan City, missy. Do you have a problem with that?"

Mary Beth bristled at the "missy" part. "Well, *excuse* me, but he's not exactly *jumping* at the moment, now is he? In fact, you can't even prove that he ever did *jump* off this bridge."

The sheriff sent her another stern look. "Is that what they teach you out in Californi-a Mary Beth Morgan? To back talk your public officials?"

Mary Beth heard her mother gasp from behind her. She ignored it. "If those officials are threatening to arrest an innocent man? Yes."

"Quit while you're still ahead, Mary Beth," Zack called out from below the bridge.

Mary Beth ignored Zack as well. "And if I were you, I'd put my efforts into pulling him back up, instead of wasting time while you threaten to arrest him.''

Sheriff Wilson's face turned bloodred. Maddie quickly stepped in front of Mary Beth and said, ''I'm afraid you'll have to excuse my sister, Sheriff. Mary Beth is just feeling guilty right now because this whole thing was her idea.''

''Maddie!''

''This was her idea, was it?'' Sheriff Wilson said, sending Mary Beth a rather sadistic grin. ''Then I guess I'll have *two* prisoners in my jail cell before this day is over.''

Mary Beth paled. ''You're arresting *me?* On what charges?''

''Disturbing the peace,'' the sheriff said, and then he turned to the group of volunteer firemen standing on the bridge and said, ''Pull him up from there, boys. Pull him up so I can arrest him *and* his mouthy television star girlfriend.''

''Pop?'' Mary Beth called out, turning to her father. ''You're the mayor. Do something.''

But when Mayor Morgan stepped forward, his wife pushed her way in front of him. ''I don't know about Zack's family, but I'm all for locking these two up, Sheriff,'' Helen Morgan said glancing over at Zack's Aunt Lou. ''Maybe if you put them in a cell together they'll have to work out their problems and stop all this nonsense that's driving everyone else crazy.''

''Mother!'' Mary Beth exclaimed.

Aunt Lou walked over to Zack when the firemen pulled him back over the railing and whacked him on the arm with her Bible. "How dare you scare me like that," she said before she turned to Mary Beth's mother and said, "I'm with you, Helen. Lock them up, Sheriff. And keep them locked up until they either kill each other or settle their differences."

MARY BETH STOOD AT THE front of the jail cell, holding onto the iron bars, her back purposely turned to Zack.

"You know I never meant for you to end up in jail, Mary Beth," Zack said for the fiftieth time.

"Don't say another word, Zack, or I'll be in here for life for first-degree murder."

Zack pulled himself up from the small cot in the cell and walked over to stand beside her. "Could we please just talk, Mary Beth. Please?"

Okay, Mary Beth thought. Maybe her mother and Aunt Lou were right. Maybe it *was* time to settle their differences. Especially before Zack pulled any more crazy stunts. Thank God she'd only given him two bogus scenarios. She shuddered to think what he might have done had she mentioned something as dangerous as tying himself to the railroad tracks and waiting for the five o'clock train they used to chase when they were kids.

Mary Beth turned to face him. "Okay. You want to talk? Then talk."

His eyes searched her face for a moment. She didn't look away. How could she? His eyes had always been one of the features she liked best about him. They were dark green like moss in the forest, with little flecks of gold around the iris that she used to tease him were sunbeams. They were also kind eyes, eyes that told her with one look that he really was sorry for hurting her.

"Damn," he said, pulling his hand through his sun-streaked hair to push it back and out of his eyes. "Now that you've finally agreed to listen to me, I don't know where to start."

Mary Beth's anger rose up again, but she pushed it down. Leaning back against the door of the cell, she folded her arms and said, "Why don't you start with the real reason you didn't show up at the church, Zack? And don't give me that crap about not standing in my way so I could go to Hollywood. I want the truth."

He stood up a little straighter, reminding her how broad his shoulders were beneath the polo shirt that hugged his body like a second skin. The way he looked in his Levi's 501's was enough to distract her, too, but she refused to let her eyes wander any lower than his face.

"I could make up a lie," he finally said, "but the main reason I didn't show up at the church *was* because I wanted you to have the opportunity to do that commercial."

"And the other part?"

He sighed. "I wanted the same chance," he admitted. "I wanted to see if I had what it took to be something other than the guy who slid into a cushy management job compliments of his new father-in-law."

Mary Beth looked away. "I don't know why taking over the dealership always bothered you, Zack. You know my father loved you like his own son.''

His voice was low and soft. ''I know he did. And I felt the same about him. But a man needs to feel like a man before he can be a good husband, Mary Beth. And I wouldn't have felt much like a man.''

''Okay. I get the picture,'' Mary Beth snapped, cutting him off. She wasn't going to give him the opportunity to shift the blame to her. Make her feel it was her fault. ''Why didn't you just tell me you didn't want to take over the dealership?''

Zack sent her a stupefied look. ''But I did tell you, Mary Beth. You just didn't want to hear what I had to say.''

''Oh, really?'' she said, pushing off from the cell door. ''What are you saying, Zack, that it was all my fault? That I was a cold, horrible, callous bitch? Because I don't remember it that way. All I remember is how devastated I was to think you could turn your back on me so easily when I thought we meant so much to each other.''

She saw a spark of anger flicker in his dark green eyes. ''Aren't you being just a bit dramatic, Mary Beth? I wouldn't call turning our wedding reception into an I'm-off-to-Hollywood-to-be-an-actress party being *that* devastated.''

''And what did you want me to do when you didn't show up for our wedding, Zack? Slit my wrists with our wedding cake knife? Run screaming from the church and throw myself into the oncoming traffic?''

''See, there you go with the dramatics again,''

Zack said. But his look turned serious when he added, "What I wanted you to do, Mary Beth, was take my calls and read all those letters I sent you without sending them back unopened. But when you sent me that note, I knew."

"Knew what?"

"That you were afraid if you did talk to me you'd end up staying right here in Morgan City without ever seeing what the world had to offer you."

Mary Beth flinched. She *had* enjoyed her freedom once he gave it to her. At least during those first few months. But rather than admit it, she said, "Well, at least I didn't go on our honeymoon without you."

"I didn't go on our honeymoon, Mary Beth. I traded in those tickets to Hawaii and went to Chicago instead."

"And it never crossed your mind that you could have flown out to Hollywood to be with me?"

"Why would I do that?" Zack demanded. "You threatened to have me arrested right here in Morgan City if I kept trying to contact you."

After a long silence, Zack said, "Now you tell me the truth, Mary Beth. If I *had* come to Hollywood. Would you have agreed to see me?"

Mary Beth hesitated. "Probably not," she admitted finally. "I was too angry with you then."

Leaning back against the bars again, Mary Beth looked him straight in the eye. "But why now, Zack? Why after six years have you suddenly decided we need to call a truce?"

His smile was genuine. "Because our quest is over, Mary Beth. We both made it. We got out of

Morgan City and we've both been very successful. But now we're old enough to step back and take a long look around us and decide what's really important in life.''

''And your definition would be?''

''The same thing it's always been. A home. A family...'' His voice trailed off and he stood there, looking at her.

''And I hope you have that one day, Zack,'' Mary Beth said, willing herself not to cry. ''I hope I will, too. But just in case you think a truce means anything other than a truce, I'm telling you right now it's too late for you and me.''

''You'll never make me believe that, Mary Beth.''

Dear God! Her mother been right about Zack wanting her back. Was he really crazy enough to think she'd take him back? *Am I crazy enough to even consider taking him back?* Mary Beth's chin jutted forward. ''Well, you'd better believe it, Zack, because that's just the way it is!''

Oh, God. Not a zinger! Zack knew she could never hold out when he kissed her like this. He'd perfected the zinger by the time they were sixteen. She'd been defenseless against it then, and heaven help her, she was defenseless against it now. It was a roller coaster type of kiss that had her heart zipping, her mind tripping, and it would have had her hands gripping the back of his head had he not finally taken pity on her and let her go.

His eyes searched her face for a moment. ''Tell me you don't still feel what I feel.''

Mary Beth looked away. "A part of me will always care about you, Zack, but…"

"Then that's the part I'll never give up on," Zack said, pulling her to him again for another for a long, deep kiss.

If Zack hadn't been the absolute best kisser on the planet, Mary Beth might have found the strength to push him away. But he *was* the best kisser on the planet as far as she was concerned. And without the ability to reason at the moment, Mary Beth simply gave in and kissed Zack back.

And then she kissed him again.

And again.

"Don't tell me there isn't any magic left between us," Zack whispered.

Mary Beth didn't try. Because being kissed by Zack Callahan had always seemed like magic to her. And so she simply enjoyed the magic until the door at the other end of the hall suddenly clanged open and broke them apart.

They weren't quick enough. Sheriff Wilson walked up to the cell with his shiny brass key ring in his hand and a knowing smile on his face. "Well, well. Looks like my jailbirds have turned into love-birds again."

Mary Beth reached up trying to smooth her defunct French twist back into place and sent the sheriff a look that should have inflicted pain.

He only smiled. "And lucky for you, Miss Hollywood, that your sister isn't as angry as your mother is. She's waiting for you outside. You're free to go."

"But what about me?" Zack protested. After their heavy petting session, Mary Beth was too confused to look back when she darted from the cell.

"The jury's still out on you, Callahan," Sheriff Wilson said slamming the door in Zack's face with a clang.

"You can't just leave me here, Mary Beth," Zack yelled from behind her.

"Sure I can," Mary Beth called back over her shoulder. "Just like you left me six years ago."

"Do yourself a favor, Callahan," Mary Beth heard Sheriff Wilson say. "Forget about Miss Wild and Free and get yourself a sweet hometown girl."

"Mary Beth *is* a sweet hometown girl," Zack insisted, his voice rising loud enough for her to hear. "She just has a temporary case of amnesia at the moment."

Mary Beth shoved open the door at the end of the hallway, but caught the sheriff's reply before it shut behind her. "Amnesia," the sheriff said with a laugh. "I could have sworn my wife told me your girlfriend was supposed to be in a coma."

ZACK FLIPPED THE CRYSTAL on his watch several times with his finger, convinced his watch wasn't working since the minutes were passing as slow as stalagmites forming in an underground cave. It had been hours since Mary Beth had made her way to freedom, yet here he sat, thinking up several ways to torture his cousin when Greg finally showed up to spring him from the slammer.

And it didn't even matter that he had the money

in his pocket to pay his imaginary bail. Zack knew Sheriff Wilson would keep him right where he sat until a member of his family went through the formality of actually showing up at the jail.

Still shaken up over the way Mary Beth had kissed him back, Zack was afraid to even hope she might be willing to leave the past in the past where it belonged and give them both a chance to start over. Sure, he'd hurt her, but did she really think she hadn't hurt him just as deeply?

Stretching out on the cot with his arms behind his head, Zack stared at the ceiling, remembering what a basket case he'd been during those months when Mary Beth refused to see him. He'd poured his heart out in long, soulful letters. Letters she'd returned unopened, letters that would have told her if she'd read them how much he loved her and that postponing their wedding didn't mean he didn't want marry her. The letters would have told her he only wanted a chance to find a career that would allow him to take care of her the way a husband should take care of his wife.

He wondered, as he had a million other times, how their lives would have turned out if they had gotten married. Would they still be together now? Would he have had the fortitude to sit behind a desk at her father's car lot, with George Morgan looking over his shoulder every second? George might have loved him like a son, but it still would have been George's business Zack would have been trying to run. Could he let go of his own business? Let someone else run it without carefully critiquing every move they made?

Not a chance.

No, he'd done the right thing by not going through with the wedding, he was sure of it. What he didn't know, was whether or not he could ever convince Mary Beth that now he could give her that life she'd started planning for them when they were ten years old.

Zack lost his train of thought when the door at the end of the hall opened and Greg strolled up to his cell.

Twirling the sheriff's brass key ring around on his finger as if he hadn't left Zack sitting behind bars most of the day, Greg had the nerve to ask, "Are you ready to get out of here?"

"No, Greg," Zack said through clenched teeth. "I've ordered a pizza and invited some friends over to watch the Braves beat the Cubs tonight."

"Suit yourself," Greg said with a shrug, and started back down the hall.

Zack yelled, "Unless you want to end up in traction, you'd better let me out of here, Greg."

Greg walked back to the cell where Zack was now holding on to the bars so tightly he thought he felt them give under the strain. "Mom said you had to promise you wouldn't pull any more dumb stunts before I set you free."

"No more dumb stunts," Zack agreed, mentally willing Greg to step closer so he could get his hands on that key ring.

"And in case you're thinking about heading over

to the Morgan house, Mom said you've embarrassed yourself *and* our family enough for one day.''

"I had no intention of going over to the Morgan house," Zack growled.

"And Mom said one of your partners called earlier today and said he needed you back in Chicago, pronto. Something about a big new account you've been working on for months."

It was all Zack could do to keep from shaking the bars like a crazed gorilla, but he let go of the bars and pointed to the lock instead. "Then get me out of here, Greg. Now."

"Say please," Greg taunted with a grin.

"Please," Zack forced himself to say.

Greg obviously saw the menacing look in Zack's eye because instead of opening the cell door himself, Greg shoved the key ring through the bars and sprinted for the door like the coward he needed to be.

5

STRETCHED OUT ON THE BED in Maddie's upstairs guest room, Mary Beth smiled when she saw that Arnold Purdy's front page column had been devoted to the threat of a new landfill at the lower end of the county. In fact, all of his daily columns over the past few days had been totally civic-minded. Going straight to the heart of the matter, as her horoscope instructed, had been good advice.

Remembering her daily horoscope, Mary Beth turned to the proper section and read: *Reward yourself with a night on the town. All work and no play makes for a dull Libran. Give yourself a chance to sparkle outside the work place.*

Tossing the paper aside, Mary Beth turned over on her back, trying to convince herself she was relieved Zack had gone back to Chicago. At least, that meant she wouldn't have to deal with him at the reunion tonight.

His leaving had also meant she hadn't had to face him again after her disastrous lapse in judgment, kissing him like there was no tomorrow in the jail cell last Sunday. She had been stupid to allow that to happen. Stupid for her, because she couldn't allow herself to fall back under Zack's spell, and stupid for him because she didn't want to encourage his insane notion that they could ever get back together again. But it did bother her. Just a tiny bit. That Zack had given up so easily.

"I still can't believe Zack gave up so easily," Maddie said when she wandered into the bedroom.

Mary Beth rolled over on her side and propped her head in her hand, always amazed when her twin read her mind. "Well, I can. I told you. We talked it out and I made sure he understood I had no intention of picking things up where we left off."

"But you said he kissed you. You even said you kissed him back," Maddie argued.

"And I didn't feel a thing," Mary Beth lied.

"Still..."

"Will you please leave it alone, Maddie?" Mary Beth sat up in the middle of the bed. "I came over here to get ready for the reunion tonight because I couldn't stand Mom grilling me exactly the way you're doing now."

Maddie placed her hands on her hips. "Well, I'm sorry, Mary Beth, but you can't blame me for wanting you back home where you belong. I want our children to grow up together. I want..."

"Zack lives in Chicago, Maddie," Mary Beth cried out. "Even if I did get back with Zack we wouldn't be living here in Morgan City."

Maddie pooched out her lower lip. "Well, you'd still be closer than you are living out in L.A. I just hope you don't look back someday and regret not giving Zack a second chance, Mary Beth. Because I know you're not happy with this glamorous life you keep trying to shove down my throat. And nothing you can say will ever convince me that you are.'' Determined to have the last word, Maddie turned on her heel and marched back out of the bedroom.

"Ahhhhhh," Mary Beth groaned as she flopped backward on the bed and pulled a pillow over her face. It was bad enough her own mind had been wandering into dangerous territory, allowing herself to contemplate if she still loved Zack enough to take him back. But having her mother and her sister constantly chipping away at her self-confidence was growing old, fast.

As for being happy, how did one really measure happy? She was happy she'd finally landed a role in the hottest new soap opera on daytime television. She was happy she'd received nothing but rave reviews, even being toasted as an up-and-coming star. But would she be happy if she gave up her new career and went running back to Zack before she got her Emmy nomination?

Absolutely not!

And with that thought in mind, Mary Beth pulled herself up from the bed, determined to make herself *sparkle* for the big night that had brought her back home to Morgan City in the first place.

Her mind drifted back to Zack.

To hell with Zack, Mary Beth decided firmly. She would worry about Zack Callahan tomorrow.

MADDIE HUNG UP THE downstairs phone and looked at her sister. "I know I told you to rub everyone's nose in your success, Mary Beth, but don't you think arranging for a limousine to take you to the reunion is carrying things a bit too far?''

"Limousine? I didn't arrange for any limousine."

"No, but your agent did. I just got the call. The limo should be here to pick you up in a few minutes.''

Mary Beth brightened at the thought. "I know you don't care for JoJo, Maddie, but see what a master planner he is?"

Maddie rolled her eyes. "Oh, I know exactly what a master planner Bozo is, Mary Beth.''

"JoJo," Mary Beth corrected, sending her sister a warning look.

Maddie ignored the reprimand. "I still have nightmares over what the two of you put me through when you were scrambling around to make the most of the alien abduction story of the century. I just can't believe anyone would place their future in the hands of a grown man who has the audacity to call himself JoJo.''

Mary Beth kept her mouth shut. There was no way she was going to reopen *that* can of worms. If Maddie got started on the alien abduction fiasco she'd personally been responsible for starting, they had the potential to end up in a huge fight that would spoil the reunion for both of them.

"But I guess if your limousine is already on its way, you'll have to go on without us," Maddie said and Mary Beth frowned.

"Don't do this to me, Maddie. We were supposed to face that snarling crowd together, remember?''

"Well, I'm sorry, Mary Beth, but Brad's still getting dressed, and then we'll have to take the baby over to Mom and Pop's, and..."

"And what am I supposed to do?" Mary Beth wailed. "Hide out in a stall in the girls' rest room until you rescue me so we can make our grand entrance together?"

Just the thought of walking into her old high school gym without at least one ally at her side was enough to make her stomach roll over. Especially since Zack's lunacy had swayed public opinion in his favor; a fact that still made her blood boil.

"You could always go for an inconspicuous drive around town first," Maddie suggested with a mischievous grin.

"Inconspicuous? In a limousine?" Mary Beth laughed.

Maddie nodded. "Exactly. Strut your stuff, sister dear. Isn't that what you came home to do?"

Maddie was right. And her horoscope *did* say to sparkle. "Why, Maddie Morgan-Hawkins," Mary Beth teased. "I'm beginning to think you have a naughty side I never knew about."

"If I have a naughty side, I learned it from you," said Maddie. "Now, let me take a look at you."

Mary Beth twirled around for her twin's inspection.

"Yes, red definitely is one of our better colors," Maddie said with her finger to her chin. She looked down at her own dress. "Of course, this modest little red dress I'm wearing looks rather shabby compared to what you have on."

Mary Beth purposely struck a pose, allowing the

side split in her strapless designer gown to show practically all of one tanned, slender leg. "Well, you know what my motto has always been."

"If you've got it, make sure everyone else sees it?" Maddie teased.

Mary Beth opened her mouth for a comeback, but the sound of a vehicle pulling into Maddie's driveway sent them both hurrying to the living-room window.

"Well, I have to admit Bozo spares no expense when it comes to showing you off," said Maddie.

Mary Beth jabbed her twin with her elbow. "It's my money he's spending, silly."

They both looked back through the window at the impressive white stretch limo as the uniformed driver emerged from behind the wheel. Once the passenger side door was open, the driver snapped to attention like one of those patient guards at Buckingham Palace waiting for the arrival of the Queen.

"Your coach awaits you, Cinderella," Maddie said, then gave Mary Beth a big hug before she pushed her sister toward the door. "Brad and I will meet you at the gym at six o'clock sharp."

"Six o'clock sharp," Mary Beth repeated, then blew a kiss over her exposed shoulder before she hurried out the door and down the steps.

"Good evening," the driver said in a deep voice, then took Mary Beth's hand in order to assist her into the back seat of the limo. "You look stunning, Miss Morgan."

Mary Beth thanked him politely, but he had his cap pulled down so low over his eyes, she wondered how he could possibly see whether she really looked stunning or not. In fact, the thought crossed her mind that it would be a miracle if he could even see enough to drive. It was on the tip of her tongue to mention her concern, but the driver quickly closed the door and sealed her inside before she had time to tell him she didn't want to go directly to the gym.

Settling herself back against the plush leather seat, Mary Beth waited until the limo backed out of her sister's driveway before she pushed the intercom button. "Driver? Are you there?"

No answer.

Turning around in her seat, Mary Beth tapped on the glass window that separated them. *"Hellooooo?"* she sang out, but he ignored her completely.

When she suddenly realized the limo was going in the opposite direction from the high school gym anyway, Mary Beth reached for the intercom button again. And that's when she noticed a florist box sitting on the long bench seat to her right.

Leaning forward, Mary Beth lifted the lid slightly and peeked into the box. It was filled to capacity with daisies, her favorite flowers. *What on earth?* Mary Beth grabbed the enclosure card. *Roses are red, violets are blue. I hope you like daisies, it's the best I could do.* Tears sprang to Mary Beth's eyes as she remembered why daisies *had* always been her favorite flowers. "Damn him!" Zack had written those exact words when they were only twelve years old. Mary Beth reached out and literally pounded the intercom button with her fist. She then did the same to the window behind her head. However, instead of following her orders to stop the limo immediately, the only answer she received from the driver was to turn up the megawatt state-of-the-art stereo system. In an instant, an old song Zack used to sing to her floated through the speakers in a deafening roar.

Fly me to the moon? I'm going to knock him to the moon!

"I said stop this car immediately," Mary Beth yelled, knocking on the window again.

The limo only picked up speed.

"I don't know how Zack talked you into this, mister, but I hope you know kidnapping is a serious offense," Mary Beth called out, absolutely fuming now.

She had convinced herself Zack had given up. She'd even been relieved she wouldn't have to deal with him at the reunion tonight. Especially since everyone would probably treat her like the Wicked Witch of the West the second she stepped into the gym. But Zack hadn't given up at all. He'd come back from Chicago to personally torment her!

When the limo and the music suddenly came to a stop, Mary Beth found herself sitting in the driveway of the old antebellum mansion on Magnolia Street that had been her dream house for as long as she could remember. Zack was definitely using every trick in the book, trying to play her memories. The daisies, the poem, even the old song he knew held sentimental value for both of them. But now he had pulled the dirtiest trick of all. If anyone knew how much she had always dreamed about living in this mansion one day, it was Zack.

Double damn him! Mary Beth thought and looked out the window at the grand old lady, called Oakmont because of the towering oak trees that surrounded it. Even in its crumbling state of disrepair, the old mansion was as impressive as Scarlett O'Hara's Tara, with its huge columns and long veranda running across the front of the house.

Her eyes stopped when she saw him. Walking down the steps in a black tux with a swagger every bit as cocky as Rhett Butler, was the one man Mary Beth could no longer put off worrying about until tomorrow.

ZACK WALKED UP TO THE LIMO and tried to open the door. It really didn't surprise him that it was locked. He tapped on the tinted window. "Open the door, Mary Beth. Please."

"Go. To. Hell!"

Zack shoved his hands into his pockets and walked up to the driver's side window. When the window slid down, Zack said, "Mary Beth won't open the door."

"Imagine that," his cousin scoffed. "What did you expect?"

"I expect you to use the main control and unlock the damn door!" Zack yelled.

Greg did as he instructed, but before Zack could sprint the thirty-five feet back to the passenger door, Mary Beth had the door locked again. "Roll her window down, Greg,'' Zack called back to his cousin.

The window slid down long enough for Mary Beth to give him a scathing look before she calmly reached over and pushed the button with the tip of her polished red finger. She sent him a satisfied smile as the tinted window zipped upward and slid back into place.

''We can play this game all night, Mary Beth,'' Zack said loud enough for her to hear him. ''But then we'll both miss the reunion. I thought you would like the idea of us showing up at the gym together and finally putting an end to all the gossip about us.''

It took a second, but the tinted window slid back down. Zack managed to keep the smile from his lips. He'd been counting on the fact Mary Beth was just as irritated as he'd been about both of them being the topic of conversation over the past six years.

''Keep talking,'' she said, but she still had that I'm-one-step-away-from-scratching-your-eyes-out look on her face.

Zack shrugged. ''What more can I say? If we show up together, think how disappointed everyone will be. They won't have anything else to gossip about.''

She thought about his statement, but she didn't look convinced. ''You mean let them think we're back together?''

Zack shook his head. ''Of course, not.'' *I can only hope for that miracle.* ''Once we get there, we'll make sure everyone knows we've decided to be friends again. End of story.''

Her eyebrow raised. "End of story, Zack? You won't read us going to the reunion together into being something more than it is?''

He should have been ashamed of himself for looking her straight in the eye and telling her a bald-faced lie. But if he told her the truth, that getting her to go to the reunion with him was just the first step of the plan he'd been working on for the past two weeks, he knew he was finished. And so Zack mentally crossed his fingers. "End of story, Mary Beth. I promise.''

She reached over and unlocked the door at the same time Greg stuck his head out the car window and yelled, "Can't you two stop fighting long enough to go to the reunion like two civilized adults?''

"Shut up and drive," Zack yelled back, then slid into the seat beside the woman he loved, praying she wouldn't kill him later when he revealed the second part of his plan to win her back.

MARY BETH STOOD AT THE refreshment table in the crowded gym, looking like a regal queen holding court. Calmly sipping her punch from a plastic cup that had Class of '91 stamped across the front, she nodded appreciatively to everyone who stopped by to congratulate her on the success of her popular new soap opera.

To say she was thrilled over the way the dreaded reunion was turning out, was putting it mildly.

In fact, Mary Beth was still laughing to herself over how shocked everyone had been when she and Zack had ridden up in the limousine together. She had finally left a few mouths hanging open over something that wouldn't come back to haunt her. And those mouths had certainly dropped open, all right. Even her twin's eyes had bugged out like one of Maddie's precious specimens.

Sending a friendly wave to someone she wasn't sure she even knew, Mary Beth was certain that Zack had been right. After tonight, all of the gossip about the ill-fated Morgan-Callahan romance would finally be put to rest. Not that the gossip about her would stop completely. In small town Morgan City? Population almost too embarrassing to list in the Rand-McNally road atlas?

No, there would still be gossip about her.

But in place of her defunct wedding, Mary Beth imagined the gossip would turn more favorable when it came to her. Like the spectacular designer gown she was wearing at the reunion, maybe. Or the fact that her celebrity status hadn't seemed to change her at all. And most importantly, how she could be friends with Zack again without it causing so much as a wrinkle in her carefully arched brow.

Yes, that was the image she would be leaving with her fellow classmates tonight. A mature, confident star in the making. A woman who was exceedingly happy with the glamorous life she had made for herself in California. And a woman who was so sure of herself, she'd even had the guts to show up on the arm of the man who had left her standing at the altar six years earlier.

But in spite of herself, Mary Beth couldn't keep from sending a brief glance now and then across the crowded gym in Zack's direction. So what if she did still have mixed feelings about Zack? After all, she reasoned, he had been her first love. Her first lover. The man she had once imagined as her husband and the father of her children.

She was pretending to be totally engrossed in the heated debate two of her classmates were having about which heartthrobs on *The Wild and the Free* were hot and which ones were not, but she kept watching Zack out of the corner of her eye. He was the center of attention among the group of guys who were listening intently to something Zack was saying. Even her own brother-in-law seemed to be hanging on his every word, though it really didn't surprise her that he and Brad Hawkins would get along. They were both what people referred to as a "man's man," both self-assured and confident. The type of man, as Zack had explained to her in the jail cell, who would never have been happy taking over her father's automobile dealership.

Well, he certainly seems happy now, Mary Beth thought with a jealous tug at her heart. She quickly looked away when one of the least favorite members of her high school senior class walked up and stopped in front of her.

"Tell us the truth, Mary Beth," said Bitsy Williams, looking back over her shoulder to make sure her classmates were following. "Have you really decided to take Zack back?"

Mary Beth sent the human equivalent of a Barbie doll and cool look and laughed just loud enough to make Zack glance in her direction. "Just because I'm an actress, doesn't mean I live in a fantasy world, Bitsy. High school sweethearts getting back together at their ten-year reunion is a scenario more suited for my soap opera."

When several of the women laughed, Bitsy's smile turned lethal. "See, girls?" she said, looking back over her shoulder again. "I told you Mary Beth wouldn't risk Zack Callahan leaving her at the altar again."

Keep cool, Mary Beth told herself, though she was seething inside. Someone had finally said out loud what had been on everyone's mind for the past six years. She could act mortified like Bitsy hoped she would, or she could rise above the insult and beat the witch at her own game.

"*Some* of us have moved on with our lives after high school, Bitsy. Maybe you should try it."

"Oh, I intend to move on," Bitsy said right back. "I intend to move right on in where you left off. Maybe Zack will actually show up for a walk down the aisle with me."

It was all Mary Beth could do to keep from slapping the silly smirk off Bitsy's face. Instead she lifted her plastic punch glass in tribute. "Believe me, I'll be the first one to toast *any* woman who makes it down the aisle with Zack Callahan."

Everyone laughed, except for Bitsy.

Sally Hughes, the redhead who had asked Zack to dinner, spoke up. "Well, don't think you won't have some competition from me, Bitsy. Especially since Zack told me a few minutes ago he's back home to stay."

Zack's back home to stay? Dear God. Wait until her mother and Maddie heard that bit of news! She'd have to break all contact with her family for the rest of her life.

"I already knew that," Bitsy said, sending Sally a superior look. "Zack said with technology what it is today, he could keep his business in Chicago and make home base anywhere he wants."

Well, fine! Let him come back home. He could even choose Bitsy or Sally to be Mrs. Zack Callahan. She didn't care. *Like hell I don't!* Well, even if she did care, she *would* survive.

"Isn't he still the best-looking thing you've ever seen?" Bitsy said dreamily, causing everyone, including Mary Beth, to look in Zack's direction. "Of course, all that gorgeous money is what really turns me on," she added on a giggle. "I can't wait to get my hands on that."

Nancy Goins, who was now thicker around the middle thanks to four kids, threw her head back and laughed. "Zack Callahan wouldn't give you the time of day, Bitsy Williams. He wouldn't have anything to do with you when we were in high school, and believe me, you looked a lot better then than you look now."

You tell her, Nancy! The gold digging little witch. Bitsy's eyes narrowed, totally spoiling the effect of her color-enhanced contacts. "At least I still have a waistline," she said tossing her long platinum pigtail for effect. "Which is something *you* haven't seen in the last ten years."

"Yeah, but I can always lose the weight," Nancy said with a laugh. "Only plastic surgery can help that wrinkled-up face of yours."

Bitsy hands were now clenched at her sides and her painted mouth was turned up in a feral snarl. "This wrinkled face still looks good enough to turn a few heads in this town, Nancy, and I think you and everyone else know exactly who I mean."

The conversation was turning ugly, fast. And here she was, trapped between them. Mary Beth quickly scanned the crowd for Maddie. When she finally found her twin talking to their high school principal, she decided to politely excuse herself and make a run for it.

Mary Beth stepped forward, but Nancy reached across her and gave Bitsy a little shove. "Ladies, please," Mary Beth began. "There's no reason...."

"Put a sock in it, Mary Beth," Nancy said and reached across her to push Bitsy a little harder. "And don't piss me off by calling this two-bit floozy a lady. She's been hanging around my husband's garage so much lately she could have bought a new car with all the money she's spent having her mysterious knocks and clangs fixed."

Mary Beth backed up against the table as far as possible, and when she did, Bitsy reached across her and pushed Nancy back. "I haven't heard David complaining about me hanging around his garage,"

Bitsy snarled. "Maybe my knocks and clangs are a lot more interesting than yours."

Still trapped between them, Mary Beth had nowhere to run and no time to brace herself for what was coming. Nancy made a lunge for Bitsy and pushed Mary Beth backward onto the long refreshment table behind them. The table collapsed with a bang under the weight of three kicking, screaming women who instantly became tangled in a human knot when the argument turned into a full-blown catfight.

Lying there, flat on her back, Mary Beth decided the only thing worse than getting drenched in sticky punch was having two crazed women on top of her in a hair-pulling frenzy.

"Get off me!" Mary Beth yelled when Nancy held up a platinum trophy to the shocked crowd that was hurrying to the rescue.

"That's my hairpiece, you cow!" Bitsy screamed in horror, but a victorious Nancy waved the hairpiece triumphantly over her head several times before she sent the platinum missile sailing across the gym.

Bitsy scrambled after her fake Barbie-style pigtail on her hands and knees, and Mary Beth made her move. She pushed Nancy off her stomach, who was now laughing so hard tears were rolling down her freshly scratched cheeks. Mary Beth then scooted backward with ease thanks to the puddle of slick chip dip she had landed in.

The first thing she did when she pulled herself into a sitting position was jerk the designer dress that had hiked up to her waist back down over her knees. She was still trying to disengage a huge piece of broccoli from her tangled hair when the band came to life at the front of the gym and the lead singer broke out with: Let's Give Them Something to Talk About.

If ever there had been a more appropriate song than the Top Ten hit that had been popular during her high school senior year, Mary Beth couldn't imagine what it would be.

"Oh, my God! You're bleeding," gasped a worried Maddie who suddenly appeared above her.

Mary Beth looked down at her cleavage and used the tip of her finger to taste the red substance. "Salsa," she told her sister, then reached up to wipe a slimy green smear from her forehead. "And don't worry, Maddie. This isn't brain matter, I think it's guacamole."

When she noticed the accusing scowl on her brother-in-law's face, Mary Beth added, "And no, Brad. I didn't start the fight."

Not that Brad was likely to believe her. His smug smile even told her that he didn't. But could she really blame him for being a bit skeptical about her denial? Her dear brother-in-law had been involved in a fight she *had* instigated on the very first day she met him.

But he could at least offer to help her up.

And it was on the tip of Mary Beth's tongue to tell him so, when a strong pair of hands from behind her slid beneath her armpits and helped her to her feet.

Mary Beth turned around and found Zack grinning from ear to ear as he looked her up and down. "First ice cream. Now this?" he teased. "Is there some new Hollywood craze we should know about?"

"Don't start with me, Zack," Mary Beth said at the same time Bitsy stomped past her and screamed in her direction, "This is all your fault, Mary Beth Morgan."

Zack looked at Maddie. Maddie looked at Brad. And Mary Beth frowned. "I'm telling you, I didn't start that fight!"

"Well, you're going to start a riot if you're not careful," Zack spoke up and Mary Beth followed his gaze to the slit in her dress that now extended almost to her armpit. "Here," Zack said, taking off his tux jacket. "Cover yourself up before Arnold Purdy has a heart attack."

For the first time, Mary Beth noticed the zoom lens pointed in her direction. She tried to hold the ripped fabric together with one hand while she waved away Zack's offer with the other. "I'm covered in slime, Zack. There's no way I'm going to ruin your jacket."

Zack ignored her. He had just draped the jacket of his tux around her sticky shoulders when Nancy's husband marched across the gym floor. The pained look on his face suggested he was having more than just a Maalox moment.

"Thanks a lot, Mary Beth," he sneered when he stopped in front of her. "Nancy's threatening to divorce me now. I hope you can sleep at night knowing four little kids will grow up without their father thanks to you.''

When Nancy's husband turned on his heel and marched out of the gym. Mary Beth wailed, "How many times do I have to say it? I didn't start the fight!'' And when Nerdy Purdy moved in a little closer with his Nikon, Mary Beth threw her hands up in the air. "I'm out of here.''

Heading for the same door the man with the fatherless children marched through, it was Zack who fell in beside her as she started down the hallway to the front exit doors of the gym. "Go away, Zack.''

Zack shook his head. "Sorry, Mary Beth. I was taught a lady's escort always made sure she arrived safely home.''

Now he's concerned about proper etiquette, Mary Beth fumed, wondering how Zack missed the chapter about never leaving a bride at the altar. "Aren't you supposed to give a speech or something?''

Zack laughed. "Are you kidding? That bunch isn't going to listen to a speech now. They'll be too busy laughing themselves silly over Bitsy's hairpiece flying through the air.''

Mary Beth paused long enough for Zack to open the exit door, then stepped out into the peaceful summer night air and took a cleansing breath to calm herself.

"What really did happen back there?'' Zack asked when they started down the steps.

"Bitsy has evidently been paying too much attention to Nancy's husband. I just happened to be standing between them when they decided to kill each other.''

"Hey, don't look so glum," Zack said, sending her a grin. "Nancy and Bitsy are going to be the main topic of conversation in Morgan City now. I think we're finally off the hook."

You jumped off the hook six years ago.

Sheesh!

She was doing it again.

Why couldn't she stop this senseless whining that was going on inside her head every time Zack opened his mouth? Should she finally go ahead and punch Zack in the nose the way she'd been wanting to do for the past six years and get it over with?

Mary Beth headed straight for the limo, reminding herself she really shouldn't take her frustration out on Zack. Not this time. He had done his best to put an *end* to the gossip about her. It wasn't his fault she had literally mooned her high school senior class. What could be more humiliating than that?

Being left at the altar, maybe?

When they reached the limo, Greg, who was sitting on the hood of the limo looking as bored as he probably was, took one look at her and said, "What happened to you? You look like a human tossed salad."

Mary Beth didn't even bother sending Greg an exasperated look. "Just take me to my parents' house, Greg," she told him. "I'm sure you're just as eager as I am for this night to be over."

It was Zack who stepped forward and opened the back passenger door of the limo. And when he did,

Mary Beth practically dove into the back seat. She thought she caught Zack giving his partner in crime a meaningful nod before he climbed into the seat beside her and closed the limo's passenger door. But she was just too fed up to care.

ZACK GROANED INWARDLY AS Greg pulled away from the curb, thinking how carefully he'd planned for this night. He'd planned to give Mary Beth her space when they first arrived at the gym, then eventually coerce her onto the dance floor and hold her in his arms while they danced to the same music they'd danced to when they had been so much in love.

He'd even carefully chosen all the memories he wanted to bring up to remind her of the special times they'd shared together. Like the time they'd sneaked up to her parents' cabin for the weekend and spent most of their time in that big feather bed. They had been so close then, so sure nothing could ever make them stop loving each other.

But now after that ruckus in the gym? He stole a sideways glance in her direction, saddened to see that the human tossed salad had anything *but* the melancholy look he'd hoped to put on her beautiful face.

But she was beautiful, even covered in slime.

Deciding he needed to make the most of what little time he had left, Zack leaned in her direction and said, "I'm so terribly sorry this night was ruined for you, my poor darling. I had so wanted it to be such a special night. A night you would remember with fondness for the rest of your days. A night you would possibly look back on as one of the most memorable nights of your life. A night…"

She cut her keen blue eyes in his direction. "Why are you talking like that?"

"Like what? I'm not talking like anything." Zack leaned forward and opened the wet bar. Picking up the bar towel, he unscrewed the top of a container of bottled water and thoroughly wet the towel.

"Yes, you are. You're talking in your phony Cary Grant voice." She took the towel without question when he handed it over. After wiping the slime from her forehead, she removed his jacket from around her shoulders and did a pretty good job of toweling herself off. Zack forced his eyes from her cleavage and back to her face when she said, "Not only did you just refer to me as 'you poor darling,' but you're using those proper British phrases. 'Remember with fondness for the rest of my days?' 'Possibly one of the most memorable nights of my life?' I know classic Cary Grant when I hear it, Zack, and you *were* talking in your phony Cary Grant voice!"

"Was I, darling?"

"See, you're doing it again! Now what's going on? The only time you ever talk to me in your phony Cary Grant voice is when you know I'm going to be upset about something you've done."

"You must be mistaken, my dear."

She reached out and actually pinched him on the arm. "I mean it, Zack. What have you done?"

Zack stalled for a moment, but he was saved from giving her a direct answer when the limo came to a slow stop only a few blocks away from the gym. Reaching out, he took her hand and brought it to his lips for a soft kiss, Cary Grant style. But he did drop the phony accent. "I haven't done anything wrong, Mary Beth. I have something I want to show you before I take you home."

IT WASN'T UNTIL ZACK opened the door and got out of the limo that Mary Beth realized where they were. "We've already had this walk down memory lane once today, Zack. And once is enough for me."

He extended his hand in her direction. "Humor me. Please. This won't take but a minute."

Common sense told her she should insist that he take her home, but in a way Oakmont had always been her home. In her dreams, at least. She couldn't explain why she'd always been so drawn to the old mansion, but she had. Even now, she could close her eyes and picture every one of its twenty-four rooms. There was a grand foyer with its sweeping staircase that always took her breath away. The parlor sat to the right and the library to the left. There was a dining room, a music room, even a ballroom that had double French doors leading out to the garden, and a kitchen at the back of the house that was so huge her Malibu beach house could fit inside that room alone. On the second floor were six bedrooms, all with fireplaces and each with a separate sitting room. Four of those bedrooms had private baths.

"Mary Beth?"

She didn't resist when Zack took her hand and helped her from the limo. She didn't even resist when he held onto her hand and began leading her along the old cobblestone path that led to the garden out back. She stopped dead still, however, when she rounded the side of the house and saw the gazebo they had played in as children twinkling in the distance.

It was still overgrown with the ancient rosebushes that had entwined themselves through the gingerbread lattice, but hundreds of tiny white lights covered every inch of it, turning it into a setting taken straight from a fairy tale.

Before Mary Beth could say a word, Zack gently pushed her forward. And when they reached the gazebo, Zack guided her up the steps and made her take a seat at a small table for two covered in a white tablecloth. In the center of the table sat an ice bucket holding a chilled bottle of champagne. Next to the ice bucket was a vase containing a single red rose. Mary Beth fought back the tears when Zack took the rose from the vase and handed it to her.

"I can do much better than daisies now, Mary Beth," he began, but Mary Beth cut him off.

"Zack, don't." She started to stand up but Zack said, "This is what I wanted to show you." He picked up an envelope from the table, opened it and handed her a piece of paper.

Mary Beth's mouth dropped open when she realized she was holding the deed to Oakmont. *How dare he buy Oakmont!* He knew how much this place had always meant to her. Maybe she didn't have the money to buy it herself. Maybe she never would. But Oakmont was meant to be hers!

"I'm going to restore Oakmont completely," he said as he popped the top on the champagne bottle. "I've already met with an architect and a contractor. It'll be a long process, but they've assured me they can make the first floor livable while the renovations are being done."

He's going to live here?

Mary Beth placed the deed back on the table, still in a daze. Zack filled two champagne glassed and handed one to her. She accepted it woodenly, seething because she couldn't bear the thought of Bitsy or Sally or any other woman living at Oakmont but her.

"To childhood dreams," he said, clinking his glass against the one she held stiffly in her hand.

"Oakmont was *my* childhood dream, Zack," Mary Beth couldn't stop herself from saying.

He sent her a bewildered look. "And that's why I bought Oakmont, Mary Beth. For you. For us."

Us? The word kept bouncing around inside Mary Beth's head until it finally landed in the common sense section. She jumped up from the table. "There isn't any *us*, Zack! *Us* ceased to exist the day you left me standing at the altar."

She pushed past him, hurried down the steps of the gazebo and began stomping across the yard with such force the six-inch heels of her bright red pumps immediately sank in the dew-covered earth. She stepped out of her shoes, and was still trying to dislodge her buried heels from the ground when Zack caught up and stood towering above her with his hands at his waist.

"Do you mind telling me what I said that was so wrong?"

Mary Beth finally pulled one of her heels free with a pop, and when she pulled the other shoe free, she stood up and faced him. "Read my lips, Zack. There is no *us*."

"Maybe there isn't an *us* at the moment, Mary Beth," he argued. "But there could be an us again if you'd give me a second chance."

She pointed at him with one of her shoes, brandishing it like a sword. "I've been trying to tell you for days, Zack, you're wasting your time. I'm sorry if you didn't find what you were looking for over the past six years, but I did. And unlike you, I'm not ready to give up the life I have now and move back home to Morgan City."

She started walking again, but Zack jogged past her and stopped in front of her, blocking her path. "I know you still have feelings for me, Mary Beth. You couldn't have kissed me the way you did at the jail if you didn't still care."

"I had a weak moment. Sue me!" was Mary Beth's only reply as she pushed Zack aside and continued making her way back to the limo. A limo she found missing when she finally reached the driveway.

She whirled back around. "You arrogant ass! You really thought this was going to work, didn't you?"

Zack stopped dead in his tracks.

"You thought all you had to do was string a few lights around the gazebo and wave the deed to Oakmont under my nose and I'd fall at your feet!"

He frowned. "There you go with your dramatics again."

"Dramatics? I'll show you dramatics!" Mary Beth drew her arm back and a bright red shoe came sailing through the air.

Zack ducked.

The second shoe was more accurate.

Marching down the driveway in her bare feet, trying to keep her torn dress and broken heart together, Mary Beth left Zack with the bloody nose she'd been wanting to give him for the past six years.

6

MARY BETH MANAGED TO GET one eye open long enough to realize the irritating noise that had awakened her was a bark. She vaguely remembered letting her dog out, but she had been so exhausted she had stumbled back to bed.

She had left Morgan City shortly after she left Zack at Oakmont on Friday night, and had barely made it to Atlanta in time to catch the red-eye back to L.A. Still, it had been late Saturday afternoon before she made it home to Malibu. She'd stopped at the kennel, dropped off her dry cleaning and made a quick grocery store trip, planning to spend the entire day in bed on Sunday so she would be rested enough to make it back on the set bright and early Monday morning.

Now, it seemed her golden retriever had other ideas about how she was going to spend her Sunday.

Pulling herself up, Mary Beth grabbed a robe from the end of her bed and glanced at the mirror on the back of her bedroom door. At least she wouldn't have to spend much time in makeup tomorrow. She really *did* look like she'd been in a coma after spending two weeks at home with Zack tormenting her every time she turned around.

Thankfully the Zack nightmare was over now. And the more distance she kept between them, the better. Maybe she did still love him. Maybe she always would. But love had nothing to do with the situation. They had chosen separate paths. They had gone their separate ways. They wanted different things out of life now.

End of story.

She headed for the sliding glass door off the kitchen, yawning as she went, and when she pulled the door open wide enough to poke her head outside the first thing she saw was Zack, standing in her yard despite the big golden retriever that was barking out a warning that he really wasn't welcome.

Her brain sent a curse word to her lips, but her heart turned a triple backflip and shouted for joy.

Wearing cutoffs, a Hawaiian-style shirt and a pair of thong sandals, he looked like the quintessential beach boy with his sun-streaked hair blowing back from his face in the soft ocean breeze. At that moment, the handle Mary Beth *thought* she had on life instantly cracked and broke.

Damn him!

She never thought he would follow her back to California. She didn't need him showing up everywhere she looked and keeping her so confused she didn't know which end was up. Flowers, poems, limos, mansions! And now a mad dash across the country to follow her home?

When was he going to give up?

"I'm not giving up as easily as I did last time, Mary Beth," he said, answering that question before she could ask it. He sent another nervous look at her dog.

It would have served him right if she stood by and allowed him to be mauled by those bared canine teeth that were keeping him at bay. But she didn't. Instead, she let out a deep sigh and called the dog's name.

"Diogee?" Zack repeated with a grin when the retriever stopped barking and obediently sat down. "How did you come up with a name like that?"

Mary Beth rolled her eyes. "D-O-G? It isn't that hard to figure out, Zack."

"Come here, boy," Zack said, crouching down and holding his hand out.

Mary Beth frowned when the attack dog she'd purchased for protection rolled over on his back, eager for Zack to give him a belly rub.

Et tu, Diogee? Mary Beth thought and stepped out on the deck. She was too irritated to care that she looked so ghastly Zack would probably run from her yard screaming in horror. She sent a disappointed look at her traitorous pet before she said, "What are you doing here, Zack? I certainly didn't invite you."

Zack stood up and smiled at her, irritating Mary Beth even more. If Zack could ignore the way she looked now, it had to be love.

"In a way, you did invite me." Mary Beth was on the verge of calling him a liar when Zack held up the canvas bag he was holding. "How could I pitch a tent in your front yard if I didn't come to Malibu?"

The tent! She'd forgotten joking that Zack could pitch a tent in her yard and she still wouldn't change her mind. When he dumped the bag on the ground, Mary Beth said, "I want you off my property, Zack. Now."

He stared her down. "And I want you *on* the property I bought for us back home, Mary Beth. So, I guess that makes us even."

"We have stalking laws here in California, Zack. Did you think about that?"

Zack rubbed his hand over his chin. "Yeah, I took that into consideration. But I'm really not a stalker, Mary Beth. I'm more of a..." He paused for a second. "I guess I'm really a *sulker.* Because I plan to sit right here and sulk. At least until you admit you do still have feelings for me."

"Then you'll be sitting in your tent until hell freezes over," Mary Beth vowed.

"Isn't that what the Eagles said about getting back together again?" Zack asked with a smirk.

Exasperated, Mary Beth stamped her bare foot. "Well, you're crazy if you think you're going to get any help from me while you're living in a tent like some contestant on *Survivor.* You'll have no kitchen privileges," she said, holding up finger number one.

"Fast food's always been my favorite," Zack said with a smile.

"There'll be no bathroom privileges," Mary Beth said, feeling rather triumphant as she held up finger number two.

"I've already found a campground right down the road. For twenty-five bucks a week they're more than happy to let me have all the bathroom, shower and laundry privileges I need.''

Holding up finger number three, she said, ''And if you think being here means the two of us will be hanging out together, reminiscing about old times, you're wrong. I have no intention of spending any time with you whatsoever.''

''But a friendly wave from your deck now and then wouldn't be too much to ask, would it?''

Finger number four turned back into finger number two, in a gesture her mother would have scolded her for making. ''Then knock yourself out, Zack. I'm simply too exhausted to argue with you any further. Sit out here in your tent! See if I care.''

''Is it okay if your dog hangs out with me?'' Zack called out when Mary Beth stormed back into the house.

''SHE'S ACTUALLY TAKING this better than I thought,'' Zack told his new buddy as Diogee trotted along beside him when he went back to his rental car to get the rest of his gear.

Had he thought for one minute that Mary Beth really did see him as a stalker, however, Zack would have packed up his tent and slipped quietly away into the night. Or into the day, as the case was at the moment.

But he knew better.

He hadn't missed the look on Mary Beth's face when she first saw him standing in her yard. That delighted ''it's you'' look of recognition that briefly passed between them. Zack would take a fleeting look like that one any day of the week. Fleeting meant hope. And hope was all he had to go on at the moment.

"We've just got to show her I'm not going to give up without a fight," Zack told Diogee as he dumped the rest of his things on the ground next to the tent. "I let her shut me out six years ago, and I've always regretted it." He looked down at the dog. Diogee wagged his tail happily. "This time, I'm not letting her off that easy. She's going to have to look me in the eye and tell me she doesn't want me in her life."

And that's why he'd followed her home.

He wasn't going to let her skirt around the issue like she did last time by refusing to see or talk to him. He wasn't accepting any curt little note, either. If he left without her, it would be because she looked him in the eye and said the words, "I don't love you."

It would kill him, granted.

But hearing those words come from her own sweet lips is what it would take to get rid of him this time.

However, after taking another long look at his surroundings, Zack wondered if he really did have the fortitude it would take to live outdoors in a tent. It certainly wouldn't be a pleasant experience, nor did he have any idea how long he would have to stay until she stopped avoiding the issue and sat down and talked to him. A day? A week? Longer?

"Well, I guess you couldn't ask for a prettier place to pitch a tent," Zack said, staring out at the ocean and the sandy beach below. "Let's go check out the beach."

Diogee barked and followed after Zack when he started down the worn path that led to the ocean. Zack half expected Mary Beth to storm out on the porch and call for her dog. He knew her well enough to know she was watching from her window.

Surprisingly they made it all the way to the beach. Zack picked up a piece of driftwood and tossed it into the ocean. Eager to please his new friend, Diogee sprang forward. The retriever returned with the stick a few seconds later and dropped it at his feet. Zack laughed when Diogee barked and shook salt water and sand all over him.

"Good boy," Zack said, ruffling the fur on the big dog's ears.

But as the dog loped off again, snapping at the water that was rushing into shore, Zack couldn't help but wonder if the success his new sidekick was having catching the white foamy waves had any correlation to the success he was going to have at winning back Mary Beth's heart.

MARY BETH STOOD AT THE kitchen window, watching while Zack played with Diogee on the beach below. She laughed in spite of herself when Zack stumbled and fell and Diogee pounced on him faster than a New York minute.

"I guess Zack will be making that trip down to the campground for a shower sooner than he expected," Mary Beth said aloud. She laughed again when Diogee reared up on his hind legs and knocked Zack back down.

When Zack stood up, took his shirt off and tied it around his waist, however, Mary Beth stopped laughing. *Heaven help me.* He'd always had a perfect athlete's body, but the chest she was staring at now was broader and more defined, and his washboard stomach was glistening in the sunlight as the droplets of water clung to his tanned skin.

Chewing on her bottom lip, Mary Beth's hand found its way to her throat, touching the place where Zack used to drive her crazy when he did that amazing little thing with his tongue. Not that her neck was the only place Zack knew how to stimulate to madness. There weren't *any* places on her body that didn't make her purr like a kitten when Zack touched them.

"And he knows it, too," Mary Beth grumbled aloud, becoming more flustered than ever thinking of him sleeping in a tent right outside her front door.

Zack's latest attack on her sanity was the last thing she needed, especially when she was due back on the set bright and early in the morning. She really didn't know how much more she could take. It had been so easy to keep him pushed to the back of her mind, when she never had to see him. Out of sight, out of mind, had held more truth than she realized.

But now he was here.

In her face.

And forcing her to deal with feelings she didn't want to deal with.

I have to get him out of here, Mary Beth decided.

Maybe if she talked to him, told him how determined she was to win an Emmy nomination, he might understand that even if she did still love him, she would always feel like a failure if she didn't achieve her goal.

Yeah, right. She could just imagine him getting a big laugh out of that conversation. She'd only been playing the role of Fancy Kildare for a little over a year. There were actors and actresses who had been in the business for ages without being nominated for an Emmy, much less winning one. He was sure to bring that up. Did the name Susan Lucci ring a bell?

Well, pipedream or not, an Emmy nomination *was* her dream. And not even Zack was going to stand in the way of making that dream a reality.

Mary Beth jumped back from the window when Zack started back toward the house, knocking the mail stacked up on the kitchen bar onto the floor in the process. She stooped down to clean the clutter up and noticed that her new *Cosmo* had opened to the horoscope section, one of the main reasons she subscribed to the magazine. Sitting down on the floor in a cross-legged position, Mary Beth read: *Ruled by lovely Venus, romance is definitely in the air for Libra on August 25. Give your heart free rein and pleasure will be your reward. Denying yourself will lead to regret. Regrets make poor bedfellows.*

Mary Beth threw the magazine across the room.

Venus was up to her old tricks again.

It was Sunday, August 25.

INSTEAD OF SPENDING SUNDAY in bed as she'd planned, Mary Beth took her frustration out on her house. She cleaned the place from top to bottom, amazed at the energy a woman can find when she's angry with a man.

She even had a pan of homemade lasagna simmering away in her oven. Zack's favorite. To torture him, she'd opened the side window in her living room/kitchen combination. He'd chosen a flat space directly below the window to pitch his stupid tent. She hoped the enticing smell wafting from her kitchen would make him choke on the fast food he claimed was his favorite.

By eight-thirty that evening, she'd taken a long shower, washed her hair and dressed in a slinky pair of purple lounging pajamas. She was going to eat her lasagna, curl up on the sofa, watch *Sex and the City,* and then go to bed. She wasn't going to worry about her horoscope, or the fact that today was August 25. And instead of romance, the only thing she intended to be *in the air* was the delicious aroma of her lasagna.

She had just served herself up a piping hot square of Zack's favorite, grabbed the remote and switched on the TV when the power went out.

Crap! Mary Beth thought as stood there in the dark. The power outages in California were beginning to be a real nuisance. And there was never any way to gauge how long the power would be off. She felt along the kitchen cabinet and found the drawer with the matches and candles that had been a necessity most of the summer. She pulled the first of the glass holders out of the drawer, lit the votive candle it contained and sat it on the bar. She placed several other candles strategically around the room, frowning because she knew if Zack realized her power was off he had to be laughing to himself.

Now they would both be spending the evening sitting in the dark!

With the last candle in hand, Mary Beth walked to the side window, pushed back the curtain and peeked out the window, trying to determine exactly where Zack was at the moment. A sudden gust of wind from the ocean billowed the curtain upward, and when the sheer fabric floated back downward it landed right on the flame from her candle.

Mary Beth screamed and dropped the candle when the fabric whooshed into a ball of fire.

She was running to the sink for a pan of water when Zack burst into the house from the deck, grabbed a throw blanket from the back of her sofa and beat the flames out with the force of a man possessed. Diogee was right behind him, barking with every blow Zack made to the curtain.

When the flames were out, they stood there looking at each other, both trembling. Each of them knew exactly what had scared Zack so badly. Zack had survived the fire that swept through his childhood home in the middle of the night only because his father had found him and taken him outside to safety. His father hadn't been that fortunate when he went back inside for Zack's mother.

"Dammit, Mary Beth, you shouldn't be so careless." Still visibly shaken, he walked over to the sofa and sat down with his elbows propped on his knees and his head buried in his hands. Diogee sat down at Zack's side and nudged his big nose under Zack's arm.

Ashamed of herself for scaring him so badly, all Mary Beth could think to say was, "Do you want some lasagna?"

He let out a deep sigh and ran a trembling hand through his hair. Without looking at her, he said, "I thought you said we weren't going to be hanging out together."

Ignoring his comment, it took a few minutes to place everything they needed on a tray. She walked back to the coffee table in front of the sofa where Zack was still sitting, placed the tray on the table and handed him a glass of wine.

"I think we both could use this right now," she said, picking up her own glass. They both took a long sip.

When she found the courage to look at him again, Mary Beth couldn't stop herself from thinking that the man sitting on her sofa had always been such a big part of her life. She knew his deepest fears and secrets, just as he knew hers. Except one. And deciding if she finally told Zack why she wasn't ready to leave Hollywood that he might go back home, Mary Beth said, "Go home, Zack. I'm not trying to hurt you. I'm even glad we've ended our silly feud. You were always..." She paused. "You were always my best friend. I've missed that."

He looked at her for a moment, then patted the place beside him. When Mary Beth sat down, he said, "I'm still your best friend, Mary Beth. And as much as it would kill me, if you tell me you don't still love me, I will leave and go back home."

Why did he have to make it so hard! She tried to say the words. She couldn't. "Love doesn't have anything to do with it, Zack. Like you told me six years ago, our timing's just off right now."

He sent her a guarded look.

"And I'm not just saying that to pay you back in some twisted way."

He reached down and rubbed Diogee's head when the dog placed its head on his knee. "Then tell me why you think our timing's off, Mary Beth, because I think our timing's perfect. We're older. We've both been successful. I know you've never been seriously involved with anyone else, and you know the same thing about me. Our families have made sure of that." He paused. "And I love you. I've never stopped loving you. And you'll never convince me you don't feel the same way about me."

Mary Beth took a deep breath. "I wish love was enough, Zack, but it isn't. Not right now. I haven't finished what I came to Hollywood to do."

He reached out and took her hand. "Why are you being so evasive? You know you can tell me anything."

"I want an Emmy nomination," Mary Beth blurted out.

He looked at her for a minute, then let out a low whistle.

"And don't you dare make fun of me, Zack. This is something I really want. And I'm not giving up until I get it."

He stood up from the sofa and began pacing back

and forth. "But an Emmy nomination could take years, Mary Beth."

"You think I don't know that?"

He stared at her.

Mary Beth stood up as well. "You had to prove something to yourself six years ago, and I have to prove something to myself now. Like I said. Our timing is off. Again. I'm sorry, but it is."

He shook his head. "I don't know what to say. Your mother told Aunt Lou you never really wanted an acting career. That you…"

"That I was just trying to spite you?"

He sent her a sheepish look. "Well…yeah."

Mary Beth sat back down on the sofa. She was the one who patted the place beside her this time. When Zack sat back down she said, "Maybe at first I did throw myself into acting trying to spite you. But if Maddie had said, 'I'm going to get an Emmy nomination,' everyone would have automatically nodded their heads and said, 'Yes, I'm sure you will.' But no one has ever taken *me* seriously, Zack. Not even you."

He started to argue, but Mary Beth cut him off. "That's why I want you to get on with your life, and let me get on with mine. I can't make you any promises right now. And I'd never expect you to wait on me while I'm out here in Hollywood trying to reach a goal I'm not even sure I can reach."

His face was solemn. "You're wrong about me not taking you seriously, Mary Beth. I can tell you're serious about this nomination. I don't have to like it, but I do know you're serious."

"Then go home, Zack. Please."

When he nodded, Mary Beth leaned forward and

kissed him lightly on the cheek. "Thanks. For still being practical enough to realize things just can't work out for us right now."

"Yeah, that's me. Good old practical Zack."

Mary Beth reached out and picked up a plate and handed it to him. He accepted it, then looked at her and said, "Can I ask at least one favor?"

Mary Beth nodded.

"Don't cut me out of your life completely, Mary Beth. I'm willing to settle for friendship if that's all you're willing to give me. Just don't cut me out of your life again."

Friendship? Now he was willing to settle for friendship? What happened to "I'm not giving up so easily this time," Mary Beth wondered, suppressing a frown. She did frown when she realized how ridiculous she was being. The whole point of her telling Zack about the Emmy nomination was to get him to leave.

Or was it?

Was she maybe secretly hoping he would stay in California with her?

Don't even go there.

"If you'll go home, Zack, I promise we'll stay in touch."

He dropped his head in defeat. "Then I'll leave first thing in the morning."

They remained silent while they both picked at the food on their plates, but she felt like such a hypocrite. Not about the Emmy nomination. She hadn't lied about that. She felt guilty about nodding politely and pretending they could be friends when all she wanted to do was throw him on the floor and demand he do that amazing little thing he did with his tongue over every inch of her body.

They'd always been hot for each other. In fact, the sex had been so volatile she'd often been surprised they didn't both burst into flames.

Stop it! she told herself. He was certainly keeping his emotions under control. Other than the time he'd kissed her at the jail, he hadn't even tried to touch her. Possibly because he knew her well enough to know coming on to her when they were still at odds would only make her angry.

But we're not at odds with each other now.

Stop it! she told herself again. She'd be insane to invite him into her bed now. Now that he'd finally agreed to go home. No! She wasn't going to think about August 25 being a red-letter romance day. Nor was she going to think about how much she wanted him at that very moment.

But she did turn to him and say, "You don't have to sleep in your stupid tent tonight, Zack. When we're finished eating I'll get you what you need to make a bed here on the sofa."

WHEN MARY BETH'S BEDROOM door closed later that night, Zack felt like the door on his entire life had just been slammed in his face. Worse yet, he knew there really wasn't anything he could do about the situation short of holding the Emmy nominating committee hostage until they agreed to give Mary Beth her damn nomination.

And even if she did get the nomination, Zack had a sinking feeling a *nomination* wouldn't be enough. Next it would be the golden statue she wanted.

Yet, who was to blame for setting her acting career in motion? He was. And now he would have to suffer the consequences.

Throwing the pillow down on the sofa, Zack stripped down to his boxers, then walked around the room blowing out the candles. She'd sure shaken him up when he heard her scream. And then when he'd seen the flames, the thought of losing Mary Beth the way he'd lost his parents chilled him to the bone. Returning to the sofa, he stretched out with a frown on his face, covered himself with the blanket and stared into the blackness of the room.

His heart groaned in agony.

Here he was, sleeping on the sofa, while the woman he loved with all his heart was only one room away.

A day didn't pass that some memory of holding Mary Beth in his arms and making love to her didn't leave another huge crack in his heart. It had been all he could do to keep from forcing himself on her from that first morning they'd run into each other at the Dairy Hut. But common sense had told him that placing any emphasis on how much he missed the intimacy they'd shared or how much he still wanted her physically would be a death sentence in winning her back. Besides, as fantastic as the sex had always been between them, the fact that they had fallen in love long before sex was even a part of their lives had always kept sex from being the main focus of their relationship.

"She turned me down, fella. For a damn statue," Zack told the dog who was stretched out in the floor by the sofa.

Diogee whined, offering his sympathy, then

jumped up on the sofa with Zack and curled himself into a ball at Zack's feet.

But at least I didn't make a fool of myself, Zack thought. No, he'd played his cards close to the vest, and he hadn't done anything stupid like falling to his knees, sobbing his eyes out, and begging her to reconsider. As much as he loved her, he still had too much pride for that. And he certainly didn't want to alienate her now that they were finally back on speaking terms. He had told her he would settle for friendship. And as much as it killed him, he would stick by his word. He tried to look on the bright side. Maybe she'd even let him fly out to see her now and then. And the holidays weren't that far away. She'd surely be home for the holidays now that they'd settled their differences. And now that he'd be living at Oakmont...

Damn! Buying Oakmont would certainly go down as the stupidest investment in his financial portfolio. The old mansion was a virtual money pit, which is why it had remained vacant over the last twenty years. Of course, that hadn't mattered when he thought he was buying Oakmont for Mary Beth. Now, he guessed he would have to restore the old mansion enough to entice some other fool to buy it, then cut his losses and learn from the experience.

"Zack?"

He was so startled buy the sound of Mary Beth's voice, Zack rolled off the sofa and landed on the floor. "What's wrong?" he called out and groaned when Diogee landed on his stomach. A tail hit him in the face as the dog trotted across the room in search of his mistress.

"Nothing's wrong. I was just wondering if you were comfortable."

"Yeah, I'm fine," Zack said, trying to get the blanket untangled from around his legs. He mumbled a curse when he heard her bedroom door close again.

Comfortable? Was she nuts? She'd just torn his heart out and stomped on it a few times, and she had the nerve to ask if he was comfortable? He finally managed to jerk the blanket free and heard the door open again.

"Zack?"

"Yes, Mary Beth," he sang out, trying not to sound as irritated with her as he really was.

"Do you think you would be more comfortable in here with me?"

She really was a sadist! "Dammit, Mary Beth, that's not funny."

Her voice was low, seductive and classic Dietrich. "Who said I was joking, dahlink?"

It took only a second for Zack to respond. "Is that you, Marlene?" he called out, suddenly happier than he'd been in six long years.

Mary Beth let out a delighted squeal when Zack stumbled through the dark and finally came barreling through her bedroom door.

7

YES, SHE *WAS* INSANE. She'd admit it. And she didn't
even care, Mary Beth decided as she drove along
the beautiful Pacific Coast Highway on her way to
the studio the next morning. Besides, how much
more could one woman take? Only a woman with a
heart of stone wouldn't have been affected by everything Zack had gone through trying to win her back.

*There was also the fire, and the fact we were
alone and four thousand miles away from Morgan
City and everyone's prying eyes.*

Yes, that, too.

*And the blow-the-top-of-your-head-off, scream-at-
the-top-of-your-lungs,   think-you've-died-and-gone-
to-*
Heaven sex!

''Mercy,'' Mary Beth said aloud, feeling her heart
race at the mere thought of how good they still were
in bed together. The sexual attraction sure hadn't
diminished one iota between them.

However, the fabulous sex was only a part of the
reason she knew she'd never love anyone else but
Zack. They'd shared so much of their lives together,
created so many memories that would always be a
part of her heart and her soul. Like the hours they'd
spent cuddled up together watching the old classic

movies they both loved, which resulted in silly role playing they'd fallen into with him pretending to be Cary Grant when he thought he was in trouble, and her perfecting Marlene Dietrich's accent when Zack had once told her Dietrich's voice definitely turned him on.

And there were a million other reasons she would always love Zack. Like last night. Him willing to settle for friendship if that's all she was willing to give him.

Of course, after last night they'd zoomed past friendship and soared right back into being lovers again.

But she wasn't going to worry about it.

Especially after Zack assured her they could work it out. She would stay in L.A. just as she'd planned, and he'd bounce back and forth from Chicago and Morgan City to L.A. to see her as often as possible. People had long-distance relationships all the time. Look at Brad and Maddie. They were even married and being together only on weekends had certainly worked for them.

Pulling into her reserved parking space at the studio, Mary Beth tried to remove the silly grin from her face that came from a long night of lovemaking and planning for a brand-new future with Zack. She couldn't. She was still grinning like the Cheshire cat when she hurried off to makeup.

She waved to several of her cast members as they welcomed her back. And when she arrived at makeup, Jon, the makeup artist, was already reaching for the magic it would take to cover her deep tan and turn her back into a believable coma victim.

"So?" said Julia Davis, the head writer who had made it possible for her trip home to Morgan City. "How was the big class reunion?"

Mary Beth laughed. "You wouldn't believe it if I told you."

Julia nodded in sympathy. "Boring, huh?"

Mary Beth really laughed then.

Thirty minutes later, she had everyone who had wandered over to hear her wacky story laughing at the mayhem that had hit Morgan City almost from the moment she arrived.

"Well, don't leave us hanging," one of the cast members grumbled after Mary Beth finished the part where she'd bloodied Zack's nose with her shoe. "Have you heard from Zack since you got back?"

"Oh, I've heard from him," Mary Beth told her fascinated friends. "Guess who showed up yesterday to pitch a tent in my front yard until I changed my mind?"

Mary Beth started laughing again, but stopped when she realized everyone else was staring at her. "What?"

"Wow," said Judy, her pretty understudy. "I'll never be lucky enough to have a man love me like your Zack loves you."

"What are you going to do, Mary Beth? Are you going to give in and marry this guy?" Ann, the woman who played Fancy's best friend, wanted to know.

Mary Beth started to answer, but Julia spoke up.

"You have a career to think about, Mary Beth. I hope you haven't forgotten that."

Dorothy, a woman in her fifties who had been married to nothing but her career for the last thirty years, shook her head in disagreement. "Trust me, Mary Beth. Careers are a dime a dozen. But a man like Zack only comes along once in a lifetime."

Julia frowned at Dorothy and patted Mary Beth on the shoulder for support. "I disagree, Mary Beth. *Men* are a dime a dozen. A career like yours only comes along once in a lifetime. And I think you're smart enough to realize that."

Deciding it would be wise not to mention she and Zack had decided to try a long-distance romance, Mary Beth kept silent.

"But I do have to admit," Julia added. "Everything you told us about what Zack was willing to go through in the name of love is almost better than a script I could write for the show."

Everyone laughed, including Mary Beth until Julia's mouth suddenly dropped open and her eyes grew so wide they were almost as big as the lenses in her designer-framed glasses. "Wait a minute," she said, shaking her finger at Mary Beth. "Your crazy reunion with Zack is perfect. For Fancy Kildare, I mean."

Mary Beth jerked away from Jon's busy hands, making him curse when she smeared the fake dark circles he was placing under her eyes. "What are you talking about?"

"Don't you see, Mary Beth," Julia said, her face animated with excitement. "The viewers will love it. We've been counting on Fancy's recovery being our big hook for sweeps week, but what I'm planning is even better."

"Oh, no you don't...." Mary Beth began, but Julia already had that faraway look in her eyes.

"I'm sorry, Mary Beth, but Fancy will have to stay in the coma another week."

"Another week?" Mary Beth echoed.

Julia nodded, confirming her spur-of-the-moment decision. "I'll need at least another week to make the arrangements."

"What arrangements?" Mary Beth was almost afraid to ask.

Pacing back and forth now, Julia stopped long enough to say, "Yes, it's all coming together in my head now. When Fancy does come out of the coma, she'll find the ex-fiancé who once left her at the altar at her bedside begging for a second chance."

Mary Beth gasped.

"We can even have him go through everything your Zack has gone through, trying to prove he still loves Fancy."

"Absolutely not!" Mary Beth fumed. "This is my life you're talking about, Julia. I'll never agree to having my personal life exploited in front of millions of viewers on daytime TV."

Julia didn't seem to hear her. She rubbed her greedy hands together. "Yes, this is exactly what we need to push us over the top during sweeps week. And I have the perfect actor in mind to make a limited appearance as Fancy's ex-lover. Dirk Devlon."

"Dirk Devlon?" Mary Beth repeated along with everyone else in the room. Dirk Devlon was a TV legend who had catapulted from the soaps to the silver screen so fast, he still had network heads reeling.

"I'm the one who gave Dirk his first big break in the business," Julia said, smiling like the cat who just swallowed the canary. "Dirk owes me a huge favor and he knows it. I've just been waiting for the right time to call in my marker. And this is definitely the right time."

Mary Beth jerked the cape from around her neck and pushed Jon aside to stand up. "You obviously didn't hear me, Julia. I'm not going to sit by and let you exploit my personal life in the name of sweeps week."

"Sure you will," Julia called back over her shoulder as she hurried out of the room in a rush. "We're talking Emmy nomination, Mary Beth. Count on it."

MARY BETH DIDN'T LEAVE the studio that evening until after eight o'clock. The thought that Zack would be waiting for her when she got home no longer cheered her up as it had when she'd left him asleep in her bed that morning.

Since Julia's brainstorm, the cast had spent the entire day talking about nothing else but Fancy's new script and the fact that the fabulous Dirk Devlon would be playing the part of her ex-fiancé. Mary Beth hadn't even had time to worry about being the icon's costar.

She had to force herself to focus on the snarled L.A. traffic. But her mind had been preoccupied, trying to decide how she was going to explain to Zack that their personal relationship was now going to be broadcast into the homes of millions of viewers on daytime television.

Zack was bound to be angry with her, as would both of their families and probably everyone else in Morgan City. And she didn't even want to think about how fast Arnold Purdy would pounce on her new story line. Instead of merciless, he would use *mercenary* as an adjective to describe her now, gleefully pointing out that hometown girl turned TV star was crass enough to sell her own soul for a lousy ratings score.

We're talking Emmy nomination, Mary Beth. Count on it.

She wished she could force Julia's words out of her mind, but she couldn't. Yet, if she couldn't figure out a way to deter Julia from putting her private life on television, she would be handing over a part of her soul. A part of her soul that also included Zack, just when they'd finally found each other again.

He'd be furious, she decided as she turned onto her street. There was no doubt about that. But maybe together they could figure out a way to stop Julia from putting their private lives on display.

After all, Zack was practical.

Zack could always solve even the toughest problems.

Zack was surrounded by reporters.

Reporters!

Mary Beth stepped on the gas pedal of her sporty red two-seater BMW and zoomed into her driveway, causing several people to scatter out of the way. TV, radio and newspaper reporters were everywhere. Zack was standing in the driveway with his hands at his waist, glaring at all of them as the lights from the TV van lit up her yard. Most of the reporters were scribbling furiously in their notebooks, but a TV reporter from a local station had a microphone pushed in Zack's face. Running back and forth in front of the TV van was Diogee, barking his head off and trying to protect his new buddy.

Vaulting from her car, Mary Beth yelled, "What's going on here?"

Everyone started running when the TV camera pointed in her direction.

"Was it your idea to have your character, Fancy Kildare, go through everything you've been going through in your own relationship with Zack Callahan, Miss Morgan?" one of the reporters was rude enough to ask.

"Is it true Dirk Devlon has agreed to play the role of your ex-fiancé?" someone else shouted.

"No comment," Mary Beth said firmly. Julia must have leaked the new plot line, Mary Beth decided frantically. She called out an order to Diogee, who stopped his running and barking long enough for Mary Beth to grab him by the collar.

Leading him beside her, she pushed past the reporters and said a silent prayer that Zack would forgive her as she started walking toward him. "Go inside, Zack,'' she said, never quite looking him in the eye. ''They'll never leave as long as we stay out here.''

He turned on his heel and stomped around the side of the house ahead of her. Mary Beth rounded the house herself, still holding to Diogee's collar. The reporters automatically picked up the chase.

But her heart sank when she saw the spectacular sunset from her oceanfront deck and the romantic scene Zack had arranged. He had placed her candles *outside* this time. They twinkled like fireflies all along the deck railing. Her patio table was set for two. Champagne was chilling in her ice bucket. Steaks, she assumed, would have soon been sizzling on the grill.

All of his careful preparations wasted now, thanks to the ambitious head writer she'd been stupid enough to think was her friend.

I'm going to kill Julia, Mary Beth thought angrily as she made her way up the stairs and onto the deck.

''Zoom in on the tent,'' she heard the reporter call out to his cameraman as she pushed Diogee through the sliding glass door and into the house.

Mary Beth took a deep breath before she walked inside. After she slid the door into place and locked it, she turned to face Zack. The only time she'd ever seen him look so angry was the night before their wedding when he'd handed her a check for her parents' expenses and begged her for the last time to postpone their wedding.

''Is this what last night was all about, Mary Beth?'' he said flatly. ''You thought if you made love to me I wouldn't be so angry about you turning our life into a script for Fancy Kildare?''

Mary Beth flinched. "How can you even ask me that question?''

"How can I not?" he shouted. "Who else could give those vultures that kind of information about us? *I* certainly didn't call them and ask them to come running with their cameras."

Mary Beth reached out and placed her hand on his arm. He turned to stone under her touch. She stepped back. "I'm sorry, Zack. I did tell some of my cast members what went on between us when I went home for the reunion. And I told you followed me back home. But I never dreamed the head writer for the show would turn our lives into a television script. And that's the honest truth."

The hard look on his face softened, but only slightly. His eyes locked with hers. "Okay. I believe you. It wasn't your idea, but what do you intend to do about it?''

Mary Beth looked away. If Julia had already leaked the information to the press, and if the reporters were alluding to the fact that Dirk Devlon had already accepted Julia's offer to play opposite her, her fate was already sealed. What could she do?

"I asked you a question," he said, his voice anything but friendly.

Mary Beth threw her hands up in the air. "What *can* I do, Zack? I don't write the scripts. I just play the role."

The muscles in his jaw twitched. "You can refuse *this* role, Mary Beth. And you know it."

Was he crazy? "Are you crazy? I'm under contract, Zack. If I walked out now, they'd sue me so fast it would make my head spin." *I'd also never work in this town again.* She decided it wise not to bring up that point. After all, Zack would like nothing better than to have her run back to Morgan City, Oakmont and him. *Don't disappoint me again, Zack. Don't walk out on me again.*

"Let the bastards sue you," he growled. "I'll pay the cost whatever it is."

"It isn't your place to pay anything, Zack."

"Why not? It's *my* life, too, Mary Beth. And I'm not interested in tuning in and being made fun of on daytime TV."

Mary Beth's chin came up. "Then *you* sue the studio, Zack. Do what you feel you have to do. But *I* signed a contract with the studio, and I don't intend to break it."

His face turned from a bloodred to a sickly pallor. Mary Beth felt as sick as he looked when he said, "You think playing a role opposite Dirk Devlon will get you that Emmy nomination, don't you? Admit it."

Mary Beth opened her mouth to deny it, but she hesitated a second too long.

"I can't believe this," he boomed. "You're really willing to let those cutthroats carve our lives into neat slices and serve it up to the public for a damn Emmy nomination!"

"That isn't true," Mary Beth cried. And it wasn't. She'd love to have the nomination, she'd admit that, but she'd told him the truth. She wasn't going to break her contract. "I told you. I'm under contract to the studio, Zack. I'm sure you take any contract you sign in your business seriously. Would *you* be willing to commit professional suicide by breaking a business contract?"

The look he sent her said he'd lost the ability to be practical Zack at the moment. "Fine. You do what *you* have to do, Mary Beth, but you'll be doing it without an audience from me. I was willing to make a fool out of myself back home because those are the same people I embarrassed you in front of. But if you think I'm going to keep grinning like an idiot while your studio makes a laughingstock out of me in front of the entire country, you don't know me very well."

Mary Beth's temper flared when he stormed off to the bedroom and came back a few minutes later with his overnight bag in his hand. "I'm beginning to think I never knew you at all, Zack." She tried to keep her voice from quivering. "You walked out on me six years ago, and now you're doing it again. Who's really the bigger idiot here? You or me?"

"I'm not walking out on you, Mary Beth. I'm asking you to come home with me." He paused for a second. "No, I'm *begging* you to come home with me." He sent her a pleading look that broke her heart. "Don't throw our future away for a bunch of people who care so little about you they'd exploit your personal life for a lousy television rating."

"Zack, please..." She couldn't think of anything else to say.

"Then I guess you've made your choice."

He turned back to face her after he opened her sliding glass door. "When you get your Emmy nomination, Mary Beth, don't come home looking for me."

Mary Beth burst into tears when he disappeared through the door. She could hear him yelling "no comment" to the reporters who were still milling around in her yard. And she was still crying thirty minutes later, facedown on her bed, when Diogee reached up with his paw and scratched her arm. Mary Beth sat up long enough to take the newspaper he had in his mouth, a routine they followed on a daily basis. She wiped at her eyes with her fingertips and performed another daily habit when she turned to see what she'd missed when she'd been too wrapped up in Zack to read her horoscope that morning.

Libra: You are destined to enjoy more than your fifteen minutes of fame.

Without even bothering to finish the rest of her daily horoscope, Mary Beth fell facedown on her bed again and cried like a baby.

IT WAS AFTER TEN O'CLOCK that night when Zack stormed into the airport terminal and asked for the first available flight to Chicago. He bought the ticket for the red-eye flight without so much as a blink. He checked what little baggage he had, grabbed his ticket and decided to kill time in the closest airport bar. Due to the late hour, he was relieved to see only two other people at a table in the back of the tiny space.

"Scotch. Neat," he told the bartender when he seated himself at the bar. When the bartender returned with his drink, he nursed his poison while he tried to pull himself back together.

There hadn't been any point in staying in Malibu with Mary Beth to slug it out. Nor would it have done him any good to argue with her any longer. She was the most stubborn person he'd ever known, and though he would always love her, this was one time he had to agree with her.

Sometimes love just wasn't enough.

He also knew his first order of business had to be to head to his Chicago office and prepare to do any damage control if his partners or any of their investors suddenly got nervous about the publicity that was sure to hit the tabloids. And he wouldn't blame them if they did get a little nervous. Wouldn't *he* be nervous if he learned the CEO of the company he'd invested in was stupid enough to hand out large sums of money on the street corner? Not to mention getting arrested for hanging upside down from a bridge, and then running off to California to pitch a pup tent in his ex-fiancée's front yard. Did any of that sound like the actions of a *sane* man. Not hardly.

What in the hell have I been thinking?

Of course, he knew exactly why he had gone to such lengths to prove he was anything but practical Zack when it came to love. Mary Beth was the reason. The Mary Beth who had made love to him last night, who had kissed him with such sweetness and sincerity and told him that she still loved him.

Not the Mary Beth he'd left a few hours ago. The Mary Beth who was so caught up in her acting career she was willing to sacrifice their future for a damn statue.

"What the hell?" the bartender said when a group of people ran past the bar and down the terminal corridor. Zack slid off the stool and followed the bartender when he walked to the open entrance of the bar to see what all the commotion was about.

"I thought it was a bomb scare or something," the bartender said shaking his head. "It's only another movie star."

Zack frowned. Dirk Devlon was standing in the middle of the terminal, surrounded by the small army he paid to protect him. He smiled his Hollywood smile for a camera that had *Entertainment Tonight* written in big letters on the side.

Even before this fiasco with Mary Beth, Zack had never liked the guy. He'd never understood why women were so crazy about him, either, but it was obvious they were from the nervous way the pretty female reporter giggled when she pushed her microphone in his direction. The rave reviews the critics always gave him also hadn't been enough to sway Zack's opinion. As far as Zack was concerned, the man couldn't act his way out of a wet paper bag.

"I'll be the first to confirm it," Dirk said with a smile as he reached up to push a dark curl back off his forehead. "The rumor about me doing a guest appearance on *The Wild and the Free* is most definitely true."

"Is it also true you'll be getting five hundred

thousand for each episode?'' the pretty woman gushed.

He adjusted the ascot around his neck and removed his designer sunglasses before he glanced back over his shoulder at a man too well dressed to be a bodyguard. ''Let's ask my agent. Ron? Care to answer this lovely young woman's question?'' When Ron sent him a terrified look, Dirk feigned surprise. ''My word, man,'' he said, his hand dramatically clutched to his chest. ''If that's all I'm getting per episode, I say we should bloody well renegotiate.''

Everyone laughed.

''But why television, Mr. Devlon?'' the pretty reporter probed. ''When you already have such a hectic movie schedule, I mean?''

He put his designer sunglasses back on before he said, ''Television was good to me once, lovey. And you can quote me on this—One should never become too famous that one forgets where one got his first start.''

The arrogant bastard, Zack thought. In addition to all the fall-out he could have from Mary Beth's latest affair with the media, he'd also be tormented by the fact that the famous Dirk Devlon would be looking into those big blue eyes of hers on a daily basis. And she always had been a sucker for a British accent. Devlon was no Cary Grant, but the fact that Mary Beth would be his love interest on the show bothered Zack, deeply. That is, until he remembered Devlon would be playing *his* role in the twisted melodrama that was his own life.

And the idea that the great Dirk Devlon would have to play the role of the character who had humiliated himself in the name of love, made Zack laugh.

"What's so funny?" the bartender asked with a grin.

"He's going to look like a real jackass on that soap opera," said Zack.

They both watched Devlon disappear down the corridor with everyone hurrying after him before the bartender looked back at Zack and said, "Are you kidding? That dude *is* a jackass, man."

Zack laughed even harder.

8

PULLING INTO A PARKING spot at the studio's executive offices, Mary Beth looked over at the shiny Mercedes where her agent was sitting behind the wheel with a worried look on his face. She'd finally pulled herself together after Zack left, and the first thing she'd done was put in an emergency call to her agent. Not that JoJo had been in sympathy with her, the jerk. In fact, she'd almost had to threaten to fire him to get him to agree to arrange for a private meeting with the executive producer.

"I still don't see why you're making such a big deal out of this," JoJo argued as they headed for the studio's impressive front doors. "Like I told you when you insisted on wearing that body suit for the *Evershine* commercial, if you're going to make it in the entertainment business, Mary Beth, you need to go with the flow. Everyone thought you were nude, anyway, so what did it matter?"

Mary Beth glared in his direction, wondering why she'd never paid attention to the gaudy gold chains around his neck and the flashy rings on his fingers before. "But *I* knew I wasn't nude, and I'm not going to apologize for sticking to my principles. Just like now. I'm making a big deal out of this because it's an invasion of my privacy, JoJo.'' And the minute she called him by his ridiculous nickname, Mary Beth realized Maddie was right. She never should have allowed herself to get involved with a grown man who was perfectly comfortable being known to the world as JoJo.

"When you're a public figure, you have no privacy," he grunted. "And if you're not careful you'll have no career, either."

Shut up, Bozo, Mary Beth thought, deciding from here on out she would use Maddie's nickname for him, at least mentally anyway. She waited at the door until he opened it and they both walked through. "Don't you think you're jumping the gun just a little? The producer might agree with me and stop Julia from using my private life as a script for sweeps week."

"If you believe that," JoJo said with snort, "then I have a great deal on some Enron stock I'd love to sell you."

When the executive producer's secretary gave them the nod, Mary Beth paused in front of the office door, took a deep breath and opened it. JoJo followed so close behind her he actually bumped into her when she came to an abrupt halt. The private meeting she thought they were having wasn't going to be private after all. Already seated in one of the chairs facing the executive producer's desk was Julia, with an extremely smug look on her face.

"I thought all parties involved in this dispute should be included in the meeting," Walter Evans informed them with a superior smile. He was distinguished-looking, as you would expect him to be, with the perpetual rich man's tan and dark hair only slightly tinted with gray.

He motioned for them to take a seat.

Before Mary Beth could kick her agent into action or say a word herself, Walter pulled a contract out of his top desk drawer and slid it across the polished mahogany table in her direction. "I think we can save everyone a lot of time if you'll look over the two-year contract you signed with the studio again, Miss Morgan. You're under contract for two more months. Or have you forgotten that?"

Mary Beth glanced at the contract, but refused to pick it up. "No, I haven't forgotten anything, Mr. Evans. I know exactly when my contract is up. And I also know there isn't anything in that contract that says I gave you the right to exploit my personal life to gain top ratings for the studio."

JoJo sent her a warning look, and Walter sat back in his big leather chair and smiled. "No one is trying to put you on the defensive, Miss Morgan. But to put it bluntly, the show will go on. With you or without you. And if you choose to break your contract by refusing to accept the new script... well...I'm sure your very eager understudy would kill for a chance to play Fancy opposite Dirk Devlon."

"Mary Beth has no intention of breaking her contract," JoJo spoke up for the first time. He laughed nervously. "Everyone knows she'd never work in this town again if she did a stupid thing like that."

You snake! He'd sold her out. He was supposed

to be on *her* side. Not hand her over to the studio with his blessing. They didn't pay him fifteen percent. *She* did!

Julia nodded politely to the producer when she stood up. "Thank you, sir. It appears this meeting is over." But she stopped beside Mary Beth's chair and looked down at her before she left the room. "Let me give you some free advice, Mary Beth. You might fool some people with that I'm-just-the-girl-next-door-and-I-have-my-principles act, but you've never fooled me. You're just as selfish and ruthless as the character you play. The minute I saw you sacrificing your own twin sister on national TV so you could get yourself in the spotlight, I said, 'That's the girl I want to play Fancy Kildare.' And if you're really as smart as your agent claims you are, you'll go right on playing Fancy Kildare. And you'll do so wearing a great big smile of gratitude on that pretty face of yours."

Mary Beth was livid. Her chin lifted in defiance. "Oh, I am smart, Julia. I'm smart enough to know free advice is worth exactly what you pay for it. But I *am* glad you realize that I do have a ruthless streak. It won't come as a surprise to you later."

"Is that a threat, Mary Beth?"

"Take it however you want, Julia."

Julia stuck her nose in the air and stomped out of the room.

Talk about a wake-up call.

Long after the meeting was over, and after her agent had slithered back under the rock he crawled out from, Mary Beth remained sitting in the studio break room waiting out her time until her brief coma-victim appearance was scheduled for the day. Nursing a cup of cold coffee, she was coming to terms with some extremely difficult truths about herself.

And she didn't like any of them.

How did Maddie ever forgive me? Mary Beth kept wondering, realizing for the first time the full magnitude of what she'd put her twin through while Maddie's life had captured front page headlines and had been on every newscast across the nation.

Funny how she'd convinced herself then she was only being resourceful when it was Maddie's life that was being exploited. And how she'd never seen herself as selfish or ruthless, only determined to make it to the big time. Now, with Dirk Devlon scheduled as her costar, she might even have a chance to really make it to the big time.

But at what price?

"Welcome to the real world," a voice said. Dorothy, the veteran actress who had told Mary Beth careers were a dime a dozen, took a seat beside her.

"You can say that again," Mary Beth mumbled, still looking into her coffee cup.

"Well, if it makes you feel any better, all actors have to pay a price for their success at some point in their careers."

When Mary Beth didn't comment, Dorothy said, "Some pay when their marriages end in divorce. Some pay when they look around and their children have grown up while they've spent the majority of their time at the studio. Others, like you, even have to let go of their principles now and then and look the other way.''

Mary Beth flinched at that remark. ''And what about you? What price have you paid?''

Dorothy shrugged. ''I guess it all depends on how you look at it. I've made good money over the years. My home is paid for. I have a nice nest egg in the bank for retirement. But I've buried most of my family now, without ever spending any real time with them. And if I live long enough to go to a nursing home, I won't have any children or grandchildren stopping by to spend time with me during the years I have left.''

''But you've had a wonderful career,'' Mary Beth reminded her weakly.

''Yes, I've had my career. And that's exactly what I always told myself I wanted. A long, prosperous career.''

Mary Beth looked at Dorothy for the first time since she had sat down beside her. ''You say that as if you don't think your career has been worth the price you've had to pay.''

Dorothy laughed as she got up to leave. ''What difference does it make? There's nothing I can do about it now.''

Could that be me in thirty years? Mary Beth wondered after Dorothy left the break room. *A woman with nothing to look forward to but waiting out her time in a nursing home with no one left to come visit?*

Mary Beth shuddered at the thought.

The only thing that kept her from walking out of

the studio and never looking back was the fact that she only had two months left on her contract. That, and the fact the executive producer had already made it clear her walking out and breaking her contract wouldn't change the script at all. They'd simply turn to her understudy. And she'd worked too hard perfecting the role of Fancy Kildare to hand it over to someone else. Especially when an actor as famous as Dirk Devlon had been called in for a guest appearance.

She consoled herself with the fact that at least she had tried to stop Julia. She'd make sure her mother passed on that piece of information to Zack's aunt Lou. *If anyone at home will ever speak to me again,* Mary Beth reminded herself.

She'd have to give her mother and Maddie time to calm down before she could talk to them rationally. She'd kept her cell phone turned off all day, already dreading what her family would have to say about the latest chapter in her life. And thinking about her uncertain future, Mary Beth picked up the paper from the break room table and turned to the horoscope section, bracing herself. *Be prepared for a big change in your life.* Mary Beth laughed bitterly. *Stop worrying about things you can't change and look to the future.* "What future?" Mary Beth mumbled. She had taken Zack back, only to lose him again. And now that she'd challenged Julia, it was highly doubtful her contract would be renewed for another two years even if she decided she did want to stay with the show. *Understanding will come, but slowly.* "Thanks for nothing," Mary Beth said with a frown.

She threw the paper back down on the table when one of her cast members called out that it was time for her appearance on the set.

MARY BETH GLANCED AT THE caller ID and waited until the phone stopped ringing. When the flashing red light appeared on her phone set, she picked up the receiver and listened to the message from her sister. "What were you thinking, Mary Beth? How can you be so vindictive? How could you sell your own life story...."

Mary Beth deleted the message. Just as she had deleted a similar message from her mother earlier. The last thing Mary Beth needed at the moment was someone else making her feel worse than she already did.

Even my dog hates me, Mary Beth thought, looking over at Diogee who had taken up a watchful post by her sliding glass door shortly after Zack had roared out of her life forever.

What was that old saying?

You always hurt the one you love.

Love. Such a mysterious, confusing and completely exasperating word. And a word she didn't have time to even contemplate at the moment.

No, what she needed to focus on at the moment was how she was going to pull herself together long enough to grit her teeth and fulfill her contract. The news on the set was that Dirk Devlon was already kicking butt and taking names. He'd refused to wait another week while Julia was dragging out the coma saga, insisting he needed to appear on the show as soon as possible, or not at all. And according to the rumors, he wasn't at all happy about having an up-and-coming actress instead of an established one as his costar.

What that would mean for her personally, Mary Beth wasn't sure. They could very well bring in some big movie star to play the role of Fancy. But it wasn't likely. Dirk was only slated for a brief appearance as would be any leading lady of his choosing.

What irritated Mary Beth most was the fact that Dirk had started out in the ranks the same way she was doing now.

Actors and their egos, she thought with a sigh. She was even beginning to worry that her own ego was getting a little too big for comfort. *Was* an Emmy nomination really worth the price she was willing to pay? She was beginning to have her doubts. Especially when she remembered Zack's final words. "When you get your Emmy nomination, don't come home looking for me."

"Venus? I could use a little help in the destiny department right now," Mary Beth mumbled aloud.

Diogee seconded her request with the thump of his tail.

WHEN DIRK DEVLON FINALLY showed up on the set of *The Wild and the Free,* it was the equivalent of Michael Jordan showing up at a high school basketball game. The only difference was that Michael

Jordan would have flashed the crowd his fantastic smile. Dirk kept his plastic-surgerized nose in the air and never looked once at any of his fellow cast members as he swept through the set to a private dressing room Julia had personally arranged for him.

"Now that's a unique individual," one of the cast members standing beside Mary Beth said.

"He's unique, all right," Mary Beth snorted. "Just like everybody else."

How she was ever going to make herself work with this man, Mary Beth didn't have a clue. Especially since the latest news on the set was that Dirk had been furious when he read the script and realized that a nobody like Mary Beth was actually going to turn him down in front of millions of his faithful fans.

Poor Dirk, Mary Beth thought. It appeared even a big name like Dirk Devlon ended up paying the price for success sooner or later, just like Dorothy told her every actor did.

She glanced at JoJo, who had begged her to let him on the set for her first scene with Devlon, possibly at the suggestion of Julia and the studio heads hoping he could keep Mary Beth in line. When he gave her a thumbs-up sign, Mary Beth frowned at him and looked away. If he told her one more time that after playing opposite Dirk Devlon the sky would be the limit, *he* was going straight to the moon when she personally punched him out! Especially if the creep kept annoying her with his lousy imitation of a cash register, doing his stupid "ka-ching, ka-ching, ka-ching" over the money he could see in their futures.

Ka-ching this, you moron. She kept her middle finger hidden behind her back, and turned around to find another greedy parasite standing right behind her.

"I need to make a few things clear before you and Dirk go before the cameras today," Julia said haughtily.

"Like what? That emotionally constipated people like you and Dirk Devlon don't give a crap?" Mary Beth said with a smile. "Save your breath, Julia. I can see that for myself."

Julia's eyes narrowed. "I'd watch my step if I were you, Mary Beth."

"A contract goes both ways, Julia. Go ahead and fire me. I have my lawyer's number on speed dial."

"I'm not stupid," she hissed. "But Dirk is already upset about the script. It's my job to see that everything runs as smoothly and as painlessly as possible. Understand?"

Mary Beth sent Julia her sweetest smile. "Painless, you say? Fine. I'll treat Dirk with the sensitivity of an angry dentist."

Literally trembling with anger, Julia looked Mary Beth up and down and said, "Listen, *sweetie.* You really don't want to screw with me."

Mary Beth didn't back down. "You're right, *sweetie.* I'd have better taste."

Julia stomped off.

JoJo glared in her direction.

Mary Beth smiled with satisfaction.

LIKE EVERYONE ELSE ON THE set who had been waiting the past two hours for Mr. Ego to emerge from his dressing room, Mary Beth's patience was growing thinner by the minute.

"According to the rumors, he always does this," Mary Beth heard someone whisper. "In fact, it's been said if Dirk Devlon hasn't kept the cast waiting for at least two hours, he doesn't consider it a good day."

"If he'd been a Pilgrim, then I guess he would have sailed over on the Decemberflower," Mary Beth grumbled and everyone laughed at the same time the great man himself took pity on the cast and finally walked onto the set.

You can do this, Mary Beth told herself when the director called for everyone to take their places on the set.

With her head held high, Mary Beth walked to the hospital bed sitting in the middle of the set wearing her sickly green hospital gown. After climbing onto the bed and adjusting the covers, she fell back against the propped up pillows and closed her eyes with the fake dark circles, wishing she really could lapse into a coma for her part of the scene.

She cringed slightly when she felt her obnoxious costar take her hand. And she almost burst out laughing when the man who didn't like to admit he was actually from Ohio delivered his lines in the phony British accent he'd recently adopted. "Fawn-cy? Dearest? It's me, Monty. Can you hear me?"

Mary Beth tried not to gag at the name he had

personally chosen for the character he was playing. A free spirit like Fancy Kildare getting involved with stuffed shirt named Montague was as likely as Mary Beth asking Dirk if she could hang out in his dressing room in hopes she might catch some of his precious fingernail clippings for her scrapbook.

But she did finally manage to let her eyes flutter open, and when she turned her head to look at him, he let go of her hand and said with a groan, "This is the woman I'm supposed to be madly in love with? That's preposterous!"

"Now, Dirk," Julia cooed running onto the set to soothe the savage beast she was responsible for creating. "Fancy's been in a coma. Remember? It would be *preposterous* if we had her looking like a model who had just stepped off a Paris runway."

Refusing to even look at her again, he had the nerve to say, "Then change the script, Julia. If you expect me to play the role up to Dirk Devlon standards, then I insist you give me a better script *and* a costar who looks better than this one does now."

"I agree," Mary Beth said right back, jerking Dirk's dark head in her direction. "If the man can't act, he can't act. I say let's make it easy for him and forget this script entirely."

Julia's face turned so white *she* looked like the coma victim, while Dirk's face turned as red as the vase of fake roses sitting on the nightstand next to her hospital bed.

Mary Beth knew she'd won round one when Dirk stormed off the set in a rage befitting a two-year-old and Julia hurried after him. She simply leaned back against the pillows with her hands propped behind her head.

That was for making me lose Zack, she thought with a satisfied smile. She already knew ka-ching, ka-ching, ka-ching was running through a few executive minds at the moment, over the horrendous amount of money their big sweeps week movie star was thoughtlessly wasting at the studio's expense.

"MADDIE, IT'S ME. Don't hang up."

When her sister didn't answer, Mary Beth said, "I'm sorry I haven't called you back."

"So am I, Mary Beth," Maddie snapped. "But if you think waiting two days to call me back means I'm not going to give you the same lecture, you're crazy."

"I owe you a huge apology, Maddie," Mary Beth broke in. "I was selfish and inconsiderate for using you like I did with that alien abduction story. I want you to know how grateful I am that you forgave me. Until now, I never realized how painful that had to have been for you."

"Zack's the one you owe an apology to now," Maddie said, refusing to let Mary Beth change the subject.

"Zack no longer has anything to worry about," Mary Beth said with a sigh. "Thanks to Dirk Devlon, even though he is an egotistical ass, the script has been changed. He insists no man in his right mind would ever do the things Zack did, even in the name of love."

"And I'm sure Zack would agree with him about now," Maddie confirmed.

Mary Beth found the nerve to ask. "Did Zack make it back home safely?"

"Like you care."

"Be mad at me if you want, Maddie, but stop acting like I'm some ogre. Of course I care if Zack made it home okay."

"He's in Chicago. Trying to run interference for all the bad publicity you've caused him. But he is safe."

"Will you make sure to pass it along that the script has been changed?"

"Absolutely not!" Maddie snapped. "If you want Zack to have that information, you can call him yourself. And I wouldn't wait around to do it, either. There are plenty of single women right here in Morgan City just dying for him to come home so they can soothe his bruised ego. Bitsy Williams for one. She's already telling everyone in town that she intends on becoming Mrs. Zack Callahan."

Bitsy? Turning Oakmont into a Barbie playhouse? I'll pull her false pigtail off again and shove it down her throat first!

"Well, you certainly got quiet all of a sudden," Maddie said, and Mary Beth frowned at the satisfied tone in her twin's voice.

"No, I didn't," Mary Beth lied.

Maddie laughed. "Sure you did. I can practically feel your rage vibrating through the phone."

"Cut it out, Maddie."

Maddie let out a sigh. "Come home, Mary Beth.

Come home now. Before it really is too late for you and Zack.''

Mary Beth closed her eyes. "I have a contract to fulfill, Maddie. That's something everyone seems to have conveniently forgotten.''

"And when your contract is up? Will you come home then?''

Mary Beth refused to answer.

"If you're irritated with me because there's nothing I'd like better than to see you come home and marry Zack, then I'm sorry. But can you really blame me, Mary Beth? Would I really be much of a sister if I didn't want to see you spend the rest of your life with a guy who loves you as much as Zack does? A man who will be a devoted husband to you and a wonderful father to your children?''

Mary Beth still didn't have an answer.

"Fine. If I'm only going to get the silent treatment, we might as well hang up.''

Before Mary Beth could answer, Maddie slammed down the phone.

"My sister just hung up on me,'' Mary Beth told the dog whose new post was still lying in front of her sliding glass door.

Even Diogee refused to look in her direction.

"Thanks for the support, traitor,'' Mary Beth scolded.

But who was she kidding. She didn't have any support. She didn't have any support at the studio, and she certainly didn't have any support when it came to her family taking sides with her against Zack.

And she didn't even want to think about the stupid script Dirk Devlon had come up with, twisting the script around so it would be Mary Beth who was doing the groveling. That was a challenge she wasn't looking forward to undertaking. Especially since Zack was certain to get a big kick out of seeing her do the groveling for a change. Maybe Bitsy Williams would invite him over so they could both laugh their fool heads off while they watched her soap together.

Bitsy Williams.

Zack certainly wouldn't have to pitch any tents in that bimbo's front yard. She'd bend over backwards in order to fulfill Zack's slightest whim.

Bitsy Callahan.

Mary Beth almost choked on those words, and she hadn't even said them out loud. Her mind sped forward, ten years down the road. Her, coming home for their *twenty*-year class reunion. Still alone and unmarried. But surely she'd have been nominated and even *won* an Emmy by then. She'd even take her statue to the family picnic on the courthouse green and display it just as proudly as Zack and Bitsy would display their children. But what did she care?

I care enough that the thought of Bitsy Williams having Zack's children makes me physically sick to my stomach, Mary Beth admitted.

Could she really stand by and let Zack marry someone else? Mary Beth looked at the phone in her hand for a moment. She didn't even have to walk back to the bar to get the numbers Zack had written down for her when they got up in the middle of the night, famished from their heated lovemaking. Being blessed with photographic memories is what had helped Maddie sail through college, and what made memorizing a script a breeze for her.

And she wasn't going to worry about the time difference, either, even though it was after midnight in Chicago. If she didn't call Zack while she had the courage, Mary Beth knew she never would.

His voice sounded sleepy when he answered.

"Zack, it's me."

She heard him breath out a long sigh.

"I just wanted to apologize for all the trouble I've caused you with media."

Still, silence.

"And I wanted you to know the script has been changed. Your life isn't going to be..."

"I don't care about the damn script, Mary Beth." His voice was cool, distant. "I cared about us. I cared about our future. I cared about having a family...."

Mary Beth's heart lurched to hear him talk about his feelings in the past tense. She broke in before she could stop herself. "Then what was all that talk about settling for friendship, Zack? What was that?"

"I had a weak moment. Sue me!" he had the nerve to say and slammed down the phone.

"Now, Zack hung up on me!" Mary Beth told Diogee. "He even stole one of *my* favorite lines."

She threw the phone down on the sofa, then stomped out onto the deck and stood staring out over the Pacific with her fists clenched at her sides. In

California she had a rented beach house she paid a fortune for every month just to say she lived in Malibu. She had a flashy sports car. She had a certain amount of fame and the potential to win that Emmy nomination if she could keep from punching Dirk Devlon in the nose and ruining his nose job.

While back home in Morgan City she would have...

No!

She wasn't going to think about home.

Or Zack.

What she was going to do was clear her mind of all confusion and concentrate on the most pressing matter at hand: taking back control from Julia and Dirk and showing everyone she wasn't beaten yet.

She smiled to herself.

Fancy Kildare still had a few tricks up her sleeve.

9

"DOES EVERYONE HAVE A copy of the new script?" asked Julia, smiling at Dirk who was sitting beside her looking aloof and completely in control. "Then let me give you a thumbnail sketch of how things have changed."

Mary Beth stifled a groan when Julia pointed to her. "After Fancy comes out of the coma, we'll keep flashing back to the past, showing how she left Monty the night before their wedding, seeking fame and fortune in Hollywood."

Mary Beth laughed. "And you really think the viewers are going to buy that Fancy Kildare is a renegade member of the royal family of England?"

Julia frowned. "Fancy ran away, Mary Beth. She left behind her royal roots and the man who loved her, and she's been guarding her true identity from the moment she hit Hollywood."

Mary Beth rolled her eyes.

"And that's what makes her outlandish role as Fancy Kildare so believable," Julia added. "In her new life, she's chosen to be the farthest thing possible from the person her royal status demanded her to be."

Dirk nodded in agreement. "It makes perfect sense to me."

Mary Beth glared in Dirk's direction.

"Let's see if I can explain it to Miss Morgan," the creep had the nerve to say when he noticed Mary Beth's scowl. "After Fancy has her close brush with death, she realizes it's time to give up her phony life in Hollywood. All she can think about is the man she truly loves and assuming her rightful place back in London's royal high society." He paused for a few seconds, looking around appreciatively at a few eager-to-please cast members who were all nodding in approval. "So Fancy goes back home. To her beloved England. And to her loving parents, the Duke and Duchess of Devlonshire."

Dirk howled at the cleverness of including his own name in Fancy's newly created royal parents. Several cast members laughed along with him, but Mary Beth wasn't one of them.

"You see," he added slowly, looking straight at her as if he were trying to explain something to the royal village idiot, "Fancy's goal now is to do whatever it takes to win back the heart of the man she once betrayed. A futile effort," he added with another obnoxious laugh, "because…"

"When did *The Wild and the Free* become *The Dull and the Snoring?*" Mary Beth interrupted.

"Do you have no depth, Miss Morgan?" Dirk asked with total disdain.

"Excuse me, Mr. Devlon," Mary Beth's perky understudy, Judy, spoke up. "I think I see where you're going with this."

Mary Beth focused on the imaginary brown spot that was quickly forming on the tip of Judy's pretty turned-up nose.

"People never really let go of their roots. Not completely," Judy said, looking around at the group sitting in a circle. "They may think they have, but deep inside, each of us is still that same person we've always been. Fancy might have more fun playing the femme fatale in Hollywood, but after her near brush with death, she comes to her senses and realizes what she really wants is the very thing she ran away from. She wants a life with the man she loves, and she wants to be back home safely in the bosom of her royal family."

"Good job, by jove!" Dirk beamed. "Excellent analogy."

In more ways than you realize, Mary Beth thought sadly.

She was still reeling from the sobering parody of her own life, when Julia said, "One more thing." She looked directly at Mary Beth. "Since *some-one*—" and she smiled facetiously when she said someone "—leaked to the press that this new script was going to mimic your own life, Mary Beth, I've come up with a perfect solution to keep the public from being disappointed now that we've changed the script."

Mary Beth held her breath.

"The public already knows you have an identical twin sister. When Fancy goes back home to London as *Edwena,* she'll find the reason Monty no longer has any interest in her, is that he's fallen in love with her identical twin, *Rowena.* The good twin,'' Julia added, getting in another barb. "The sister who is loving, kind, loyal and who will make Monty the perfect wife. Everything Fancy never was and never could be.''

Like me, you're insinuating.

"And though Dirk and I both have extreme doubts about the scope of your acting abilities,'' Julia said with great satisfaction, "since we're playing up the identical twin hook, I have no choice but to let you play both roles.''

Mary Beth felt the heat creep up her neck at Julia's insult.

"But you will have to overcome your irritating Southern twang in the role of Fancy's twin, Miss Morgan,'' Dirk said, pretending to shudder. "A believable British accent will be absolutely mandatory for the role of Rowena.''

A believable British accent, Mary Beth seethed. A man who sounded like a cross between Hugh Grant and Fred Flintstone was concerned about *her* believable British accent?

Well, she thought smugly, she had a little surprise for both of them. Dorothy, bless her heart, just happened to sneak a copy of the new script out of Julia's office so Mary Beth wouldn't be caught with her panties down, so to speak. And thanks to her sainted friend, Mary Beth already knew the new script inside and out.

Standing up from her chair, Mary Beth tossed her long pale locks over one shoulder and walked toward Dirk with the sensuous sway that had made

Fancy so popular. Using the words she had memorized straight from the script, Mary Beth looked him up and down and said in Fancy's low, sexy and definitely *Southern* drawl, "Your lips say you're in love with my sister now, Monty, but that hungry look I see in your eyes calls you a liar."

Dirk, who had sat up straighter in his chair when she made the advance in his direction, sent Julia an annoyed look. And when he did, Mary Beth changed her posturing and adopted a look so pure and innocent, he blinked in surprise. In perfect, clipped English diction that would have made the Duchess of York proud, it was Rowena who fell to her knees and took Dirk's hand. "Monty, I beg you. There's no hope for you if you listen to such foolishness from my sister. Edwena betrayed you once before. She'll do it yet again."

The cast rose to their feet and actually applauded. Even Julia.

But not Dirk. The great one remained seated.

He also kept a tight-lipped grimace on his face for the remainder of the afternoon while the cast worked patiently through Fancy's new script.

DRESSED IN A CLINGING BLACK sequined evening gown, Mary Beth gazed around the crowded room that was filled to capacity with the who's who of Hollywood daytime television. Her eyes fell on Walter Evans, the executive producer of *The Wild and the Free* and she gave the man a polite nod. He smiled at her, then lifted his champagne glass in a toast. She found it rather ironic the same man had been ready to kick her to the curb only a few weeks earlier.

Of course, that wasn't going to happen now. Not when the ratings for sweeps week had far exceeded any of the numbers the producers had even hoped for; thus the reason for tonight's party. Dirk Devlon had even postponed his return to New York to celebrate the big victory.

A group of smiling cast members were gathered around him now, while he regaled them with another one of what Mary Beth suspected was a self-serving story. If there was one thing she had learned about Dirk over the past few weeks, it was the fact that he never said or did anything that didn't call attention to himself.

Mary Beth stiffened when Julia actually had the nerve to walk up to her, give her a hug and air-kiss both cheeks. When she stepped back, she said, "I know we've had our differences, Mary Beth, but I'm willing to put those behind us if you are. I can't tell you how impressed I've been with your talent over the past few weeks."

Mary Beth managed a curt thank-you, and Julia smiled. "And I wanted you to know I have some wonderful ideas about what Fancy might get into after she returns to Hollywood. She'll still be devastated, of course, because Monty wouldn't take her back, but I think I can help take her mind off Monty. I hear the new heartthrob over at NBC isn't happy. I'm going to call him next week and see if we can't entice him to come play with Fancy for a while."

Julia laughed and Mary Beth took a sip from her

glass, trying to appear interested. Rather than thinking about a hot new co-star, the only thing on her mind was sticking it out at the party long enough to make an appearance. Over the last few weeks, she'd found it more and more difficult to play the silly Hollywood game. And she'd had enough of the phony people in the room to last her a lifetime.

"And don't mention a word," Julia whispered as she leaned in closer, "but Dirk's already agreed to return for the next sweeps week when Fancy is invited to Monty and Rowena's wedding. You'll play the double role again, of course. It's been such a success we need to milk it for all it's worth."

After dropping that bit of news, Julia hurried off to mingle, but JoJo slid right into the vacant space beside Mary Beth. His slicked-back hair held so much gel Mary Beth was surprised it didn't slide right off his head. He gave her a wink and said, "I've been working the room and doing a little schmoozing and the word is you're a definite shoo-in for an Emmy nomination. Didn't I tell you sticking with that role would be in your best interest?"

An Emmy nomination. But did she dare hope to believe it? Everyone else seemed to think it was a possibility. And even she had to admit she'd done an outstanding job playing the double roles of Edwena and Rowena. *But an Emmy nomination?*

JoJo jarred her from her thoughts when he put his hand on her elbow. "I just want you to know I've already made it clear to the big boys that keeping you is going to be expensive. If they want you to sign another contract, it won't be for the chicken feed they gave you the first time.''

Though what he said should have pleased her, his statement made her mad enough to spit. "Why are you threatening the big boys now, JoJo?" She was through being nice. "What happened to your go-with-the-flow philosophy? Why couldn't you have played the hard, tough agent when I needed you to stand up for me?"

He paled, obviously realizing she was only a second away from cutting him loose. "Now, Mary Beth, I was doing what I thought was best for you. And even you can't say I didn't do the right thing. We've got clout now, Mary Beth. C-l-o-u-t clout."

She hated the annoying way he spelled out words.

"You're the hottest thing on daytime TV," he added. "And everyone in this town knows it."

Mary Beth was amused to see him so shaken. He motioned to one of the circulating waiters, their trays filled with champagne glasses. JoJo grabbed a glass and polished it off in one easy gulp. "I've brought you this far," he was quick to remind her. "And you're going to realize how much you really need me when I bring you that contract to sign in a few weeks."

JoJo scurried off, probably afraid she was going to fire him on the spot, but Mary Beth barely noticed. Dirk Devlon had her in his sights now, and the great one himself was strolling leisurely across the room in her direction. Every eye in the room was following each step he took.

"You look ravishing tonight, Mary Beth," he

said, pausing to look her up and down. "Simply ravishing. And one day," he said, raising his voice loud enough for everyone to hear, "I predict that you will look back on this night as one of the most memorable nights of your life. Because everyone in this room—" and he dramatically used his champagne glass in a sweeping gesture around the room "—already knows you have an incredibly bright future ahead of you. And that includes me."

He made a formal bow then, and reached out and brought her hand to his lips for a kiss.

Everyone clapped in approval.

Mary Beth managed to mumble a thank-you, but the tears running down her cheeks had nothing to do with Dirk's unexpected praise. It was the memory of someone else's phony British accent and kiss on the hand that actually made her cry.

10

ZACK MOTIONED FOR GREG to keep backing up. The truck eased backward, closer to the spot Zack had chosen to unload the lumber. "Stop," Zack called out, then walked to the back of the truck and let down the tailgate. Greg left the truck and came around back to help as Zack paused to look down at the ringing cell phone clipped to his belt.

When he didn't take the call, Greg chuckled and said, "I bet I can guess who that was."

"Shut up. It isn't funny," Zack grumbled.

"Sure it is," Greg said and laughed. "Mom even heard down at the beauty parlor that Bitsy is already looking through catalogs trying to choose a wedding dress."

"Like that's going to happen," Zack said with a snort. "Can you imagine a life with a woman who can talk nonstop for five straight minutes without taking a single breath? And I should know. I timed Bitsy yesterday when she stopped by to drop off another one of her damn casseroles."

"At least you're eating well," Greg threw in and reached out to pat Zack's stomach.

Zack threw the red warning flag he'd just taken off one of the boards and hit Greg in the face.

The slap in the face didn't stop Greg's teasing. "Yeah, give Bitsy another week or two and you'll probably be willing to marry her just to get her to shut up."

"Believe me, I've been tempted to use my caulking gun and glue that fake pigtail right across her mouth."

"You've done crazier things," Greg reminded him, then pulled himself up into the back of the truck to get a stubborn board that wouldn't budge.

"And Mary Beth's latest success on her soap opera certainly hasn't helped matters," Zack complained.

"Her success hasn't helped your foul mood, either," Greg mumbled.

"Now Bitsy's more convinced than ever that Mary Beth isn't coming back. I guess she thinks that makes me fair game."

"And what about you? Have you finally accepted the fact that Mary Beth isn't coming back?"

Zack grabbed the two-by-four Greg handed him and slammed it to the ground. "Yeah. I accepted the fact Mary Beth wasn't coming back the day I left Malibu."

"Good," Greg said as he hopped off the back of the truck. "Because I ran into Maddie at the post office a little while ago and she told me Mary Beth had received so much acclaim playing that double role on her soap opera, she was a guaranteed shoo-in for an Emmy nomination."

"Well, bully for Edwena, Rowena *and* Mary Beth," Zack barked.

He'd never admit it to Greg, but even though her most recent success had permanently sealed his own fate, Zack was definitely proud of her. Greg wasn't the only one who had talked to Maddie. Maddie had stopped by last week with little B.J. and told Zack how horrible Dirk Devlon had treated Mary Beth on the set. She'd also said the studio was so thrilled with the sweeps week rating they were offering Mary Beth more money and a five-year contract. Maddie had begged Zack to go back to Malibu and bring Maddie home, even if he had to bring her home kicking and screaming.

Like that was an option.

With a possible Emmy nomination, more money *and* a five-year contract, Mary Beth never would be willing to leave Hollywood. He'd predicted that two months ago.

Of course, he had no one to blame but himself. He was the one who had pushed Mary Beth in front of the cameras in the first place. And he had been the one so determined they both needed to experience life outside Morgan City before they got married, settled down and raised their family.

Practical Zack.

He was practical, all right, he thought. Practically the stupidest man on the face of the earth.

Once they had unloaded all the two-by-fours, Greg drove away to pick up another load of lumber. Zack turned up the collar of his jacket against the cold. The fact that it was only a week until Thanksgiving didn't seem possible. Of course, since he'd left Malibu, most of Zack's days had been nothing but a blur.

After Mary Beth had called him with the news about the script, he didn't have to worry about his partners or his investors jumping ship. That's when he'd come back home to Oakmont to oversee the renovations. The contractor had a full-time crew working on the major repairs, but Zack often worked late into the night himself.

It helped him keep his mind off Mary Beth.

Some of the time.

The lower level of the old mansion was livable now, by his standards anyway, and though most of the big renovations wouldn't start up again until the Spring, he planned to work through the winter, doing what he could inside so he might entice a buyer. Then he would sell Oakmont. He would hand it over to someone who would hopefully have children to play in the old gazebo like the children he dreamed he and Mary Beth would have one day.

Dammit, I need to stop torturing myself.

He and Mary Beth weren't getting back together and they weren't having children.

Mary Beth wasn't even coming home for Thanksgiving. It was contract negotiating time, she had told Maddie, and Maddie had been fit to be tied because she said Mary Beth was literally bubbling with excitement when she called to tell her about her new contract.

The holidays. Zack sighed. Since he and Mary Beth had broken up, it had always been the toughest time of the year for him. Now, it looked as if he would be making it through another holiday season without her. But in spite of the empty feeling he had inside, remembering how Mary Beth had always saved the wishbone from the Thanksgiving turkey until New Year's Eve made Zack smile.

She'd been so adamant about saving that wishbone when they were kids. At the stroke of midnight, they had always rung in the new year together by breaking the wishbone and always wishing for the same thing. "That way, it won't matter who gets the short end," Mary Beth had told him with a pixielike grin that first year he'd come to live with his aunt and uncle. "Don't you see, Zack? If we both wish for the same thing, our wishes will always come true."

Well, he certainly wasn't going to ask Aunt Lou to save the damn wishbone for him this year. And he wouldn't be making any pointless wishes, either. Until his cell phone rang again, that is. Then Zack decided he might be asking Aunt Lou to save that wishbone so he could wish Bitsy Williams would find someone else to torture and leave him the hell alone.

MARY BETH WALKED THROUGH the doors of Granita, the latest Wolfgang Puck in-spot for celebrities on West Malibu Road. Not only did she look like a million bucks in her jeans, thigh-high boots and red cashmere sweater, but she felt even better. It always overwhelmed her that anyone would recognize her off the set, but several big names *she* had no trouble recognizing nodded cordially as she made her way through the crowded restaurant.

She headed for a table where her agent was already seated, deciding JoJo looked as out of place as she felt. He had added a few more gold chains around his neck, but thankfully he only had ten fingers. Several diamonds flashed as he waved in her direction.

When she stopped at the table, JoJo jumped up and pulled out her chair. "Did you see those heads turn?" he asked with a grin. "You're hot, pretty lady. H-o-t hot."

Mary Beth fought back the urge to wrap a few of the chains tighter around JoJo's neck and waited until he sat back down. Like magic, he produced what she already knew was her new contract from his expensive leather briefcase.

"I'm glad you're already sitting down," JoJo said proudly, "because when you see the dollar amount I held out for, you're not going to believe it."

Mary Beth accepted the contract, but before she even turned to the second page, JoJo already had his pen out, eager for her to sign. He was practically breathing down her neck, but Mary Beth ignored him completely and stared at the dollar amount for a long, long time. She finally smiled and reached for the pen which JoJo was more than happy to hand right over.

"Didn't I tell you I would take you straight to the top?" He dropped back down in his chair with a relieved sigh.

"Yes, that's exactly what you told me," Mary

Beth agreed, sliding the contract back across the table.

And then she stood up.

"Hey, where are you going? I thought we were having lunch."

I've bought your lunch for the last time, Bozo, Mary Beth thought. "I'm going home."

"You didn't tell me you were taking any time off for Thanksgiving."

Mary Beth didn't answer, nor did she wait for JoJo to blow a gasket when the signature he found on the dotted line read: Hopefully, Mrs. Zack Callahan.

She was already back outside when JoJo finally caught up with her. "Are you crazy?" he yelled, trying to keep in step.

"Certifiable," Mary Beth told him as she continued walking across the parking lot.

"I don't believe this," he gasped. "Nobody would turn down an offer like the one I just got for you. Nobody!"

"The Duke of Windsor gave up the bloody throne in the name of love," Mary Beth said in her perfected Rowena accent. But in her own voice she added, "I hardly think giving up a role on a daytime soap opera is that unbelievable."

She stopped in front of her new Ford Explorer, and JoJo frowned. "Where's your BMW? Riding around in that thing isn't going to be good for your image."

Mary Beth patted the golden head that popped through the window she'd left half open. "The

BMW is history. I can't very well move cross country in two-seater sports car.''

"You're really serious about this," JoJo croaked, sweat popping out on his brow.

"Have a great life, JoJo," Mary Beth told him as she unlocked the door to her new SUV and slid behind the wheel.

"But what about your Emmy nomination?" JoJo pleaded, holding on to the side of the Explorer as Mary Beth slowly backed up.

"Oh, I'll show up at the awards ceremony if I'm nominated for an Emmy," Mary Beth said with a laugh. "I might be pregnant, but I'll definitely show up."

"Pregnant?" JoJo yelled, his face turning redder by the minute. "Is that what this is all about? You're giving up the career of a lifetime to go home and make babies with that idiot who's been following you around?"

"If he'll still have me," Mary Beth confirmed as she shifted the Explorer into Drive.

JoJo stepped back from the Explorer with his face twisted in an ugly snarl. "You ungrateful little bitch," he yelled. "I should have left you on that street corner in Atlanta where I found you. I thought you had potential, Mary Beth, but I was wrong. You're nothing but a small-town Georgia hick!"

"And proud of it," Mary Beth yelled back and roared out of the parking lot. When she looked in her rearview mirror her irate ex-agent was still shaking a diamond-clad fist in her direction.

Mary Beth laughed. No more greedy agents. No

more pushy head writers. No more egotistical co-stars. And no more acting out life in front of a television camera instead of living it. She was a home-town girl after all, who had been trying to convince everyone, including herself, that she was someone else.

And as for her Emmy nomination?

Well, she had the *promise* of a nomination.

That was good enough for her.

People would call her crazy for walking away when her acting career was at its peak, that's for sure. And she'd probably never win any awards teaching college level drama classes. But by the time her twenty-year high school reunion rolled around, she would hopefully have more than a statue to take to the family picnic. She and Zack would hopefully have children of their own romping across the court-house green.

Reaching out, Mary Beth smiled and rubbed Diogee gently behind the ears. "Let's go home, fella. Let's go home and see if Zack will still have us."

The big dog barked and gave Mary Beth's face a happy, sloppy lick.

Diogee settled back down in the passenger seat while Mary Beth reread the clipping she'd cut out of the morning paper and taped to the dash of the Explorer. As far as she was concerned, Venus had sent her a personal message. *Libra: Look past the glitter to find true wealth. Follow the truth you feel in your heart. True love transcends all boundaries and has no end. Embrace it and you can hold eternity in the palm of your hand.*

A LOUD BANGING ON THE FRONT door awakened Zack early on Thanksgiving morning. He sat up in bed and felt his stomach roll over at the thought of piping hot turkey and dressing casserole.

"I'm going to kill that woman," Zack grumbled when he pulled himself out of bed.

He didn't bother looking for a shirt. He grabbed a pair of jeans from the floor beside his bed, stepped into them and headed through the house, still half asleep. When he stubbed his big toe on the five-gallon can of paint sitting in the foyer, however, Zack snapped wide-awake.

Cursing under his breath, Zack limped to his front door, fully prepared to tell Bitsy once and for all to politely buzz off. What he wasn't prepared for, was the big golden dog that almost knocked him down when he opened the door.

"I came to return your tent," Mary Beth told him when he finally managed to force Diogee into a sitting position.

Zack glanced at the canvas bag slung over her shoulder, and though he didn't invite her inside, Mary Beth strolled past him and set the bag down on the floor.

After taking a long look around, she smiled at him and said, "You've done wonders with this place, Zack. I always knew it could be beautiful again."

Zack closed the door, trying to imagine what Mary Beth standing in his foyer might mean. He mentally punched hope in the nose when it sprang forward to tease him.

Maddie had said Mary Beth wasn't coming home for Thanksgiving. So what was she doing in Morgan

City now? She'd probably come home to smooth things over with her family.

But if she thinks she'll get anywhere trying to smooth things over with me, she's...

"I think you still have a pair of my shoes," she said, cutting off his mental raging.

Shoes? Tents? What did she think he was doing on Thanksgiving morning? Having a damn yard sale?

"Yeah, your shoes are around here somewhere," Zack said, but he frowned when he remembered his bloody nose.

"You certainly don't seem to have the holiday spirit, Mr. Callahan," she had the nerve to say as she followed along behind him as he went from room to room.

Holiday spirit? Was she kidding? And who did she think she was waltzing through his door and reprimanding him for not having any holiday spirit!

When he finally saw her shoes sitting on a book-case shelf in the library, Zack snatched them up and handed them over. "Anything else?"

She looked around the room. "Maddie said you were planning to work inside all winter and try to get this place ready to sell."

"That's right," Zack said, and because he knew it would irritate her, he added, "The sooner I sell this place, the better."

He didn't get any satisfaction when she tossed her hair back over her shoulder and smiled. "Need any help?"

He frowned. "Who did you have in mind?"

She shrugged. "Me. I'm unemployed."

Zack threw his head back and laughed. "Yeah,

right," he said, frowning when he looked at her again. "Last I heard you were a guaranteed shoo-in for your Emmy nomination, and you were ready to sign a five-year contract with the studio."

She took a step in his direction. "That's why I'm here."

"To rub my nose in your success?" Zack thundered.

She pushed him backward and pinned him flat against the bookcase. He blinked when she said, "No. You told me when I got an Emmy nomination not to come back home looking for you. So I wanted to come home now. *Before* I even know if I have the nomination."

She leaned forward and kissed him softly on the lips. "Besides, the only Emmy I'm concerned about is the type of Emmy *you* can give me."

Zack gulped when she ran her hands up his bare chest.

"And what kind of Emmy would that be?"

"The kind that could come right along behind Zack Jr., Annie and Betsy. *Emmy* Callahan. I think Oakmont is big enough for four children instead of three, don't you?"

Zack was dead serious when he said, "My heart can't stand any more games, Mary Beth. If you're not home to stay..."

"Oh, I'm home to stay, Zack. What about you?"

"I'm not going anywhere."

"Any pressing phobias about walking down the aisle this time?"

"Nope."

"Can I get that in writing?"

"You can," Zack assured her.

Mary Beth held up her shoe as a threat. "Are you willing to sign that document in blood?"

"Why you little…"

MARY BETH THREW HER SHOES down when Zack lunged in her direction. They darted off through the house, much the same as they had done when they were children, Diogee barking at their heels.

But when she ended up in the back room Zack was using for his bedroom, she was trapped with nowhere left to run. She turned around, hoping to escape, but Zack slid sideways through the door with a playful gleam in his eye. He maneuvered Diogee gently back out into the hallway, pushed the door shut and turned to face her.

"Come hither, Rowena, you saucy English tart," he said in his phony Cary Grant voice.

Mary Beth laughed when he started walking in her direction. Her heart was beating faster with every step he took. "How dare you throw Marlene over for a stuck-up prude like Rowena!"

Zack pushed her backward onto his bed. "Marlene is much too worldly for me, darling. I'd much prefer a woman who wants to make a home, have tea and have a family with me."

"But Marlena is *soooo* much sexier," Mary Beth argued in her slow, sexy accent. She held her breath when Zack unzipped her parka and slid his hands beneath her sweater.

"But movie stars can be such a troublesome breed, darling. Don't you think?" Zack kissed her again.

"What about hometown girls?" Mary Beth teased, dropping the accent. She forgot the question when his fingers found the way to the zipper in her jeans.

"Oh, yeah." He growled low in his throat. "Hometown girls definitely turn me on."

Mary Beth moaned when Zack did that amazing little thing he always did with his tongue up the full length of her neck.

When he pulled his head back, he turned her face to look at him. "Welcome home, Mary Beth. I'll never give you any reason to regret coming back home to me."

She could see the depth of the love he felt for her reflected in his eyes, but Mary Beth couldn't resist pushing him away. "I'll believe *that* when I see you standing at the altar, Zack Callahan!"

"Don't say you don't believe me, Mary Beth," Zack threatened.

Mary Beth squealed when Zack began tickling her all over. "I believe you. I believe you!" she kept yelling, but Zack wouldn't let up.

Her peals of laughter grew louder and louder.

So loud, Diogee finally knocked the door open and bounded into the bedroom fully prepared to join in the fun.

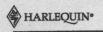
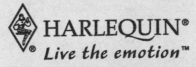

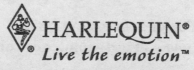

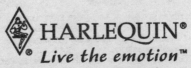